# CATAMOUNT

by

Woody Knowles

**CATAMOUNT**
**A novel by Woody Knowles**
is an original publication of ***G. F. Hutchison Press***.

G. F. Hutchison Press
319 South Block Avenue, Suite 17
Fayetteville, AR 72701


ISBN: 978-0-9796279-4-1



Printed in USA

PR 10 9 8 7 6 5 4 3 2 1

## DEDICATION

This book is dedicated to Pamela Powers,
who left this world too soon.
When the roll is called up yonder,
she'll be there.

# IN APPRECIATION

The author wishes to acknowledge the assistance and the friendship of three important people.

I met *Shannon Edward Lacey*, when he decided to run for congress. I had the privilege and the honor to write his speeches. With less than a thousand dollars, no organization, and no name recognition, we got fifteen percent of the vote in a three way primary election, in which we were outspent ten and twenty to one, respectively. The author would like to believe that the speeches helped. After the campaign, Shannon came to visit my home in the woods, and I related some of the locals tales about cougars and black bears that are occasionally seen in the area. He thought, and I agreed that it would make a good story. The detail of the military equipment and the weaponry used in this book owe much to his research. (The author was twenty to thirty years behind the times on such matters.) He also researched the big cats, which was also invaluable. It is all much appreciated.

During the writing of this manuscript, I was also trying to market my first completed work, entitled "I love you always, forever: A story of war lost." *Calvin Boyd* and *Pamela Powers* welcomed me into their home as we searched the internet for leads. He and she also read portions of both manuscripts and offered their thoughts. Pam had to go into the hospital for a chronic condition. Shortly thereafter she passed from this world. She is now in a better place. The kindness and the assistance of both of these people was, and is, greatly appreciated. They were and are friends.

About the author: The author lives upon a woody knoll, riding towards his next adventure, and towards his final reward.

The characters and their actions in this book are fictional. Any resemblance between them and anything that has actually happened is strictly co-incidental. The towns and lakes are also fictional as are the judges and the politicians. This is a story that could never happen in today's modern world - **OR COULD IT?**

# TABLE OF CONTENTS

# CHAPTER ONE:
## Ol' Bessie

Hot steam rose from Jack Morgan's cup of coffee. He liked how it kept his insides warm on those cold days – and it most certainly was a cold one. Rain and sleet had been drizzling down for what seemed like forever. Jack felt comfortably secure in his American made, four-wheel drive, Chevy truck. Its four by four treads gripped the road like nothing else. A grin of satisfaction worked its way up one corner of his mouth as he recalled how, on more than one occasion, his Chevy and his come-a-long had pulled stalled and lost vehicles out of ditches and ravines. The environmentalists (hippies) wouldn't appreciate, nor would they ever understand, the sheer beauty and the raw power of a big eight-cylinder engine with enough horses under the hood to power a tank. It had saved a lot of heartache and a great many people who had found themselves stranded. Those tiny, so called, "Earth Friendly" cars, just couldn't cut mustard out in the wild.

"Forget the dumb stuff," he said, to himself.

Jack had to make an extra trip to the store that day. His dog, Bessie, had jumped her line and gone off into the woods somewhere. He knew that she'd come back smellin' like some road kill, and he was going to be prepared with flea and tick killer, flea soap, and pet fresh! He also wanted to get another line. This time it would be a heavy gauge wire that Bessie couldn't chew through.

"Damn that dog," he muttered to himself.

Bessie was a good beagle. She had a lot of wood smarts and was a good hunting dog. She was loving and when she would put her head on Jack's lap and look up at him with those big brown eyes, his heart would just melt. But she had a mind of her own and that could and did get her into big trouble out there in the wilds of the Appalachian foothills.

The headlights cut across the parking lot of his faithful I.G.A. store. The fog was thick. It was hard to see. In a way Jack liked the mist. It tended to make him feel alert and alive. These were the types of days he used to curl up by the fire with Sue. The memories of those times warmed his heart better than coffee could ever do. He loved her with all his being. It was painfully unfortunate that God had taken her so soon. But he was glad that the brain aneurism took her quickly and that her suffering was minimal. Jack missed her greatly but he had many friends to lift his spirits for which he was thankful to the Lord. Sometimes he wondered how he could have survived without them.

Earl Johnson, the owner of the I.G.A. store, was one such a friend. He'd been a friend of the family since before Jack was born. He filled Jack's refrigerator with food when Sue died. He was just that kind of a man. He was into his late sixties now but was fighting it well. He still had his hair and his grit. The two men's eyes met as Jack walked in. Jack smiled and asked him how he'd been doing.

"Fine," Earl offered.

Then he started in.

"Ya know, Susan's gone Jack. She's been gone for five years now. She would want you to enjoy your life and be happy. I know you miss her but it would be a lot better if you would move on and find someone, rather than trying to hold on to something that's dead and gone?"

"I know Earl. But you haven't lost a wife. It's not something you just turn on and off on any given day."

"Maybe so, but it is possible to heal even broken hearts. The question is, are you willing to allow the healing process to begin?" Earl said, pressing the issue.

"The chances of finding someone like Sue are real slim." Jack replied thoughtfully.

"You're right. No one else will ever be Susan. But someone else could be very special in her own ways. And you could love her for who and what those are. There is more than one good guy or good gal in the world. A good woman can mend just about anything. Hey... That's what we'll do – we'll go shopping for a wife for you! I say this coming Friday we'll go down to the tavern. There's bound to be some fine ladies there. What do ya say?"

"I don't know," Jack mumbled hesitantly.

Earl was insistent.

"Oh, come on! What will it hurt?"

"Alright Earl, you win," Jack said, clearly reluctant about the scheme. "We will go."

"Alright that settles it. Friday night at eight o'clock, don't forget." Earl insisted.

"I won't," Jack agreed silently taken with the humor of his friend's enthusiasm.

Jack picked up the items he needed and headed for home. He lived in a modest two-story home in the country located in the Ohio valley. Jack's home overlooked a large cornfield with a wide stream flowing through it. The field was situated in a valley between two sizeable hills. Deer and wild turkey came out from the timberline to graze. There was a magnificent majesty in how the hawks circled high above the field. During the fall one could sit on one of the big rocks atop one of the hills and watch the fog roll in. The cadence of the woodpeckers echoed for miles. It never ceased to be breathtaking.

Bessie didn't come home that night, nor would she ever. It bothered Jack a great deal. Where did she run off to? What had happened to her? Had she wandered off too far and got lost? Did some farmer shoot her? Did she tangle with a pack of wild dogs? Maybe Jack would never know. Maybe...

His thoughts drifted back. He got to thinking about how it had been when he was a young boy growing up. He had a beagle named 'Hound'. Hound was all they ever called him and he took to it well. When Jack was nine ol' Hound became his inseparable companion. They hunted together, walked together, and, with some persistence, he even got the dog to fetch a stick. Hound wasn't too much interested in sticks. One seemed just as good as another as far he was concerned, but he humored his master. He was good that way, and besides, he loved being petted so it seemed a fair trade. He slept outside the boy's door at night because that was as close as he was allowed by 'the house rules'. Mornings would come and he would follow the boy wherever he was allowed. Summers found them always together. During the fall and winter months, however, school got in the way. But every day after school hound was at the door waiting for his friend.

Their lives continued pretty much like that until the boy turned sixteen. Then something called 'girls' came between them. The boy gave him an occasional pat but more and more, instead of their going off together for walks and adventures, his 'ailing' master seemed to spend all of his time in front of a mirror combing his greased hair. Even as a dog he knew all of that wasted time would not actually make it stay in place once he walked or ran a few paces. It never did, of course, but humans never seemed savvy enough to figure that out.

Jack smiled. He could almost sense that old dog chuckling at him from the next world. He remembered how bad it hurt when he got home from school and discovered why ol' Hound hadn't been there waiting for him at the end of classes that day. His father looked sad. Then told him the bad news. Some hot-rodding teenagers peeled out by the house, burning rubber. The house's canine centurion had gone out to investigate and to give the intruders a thoroughgoing barking.

One of the young drivers, if you could call him that, swerved at the dog – probably just to scare him. The right front wheel caught hound's head and smashed it. The dog died instantly and the kid squalled on down the road.

Jack never did find out who had done it but for years hoped that he would so he might in some way return the favor. They buried ol' Hound in the back yard, and the boy even put a little cross to mark the spot. He didn't get another dog.

He mused out loud, "I'd like to have another beagle," and by either sheer coincidence or by an act of God (he was never quite sure in his mind, which it was) he heard a scratching at the door.

"I've got to be hearing things", he muttered.

The scratching persisted and he opened the door. There, right before his disbelieving eyes, was a bloody, trembling, half-starved, beagle pup.

"Well I'll be a son of a ...", he said.

Then he caught himself.

"If my wishes are starting to come true, I'd better be very careful," he chuckled.

He carried the pup into the house and washed the blood off in the tub.

"A female," he said out loud.

Then he put peroxide on the gashes and cuts, and dried the dog off with an old towel, which was past redemption anyway. He poured some milk into a bowl and the pup greedily lapped it up, then whined for more. Jack was in a benevolent mood so he fried up some hamburger and plopped it into the bowl.

"Don't you think that this is the way it's gonna be," he told her. "Starting tomorrow it's kibbles for *you* and hamburger for *me*." Bessie looked up and gave him her best doggie smile. She suspected that Jack would not be firm in his resolve and that meat scraps and other table delights would often come her way – there at her new home. She was right, of course.

Jack figured that someone in the city had dropped her off out there – just to be rid of her; city people were like that. They would just toss dogs out in the middle of nowhere and then drive, relieved, back to the city. Most of the dogs would either starve to death or be eaten by one critter or another. A few would go wild and run with packs of wild dogs that lived like the inferior wolves that they naturally were. They would survive long enough to terrorize flocks of sheep or chickens before a farmer would shoot them. A few lucky ones, that managed to wander onto the right place at the right time found homes without a dog. Happily, it would soon become a home *with* a dog: a rare happy ending for all concerned.

Such was Bessie's luck – and Jacks. She grew to be a wonder on the hunt. She was a survivor. Unknown to Jack, of course, she had managed to stay alive for six days as an abandoned pup. She had found a hole under a stump that had once housed groundhog and made it into her temporary digs. She had eaten some tasty grasshoppers. She also stumbled onto a field mouse and had actually caught and eaten him. But, she could not find enough. She was slowly starving to death.

A coyote had spotted her and decided that puppy was just what had been missing on his menu. He sprang at her from his place of hiding. His jaws closed on the back of her neck and tore skin and gashed her head. Luckily, the bite was a glancing one. In terror, she made her way into her hole. It was just big enough for her and just small enough so that the coyote's head could not enter. Shivering in fear, she had waited an entire afternoon and night before she ventured out again. By then hunger drove her to her search.

She was at her pitiful puppy wits end when she came upon a dirt road. She followed it for a hundred yards or so. She saw a house; throwing what little she knew of caution to the winds, she bounded up the stairs and onto the porch. She scratched at the door. There was no answer but she was persistent. Finally, Jack opened the door and, as they say, the rest was history.

Bessie was not a purebred. Jack figured she was probably mixed with some kind of coonhound. She was too long legged for a beagle but man could she hunt. She worked the circle and always brought the rabbit right around to where she knew Jack and his fire stick were waiting. She was good as gold. When the hunt was finished she would follow him into the house, curl up in front of the door, and wait. She wasn't sleeping, she was patiently waiting for the reward she knew would be coming as a result of her diligence on the hunt. She was seldom disappointed. Jack would fix his supper while she lay in wait for the bounty he'd inevitably share with her after he had eaten. Then she'd pounce on her bowl and gorge herself. After they had eaten she would hop up on the couch and lay her head on his lap while he read the paper. He would reach down and give her a pat. It was all that she ever asked for in this life. She would close her eyes and sleep right there – in doggy heaven.

It was late November while they were on such a hunt that they first saw the huge paw prints that told Jack something out of the ordinary had passed through.

"That's no dog print and no Bobcat either." Jack surmised.

He didn't want to acknowledge what he thought it was.

"There hasn't been a painter cat round these parts in sixty years," he whispered to himself.

If he was right it meant big trouble on the hoof and he knew that he *was* right. The deer herds were growing each and every year because of the good conservation efforts paid for by hunting licenses. It was not surprising, therefore, that their natural predators, who had left for points south or north in search of food, would begin to follow the herds as they multiplied. He had seen coyotes and even some red wolves for the first time in years. But a *painter*? He was about to dismiss the possibility when his eyes examined the tracks again.

“A painter, and a damn big one at that,” he said aloud.

Judging from the size of the paw prints, it could be as large as 180 pounds of pure predator. A painter could break a buck’s neck with one blow of its massive paw. And a kid, out playing in the wrong place, had no chance at all. A chill worked its way down his spine.

This was not good news. He'd have to be careful whom he told. The people in town, down below, would swear he was crazy. They feared both the wilds and the folks who lived up in those hills. He would warn his neighbors – those who would listen. A painter meant real trouble. Only the old timers knew how much trouble. He had heard their stories as a boy. Now, it seemed, the old times were coming back. A painter meant dead sheep and cows and sometimes, dead people.

As time passed, no more tracks were found. He passed it off. Maybe he had been seeing things. Maybe...

Later that winter he found the first deer carcass. Bones and hide were all that were left and the carcass was half-buried with stick and things – the trademark of the big cats.

"No doubt about it," he said. "There *is* one about."

Bessie barked and the hair on her back stood straight,

producing a scruffy ridge along her spine. She sensed trouble. Nothing came of it that day.

The rest of the winter passed uneventfully. There were no further signs of anything out of the ordinary.

It was early spring when Bessie, during one of her frequent wanderings, came upon Sammy. Sammy was not your normal type dog. He was short tempered and vicious and he had the pit-bull breeding to back it up. He wasn't all that big – maybe fifty pounds – but he had tangled with the biggest and had always come out on top. His owner was George Hogan who lived about a mile down the road from Jack. He bred pit bulls and sold the pups. He also had lived in those parts all of his seventy-five years and was a hunter and a fisherman of some renowned. He was also known as a spinner of wonderful tales. Jack knew him well. George always said, "It's not that a pit bull fights any more than any other dog," then he'd grin, "It's that when he does, he's always the last dog standin'."

George kept Sammy fenced in so he wouldn't get loose. The dog was one hell of a fighter and guard dog, but he had no more woods sense then a piece of cardboard. If he were to get loose, he would like as not take off in one direction and three miles down the road forget which way he was going.

"He'd probably starve to death before he figured it out," the old man mused.

Most dogs couldn't get within twenty feet of the fenced-in yard without his vicious nature asserting itself. But then, again, most dogs weren't Bessie. She walked right up to the fence, sniffed noses with the old boy, and proceeded to walk all the way around the yard looking for a soft place to dig. Digging was one of many things she did far better than the average dog. Sammy, far from growling and threatening her, was soon helping her dig from the inside out. The tunnel was completed and Bessie and Sammy were chasing, playfully, around the yard inside the fence.

George heard the commotion and went outside to take a look. He rubbed his eyes in disbelief. No dog had ever dared nose up to the fence without engendering the wrath of Sammy, but again, Bessie was no ordinary dog. George ran out into the yard. Bessie took one look at him and ran to the tunnel with Sammy in hot pursuit. Both of them emerged on the outside of the fence and ran off into the woods at full speed. Ol' George called and called but that day the dogs were listening to a stronger calling.

George gave up. He got into his truck and drove over to Jack's in the hope that Bessie had led Sammy there. Jack saw the pickup truck enter the drive. He walked toward it and motioned George in for coffee.

"*Your* dog led *my* dog off into the woods," George began. "And that dog of mine is liable to get into big trouble, maybe kill other dogs or, God forbid, someone's live stock. He'll never be able to find his way home."

"If he sticks with Bessie he'll be alright," Jack offered.

"She knows these woods like the back of her paw. But this does create a major problem."

"What's that?" George asked.

"What kind of God-awful pups would the two of them create?" Jack asked.

George got a sick look on his face.

"Pit beagles?"

He just shook his head. Then Jack began to laugh.

"They'll hunt all day – just don't try to take the rabbit away from `em!" George roared.

"That's just about the size of it," Jack said. "They'll either make it back or they won't. We'll never find `em on foot. They'll come home when they get good and ready."

Jack could hold it no longer.

"There's a painter about. I've seen the tracks and I found a deer carcass half buried in the woods."

"Come on," the old man said, giving Jack a skeptical look. "There hasn't been a big cat in these parts in years."

There's one out their now," Jack said nodding with certainty.

The old man sighed. "I sure hope you're wrong."

"It's out there, okay," Jack affirmed emphasizing his words.

A look of awe washed over the old man’s face.

"I was just a boy when I saw the last one in these parts. It killed cattle and horses. It ate dogs for breakfast. At night, you could hear it scream. You grabbed for your gun and you're flashlight and ran outside to save your animals, but through it all, you seldom saw it. You were soon one animal short of what you were before the scream. Men and dogs would take chase but it appeared to just vanish into thin air. The only time you had a chance of seeing it was when you were in the woods without a gun. It would know. Somehow, it just knew. Sometimes it would appear on top of a ridge and give you a long, lingering, look. It was a look that would send fear up a grown man's spine and make the hair stand up on the back of his neck. If you were smart you showed no fear, just quietly worked your way back to the house and your gun. If you showed no alarm you would be okay, most of the time, but God help you if it smelled fear. They really only fear the gun you carry. They don't fear you at all. Those eyes are the devil's own, and those teeth and claws "...

The old man sighed.

"I sure hope that you're wrong."

A week later Bessie came home alone. She was a little early by Jacks reckoning. Ten days would have been a more typical outing for her. She scratched at the door, went to her bowl, and gorged herself. Then she collapsed and fell into an exhausted sleep.

"Where is Sammy?" Jack had asked.

She looked up at him, whined a pitiful whine, and dropped her head back to the floor. In the morning she started to whine again.

"What's the matter girl?" Jack had asked.

She headed for the door. Jack followed her outside. There on the porch lay Sammy's collar. She started to whine, as she picked it up in her mouth. It was not good news.

Jack called George on the phone and told him to come by the house, pronto.

"You better bring your rifle," he suggested.

Within five minutes George was there. It was only then

that Jack noticed Bessie was limping on one of her back legs. He looked her over. There was a gash on the leg that had clotted over. George, also, took a look.

"Whatever she tangled with came within a hair of killing her," George allowed.

Bessie whined and barked, offering starts and stops, indicating that she wanted the men to follow.

The three of them went into the woods. Bessie was following the same trail she had followed home. The men could see the tracks in the snow that she had left earlier. They followed her for about three miles. At the base of a boulder strewn hill she started to climb. They called her back. The men were tired and sat down to take a breather before undertaking the uphill climb. They used the break to eat the sandwiches they had brought along. Jack offered Bessie a bite, which she took and disposed of in a single gulp.

Fifteen minutes later they were on the trail again. It went up a slope toward a rock ledge. Bessie started to whine. They climbed to the ledge and looked down the other side. There were tracks everywhere; there was blood in the snow. They worked their way down the slope. Halfway to the bottom the grade became more gradual. They saw where the battle had taken place. George took one look at the monstrous cat tracks and let out a whistle.

"You were right," he said, shaking his head, "A catamount, and a *big* one."

The tracks told the story. Two sets of dog tracks, one larger then the other, and cat tracks ahead of them. They had been chasing the cat when the cat suddenly stopped and turned on them. They saw the larger set of dog tracks skid to a stop. The smaller set circled the combatants. It was clear what had happened. When the cat turned, Sammy, true to his pitbull heritage, charged in for the throat. Bessie had circled, and true to her hound pedigree, had attacked from the rear, drawing the cat's attention away from the pit bull it was mauling. The pit bull had managed to clamp his jaws near the cat's shoulder. That had been far from enough, however. The cat, with its rear claws, disemboweled it, leaving a huge quantity of blood in the snow. Then it turned on the beagle. Bessie had been lucky. The pit, in death, still maintained his hold. The cat had to unlock the dead dogs jaw before it could take up the pursuit.

Bessie had run to a small hole between two boulders that opened into a cavern behind them and there she had waited in safety. The cat had tried, but failed, to dig away enough of the rock so it could follow. It soon gave up and returned to Sammy, dragging his remains into a nearby thicket, where, it had eaten the remains. The men followed the tracks into the thicket. Only bones and pieces of hide remained of what had been Sammy. Bessie's tracks went to the grisly cite and then backtracked towards the way they had just come.

Blood spots followed the cat tracks in the other direction. That was the worst news of all. The cat had been wounded and clearly didn't have the full use one front paw. A wounded cat was capable of anything. The men realized that there was no way of overtaking the cat on foot without carrying provisions for at least a week. They also realized that there was a wounded cat on the loose and that trouble walked with that cat; now, anything or anybody in its path was in danger, gun or no gun.

"A wounded cat can jump a man from a tree or a ledge or most anywhere," George said. "Any shadow should be suspect. A cat's powerful back legs would have him on top of a man well before he had any chance of mounting any sort of protective defense."

Jack had come prepared and poured plaster of Paris into one of the more pronounced tracks making an imprint they could carry back with them. The authorities would have to be notified. Somewhere out there, Death was lurking on four legs. They had to have proof or no one would take their claim seriously. Jack had suspected the worst and had been right.

*It was beginning.*

They had gone about a mile towards home when they heard the unmistakable scream. They stopped and looked in all directions but saw nothing. The cat had put them on notice, There was no place of safety, there. Bessie growled and started in the direction of the sound. Jack called her off because there was no time and because something told him to get back to the house. He wasn't afraid of the cat, Jack told himself, but he wanted to be better provisioned when he did go after it. Truthfully he was tired and more than a little concerned. First, the authorities must be notified.

When they got home they called the game warden and told him to meet them at the house right away. They had proof that a catamount was in the vicinity. The warden tried to reassure them that such was simply not possible. But he had enough respect for those two that he went out to the house to hear them out.

Sam Macafee was a big built man with big hands and a big, old fashioned, handlebar mustache. He was a throwback to another day and chafed badly under the new way of doing things – codified things with which he was ordered to comply. He and Jack knew each other well. They would often laugh at the "idiots who think the hills are like a Disney movie with cute cuddly little animals all of whom were angelic, in contrast to mankind, the villain."

He'd laugh.

"But that's what the university's are graduating nowadays. The governor even puts these know it all hippies in charge. It's a real pain in the butt to try to tell these idiots what's really going on out here," he would say. "And they don't listen anyway. What the hell do I know?" He'd snort, "I've just lived in these parts all of my life."

Sam's car pulled into the drive. He got out. George and Jack were waiting for him.

"Okay," Sam began, "So what's all this I'm hearing about a big kitty?"

Bessie snorted. Sam looked down at her and began to laugh.

"So they got you convinced, too. Huh?"

Bessie snorted again. Jack invited Sam inside and handed him a mug of coffee. The three men took seats at the table.

"Okay", Sam began, "So what makes you think there's a lion in the woods?"

Jack reached into his jacket pocket and laid the plaster of Paris imprint on the table in front of him. Sam examined it scarcely believing what he saw.

"Holy mother of God!" He whispered. "There's only *one* animal that could make this kind of track."

"A catamount," George said.

"A catamount," Sam agreed with a set of slow, deliberate, nods.

Jack related the story of what had happened and what they had seen in the snow.

Sam looked down at Bessie and said, "I'm sorry for doubting you girl."

Bessie looked up at him and wagged her tail. The big man had been forgiven.

Sam put the evidence in his coat pocket. He was ready to leave.

"If we *have* got a wounded cat on the loose we better be ready for anything. You guys have no idea how complicated you have just made my job."

In truth they did.

Sam was not looking forward to the report he was going to have to file and the idiocy he knew it would bring in response. It would take several long days at the very least. Sam pulled out of the driveway and wound his way down the little mountain road.

From the top of a rocky knoll the cat watched the car pass out of sight. It then strolled majestically back into the woods.

Sam got back to the office and filed his report. He tagged the plaster cast of the footprint as 'Exhibit A', and stored it in a safe place. Then, he made the report in person.

His superior was a woman named April Gillespie. She had taken all of the right courses and her family had all of the right connections. She had the requisite amount of experience in dealing with the wilds – a six-month internship at a national forest out west. She belonged to the Sierra Club and had been active in getting the wolves re-introduced into Yellowstone. That took place over the loud protests of the farmers whose families had finally managed to rid the area of the deadly sheep and cow killing plague. The hippies, with degrees and the law on their side, re-introduced them and forbade the residents to shoot the animals, even when they threatened their livestock, their poultry, and their children. In self-defense the locals developed a policy to defend themselves from the wolves, the environmentalist ideologues, and, most of all, the government, which, of course believed it knew far better than they did what was good for them. The policy became known as, "Shoot `em, shovel `em, and shut up." For the most part it worked quite well, except for the occasional bungler who had the unmitigated stupidity to get caught. Then, there was jail to serve and fines to pay. ‘How dare you defend yourself, your loved ones, and your property, when the government knows what is better for you than you do?’

At first sight of the evidence, April launched her convoluted logic.

"The endangered species act," she announced, "forbids citizens from hunting cougars. The state could mount a capture and relocation effort, but that might cause a panic; and worse, every deer hunter would be out there breaking the law trying to kill it. And how would the state be able to prove otherwise, short of catching someone with the carcass, in which case, the majestic animal would already be dead."

She droned on.

"So, the solution is simple. There simply is no cat. Tell the people who made the plaster impression of the track that it was just a big bob-cat."

"Those are woods-wise men," Sam answered. "They are not gonna buy that line of crap!"

April gave Sam a look. It didn't matter who was right. It only mattered that she had the authority.

"If you can’t make them buy it, then we will have to get another game warden who can."

There was a calm iciness in her voice.

"So, make sure you can get them to buy it?"

Sam answered.

"I'd like to see *you* try. And by the way, I'd also like to see you explain to the first family of a young child killed by that cat why the policy was to do nothing about it."

April responded.

"Mountain Lions won't attack people."

Sam had heard enough.

"Oh yeah! How about those joggers in California that were killed last year? Only then was the cat hunted down, and by a government hunter, mind you, because it was still illegal for the citizens to defend themselves against it."

"This cat has committed no crime." She answered, "And officially, this cat does not exist!"

With that she ended the meeting leaving Sam somewhere between resigning and just being flat out exasperated.

"What the hell. I've got kids to feed. To hell with that broad!" He muttered to himself, as he left.

He got in his car and drove over to see Jack to tell him the good news. Jack would know what to do. He and Jack had both served in `Nam, so they both understood orders that made no sense, that were to be `officially' followed to the letter, and which were unofficially carried out in a slightly different manner. Jack had been a platoon leader so he understood well.

"So that's it?" Jack chuckled. "It doesn't exist. Well that solves everything."

Then he grinned, and added, "I can't hardly be arrested or charged with hunting something that doesn't exist now. Can I?"

"I don't see how you could," Sam answered, "unless you are caught with the non-existent creature's carcass. And I cannot imagine your being that stupid or careless, especially when I'm not looking for you to be hunting a non-existent beast. I can't arrest a man for snipe hunting can I?"

"You've got a hell of a tough job," Jack offered.

"I'd quit but then they might find a fool who would actually try to enforce this garbage. All I can do is wait for the country to wake up and elect people to office who will appoint someone with a little sense about such issues. By the way, if you are asked, I told you that it was a bobcat track you took in plaster."

"Right!" Jack chuckled, "And I am Little Orphan Annie."

"Glad you got the picture," Sam answered. "It's time for dinner so I'd best get to movin'."

"Take care Sam," Jack smiled.

"Got too," Sam said with a grin.

Jack escorted him to his car. Sam honked and then drove for home. He still didn't believe the dangerous idiocy that his 'superior' had just doled out.

"That's just about the topper!" Sam said with disgust, to himself. "The cat does not exist but hunting it is a crime. Better lock up the boy scouts for huntin' snipe. Since no one has ever seen one, it must be endangered too."

He wiped the sweat from his brow, pulled into his drive, and prepared for supper. It would be a whole lot easier to digest than this day had been. Jack called ol' George on the phone and filled him in on the insanity. George responded like Jack knew he would.

"That son-of-a bitch killed my dog; so now I'm gonna kill that non-existent son-of-a-bitch!"

"I like your attitude, George, and so I'm gonna help you do it, just to be neighborly, you understand."

"I was hopin' you'd say that," George chuckled. "It has to be found before that devil kills a ki d."

The next morning, George and Jack took Bessie with them. George was retired and Jack had a week's vacation coming. They provisioned up and set out to kill that non-existent cat. It was probably better that way. At least the hunters were men who knew how to hunt and how to shoot. Jack packed his old army folding 'entrenching tool' in case shoveling became the order of the day. And with all of the idiots now in positions of power there was a lot of that needing to be done – all the way to Washington.

They hunted for five days to no avail. At least for the time being the big cat really seemed to have become non-existent in their neck of the woods. The cat would not be heard from for some time. But it *WOULD RETURN*. Jack and

George both knew it.

Eight uneventful weeks passed.

Bessie disappeared for a period of several nights. When she came back it was apparent that she had dropped her pit-beagle pups, somewhere. Patiently, Jack just kept her fed. He'd find out where she dropped her litter when they were a little older.

"Man, I'll bet their gonna be ugly," he whispered to himself. "Butt ugly!"

It was her first litter. Six pups. Two died on the way out, so that left four. They were weak little pups. Pit bull puppies usually are, at birth, far weaker than beagle pups, but they made up for that later. For some reason, two more died quickly. That left only two: A predominantly black one and a predominantly brown one.

Four weeks later, Jack decided that Bessie was not going to voluntarily take him to the pups, so he went looking. He heard whining and squeaking in the barn. Bessie tried to lead him in the wrong direction. 'Maybe she thinks I'd kill `em, for being so cross-breed, ugly,' he thought to himself.

"It's okay", girl, he reassured her. "I won't hurt em."

Bessie still had misgivings. Jack located the two pups and, with Bessie at his heals, he carried them into the house. They were every bit as ugly as he had imagined. His eyes hurt just looking at them. He called George to come on over for an introduction. George rubbed his eyes, as well.

"Two ugliest pups God never created!" He offered. "But only two survived. It could have been worse."

"Yeah," Jack laughed, "Like ten of `em!"

Bessie was clearly offended and no amount of patting was going to change that. She alone knew what she had there, and the stupid humans were just going to have to find out for themselves. She sulked into another room, snorted, and lay down.

"What are you gonna name them ?" George asked.

"How about `Useless and Worthless'?" Jack offered.

"Two many syllables," George declared. "Besides, nature's given them a bad hand in the looks department, so give them a break."

"How about `Blackie and Brownie'?" Jack said.

"That's not bad at all. It's easy to remember and it's truthful." George allowed.

And so it was, that Blackie and Brownie got their names.

In three months time, Bessie started bringing game to them in their lair in the barn. Jack had returned them there because it was a good safe and protected place for pups, or so he thought. He had tethered Bessie to a line that ran to the barn and he introduced the pups to canned dog food. That was not acceptable to Bessie. If pups are going to become woods smart, then they are going to have to be able to kill and eat all manner of critters that are smaller than they are, unless they have quills or stink glands. She would break her line and run off in search of such critters as she deemed appropriate to present to her pups. She never killed them outright. She made the pups kill and eat them. They were both quick learners – especially the black one. The pups grew by leaps and bounds. They were getting better looking as they grew up, too – especially the black one. He was the larger of the two and would grow to be the size of his father. The brown one was only slightly smaller and was less physically capable than his brother. But he *was* half pit bull and would eventually become formidable in his own right. Blackie, however, would become the better fighter.

One day in late autumn Bessie broke her line and went for a hunt. Something hit her nostrils like a hammer. It was a smell she remembered, hated, and most of all, feared. She smelled big cat. She knew that it was near the barn – and her pups. She dropped the field mouse she had been carrying and allowed it to scurry to safety. She headed for the barn on a dead run. At the door to the barn, sniffing at the stairway that led to her pups, was the painter. Bessie didn't even slow down. At a full run she charged the cougar's from behind. Adrenalin flowing, she bit the cat's tail in a way that had to have hurt. Like a flash the cat turned around only to see a fleeing Bessie headed for the timber. The cat was immediately on her tail. Bessie circled around a tree. The faster cat was right there. It took all she had to elude its front paw as it was extended in full flight. There was more than just a little luck involved. The cat still had a bad shoulder. It had not fully healed from the bite inflicted by Sammy's crushing jaws. It provided Bessie a momentary reprieve. She ran further up the hill leading the big cat further away from her pups. The cat closed and its huge front paw finally knocked Bessie down. Its fangs quickly brought Bessie's end. The cat had forgotten the pups. Game to the end, Bessie fought unto death. She must have had a doggie smile on her way out, because she had fulfilled her mission – if at the cost of her own life. Her precious pups were safe.

Jack heard the commotion and ran outside with his flashlight and his gun. The last sound Bessie heard was the sound of her master's voice calling to her. She didn't have the strength to offer up her familiar bark in return. Everything went black. Her struggle was over.

Jack called and called. Only silence answered him. He went up the stairs and checked on the pups; they were fine. On impulse he carried them into the house and made a place for them in the basement. Something told him that Bessie was in trouble. He felt bad. He was right, of course. Bessie never made it home.

Months later the black puppy lead him to his mother's bones. Only then did Jack understand that both of the puppies parents been killed by the same cat. Months later he would learn Bessie's final secret: That the puppies of the pit bull and the beagle, especially the black one, would inherit Sammy's strength, jaw pressure, and fighting savvy, as well as the best of Bessie's hunting instincts – her nose for game, (in their case, deer was the game rather than rabbit), and her woods smarts. Her puppies would eventually become the instruments the men would use to neutralize some of the cat's advantages. Blackie and Brownie would work to avenge their parents' deaths. They had been bred for that job.

## CHAPTER TWO
### Blackie and Brownie

On Friday, Jack kept his promise to Earl. They went out to have a turn at the tavern. There were women present, but none that interested him.

So, instead of mingling, he and Earl talked. Jack told him about the big cat. Earl was dumbfounded.

"A painter in these parts?"

He almost whispered.

"Old George Hogan was probably the last man in these parts to ever see one. But I remember my dad talking about them. He used to talk of them often. Being a young kid, I was curious. I would have liked to have seen one. My Dad told me, `I always wanted to see a twister, but one day one came and carried away the barn. Only then did I realize what a terror it was.' Then he looked at me, and said, `that tornado, and that cat are a lot a like. They're almost supernatural in their sheer power and in their ability to kill and destroy. A big cat like that will prowl in the night and kill anything that is smaller than he is. It might be a deer, a sheep, or even a human. Then he might get to feeling frisky and kill that which is bigger than he is, like a horse or cattle. Even a big bull, as powerful as he is, isn't safe. A wounded cat will always go after livestock because they are fenced in and slower than the normal wild prey.'

The old folks talked about their screams in the night. They were known to kill and carry off kids. Then I realized that as usual, Dad was right.

"I was lucky, never to have seen one on the loose."

Jack told him of the killing of Sammy, and of the position of the State Department of Wildlife on the issue. Earl just shook his head.

"That figures. The Government always wants our

money and then, instead of being there to help, they get in your way, and spend that money to regulate your life and then tell you what to do. They don't like to be reminded that it's the little guy that is paying their salaries. They really do think that it is their God given right to run your life for you."

Earl asked, "Do you see any women here that interest you?"

Jack laughed and said, "I wonder if any of them owns a good boat and motor?"

He then continued: "I think I'll take a pass. I don't have a bad life out in the woods. I can hunt when I want to and fish when I want to. I can do pretty much what I want to do when I want to do it. It would take someone pretty special to make me want to change. There is nothin' wrong with `em, but I'd probably have better luck goin' to a church than out at a bar. The plain truth is I'll know it when I see it, and, until then, I'm not gonna worry about it none. Not many women nowadays want to be a wife or a mother. They think that they can do whatever they please and still have a husband and kids. Not Sue. She loved to take care of me and the little ones. She never had to work outside the house and she never wanted to. The time we had together was more important. When I lost her I lost more than most ever had."

Earl nodded his head. He knew that Jack had not really come to meet a woman. He was there because a friend had asked him to come. The two men talked for a while and then adjourned to their own lives. Jack drove home. His thoughts drifted back to his life with Sue. They had always been happy. They had each put the other first. Because of that they were inseparable—until her death. He had looked, of course, but the price that was now being asked was just too high.

When he got home, the pups were raising hell in the basement. The black one was always picking on the brown one. He wondered what he might do about that.

"I'll have to talk to old George. He knows more about dogs than anyone I know."

Jack broke up the dogs and spanked the black one—not hard, but just enough for his message to get through. The pups were growing fast. In about a month he would start taking them out to give them their first hunting lessons. Suddenly, they actually seemed to be getting better looking. Jack chuckled at the realization.

"Maybe Bessie was right about you two."

The puppies barked. Jack played with them for a while. The black one had the beagle coloring except he was primarily black. He had a small white beagle tip on the very end of his tail and he had beagle ears. His body structure, from his chest to his jaw, was pure pit bull. Brownie was just brown all over, with brindle markings. He was slighter of build than Blackie. His jaw was not as strong and his inclination was to be the follower. It would later turn out that he had Bessie's nose for game and would bay like a beagle on the trail. Both Dogs would weigh in the fifties. Bigger than any beagle, they were both endowed with a hound's endurance on the trail.

In the morning Jack called George and asked him what he could do about Blackie's total domination of Brownie, or, if anything could be done at all. George knew right away.

"Sounds like you've got an overdog and an underdog." You will have to separate `em. Walk and hunt them separately for a while. Otherwise the underdog will listen to the overdog and not to you. It's the wolf that left in the dog. One leads and the other follows taking his orders from the leader. Work `em separately and they will sooner or later get the idea that you are the leader. Then, they will work well together and do so under *your* commands."

"Thanks George," Jack said.

"You bet," George answered. "By the way, are they maybe getting better looking?"

"You know they *really* are." Jack answered.

The two men prolonged their chuckles as they hung up the phones.

Jack went out to his garage and began building two doghouses for the back yard. He would have to keep the dogs chained to their respective shelters. He wasn't sure whether the beagle or the pit bull would dominate in terms of their temperament. If it was the pit, Jack didn't want someone to get bit or hurt.

It turned into an all day project. They were the traditional wooden structures with peaked roofs. He used pieces of roofing materials left over from when he roofed his home. Once finished, he set them some thirty-five feet apart. He had bought two, twenty-five foot, chains. He staked the ends far enough apart so each pup had comfortable access to its own house and could get out and exercise, but not get at each other.

Then, he introduced Blackie to his new chain and house. He had bought the black dog a black collar and the brown one a brown collar. It was only fitting, he allowed. He brought Brownie out next and repeated the procedure. The pups clearly didn't like the arrangement and announced their objections with prolonged barking and howling. Eventually it subsided to whines and whimpers. Jack took a drive to get away from the noise. In the city, people would have complained about the noise, but out there the nearest neighbor was a mile away. The dogs could cry till the cows came in if they wanted too. No one would notice.

Jack drove into town and stopped at the store for provisions. He bought two metal drinking bowls and two food bowls for the dogs. He also stocked up on dog food. That finished, he picked up the necessary dog licenses before returning home.

Something was wrong. There was no barking and no crying. Something told him to get to his gun. Something made the hair stand up on the back of his neck. Something... It felt like it did when he "smelled" the cong in Nam. He slipped into the house and grabbed his handgun. He opened the back door. Both dogs were growling from inside their doghouses. Still, Jack saw nothing.

Closing the door behind him, he slowly descended the steps from the back deck. The 'back yard' was a small clearing with the distant tree line marking the end of the 'yard' and the beginning of the woods. He stepped lightly. Obviously buoyed up by his presence, the dogs came out of their houses now and strained at the end of their chains. But still, Jack saw or heard nothing out of the ordinary. He leaned down and petted the dogs before he began walking the perimeter of his yard.

He stopped by his ‘garden spot’. There, in the freshly tilled soil, he found his answer. It was a single paw print. It was as fresh as home baked bread straight from the oven. It was huge. Jack's eyes scanned the tree line and then the field, which separated him from it. Nothing... He looked for more ‘sign’. Not another trace...

"It's gone now," he mused out loud. Dusk would encompass the area in about an hour. That would dramatically shift the odds—in the cat's favor. Suddenly, he heard a bone-chilling scream. He reckoned it was a quarter mile or so into the woods. The catamount had announced its intentions.

The dogs were still young—far too young and untrained to be useful in trailing a cat. On an impulse he went into the house and got his rifle. He put a leash on Blackie and said, "Go get `um' boy."

He placed the dog’s nose on the track in the garden. The black pup growled. It was almost as if he understood. He pulled away, nose to the ground and growling. Jack followed. The pup, now nine months old, followed a scent that he instinctively both hated and feared. He led Jack past the barn in which he had been born. Then, he climbed the grade toward the road. Without hesitation he crossed it and entered the woods. He was not baying or barking. He was growling a most serious and prolonged, low, growl. It was the fight-to-the-death growl of the pit bull that lived within him. Brownie barked and cried not quietly accepting that he had been left behind. He wanted a part of it, too.

A mile ahead of them, and moving at full diplomatic speed, the cat stalked ahead. He was not really running yet neither was he walking as he steadily made his way towards the interior of the woods and the rock strewn hills ahead. He winced as his front right paw hit the ground awkwardly. Still, he proceeded onward even though he couldn’t shake it off.

Back when Sammy had locked his jaw on the big cat's shoulder, muscle and sinew had been mangled. The bone itself had cracked and a piece of it had fragmented. It lay suspended in tissue, waiting for just the wrong kind of movement to snag up the works and cause pain. It shot through the right front leg like an electric shock. There was worse news. Arthritis was attacking the bone and muscle of the right shoulder of the cat. Sammy, on his way out of this world, had let the cat know what the words "pit bull" meant. The cat could not soon forget.

Blackie led Jack to the base of the same hill that Bessie had led him over when he and George had found the dog and cat battle scene—where Sammy had been killed. Jack stopped. The sun was getting ready to set.

Unknown to him, less than a mile ahead on a rock ledge, concealed by trees and brush directly in front of it, the cat waited. It was running no more. It was waiting. Its leg was throbbing. The cat wanted to have it out right then and there. It opened its mouth wide revealing its horrifyingly surreal teeth in a silent snarl. Its eyes were slits and they glowed green with hatred. They sparked with an ancient fire, as old as time: the predators' gaze, the look of the ancient, and the unafraid. Look and see the depths of hell and prepare to enter the next world. This was the big he-Catamount, the king of all the North American beasts, and he was waiting and biding his time. The invitation was out. The cat spoke without words: "Enter my kingdom—if you dare."

Jack called Blackie to a halt. It was getting too dusky. The sun was just beginning to set. Something primitive within Jack was at work; something deep within all primates; instilled in another time when lions and leopards ate monkeys on a regular basis and later when they ate men. They would strike at night when their vision advantage over the man was the greatest. Night, when they could see as in daylight and the man could not. His tools were not as effective then. His fears were greater, too. For inside him he knew that he was no physical match for the great cat. He became merely a prey animal and like all of the prey animals of the wild places, he found himself looking over his shoulder in fear. His hair would stand up on the back of his neck. Something would tell him that he was not the master there. His master waited ahead for him with unimaginable strength and natural weapons the likes of which inspire nightmares: Razor like teeth and claws, like knives and chisels, packaged in a beast of steel and sinew with grace and balance as well as raw power.

His instincts told him: "A catamount was waiting."

The hunter would soon become the hunted.

"It's getting dark Blackie. We'd better head back to the house."

The pup growled. Something primitive was stirring within him, too: The beagle instinct to trail game, and the pit bull instinct to fight without fear or mercy. By instinct, the dog within him hated all cats. The puppy was becoming a dog.

He obeyed his master and they turned around. They continued back down the trail toward the house and the tools within it, which represented the only source of fear the cat possessed. Suddenly, Blackie started to whine and cry.

"What's a matter boy?" Jack called out. Blackie pulled towards the base of a tree, which was surrounded by under brush.

"What ya got there, boy?"

Blackie entered the brush up to his shoulders. Jack pulled him back and went for a look. What he saw filled him with rage and sadness.

"Bones," he said. "Too small for a deer..."

His voice trailed off. His eyes located the scull of a dog. Beneath the head was a strap of some kind. No... It was a collar. In the fading light Jack reached into the brush and took hold of it. He gave it a gentle tug. The bones fell apart as he drew the strange piece of leather from the rubble. It suddenly became clear. It had belonged to Bessie. Blackie sniffed and whined.

Jack put it into his coat pocket and he and Blackie continued toward the house. They heard a scream. It sounded fairly close: too close there in the—dark. Jack led Blackie into the house and turned on the lights. The mercury vapor light lit up the back yard. Brownie was crying near his house.

Across the road, two glowing eyes watched the lights come on. They gazed intently but the cat had no desire to do battle there. It was the man's territory and he ruled there under his artificial sun. The cat would wait for another day and time at a place where he knew he had the advantage. Sooner or later his chance would come. He screamed a bone-chilling scream, then turned to stalk the woods for easier prey.

A few miles away he came upon sheep in an enclosed pasture. With an ease that was a sight to behold, he cleared the fence, jumped onto a sheep, and broke its neck with one powerful blow from a front paw. He tore it apart and devoured it. Eventually satisfied, he dragged the carcass away into the brush.

The sheep dog growled and barked. From out of the darkness the cat appeared, jumped, landed upon, and dispatched it, before another sound was made. Then it secured the rest of the sheep carcass in his jaws and jumped the fence. Once across the road and into the woods, it stored the catch in some brush and half buried it. It then climbed a nearby tree and lay out on a large branch. It yawned, much in the manner of a housecat, and took its rest.

It was 6 a.m. when John Phillips got out to his sheep pasture. Things looked pretty much as the always did. He walked into the field and called to his dog. Strange, he thought, the dog was nowhere to be seen. Usually this was the time he fed and watered him. He called out again as he began looking for him.

Fifty yards down the fencerow he understood why. The ground and the brush around it marked the spot where the sheep had been killed. Thirty yards away he found his dog—dead. The ground was splattered with blood. Its neck had been broken and its throat was torn out. He saw the paw prints.

"Oh my Lord," he whispered.

He ran back to his truck and drove to the house. He called Sam Macafee.

"Game warden Macafee," Sam answered as he picked up the phone.

"Sam," John said, "This is John Phillips. I need you to come out here. Something has happened that you have to see with your own eyes."

"What is it?"

"Something killed one of my sheep and my sheep dog. There are paw prints out here big as saucers— something that you will have to see to believe."

"What do you think they are?" Sam asked.

He knew in his heart what it was.

"I just don't know," John answered.

"I'll be right out, John."

Sam hung up the phone.

He called Jack.

"Hello," Jack answered.

"Jack, this is Sam. Have you seen that non-existent cat again?"

"Sure have," Jack answered. "He made an appearance last night. I took Blackie out lookin' for him but he must not have existed, because we only heard him; never saw him."

"He was busy. I think he ate one of John Phillips sheep and killed his sheepdog last night. John doesn't know what it was. You want to meet me out there and have a look see?"

"Yeah," Jack said, "I'll meet you out there."

"Thanks," Sam answered.

He hung up the phone.

"So now it begins in earnest," he whispered to himself. "The cat likes the easy prey to catch. No farm animal will be safe until we get him."

It was Saturday morning. Jack's truck pulled into John's driveway. He stopped and got out.

"Mornin' John," he called out. "Sam told me to meet him out here. Said you've got a sheep and a dog killed."

"Jack, you're not gonna believe the tracks I found out there."

"I just might," Jack said. "I've seen `em too."

"What in the hell is it?" John asked.

"Let's take us a look and see for sure, first. Sam will be along in a few minutes."

Jack didn't want to let the cat out of the bag, so to speak, until he was sure. He let Brownie out on his leash. It was time for his first cat lesson. He was following George's advice and it was working. Back home, Blackie was having a fit. Brownie remained fully obedient and sat upon command.

Soon, Sam's truck pulled in, and he got out.

"Well let's see what the excitement's all about."

John led them to the field where they followed him down the fencerow. It was pretty much what they expected.

"What in the hell could have done this?" John asked.

"We know." Sam answered. "But officially it doesn't exist in these parts, or at least hasn't in sixty some years. Some call it a painter; some a panther; some a cougar. But it's the king catamount. And it's a big one."

"I just can't believe it", John said, shaking his head. "Where could it have come from?"

"I don't know," Jack answered, "but it is here now."

Jack mixed and poured plaster of Paris into the print. Then he led Brownie to another one and let him get the scent. Brownie began to growl. He wanted to follow the trail. It led to the fence and then off into the woods. Jack had to rein him in. Officially, it was still illegal to hunt them.

Sam took the report in a very professional way, collected the print, and left. He wanted Jack to fill John in on the unofficial details while he lit the fire under a certain lady who's policy led to this mess in the first place.

Jack explained to John what the situation was, and the box it had put Sam in. Then he said, "I'd start by carrying a big caliber handgun whenever you're in the fields. Also, I'd like permission to hunt you're ground for a certain unspecified cat, that we're told does not exist."

"That's easy," John answered. "Do it anytime you like. I'd like to go with you."

"Good," Jack said. "Let's put Brownie on the trail."

That morning, the hungry cat had finished the rest of the sheep. Then, it had moved deep into the woods and went high into the hills where it found a comfortable ledge and settled in for a nap.

By the time the men began the hunt he was miles away. The men followed the trail to the kill. Then, they followed the trail for miles beyond. Brownie recognized and hated the scent. He was able to follow it, as Blackie had before him, but the cat had too big a lead. After five hours the men gave up and turned for home.

Above them, from a high ledge, the cat's eyes were on them. Taking the prey had been easy. A time of plenty had come for the cat. Slow, unsuspecting, sheep and cattle were child's play compared with the fleet deer. His eyes focused on the dog. He seemed to understand that this man's dogs presented a problem. They could bring the men and their guns to his very doorstep. He would have to reckon with them—and soon. Most dogs were no problem, but those two... . The cat had marked them for death. One day he would lead them off into the woods allowing them to trail him. At the opportune moment, he would turn and they would bother him no more. He yawned, showing his teeth, and stretched, flaunting his claws. He would enjoy it!

When they reached John's house the men had coffee. Jack and Brownie then headed for home. Jack decided to build a chain link fence enclosing each of the Dog's houses so that they wouldn't have to be tied. That way they would have half a chance if the cat came by day. At night he would let them in the basement. He needed some time, wanting them to grow to maturity and come to work well as a team before he would hunt the cat in earnest. He would need any edge he could find if he were going to get this cat and no one knew that better than Jack.

Sam had another report to file. It was only a matter of time before, even a certain Ms. Gillespie, would have to come to grip with reality and allow the state to capture or kill the cat. Back at the office he filed his report. He prepared himself for the confrontation. The wait was not long.

"What is this about another cat track?" She asked. "I thought we were clear on this cat business?"

"It killed a man's sheep and his dog. And it is not gonna stop there. It will keep killing until it's stopped. The worst case scenario is that it may not stop at livestock." Sam answered.

"A majestic cat like that is worth a thousand sheep," She said flatly.

"That's a fine position to take if the money is not coming out of your pocket."

"Our policy has not changed and is *not* changing. Is that clear?"

She was pulling rank now.

"Okay," Sam stated. "But note in the record that this policy was implemented over my objection."

"Does that mean that you are not a team player?" She asked, a snide threat implied.

"Call it what you like," he answered, "but put it in the record. And ma'am, I've been here eighteen years and have a clear record. If you want to fire me for objecting on the record, then you better read the personnel regs. I can also only be fired for cause. You have been here less than one year. I don't believe you could make a firing stick."

Sam's eyes shot fire. It stunned her.

"Very well; your objection is noted. This conversation is over."

Sam left the room before his temper exploded. He thought better than to give her a legitimate reason to fire him. He walked out of the building and got into his truck. The squalling of his tires as he left was intended as one last way of emphasizing his descent.

After he left Ms. Gillespie got on the phone. She was calling the state central office to report his actions. Her boss and she had enjoyed many cocktails and dinners together. When she had first applied and been given the position—over several more experienced people—the rumor mill had them sharing much more than dinners. She sobbed at the fact that mean ol' Sam had demanded that his objection be noted.

"And Robert," she began, "Some men are just chauvinist pigs. They have to kill a beautiful cat just because it is out there. They have to shoot, and maim, and kill, just to feel powerful. It is so wrong to make a beautiful cat pay such a horrible price just to satisfy the killing instinct of a brutal man. What can I do Robert?"

Robert Sanford was second in command in the state Department of Wildlife structure. He was a very powerful man.

He had worked in the governor's campaign and many felt he had made the difference. The appointment was made strictly in recognition of his service. He became more and more influential. He was in his late fifties, balding, overweight, and brilliant.

"Why don't you fly down to the capitol this Friday evening and we can give this matter the attention it deserves."

"Why Robert, that's a wonderful idea. I have a few outfits that you haven't seen yet."

"I'll pick you up at the airport. Let my secretary know your E.T.A., and I'll be there."

He smiled.

"Okay, Robert, I just can't wait to see you and to have you see me."

She purred, as she hung up the phone, smiling a triumphant smile.

"Men can be controlled so easily," she said out loud.

She left the office.

"I simply must pick up just the right lingerie," she whispered to herself.

She then continued, voicing the attack she planned to initiate.

"Poor Sam Macafee. You have no idea what you're up against. I will get rid of you and as many of your fellow Neanderthals as is possible. You will be example number one."

She entered her car. There was shopping to do. She *did* have an amazing figure and she was clearly well practiced in using it to her best advantage.

Some miles away, Sam got out of his car and walked into his home. Supper was on and Sally had his place all ready. His two kids were off at college so it was just Sam and Sally again, like it had been back when it all started.

"How was work honey?" she asked him as he took his place at the table.

"Don't ask," he said. "Lets just say that it is great to be home."

"Is that Gillespie woman giving you a bad time again?"

"She sure is."

Sam was still livid. He told Sally about the cat and what had happened. He related Ms. Gillespie's, and therefore the state's, position on the cat.

"She can't really get away with that. Can she?"

Sam sighed, a tired look crossed his face.

"Don't bet on it. But I thought about our two kids when they were little. How would we feel if there was danger out there that the state kept from us? What if a cat like that killed one of our kids? I just couldn't live with not at least going on the record in opposition? If a kid gets mauled, at least his folks will know that somebody tried to get the truth out."

Sarah got up, and hugged her husband.

"I want you to know, Sam Macafee, that I think you are wonderful, and that, however this turns out, you are my hero!"

Sam hugged her back.

"This more than makes up for all the bad that has happened, this day."

* * *

Spring soon became the summer. Jack finished the chain link fence around the two doghouses. For a while he had a separation fence to keep the two dogs apart the way George had instructed. Jack worked each animal separately and the progress had been remarkable. Both dogs were becoming excellent hunters and trackers. They were also learning one other vital skill; when they were called off a trail, they were learning to return to Jack immediately. He trained them using a silent dog whistle. Jack would praise and reward them with a treat every time they did return and would scold them when they did not. There was good reason for this training. If they would be on the cat's trail and get too far ahead of the men and guns, the cat could turn and kill both of them before the men, and the guns could arrive. Immediate obedience would be vital if they were to work together as a unit. The dogs would need all of their woods smarts, fighting ability, and their willing team work with the men, if they were ever to have a chance of success against the cat.

By the middle of summer, Jack removed the separating

fence between the two doghouses so the dogs could share the whole enclosed yard. They were no longer pups. They had their size and were well on their way to becoming the kind of dogs Jack was going to need on the upcoming hunt he was planning.

The cat had made itself scarce for the last three months. It was haunting a different part of its wide range. Forty miles away, though, farmers were losing dogs, sheep, and cattle. It was beginning to make the papers. The official story blamed every thing from wild dogs to coyotes, to anything the Division of Wildlife could think to blame—but never a word about a cat. Farmers were getting suspicious.

Whispered rumors were rampant. Something was out there and it was killing dogs and livestock with regularity over a five hundred square mile range. Sam had been reprimanded four times, all over petty stuff, but the employees union had come to his aid. His on-going battle with Ms. Gillespie was growing fiercer each day. So far he had been able to get by, with "no comment" when he was asked about the latest livestock kill. He could not and would not remain silent much longer. His job was in the balance.

His wife had gone to work—just in case. He knew that sooner or later the cat would do something that he could no longer remain silent about. In the meantime, his stalemate with Ms. Gillespie continued. Her tryst had resulted in increasing pressure on him, but his seniority and civil service protection were strong bulwarks against her attempts. His relationship with her was icy at best. There had been a long series of on-the-record objections to her head-in-the-sand policy where the cat was concerned.

The cat obliged by staying away long enough for the men and the dogs to get ready. Now they worked as a team. Now their instincts had been tempered with discipline. They had trailed deer together, although Jack had not been trying to hunt deer. Using dogs to bag deer was illegal and Jack hunted well within the law. It was the perfecting of the instincts he was interested in. He marveled at how they would work a field and drive the deer right to the concealed 'hunters'. The dogs would then move away from the deer towards the men. The deer's eyes would stay riveted on the dogs with not one thought of what might be concealed in the woods down wind. Jack could have shot a hundred deer if he'd been the type to cheat. But deer hunting was not his object. Working the dogs was. They were now ready. The next move was up to the cat. The dogs were big enough, that he didn't need to bring them in the house at night. Should the cat arrive, they could now last long enough in safety, fighting in tandem, for Jack to get to his gun in time to get a shot at the cat.

He talked with George about training them in that way because most dogs that chase deer are worthless when it comes to chasing cats. George had re-assured him.

"With these two dogs," the old man said, "When it's a choice between deer and cat scent, they will choose cat. They have learned since they were small that cat is their enemy. With most dogs it's a problem, but not with these two. They do know the difference. They are also smart enough to pick up on the difference in your attitude when you are just exercising them and when you are after cat. These dogs are cat smart. That is rare in dogs but these two are."

That had put Jack at ease on the subject.

Blackie was the fiercer of the two and by far the most powerful, but Brownie had more of his mothers nose for game and was the faster of the two dogs. Sometimes they would work together and sometimes they would split up working the deer to the middle of a field. The men could have shot them blindfolded! As Jack watched them work, he saw much of Bessie in them. He saw a lot of Sammy as well. At home they were guard dogs. They would alert him to anything that was there that shouldn't have been there. They had perfected growls and vicious snarls and barks, which convincingly suggested they would tear whatever it might be limb from limb. The beagle in them, however, had removed any hateful edge. They had all of the pit bull capacity, but their spirit was gentled by their beagle temperament. They would not attack without reason and they were not vicious for the sake of viciousness. They could be petted, and to those who knew them, they seemed like big beagles. To strangers and those who seemed to pose a threat, all of the pit bull ferocity and capability emerged.

Jack smiled. Bessie had been right about these pups all along. They were both worthy to be proud of.

## CHAPTER THREE
## The Lamb People

One crisp, though not bitter, cold November day, Jack took both dogs for a walk down the gravel and dirt road that ran past his house. The weather was more reminiscent of October than November. It was a good day to work the dogs. Because of the presence of the cat in the vicinity, Jack had taken to the habit of carrying his holstered colt strapped on his hip. He half-laughed about it because he must have looked like he was out of some western movie. He wore a coat over it so as not to advertise its presence. He'd rather face concealed weapons charges than to get chewed alive by a non-existent catamount prowling the woods that might get ideas. He was also using the walk to train his dogs. He needed them to be completely obedient to his commands if they were to be of any use to him on a certain hunt he was planning.

He soon arrived at a trail that crossed the road and entered the woods. It was a deer trail. Often, deer were seen crossing the road there and once in a while a car would hit one at night. The terrain was perfect for Jack's purposes. He needed his dogs to learn to come to heel on command. He wasn't about to have to put them on leashes when he went for walks, either in town or out along these old country roads. He'd gotten a good start with Blackie. He'd been working them separately, as George had suggested, and Blackie had discovered a groundhog hide. Someone had shot and skinned the groundhog, leaving the head and the feet in the hide. The rest had been skinned out. Blackie soon had the hide in his mouth, and, as was his instinct, began gnawing at it for any meat remnants he might recover. True to his instincts he began to shake it as if he were killing a rat or a coon.

Jack had an idea. "Drop it!" He shouted. Blackie looked right at him and instead of following his command, he gave Jack his mischievous doggy smile that as much as said, "You can't catch me, and I've got it, and you can't have it." Jack pulled his 45-caliber colt out, and repeated his command.

"Drop it!"

Blackie began to shake his prize and trot away, his eyes still fixed on Jack. He was clearly asking, "What can you do about it?"

Jack pointed his colt in the air and it belched fire and smoke. It roared out with an earth shaking **"BOOOOM"** that shattered the quiet of the woods. Blackie was on the verge of urinating himself—or worse. His 'prize' hit the ground immediately and Blackie crawled back to his master, belly to the ground, signaling his sincerest apology. It let his master know that his attitude was now **completely** adjusted. He came to heel. He had asked the question and he had gotten his answer. The issue was now resolved.

Jack tried hard to suppress a grin or worse to follow his desire to pat the dog and to say, "That's okay boy." Instead, he walked to the hide and gave it back to the dog. The dog was not about to believe his good fortune. With some initial reservation he picked it up and walked by the man's side chewing and shaking it. Then he started to run ahead.

"Drop it!" Jack commanded.

This time Blackie let the hide hit the ground as if it were poison. He immediately came to heel.

"Good boy!"

Jack called out and reached down and petted his dog's head. Then he gave the dog the hide again and allowed him to keep it without further interference. Blackie gratefully chewed his prize and walked at his master's heel.

This time, both dogs were along. It was Brownie's turn to learn the lesson. Blackie was staying at Jack's heel and Brownie was taking his cue from Blackie. So, they walked the trail one dog on each of Jack's heels. Then, Brownie's nose picked up the scent of deer. He bayed and started off on his own.

"Drop it!" Jack commanded.

Blackie hit the ground at his master's heel. Brownie looked at Blackie in disbelief. There were deer ahead, his instincts told him. He looked back at Jack as if he were nuts. Then he grinned his mischievous doggy grin and darted on ahead. Blackie wore a worried expression. Jack petted him and said, "good boy." Then he commanded.

"Brownie: **DROP IT!**"

He pulled his 45 out of his holster. Brownie forged ahead. Jack pointed his gun in the air and pulled the trigger. **"BOOOOM"!** Brownie hit the ground and crawled back to his master. Blackie gave him a look, which as much as said, "See, I tried to tell you." Blackie got a pat. Brownie got the message.

Then Jack shouted:

"Go get `em boys!"

Brownie let out a joyful bay and the two dogs were off at full gallop. Jack followed them to the field on top of the hill, and waited behind some trees, well out of sight. Soon, Brownie was in full bay and he heard Blackie barking and growling. The dogs had split up. He heard a scream that could only have come from one animal. The dogs were reunited. Jack ran out into the field. He blew on his dog whistle. He was not prepared to take on the cat just yet, and certainly not with a pistol. He ran across the field. He heard fighting just ahead. Then he saw his dogs turn and come to heel. They went forward together.

There, just ahead on the ground, was his answer. A full-grown buck lay on the ground. Its neck was broken. He was kicking his last. The dogs had apparently chased the buck into the awaiting ambush of the cat. It had jumped on the buck's back, and with one surgical bite, severed the deer's spinal cord. The buck was as good as dead when it hit the ground. Brownie burst into view by himself. The cat charged him and the fight was about to begin when Blackie entered the fray from behind. The big cat whirled to respond to the second challenge just as Brownie's teeth hit home. The cat's tail burned as if on fire. In an instant it turned to kill the brown dog. Blackie's teeth hit the tail higher up.

It was at that point that Jack blew the whistle and both dogs, true to their training, broke off the attack and ran toward the spot where they had heard the whistle. The cat mounted his pursuit but when it caught sight of Jack running towards them, gun in hand, it stopped. With a magnificent leap, the big cat simply disappeared from view, jumping over a stand of ten-foot high brush. There was no sound of a landing, no rustling of brush or leaves, not one giveaway. Not even a hint that the cat had seconds before been in plain sight. It simply had vanished. Jack looked at the dead buck and marked it in his mind. He and old George would visit the carcass later when they had some big caliber weapons that could deal with whatever the cat might have to offer. Maybe they would get lucky.

Jack fought off the eerie feeling that it was he that was being watched. He moved down the middle of the open field so that he might see anything moving in his direction. His hair bristled on the back of his neck. The dogs, true to their training, were right where they should be: one at each heel. He was proud of them! He patted them.

Jack's instincts were quite accurate. The cat was watching every move he made. It was probing for any sign of weakness. One hesitation, one slip, or any sign of weakness whatsoever, and he would show them just how close he was. The dogs both began to growl. The cat narrowed its eyes and yawned presenting its teeth. It was moving slowly and without sound, concealed in brush. Jack, by moving to the middle of the field had thwarted the big cat's ambush plan. Its tail was still in great pain. He wanted to kill both dogs. Quiet rage was surging through his veins. The cat worked its way around the corner of the woods where woods met field. It set up another ambush. Again, the dogs started to bark and growl. The cat was discovered again. Jack drew his gun.

The dogs wanted to bolt and go after it.

"Drop it!" Jack commanded.

Both dogs obeyed. The cat had counted on both dogs

pursuing it. It wanted to lead them deep into the woods where the man and the gun could not follow. He wanted them to chase him far ahead of the man. Then the cat would double back. Then he would kill, first one, and then the other dog. Then it would be the man's turn. Neither dog budged from Jack's heels. Then and there the big cat marked all three of them for death.

It would have to come at another time and place that would favor the cat and not the man. Silently, the cat crept away. He went back to his kill and gorged. Then he covered what was left of the big buck with twigs and leaves. He knew that the man would be back. He was counting on it. He would be waiting for him. Then he would work his way down the hill to the den of the man. First, he would kill the dogs and scream in triumph! He extended his claws and raked the ground. He was going to enjoy those kills.

The dogs had quit growling and the hair again lay flat on the back of Jack's neck. He could sense that the immediate danger had passed. He took another game trail that would cross the road further down. He was thrilled that his dogs had responded so well. They still had many lessons to learn before the three of them engaged the cat, but so far their progress had been spectacular!

About a mile down the game trail, Jack spotted the road below. They worked their way down the hill toward the road. It cut through the bank where the trail met it. Jack worked his way halfway down the bank and then jumped down to the road. The dogs matched his steps, and the three of them hit the pavement at virtually the same time.

Their sudden appearance on the road left four startled walkers shaking.

"I'm sorry," Jack offered. "We didn't mean to startle you."

Edgar and Victoria Salem had been walking with their two children, when suddenly Jack and his two dogs dropped out of nowhere. Victoria screamed and the children stood frozen. Edgar moved as if to hide behind his wife. He was a very smallish man and she a very large and dominating women. Jack explained that the brush was very thick where they made their 'entrance' and that he had not seen them.

"That's quite all right," Victoria announced. "Living out here in the middle of nowhere, we have come to expect the unexpected."

She and her husband were city folks who really should have stayed in the city. They had been hippies in the sixties and had moved out into the woods to 'commune with nature'. Their children had come late in life and they wanted them to grow up in a rural setting. But, they wanted to have nothing to do with the 'indigenous hicks' who for some reason, unknown to them, populated the area. They had moved into the old Smith place a few months before. They were churchgoers, but their most unusual church was in the city. They believed in God, but they were strict vegetarians and strong animal rights devotees. She was strongly into women's lib and he followed her every command. They thought that the 'locals' might be converted to their 'wisdom' if they proselytized. Jack had heard many stories about their attempts to re-educate the ignorant.

Jack was a patient man, but his patience had its limits. Some years before, Jehovah's Witnesses began visiting his home while he was working. They wanted to convert Sue to their wiser system of beliefs. Sue had been very nice to them, as was her nature, and had invited them in for coffee. They started in on her and they wouldn't quit. Finally, she told them that she and her husband were Baptists and that it was not about to change. She had been social but she had not wanted to be cross-examined about her religion. She thought that had ended the matter, but a few days later they were back and at it again. She wasn't as nice that time, and kept the conversation on the porch. Soon, she made an excuse and went inside. The next time they knocked she didn't answer. But they kept coming back. She realized that she was in over her head. She told Jack about the encounters. Jack pulled her into his arms and chuckled.

"Some people you just cannot be nice to. It's okay," he assured her. "You did your best but now it's up to me to make sure they get the message."

Jack knew that Jehovah's Witnesses were people who didn't believe in the *Pledge of Allegiance*, or in the display of the American flag.

On the day that they typically dropped by, Jack stayed home from work with a 'bad case of the flu'. He had hoisted a large American flag on the flagpole on the porch. Then he had gone inside and waited for the arrivals. Soon an older car pulled into the drive.

"That's them," Sue announced, in horror.

An older and very fat and ugly lady got out of the car accompanied by a pretty young lady and a teenager. Together they marched up to the porch. They recoiled in horror when met by the flag, in much the same way as a movie vampire recoils at a cross being flaunted in their direction. Nonetheless, they ascended the porch steps and were soon knocking at the door. Jack stepped out onto the porch.

"Hello" he said.

"Is the Misses home?" the old crohn asked.

"Yes she is." Jack answered. "But, I am the head of this household and you are going to have to deal with me if you want to do any business with this family."

"Very well," the old crohn croaked.

Then the young pretty girl took over in an abrupt and obvious change of tactics.

"Can we come in and talk about our Lord?" She asked with perfect gentility in her voice."

"Sure," Jack answered, "as soon as you answer one question for me."

"What is it?" Clearly, she was getting ancey.

"Well," Jack began, "I have heard a very unsettling rumor about the Jehovah's Witnesses; one that I am sure you can clear up for me. That is, that you won't salute an American flag or say the pledge of allegiance to our great country. That isn't true of course. Is it?"

"Well," the pretty girl began.

The old crohn interrupted.

"We believe that God and his will are superior to any

national creed."

"So do I," Jack agreed. "But this great nation was founded by God fearing men and our constitution says that God granted us `Certain unalienable rights.' That is what our very freedom is based on. I fought for this country and those `certain unalienable rights.' I served two tours in Vietnam and lost half of my unit twice. I prayed for the salvation of every one of those American boys we buried. God blessed this nation. No one comes into my house that won't salute her flag and won't say her pledge of allegiance. Are you loyal Americans? Will you salute our American flag? That's all you have to do and then we will talk with you as long as you like."

"We cannot and we will not," the old crohn answered.

"Then this conversation is over!" Jack stated with finality. "I'll have no truck with people who sponge off of our God given rights and freedoms without any loyalty to this nation, who's very constitution is based on the Bible."

"Very well," the old crohn answered.

They turned around, walked to their car, and left.

When Jack got back inside, Sue hugged him hard and they went directly to the bedroom. Later, she would laugh about how easy he had made it look and she would imitate the old crohn as she stomped off of the porch and into the car.

"Now," Jack told her, "they will not try to raid the chicken house when the rooster is away. If they come back, you tell them that your mean old husband set down the law, and, if they want to talk they'd better salute that flag and say the pledge." Then he laughed. "I may have laid it on a little thick, but deep down, I meant every word."

"Got ya!" Sue said, and she saluted. Then she grabbed her husband and hugged him again. True to his prediction, they came one last time while he was away, but Sue gave them the same terms and they left. That time it was for good.

"And good riddance," as Sue had put it.

As it turned out, the young woman and the child later became Baptists. She had been so taken in by the old crone that she was about to divorce her husband because he would not join her new church and share in her new faith. What Jack said made her think. She began to realize how far off the deep end she had plunged. She made up with her husband and she and her child went home to him. Her husband, Joe Jessip, sought Jack out and told him that he owed him a huge favor. Jack told him that he could pay it back by helping someone else who needed it down the line sometime. They became good friends. After Sue passed away, they visited often. They remained friends over the years.

Victoria asked Jack where he and his dogs were going. Jack knew what was coming, so he decided to throw some fuel on the fire and see what happened.

"I was just getting the dogs ready for the hunting season," he offered, as matter of factly as possible. Victoria's face fell.

"You don't kill beautiful animals. Do you?"

"Yes, ma'am. I have hunted all of my life. These two dogs are natural deer dogs, although I don't use them for that. It is something to see them work."

The two children interrupted.

"Can we pet the doggies?" The little boy asked.

His name was Marc and he was about seven, Jack guessed. The little girl looked to be five and she loved the doggies too.

"I guess that wouldn't hurt." He looked at his two dogs and gave a command: "Blackie and Brownie, **DROP IT!"** Both dogs hit the ground at Jacks heels.

"What is your name?" Jack asked the little girl.

"Teresa," she answered. Then she proudly held up five fingers. "I'm five."

"That's very good," Jack said. "Would you like to pet the doggies first?"

"Oh yeah!" She squealed.

She moved toward Blackie. Blackie growled.

"Blackie be quiet!" Jack said harshly, "It's okay boy."

Blackie looked up at the little girl and the beagle immediately surfaced. His tongue came out, and he began to wag his tail.

"Good boy," Jack called out.

Then Teresa began to pet him.

"OOOH! YOUR SUCH A NICE DOGGIE!" She squealed.

Jack was now reassured that Blackie would stay in beagle mode while the little girl petted and fussed over him. He turned his attention to Marc and asked.

"Would you like to pet Brownie?"

"OH YEAH! THAT WOULD BE NEAT!" He said, with childlike excitement in his voice. Brownie was wagging his tail too. Eventually the kids switched dogs and the petting began anew.

Edgar warmed up a little and noted that the dogs were extremely well behaved and well trained. Jack smiled.

"It's a lot of work but these two have really taken to it well."

"How do you get them both to heel like that? They don't even need leashes."

Jack smiled and answered. "Just a lot of work and patience. And two good dogs that really want to learn."

"They are wonderful dogs!" Teresa squealed. "Momma could I have a doggie like that?"

"Now, you have a nice kitty. Don't you?"

"Yes mama, but these dogs are neat!"

Jack looked at Marc. "Do you have a kitten too?"

"No," he answered, "but I do have two lambs."

Edgar quickly mentioned. "It's good for kids to raise animals. It teaches them a lot."

Jack nodded his agreement without mentioning the seeming contradiction of vegetarians raising sheep.

Victoria looked at Marc, "And what do sheep give us?"

"Wool," the boy answered as if he were responding to a teacher at school.

"And what do the lambs teach us?" She prompted.

"That God wants us to be gentle in all things." The boy answered.

He looked up at Jack. Something within him could not be silenced.

"Do you use a gun when you go hunting?"

It seemed an odd question to Jack, but he answered.

"Yes, I do."

Edgar quickly added, "Some people shoot the pretty deer."

Now Jack couldn't avoid the subject. He had tried for the sake of the children. He really had. Victoria now bored in.

"The deer should be free to roam and just live as God intended all of us to live."

Jack answered: "Ma'am, if no one hunted the deer, they would over populate and starve to death slowly. That is a terrible way to die. This way they give us meat, and sport, and they grow in numbers every year. Our hunting licenses pay for the monitoring of the herd so they continue to thrive. Did you know that we now have more deer than we did one hundred years ago, in these parts? So you are free to see their beauty."

"That's the excuse that is given." Victoria sneered. "But, if man had not killed off all of their natural predators, hunting wouldn't be needed."

"Ma'am," Jack answered, "I don't believe that you would want to be raising children with wolves, bears, and mountain lions around, especially if you do not have any guns handy." He really wanted to warn them. "In fact, there is a mountain lion in these parts right now. Watch your kids closely."

Victoria didn't believe him for a minute. "Don't scare the children with you're tall tales. Besides," she looked at her children, "The animals are our friends. If we don't try to hurt them, they won't try to hurt us."

"Yes mama," the children said.

Then she continued. "The Bible tells us to beat our swords into plow shares, and the lion will lay down with the lamb."

Jack looked at her and said, "I believe that God is speaking of the next world in that statement: not this one. `For there will always be wars and rumors of war,' in this world."

"We don't want to wait for the next world to have peace and love and harmony. We can have it that way right here and now. Can't we children?"

"Yes momma," they answered. Jack didn't want to argue in front of the kids.

"That is the wonderful thing about living in the United States of America," he said. "I am free to hunt, and you are free not to. I am free to eat meat, and you are free to eat vegetables. I am free to interpret scripture the way that I see it, and you are free to interpret it the way you want to."

"Victoria said, "We believe that hunting is evil and should be banned. Guns should be banned too."

Jack had enough. "And freedom? Should that be banned too?"

"The freedom to do harm to innocent animals or to innocent people should be banned," She said.

Jack answered: "You will never see that end in this world, when it comes to people doing harm and evil to other people, or predatory animals eating prey animals if they are in proximity to them. I wasn't kidding about the lion. Be careful, and I would still advise that you get a gun. There is a big difference between a prayer meeting, and a bear meeting."

"Just what do you mean by that!" Victoria snapped back.

"Just that a preacher is good for a prayer meeting, and a gun is good for a bear meeting," Jack answered, matter of fact. "Well, it's been nice talking, but me and the dogs have got to get back to the house."

With that he tipped his hat and called out to the dogs.

"Blackie and Brownie: **move out!"**

On command, the dogs rose to their feet and formed on Jack's heels.

"Goodbye mister. Goodbye doggies." Teresa called out."

"Goodbye Teresa." Jack called back.

"Goodbye mister." Marc called out.

"Goodbye Marc," Jack answered.

"Children!" Victoria called out. "You two march for home: right now!"

"Yes mama," they said in unison.

And so they departed in opposite directions.

"Those poor kids," Jack whispered out loud. "They just wanted to play with the doggies. If they were given half a chance they would be all right."

He had heard that their mother home-schooled them rather than exposing them to the public schools. He didn't mind that idea. With all of the so-called sex education and so-called liberation-in-all-forms ideology being taught as fact, Jack might home school his own kids had they still been in school. But still the kids haunted him, being raised as they were in what seemed to him to be such an unrealistic and strange ideology. He wished them well.

Soon he was home. He put the dogs in their fenced in yard and fed and watered them. Then he went in to call George. The phone rang three times before George picked it up.

"Hello," an old and strangely grumpy voice answered.

"George."

"Yeah."

"This is Jack."

The old man's voice perked up.

"Hi Jack. How are you doin' there, young fella?"

Jack laughed.

"Pretty good there, *old* timer."

George started to laugh.

"Well, what is it that made you call this old relic?"

"I need your help."

"Oh yeah. What with?"

Jack related what had happened with the cat and about the dogs finding the deer carcass. He wanted George to go with him, without the dogs, to set an ambush for the cat at the site of the kill. George turned dead serious.

"Did the dogs injure the cat?" he asked clearly concerned.

"I don't know". Jack answered. "I blew the dog whistle as soon as I heard the fight began."

He then related his sense that the cat had set and abandoned two ambushes on their way home.

"Better get over here quick. And bring the dogs! I've

been through something like this before and I smell trouble."

"Okay", Jack said, "We're on the way."

Something about the way the old man had spoken upset him. 'He knows something,' Jack thought to himself. He got in his truck and the dogs upon command jumped into the bed. They were off.

Before long they pulled into George's driveway. The old man was waiting.

"Better kennel the dogs here for now," The old man offered.

He opened the gate and let the dogs into his fenced-in enclosure. Then the two men went into the house. George poured the coffee. He began.

"The cat saw you and knows that you know where the kill is. Right?"

"That's probably right," Jack answered.

George continued.

"My father told me a story once. They had caught a cat on its kill. They wanted to set an ambush for later. But the cat knew. It was waiting for them to return. When they did, it doubled back to where the dogs were kenneled and killed them. That done, it worked its way back to the men. It waited until the sun had almost set and then it struck. It killed one of the men and took him off into the woods. When they got back they found the dogs dead.

"This cat looks at us as enemies, but not yet as food. It has not yet tasted human blood. If it ever does, then we have an entirely different problem on our hands. Once a big cat tastes human blood it goes crazy. It likes the taste so well that we become its first choice. That's when it becomes the real danger. In India one leopard reportedly killed over 400 people before they finally got it. The hunter who killed it tried and failed a hundred times over five years before he finally got lucky. Once a cat tastes human blood, it becomes something all together different. If the dogs hurt him, he will mark those dogs for death. Then, he will systematically hunt them down until it kills them. It senses that they may be on to him; that they will track his specific scent to his lair. You may think that

I'm crazy, but you better realize that a leopard is smaller than that mountain lion. It isn't as good a hunter either. Of all the big cat's, the catamount is the best hunter of them all. Eight out of ten times it gets its prey. By comparison, an African lion hits pay dirt only one in ten times, and a tiger, three in ten. What we are up against is the most efficient predator God ever created! Pound for pound it is many times stronger than a tiger or a lion. A leopard is just as strong pound for pound but a leopard is smaller. Part of the reason that the big cats of India and Africa got away with killing so many before they were put down was because most of the people didn't have guns.

"The wolves here are unique. They hunt in packs and there are so many of them that the big cats, or even grizzlies, would not want to confront them alone. Of the big cats, only the African lion hunts in packs or prides. Run amuck of several lions at the same time and you have even bigger trouble than we would have with this cat if it turns man-eater. Most big cats that turn man-eater are either old or weak or are injured. But from time to time, a young one gets the taste of human blood. In a place in Africa called Tsavo, two young males in their prime got the taste of human blood. They killed man after man, in twos and threes, and carried them off. By the time they were done they killed hundreds and completely stopped a bridge building project until a hunter got lucky and killed the first one. He had to kill the second one when it was coming after him and after it had already killed three men armed with rifles. That man only killed that cat after putting eight holes in him. And he was damn lucky at that.

"If your dogs drew blood and got away because you whistled them off, then that cat knows that you and they are a danger to it. And it still believes that it and not you and your dogs are king of the woods and the hills. It sees you as another predator challenging its supremacy. It fears your gun but it does not fear you. Yet a man poses attack problems that no other creature of the woods does. He stands upright, for one thing. A deer, or any other four legged animal, gives him the chance to land on his back and deliver either a precision bite to the neck which severs the spinal chord, or he'll hit him with one blow of his mighty paw and break its neck. Such power does this cat have that its blow has been known, not only to break the neck of a bull elk, but to actually drive its antlers into the ground and stick there! But a man is upright. He can't jump on his back. He has to go for him face to face. In that position the cat cannot get the leverage to launch a paw to the head from above. That is why big cats tend to back off if it's an eyeball-to-eyeball confrontation. They like to attack from behind. Then killing a man is easy. Even a tiger will generally not tackle a man face to face. Of the thousands and thousands of men tigers have killed, its almost always from behind. Indian natives often wear masks on the back of their heads so that the tigers think they can see them. It works too. If a big cat strikes from behind he is in control and he knows it. That way he knocks you down gets on your back and suddenly you're meat. Eyeball to eyeball a man can usually back off a tiger or a leopard. If it's an African lion, though, hunting in teams like in Tsavo, they will attack at any time, especially once they have tasted human blood.

"Be glad that we are facing a solitary catamount. Let me give you an idea of what we are facing. A catamount that weighs, lets say 150 pounds—and the one we are looking at is much bigger than that—but at just one hundred and fifty pounds, that cat can carry nine hundred pounds worth of buffalo or elk up the sheer face of a rock cliff in its jaws. It could damn near drag a moose up into the crotch of a big tree. Its jaws are such that when it bites the neck just below the head, from behind, its fangs will hit between the first and the third vertebra and sever the spinal chord killing the prey instantly. Or, it can use its paw. What I'm saying is that if we are gonna stake out a carcass that the critter knows we have seen, we better be prepared for anything."

"Where did you learn all of this?" Jack wondered aloud.

"Cats," the old man said, "have always fascinated me. My father got the last one in these parts when I was just a boy. I grew up with his stories about them. One of his stories was the one I told you about the `ambush'. They tried to set at his carcass. If we were smart, we would leave the dogs kenneled at your place and post a guard so that if the cat decides to leave us at the carcass and use that opportunity to sneak down and kill the dogs, a man with a gun, in concealment, would be waiting. That's how dad got the last one in these parts. But, the hell of it is, there are only two of us. Unless this cat is a young and inexperienced one, the ambush won't work. When you have the time," the old man went on, "you can borrow these books. You will need to know what's in them, if you are gonna get this cat."

The two men decided to leave the dogs safely kenneled at George's house and hope they got lucky with the cat at the sight of the ambush. They set out in Jack's truck. He stopped by his house to get provisions. George loaded his stuff into the truck. They pulled in to Jack's driveway and went into the house. Jack got his rifle and jacket and a good pair of leather boots. He changed into his thermals, because in the evenings, the temperature would drop.

George had a surprise for Jack: Two facemasks to be worn backwards to make the cat think that they could see behind them. Jack was resistant to the idea.

"Damn. What is this? Halloween?" He protested.

"I'd rather have a cat die laughing, than to be attacked from behind by one." George answered. "Big cats are big cats when you get right down to it. Better safe than sorry. Eh?"

"Okay, okay," Jack agreed. "But never a word to anyone about this. Huh?"

George couldn't resist.

"Okay kitty: Here comes ol' four eyes and his friend."

The two men shared a laugh. They turned onto the road to the game trail Jack had taken earlier with the two dogs.

They were soon at the field. Instead of taking the direct route to the kill, Jack went clear around the field on the other side from the kill, then worked his way in toward it. Fifty yards away, he stopped behind a tree. George worked his way behind another tree some thirty yards off to the side of Jack. He was nearly twenty yards closer to the carcass. One hundred yards behind them, and up in a tree, the cat had been watching it all. He worked his way out of the tree and down to the ground, keeping the trunk of the tree between him and the men. There was no way the men could see him.

Once on the ground, the cat snarled quietly, then slowly worked its way toward George. With the brush between it and George, it inched closer. It got to within twenty feet—almost within striking distance. Its tail began to twitch in anticipation of the spring and the strike. Then, it stopped dead in its tracks. There was the man with his gun, pointing towards the kill. But something was wrong. The cat saw the man's eyes looking right at him. His belly hit the ground. Deftly and without sound, it worked its way away from George and gradually circled around behind Jack. There were no dogs to give him away. He got behind Jack and stopped dead. Jack's eyes were on him too.

He worked himself away from Jack and down the hill towards the house. The dogs were not along. They would be in the yard—alone. The cat began to run in anticipation. He darted across the road and into the brush and trees on the other side. Then he circled to where the fence was. He didn't hear them barking and they should have been. He inched his way to the fence and jumped it, landing on Blackie's doghouse. Nobody was home. In rage, he jumped to the ground, backed up against Blackie's house, scent marked it with urine, and then did Brownie's as well. It was his insult. Then he went up the stairs to the back porch. The man must have locked the dogs inside. With one leap it broke the back window and was in the house: No dogs.

The cat was by then enraged. It smelled the man's scent everywhere. It entered the bedroom. The scent was strongest, on the bed. He leaped upon it and scent marked the bed. Rage consumed it now. It tore and rent with its claws, shredding the mattress. Then, in much the same manner as a house cat, it crapped, covering it with the torn stuffing from the bed. As quickly as it had come it was gone out the back window.

The cat was now going to settle with the men: Eyes or no eyes. Dusk settled over the hills and meadows. Now the odds were in his favor. The big cat moved along the trail the men had taken. It heard noise and talking. He leapt, without sound, behind some brush. The men were coming. George and Jack had waited for any sign of the catamount. They heard and saw nothing. George turned around and moved twenty feet to his left. Then he stopped dead sill. There, in a sandy bank, he saw the tracks of the cat. He hollered for Jack. Jack came running. Goorge showed him the tracks.

"That cat was right behind me," He said, as a chill shuddered down his back.

Then they went to Jack's tree where they found more tracks.

"That cat got behind us both. That could mean only one thing. It was going to strike!" George said.

"The eyes saved us. That's all I can figure. I wonder if it went after the dogs in their kennel?"

"Let's go find out." Jack said.

The two men walked rapidly down the trail. The cat watched them pass by. With both of them together, guns at the ready, the cat didn't like the odds. It stayed concealed and waited until they were out of sight. Then it unleashed a blood-curdling scream. The men were on the road when they heard it. They were not about to go chasing after it into the woods in the dark. For the moment they were thanking their lucky stars and their extra set of ‘eyes’ for their good fortune.

When they entered the house they found it was a wreck. Jack went into the bedroom and cursed. The cat had torn the bed limb from limb and had urinated and crapped. The odor was everywhere and so potent he felt like throwing up.

George's face was ashen.

"I knew that the cat didn’t fear a man's dwelling and that they were known to come in after people through windows. But I've never seen or heard of anything like this. That cat has declared war on you and the dogs. It's an open declaration."

George helped Jack carry the mattress outside. They were going to burn it. Before they did though, they called Sam MaCaffe to have him witness the carnage.

"He's not a man-eater yet, but that cat is just about to cross the line. He has challenged you and your dogs to a fight to the death. There is no doubt about that. If I were you, I'd let the dogs come in at night and I'd advise you to sleep with a gun in easy reach. You might consider installing bars on the inside of the windows just as a precaution," George advised.

Jack got on the phone and called Sam Macafee.

"Hello," Sam answered.

"Sam," Jack began. "I need your help, bad."

"What is it?" Sam wondered aloud.

"It's the cat, Sam. It broke into my house and scent marked the place and tore up my bedroom. It broke a window getting in. It has declared war on me and my dogs."

Sam was stunned. He had never imagined such a thing. He'd heard the old folk stories about such things, but he'd always thought that they had been stretched a bit, much as a fish story might be. Now he wondered.

"I'm on my way."

He hung up the phone kissed his wife on his way out the door, jumped in his truck, and spun gravel as he moved out towards Jack's house. Even as he raced to the scene, he wondered what he was going to be able to do about it. Maybe he and Jack could figure a way to blow the cover on the big cat without his boss being able to silence the story. Maybe the police and the press should be notified.

Sam soon pulled into the drive. He got out of his truck and walked to the door. Jack let him in and immediately his senses were assaulted by the petrifying odor of the cat. He almost gagged! Jack showed him the bedroom and the broken window. Then he showed him the tracks out by the dogs' houses. It was all too clear what had happened.

"The fat is in the fire now," Sam said. "The genie's out of the bottle and there is no way to put it back. If I were you, Jack, I'd call the police and the press. Tell them you called me, too. That way it wasn't me who `broke the story' and there will be nothin' Ms. Gillespie can do to silence the story. That will untie my hands and maybe we can finally get rid of that cat. I can't see how they could quiet this down. Go make a plaster cast of one of the prints outside and don't tell them that you were hunting the cat. It just broke in while you and the dogs were out. Then maybe we can get some action."

Jack was uncertain.

"I'd like to warn everybody. But that cat has declared war on me. I'm not about to turn my house into a prison with bars. I think maybe it's time me and the dogs had it out with the cat. They are just about ready. If they can tree that cat, then maybe I can kill it. I think that the dogs can find it's den and I can finish this nonsense once and for all."

Sam and George had grim looks on their faces.

"It might work," George said, "and it might not."

Sam fists were clenched, and his face was set. "We have got to alert the people. They have a right to know."

"And what if you're wrong, and a way is found to shut up the story and you get fired?" Jack answered. "My way doesn't risk your job."

Sam just laughed.

"My job is to tell the truth to the people when an animal threatens their safety. Up until now, it's been dogs and livestock. Things have changed. As you said, it has declared war. It's time to finish that cat and to alert the people."

George looked at Jack.

"Sam is right. This is bigger than just you and that cat. What if you just wound the cat and it starts killing kids? Do you want that on your conscience?"

Jack shook his head. They were right and he knew it.

"Okay, okay. We'll do it your way. But I still want a crack at that cat."

Jack called the paper and the police. They arrived about half an hour later. They were stunned. The photographers took pictures, and reporters interviewed Jack and Sam. George, as agreed, went home and got the dogs. He would be back a little later. The police did the interview and took pictures of the bed. Samples of the cat's feces and the plaster of Paris track were given to Sam in full view of the photographers. It would be in the morning edition of the paper. Sam was asked point-blank what he thought it was, and this time he didn't say "no comment." He announced that this was the work of a cougar. The police took the report and the media reporters left. That was about it, Jack thought.

In the morning two vans pulled into the drive. The television crews piled out with action cams and they came in and surveyed the damage. They interviewed Jack. They seemed skeptical. He showed them the paw prints and the torn up mattress, which had been tossed into the back yard. Then they left. As a precaution the dogs had been tied to their doghouses, so nobody got bit.

Once they were gone, George came over and they made coffee. George brought a copy of the morning paper. It had a front headline that read: COUGAR TEARS UP HOME. It had pictures of the mattress, the plaster of Paris paw print and it quoted the police as saying it was the darndest thing they had ever seen. They quoted Sam Macafee as verifying that it was indeed a cougar. Pictures followed on the nightly news.

When Sam got to work that morning he was immediately fired. Ms. Gillespie did that job personally. The State Department of Wildlife denied that the track was that of a cougar and claimed that the feces were that of a bobcat. It was asserted that the bobcat might have rabies, and an alert was put out. By the time Ms. Gillespie and her boss in the capitol got done with the press, they had actually been convinced that the story was a hoax. Sam had asked her why in front of her boss.

"We don't want a panic," was their answer. "Besides," Ms. Gillespie said with cold hatred, "The cat has harmed only property and that was not sufficient to kill it." She' had called an old family friend at the newspaper, and told him that it wasn't a cougar, and that they'd fired Sam Macafee for incompetence and for creating a hoax.

Sam walked out the door in disgust. He had finally had enough. He went to a lawyer and brought a sample of the feces to his office. He had the lawyer contact an independent expert to verify what it was. He called Jack and asked him to take another paw print. This was done and forwarded to an independent lab for analysis. He was going to sue to get his good name back.

He went over to Jack's house. If the fix was in, he was at least going to fight back. He could not comprehend the cold-blooded nature of those he fought. That cat was more important to them than any people it might kill. He was wrong. They wanted to get the cat and tranquilize it. Then they would relocate it. Nobody would be the wiser. Ms. Gillespie's figure was paying big dividends, for her. She had gotten rid of her first Neanderthal.

The days that followed were filled with activity from the Department of Wildlife. Helicopters hovered over Jack's land. Men and dogs were engaged in sweeping the area to find a rabid bobcat. No one asked why they carried tranquilizer darts instead of bullets if they were out to kill a rabid bobcat. The hills were alive with the sounds of baying coon dogs and helicopters.

The cat had, of course, heard the commotion and, keeping its composure, stayed in its cave until he heard the dogs coming for it. Then, he lit out the back way and, without leaving deep cover, worked himself out of harms way. By the time the dogs located the den it was late afternoon. In a matter of two hours the sun began to set. The cat stayed in cover and just kept moving. One persistent coon dog had worked its way well ahead of the pack. At dark the dogs were called back. All but one returned. It had stayed on the trail, as a coon dog would do at night.

It had miscalculated badly. From out of nowhere the cat was on it and by himself he was unable to do much. In the darkness, the cat concealed itself on a rock ledge above the trail. The dog had worked its way up the rock-strewn trail. The cat sprang out of the darkness. It hit the dog from behind and administered one powerful swipe of its huge front paw. It was over in seconds. The cat feasted. It covered the uneaten half of the dog with twigs and branches.

Then the cat, as if sensing that the hunt was on, simply left the immediate area. It traveled north by northeast all night. It revisited another den. At daylight it curled up and went to sleep. It had traveled almost thirty miles that night and it wasn't stopping there long. The next night it covered thirty more. The men and dogs combed the area and found only scent that was growing colder and colder.

Finally, in defeat, the pursuers treed a bobcat that was promptly shot. The claim was made that they had gotten their cat. The carcass was displayed before the T.V. cameras. Then the Department of Wildlife proclaimed victory and left. Their experts correctly assessed that the cat had simply left the area, and therefore it had been "relocated." The missing dog was never found and therefore was 'presumed lost'. At the end of the third day the men, women, and helicopters left the area, the problem presumed solved.

Later in the week, Jack and his dogs were walking down the road when he ran into the lamb people again. They snubbed him and would not allow their children to talk to him or pet the dogs. The misses made one snide comment about the cougar hoax and he didn't even try to explain it to them. They knew it all anyway, he figured. He had tried to warn them. He had tried to warn the people. He had notified all of the proper authorities. Sam had been fired. Those who knew Sam believed him. Those who believed his story had loaded up their rifles and shotguns and remained on the lookout. Those who did not had at least been warned. For the time being, they were safe. It was the calm before the storm.

## CHAPTER FOUR
## The Bare-Assed Buck

As time progressed Jack's relationship with the lamb people grew quite nasty. They, and the long time locals were at sword points. They spoke to fewer and fewer people. The young boy, Marc, and the young girl, Teresa, secretly liked, and were immensely curious about, their neighbor, Mr. Jack, and his dogs. Marc wanted to learn to shoot a gun and go hunting. Such thoughts were strictly prohibited in his home so he dared not speak of them. His sister wanted a dog, "like Blackie and Brownie," and she did ask. She was severely reprimanded for having such thoughts. But she was immensely curious. On days that were not too cold, they took to walking their lambs on rope leashes and often they would walk past Jack's house.

Sometimes they would see him and they would call out, "Hi Mr. Jack." He would always wave and say, "Hi kids. How are you doing?" They would try to start conversations with him but he always seemed to have things he had to do. They wondered why. He couldn't tell them but he didn't start or continue conversations with them because he did not want to get them in trouble with their parents. Also, he didn't want their parents to have even the remotest excuse to invent a lie about him or twist his conduct towards the children that could seem like something that it never was, just because they didn't like him. So the children were kept at arms length. Sometimes it hurt their feelings. He was never mean to them in any way but he was *always* busy. He worried about them walking their lambs with a cat about. It was made worse by the fact they had been taught it wouldn't bother them if they didn't bother him. Jack was more than a little frightened for them, but there was nothing he could do. Sometimes he would take his gun and his dogs into the woods after they had safely passed from view. He followed and watched to make sure they made it home safely. They never knew about that, of course.

Deer season was approaching. Regardless of any logical, fact-based, arguments to the contrary, the lamb people believed that deer hunting should be stopped. They invited friends down from the city, many of whom went to the same liberal and peculiar church that they went to. Often they planned and discussed what they could do to stop the outrageous killing. They held animal rights meetings in their home. Jack didn't know it but one of those who attended frequently was April Gillespie. The same April Gillespie that had doctored the cat evidence that Sam had presented and had gotten Sam fired. Jack had been able to get Sam a job in the factory where he worked. The Macafee's were at least eating, with both of them having to hold down jobs in order to keep things going.

There was considerable animal rights activity out west, but until now very little had filtered into the Midwest. That was about to change. As deer season came activists began harassing hunters on the public hunting lands. They would send college age kids, dressed in deer and rabbit costumes, to taunt hunters and to chase away game to 'save' the animals. The problem was that in this remote area people hunted their own private ground and arranged with their landowning friends and neighbors to hunt their private land with permission. The trespassing laws made it a crime for animal rights people to harass hunters, either on their own land or on land that the hunters had permission to hunt. The animal rights activists, (the locals called them hippies, weirdoes, or worse), could be charged with trespassing and jailed, fined, and dragged into court for such activities.

Ms. Gillespie had a two-pronged strategy to address these 'archaic legal barriers': first, she and those of her wealth and persuasion, campaigned to have 'endangered' animals protected. This was pretty well accepted by many people. The problem was that the 'environmentalists and their allies in the academic community, began to do 'studies' that were biased at best and outright lies at worst, in order to twist information. They used those claims to include non-threatened animals on the list of endangered species.

They had no regard for the truth. Just as cat paw prints, set in plaster of Paris could be called bob cat tracks, and cougar feces could be called bobcat droppings, so too, healthy populations of animals could be called endangered because they weren't often seen in a particular area. They would create a so-called 'sub-species' that supposedly existed only in that area and that sub-specie could be called endangered.

Division's of wildlife could overcome property rights of land owners by proclaiming that the state 'owned' all of the wildlife, and if 'the people' (meaning the state), owned all of the wildlife, even if it was on your land, the State Department of Wildlife could legally trespass on anyone's land for the purpose regulating 'the peoples' wildlife. So, if the people own all of the wildlife, then the individual owns nothing. It could be argued that the property rights of the individual had been taken from him by the state, and the state could trespass at will. They could also proclaim a 'protected habitat' and force the property owner to sacrifice his land 'for the public good' with no compensation. As Orwell pointed out, if the 'people' own all of the property, then the individual owns nothing.

When state regulation wouldn't work, a smear campaign sometimes would. Ms. Gillespie had run an ad campaign using taxpayer money supplemented with other funds from well healed, socialists, to stop the hunting of non-endangered species. One such campaign was to stop dove hunting. Doves were abundant everywhere. But television ads began to appear to, "Stop the shooting of the symbol of peace," and to reclassify it as a songbird rather than a game bird. Since most of America now lived in cities rather than in rural areas, the appeal caught on and dove hunting was banned in the state. In the name of the 'bird of peace' a majority of the non-hunting public had curtailed the rights of a specific category of people—in this case hunters—from enjoying recreation, simply because a majority of the people didn't choose to hunt this species, or, quite typically, any species at all.

The second part of the strategy was to trespass, get arrested, and then to sue the landowner, in court, for stopping their 'freedom of speech', or some other such nonsense. It doesn't take Einstein to figure out that the right to speak your mind does not give you the right to enter someone else's property and physically impede his activity, on his land, just because you don't personally like that activity. To say that you dislike what's going on, can be done anywhere, without impinging on anyone else's rights; but to storm onto someone's land and try to disrupt that activity is clearly trespassing.

Nonetheless, big money can tie up the courts indefinitely with delaying tactics, and with huge expenses for the little guys. So, by dropping huge sums of money into lawyers' pockets, the activists could simply sandbag the property owners out of their property and civil rights, draining them of the money it took to fight back and win in a court system that more and more seemed to be controlled by aristocratic socialists with deep pockets. The State Department of Wildlife was covertly in their corner and big money was there to back them.

Sam was waiting for his attorney to get the lab results so that he could get his good name back. He couldn't wait. He, George, and Jack, were going to meet Earl Johnson at the restaurant across from his I.G.A. store. Soon the four of them would be shooting the breeze and contemplating a big deer hunt. Earl had some distressing news. Some hippies had disrupted his hunt on opening day of the deer season by storming across his barbed wire fence and past his no trespassing signs, chasing away a big buck he'd had in his crosshairs. The college kids wore deer and rabbit costumes and simply refused to leave. He wanted to shoot in the air to give them the idea that trespassing was a bad idea but had thought better of it.

"Oh, the sheriff would arrest them all right," Earl said with a sigh, "but then it would go to court and they would bankrupt him. This old boy is a lot smarter than that, thank you very much."

But he had a better idea if his friends would just help him out. There was instant agreement.

The plan that Earl had in mind would take some doing. He'd requisitioned some new no trespassing signs from his store. Some signs read: **NO TRESPASSING;** others read **BEWARE: PATROLLED BY GUARD DOGS;** another set read, **ABSOLUTELY NO HUNTING WITHOUT OWNER PERMISSION.** A final set read, **TRESPASSERS WILL BE PROSECUTED.** They went down to the hardware store and picked up metal fence posts, fencing material that could be stretched between the posts, and fasteners to secure it. The men drove to Jack's house. Jack made coffee. Refreshed, the men broke out sledgehammers and were soon on their way.

Earl, and George's land connected with Jack's property, which sat in the middle. Earl's was on the east, and George's on the west. For years they had an agreement among them that each could hunt the other's land. Sam had open permission as well. Now they would make this informal arrangement formal and legal. They filled out the permission to hunt forms and each carried it in their wallets until it could be formalized further. Then they went into the woods with the sledgehammers, the metal posts, and the signs. They also brought hammers and nails. They started by posting the 'Patrolled by Guard Dogs' signs on Earl's already fenced-in land. They did a liberal posting all of the various signs on Earl's land. Blackie and Brownie were along for the walk working the outing for every pat they could get.

When finished they crossed the road to Jack's house, and re-loaded on coffee. The two dogs lay quietly under the kitchen table. George spoke.

"Man that's heavy work for an old man."

The others laughed.

Jack agreed; "For any of us. It seems we're all out of shape."

Soon they re-crossed the road, and drove the posts along the front of both George's and Jack's land. They could now retire the sledges and, to a man, they were glad that the worst part was over.

It was time to string the fence to the posts. This was backbreaking work in its own way. Every so often they would post a gate and anchor it to two posts and attach the hardware from the hinges to catches and locks for each gate. They posted one of each of the signs, side by side, at each gate, so that no one could claim that they had not been warned. Then they strung the fence. It couldn't be barbed wire, except for one row at the top of the fence. The rest was square mesh, so the guard dogs would be fenced in. George and Jack settled for three strands of barbwire to separate their land in the middle but they had to string regular fence on the west end of George's property. That way the dogs were fenced inside the enclosure. They had strung what felt like miles of fence before they finished. They still had much to do.

A vanload of hippies passed by and blasted rock music in their direction. They saw no one hunting, so they went off in another direction to find others to prey upon. At the end of the second full day of hard work, the fence was all but completed. The signs were posted.

Then they drove over to Earl's House to meet Hansel and Gretel. Earl opened the door to his home and there they were: two of the fiercest looking Dobermans God ever created. They knew and were comfortable with all of the men. They had been friends for many years, so they acted like big puppies. They whined, rolled over on their backs, and wanted to be petted. Hansel was a big male who went well over one hundred and twenty pounds. Gretel was a big female who weighed in at a very formidable eighty pounds. They were both obedience and attack trained. Earl was getting up in years and his dogs were good insurance against any young punk giving an old man a hard time. They hadn't confronted the cat because they were routinely fenced in the yard by day and night. When Earl was absent from the house he let them inside. In all the years he'd owned them no one had ever tried to break into his home. It was no wonder.

Earl's wife Michelle loved the dogs. She also had

supper on for everyone. The men ate until they could eat no more, said their thanks, and retired to their homes for the night. They would meet early in the morning at Jack's to finish the fencing and the posting of the signs across the land. They still had to finish the west wall of George's land and post the signs there before the rest of the plan could be implemented. The 'plan' was expensive in terms of fence costs, and costly in terms of labor, but the job was nearly complete. At six o'clock they resumed work and by days end had George's land all fenced in.

The plan was simple: the dogs were to be released into the posted lands at four thirty in the morning. Earl's dogs would patrol his fenced in lands while Blackie and Brownie were set loose on Jack's. George had replaced Sammie with two pit bulls from Sammie's bloodline. Friends he had sold pups to, let him pick two from Sonny, and a pure bred bitch. Sonny had been sired by Sammie. All of the dogs were well acquainted so, as long as each stayed on his own land, there would be no conflict. They would nose each other through the fences. The men and the dogs all knew and liked, or at least easily tolerated each other. They met at George's after the work was done and called the Sheriff's office.

Hal Bonner had been the county sheriff for twenty years. He was so well thought of in the region that he hadn't faced a serious challenge at the polls in years. He ran a highly efficient, corruption free, department and he'd never lost sight of the fact that he was a public *servant*—not a public *master*. Whenever Earl called him with a problem, he didn't send a deputy; he came himself. Earl, Jack, George, and Sam were all life long residents of the area. All four were well thought of. Hal had believed Sam when Sam told him that the cat was a cougar and not a bobcat. He could tell that from the size of the paw prints he saw. He didn't like the new Governor and the leftwing animal rights crap that was now coming out of the statehouse. To seal the matter, he had been a life long dove hunter until the state started the songbird double-talk.

"No songbird ever tasted as good as a dove." He'd said sadly.

When the men filled him in about the animal rights idiots that were invading the private property of the local citizens, the sheriff stood solidly in the corner of the locals.

George, Jack, and Earl had each set up a blind that was well constructed and well camouflaged; one on each of their adjoining properties. A deputy would occupy each one. The dogs involved were all well trained enough so that with one word from their master the deputies were as safe in the blind, as they would be in their own houses with the doors locked.

There was a legal technicality involved. If one citizen accused another of trespass it was citizen's word against citizen's word. The deputies would have to make a determination. It could drag out in the courts for a long time that way. But, if a citizen was harassed and a deputy had witnessed the infraction, then, the county prosecutor picked up the legal tab. A suit against the landowner would mean a suit against the county sheriff's department and the county prosecutor, and, as the adage goes, "It's hard to sue city hall." If the dogs responded after the property had been trespassed upon—in spite of signs and warnings—then no charges could be brought against those dogs. They had acted within the law.

It was explained that Blackie and Brownie would be used to herd deer onto Earl's and Jack's property. The three and a half foot fences were nothing for deer and dogs to jump, but posed a legal barrier to a trespasser, since the lands were posted. The deputies would arrive at four in the morning and would be escorted to the blinds and introduced to the dogs. The men who owned land would not be hunting that day. They would only *appear* to be hunting. Blackie and Brownie, in herding the deer into the posted area, would not be violating game law against using dogs to hunt deer because the men had sworn an oath that they would only be appearing to hunt and were not actually hunting deer. They were hunting trespassers.

The deputies arrived on schedule at four in the morning. They parked in behind Earl's home so their vehicles would not draw attention. The men were introduced to the dogs and became quick friends. By five o'clock they were in the blinds. Jack and George went to tree stands on Jack's property, while

Sam and Earl took two tree stands on Earl's property. Hansel and Gretel were told to lay motionless in the brush behind the tree Earl was in. All of the tree stands were within sight of each other at a distance of about a hundred yards. The blinds were close to the fences. The trap was almost set. They waited until seven o'clock to send Blackie and Brownie into the field to bring the deer. Within twenty minutes, fifty had been driven over the fences onto Jack's and Earl's property. Deer were literally everywhere.

The men didn't have long to wait. Two vans full of animal rights activists, arrived and parked their vans on the grassy bank by the side of the road that belonged to Jack. They walked up to Jack's newly constructed fences, cursed, tore down a section of fence, and scrambled over it. They were wearing deer and rabbit costumes. Blackie and Brownie were lying in brush out of sight behind Jack's tree. Their inclination was to get up when they heard the hippies attacking and scrambling over Jack's fence.

"Shhhhhh," Jack whispered.

Drop it".

Both dogs hit the ground and did not move from the spot. Earl commanded his dogs to lie down and not to move. They also obeyed.

Soon the hippies came to the fence between Jack and Earl's property. There was Earl again. And again he had a bead on a big buck. The same hippie in his buck costume climbed Earl's fence and scared away the deer. Earl spoke.

"This makes the second time you have trespassed on my land and ruined a shot I was about to take."

"Shut up old man!" the 'buck' replied. "You are oppressing deer and I am going to stop it."

He started to dance around, playfully shooing at the deer. When he got within ten feet of Earl's tree Earl made a hand motion; Hansel and Gretel bore down on the hippie, teeth bared and barking.

"Oh shit!" The hippie shouted and proceeded to run for the fence. He got halfway up it when Gretel and Hansel converged on him. Gretel snapped at his left buttock and

Hansel at his right. The shrill sound of fabric tearing could be heard. When the hippie hit the ground on Jack's side of the fence it was apparent that something was missing—the seat of his buck costume as well as the seat of his underwear. In back, from just below belt level to his knees, he was 'buck' naked.

Jack called out from his tree stand.

"Hot damn! A bare-assed buck!"

The other 'bucks' and 'does', and all of the 'rabbits' headed for Jack's fence on the run. Jack called out again.

"Blackie and Brownie: Stop `em."

Earl called out.

"Hansel and Gretel: APPREHEND!"

Hansel and Gretel cleared the fence with ease. Blackie and Brownie circled ahead of the hippies and stopped them dead in their tracks—teeth showing, barking, and growling. No body doubted that they meant business.

"Trespassers! Stop dead in your tracks," Jack shouted! "That's the only way you will keep from being bitten!"

They didn't need much in the way of persuasion immediately coming to attention like statues in a formal garden. Hansel and Gretel came in behind them.

Earl hollered, "Guard!"

Jack called out, "Sit down on the grass and don't move a muscle or they'll eat you alive!"

The trespassers, right down to the last buck, doe, and rabbit, complied without exception. The bare-assed buck started to say something foul when Blackie grabbed his leg in his vice-like jaws. He growled and snarled but did not close his jaws completely. The hippie sat down and Blackie let go. But so much as a wiggle out of any of them and all four dogs showed teeth, growled, and moved for them. The 'animals' got real quiet, real fast. One of the 'does' tried to make friends, by saying "Nice doggies." Hansel grabbed her arm and growled. She urinated and shut up.

At that point the men descended from their tree stands and approached the detainees. When the bare-assed buck started to mouth off, Gretel grabbed his privates and growled. He turned white and got as quiet as a mouse.

"Let go Gretel," Earl ordered.

Gretel released him and looked the look of impending death into hippie's eyes. The bare-assed buck passed gas and shook with fright.

The sheriff's deputies crawled out of their blinds. They called for a paddy wagon. They walked up to the intruders attaching handcuffs and leg restraints. The dogs were called off. The hippies started to spew their well-practiced complaints about the excessive use of force being used by the landowners in apprehending them. There was the usual talk about the 'pig' brutality, to which they were being subjected. The deputies smiled and read them their rights. Soon the paddy wagon arrived and all of the 'paddies' were put inside. One deputy stayed to get statements from the landowners. Then he joined the others at the police station.

The trespassers were processed at the police station, outfitted in county orange, and locked together in one big holding cell. Procedures were adhered to meticulously. Each was allowed his one phone call.

The bare-assed buck was the only one of them who didn't seem to mind the colorful jump suit. He'd been through the entire processing with his backside hanging out and seemed relieved that his tail was finally covered. He hadn't appreciated the chuckles coming from the female officers and secretaries, or the gawks from the civilians in the building while he and the others had been so ignominiously paraded about during their processing. They wanted to be set free, but bail would not and could not be set until the next day. They would have to spend the night in jail.

The lamb people got the call. They in turn called Ms. Gillespie and all of the parents involved. The next afternoon Bail was set and paid.

It was about at that same time when the protesters got the bad news from their high priced attorneys. The Sheriff's deputies had witnessed the entire encounter and the county prosecutor had picked up the charges. It was not going to cost the landowners a penny. To sue them, was in effect suing the county sheriff's department and the county prosecutor. The deputies had been in on, and had approved, the entire operation! The young people who participated might get as much as six months in jail for trespass and disorderly conduct, and for damaging Jack's fence when they entered. If vandalism were an added charge it would mean major trouble. They were instructed to meet with the judge in thirty days to make a plea and to set a court date. The animal rights group had met at the lamb people's home and no further harassing activities were planned until after the court date. Any proven involvement by the group could result in fines or jail time, or worse. They didn't know what to do.

The following day the four men went deer hunting for real. They each got their deer. They celebrated together. It had been worth all the money spent and all of the hard work and planning. The dogs got extra deer bones and hearts. They had earned them.

A month later—by then it was January—the hippies went to court. They demanded a jury trial. The trial date had been set for right after the Easter holiday. In the mean time the relations between the lamb people and everyone else in the region became as frigid as the January weather.

The catamount had not been seen in quite some time. Reports of missing dogs and livestock were rampant just to the north. The cat was getting ever bolder. It was attacking more by night and less by day. It was changing its habits. It was bothered by the helicopters and large numbers of dogs coming after it. At night those things did not happen. Only when easy prey was in sight would it attack by day. It steered clear of the area where the men, dogs, and helicopters appeared. Soon, as one area heating up, another would cool off. He had not forgotten the score he had to settle with one man and two particularly troublesome dogs. He returned, in early March.

Sam Macafee got the news he was waiting for. The independent lab and their experts confirmed what he already knew: that the prints and the feces were indeed those of a mountain lion. He went to his attorney. The two men were overjoyed and displayed it with the whoops and hollers of nine year olds.

Sam called a press conference. Only one reporter showed up. Then next day's paper carried a small article, buried in the back of the paper. It reported the findings without comment. Things regarding it had been quiet for some time. Neither the paper nor the local television station had reported any livestock losses in the immediate area since the 'rabid bobcat' had been taken. They wanted to believe what they wanted to believe. Ms. Gillespie had emerged as the heroine. Sam Macafee, the villain. The media reported the independent experts findings—and said nothing more.

March came in like a lamb—warmer than it had been in years. The children began to walk their lambs again. On a particularly nice day, Victoria and Edgar went walking with Marc and one of his friends. The two boys and the lambs moved far ahead of the others. Teresa and one of her friends were having a tea party back at the house. Grandma was acting as hostess. Everything was beautiful. The boys had run well ahead of the adults. Victoria told them to stop and wait. They did and the parents hurried to catch up.

Suddenly, the lambs started to bleat and to tried to pull away from the children. Clearly, they were frantic about something. Victoria started to run towards them, cursing her husband as she ran for lagging behind. She was within ten yards of the children when one of the lambs broke free. In one horrifying second, a black blur flew through the air and landed on the lamb; the lamb fell dead. The children, and the parents recoiled in horror.

"My God, it's a panther!" Victoria screamed. "A panther!"

She clutched the two boys and backed away. The catamount calmly picked up the lamb in its jaws, climbed embankment, and sauntered into the woods. As quickly as it had appeared it was gone.

They were in sight of Jack's house. All animosities were quickly laid aside. Edgar and Victoria Salem were suddenly frightened—frightened that the cat would return for them and the children. They ran, screaming and crying, up to Jack's front porch. Jack opened the door. From the fear he saw in their faces he knew immediately that something was terribly wrong. Victoria could not speak. The children had horror written on their tear-smudged faces. Edgar eventually managed to speak.

"We are terribly afraid. Can we please come in?"

Without hesitation Jack invited them in and had every one sit around the kitchen table. Blackie and Brownie were inside after having devoured deer meat and bones. They whined at the back door, and acted strangely. Any thoughts about the cat were the last things on Jack's mind. Presently, Victoria screamed the explanation.

"A panther killed our lamb and carried it off. I thought it was going to come after me and the children!"

She was sobbing.

"Where is the other lamb?" Jack asked.

"I don't know," came the answer.

Jack reached for his rifle.

"Ma'am, you and yours just wait here a minute. Blackie and Brownie, Drop it!"

The remnants of the deer bones hit the floor and they were immediately on his heels. He grabbed his dog whistle on the way out the door. He and the dogs ran down the road. Then he caught sight of the remaining lamb running just ahead on the bank by the field.

"Go get him boys," he called out.

The dogs raced ahead and herded the lamb back in Jack's direction. Jack grabbed the rope and led it home. He put the lamb and the dogs in the enclosed back yard. He went back inside. From deep within the woods the cougar screamed, re-issuing its challenge.

Jack called George and asked him not to spare the horses on his way over. A few minutes later George pulled into the drive. By that point, Victoria and Edgar had regained their composure.

"Your other lamb is safe now. It's fenced in the back yard with Blackie and Brownie." Jack reassured them.

George rushed in the door asking, "What in the..?"

He saw the Salem family at the table and the horror in

their eyes.

"The cat?" he asked.

"The cat." Jack answered, nodding. "It took a sheep virtually out of the boy's hands."

"He's getting that bold?" George said, more a statement than a question.

"Yup." Jack answered.

Jack looked at Edgar.

"Would you like me to loan you a gun?"

"No," Ed and Victoria said as one.

"We still don't believe in guns. But could you escort us safely home?"

"Certainly," Jack said.

Guns in hand, he and George with the two dogs, were soon escorting the family and the sheep safely down the road to their house. They put the sheep back in its pen. The Salem's invited them in. Once they regained their composure, Jack made the offer again.

"I could load a gun with blanks so the noise would scare the cat off should it come back."

Victoria looked at her husband and for the first time in Jacks memory, her voice was soft.

"Oh Edgar, I think that is a good compromise. What do you think?"

"I'm all for it," he said, with more firmness in his voice than Jack ever remembered.

Jack told them that he'd have the gun and the blanks to them before dark. Then Edgar left to drop their children's friends off at their home. My, did they have a story to tell their parents!

Teresa walked into the Salem's living room. Her eyes were wide.

"Marc and Jon said that they saw a great big panther in the woods. Is that true?"

Seeing Jack there she sensed that something was wrong.

"We aren't sure what happened, honey. Mr. Jack and his dogs are gonna go and find out," she offered. "It's gonna be all right."

Teresa's face was all worried. Katy had been her favorite lamb.

"Mama, do you think Katy will be alright?" Victoria turned her head and her eyes met Jack's. She didn't want her five year old to be afraid. Teresa's face filled with questions.

"Momma, what's a Panther?"

Victoria's eyes searched for an answer.

"It's like a big kitty. Don't worry Teresa. The lamb probably just wandered off."

"Momma, what do I do if I see a panther?"

Victoria asked, "What would you do if you saw a big kitty?"

"I might want to pet it." Teresa answered. "It won't hurt me if I don't hurt it. Will it mama?"

"No baby." Victoria answered.

"That's good." Teresa said. "I was gettin' a little bit 'fraid."

Marc had been lectured by Grandma to keep the killing of the lamb from Teresa so not scare her. Grandma Salem also suggested that the live ammunition, which Jack had first offered, be accepted. Victoria made no comment.

Grandma soon left for own her home.

For Teresa's sake, Jack changed the subject.

"George and I are gonna see about the other lamb." Then he left. Soon, he and George found the blood and the trail. The dogs were kept close as it was too late in the day for a prolonged excursion. A mile into the trail they found the half buried carcass. Jack shook his head. He was amazed that even after they had seen the catamount attack and kill the lamb, right in front of their eyes, that they still didn't want a gun, with live ammunition. Suddenly, it occurred to him what had happened: They had beaten their swords into plowshares, and the lion *had* laid down with the lamb—and feasted!

He hoped that he could show them the error of their ways before anything truly tragic happened. That evening, as promised, he loaned them a rifle and some blanks. He also told them that if they saw the cat they should give him a call. He also casually mentioned that if they should change their mind, live ammunition was available. They politely refused, but thanked him. They were privately embarrassed by the entire spectacle. Could they really have been so wrong about so many things? Surely the cat was just after the lamb and not them. Surely!

Victoria swore Marc to secrecy about the Panther.

"There is no need to scare your little sister. You have got to be the big brother now and look out for her."

Marc nodded.

"Sure mom. But it sure scared me."

"I know. Me too."

Marc looked his mom dead in the eye.

"I'd like to get a gun and learn how to shoot it, in case that panther comes back."

His mother smiled that special smile which recognized the boy's need to establish his manhood separate from his mother's protective, feminine, instincts. She showed him Jack's rifle.

"It's loaded with big noise makers so that it will go `bang' and scare the cat away without hurting it."

Mark looked at his mother.

"That cat killed Katey. Katey didn't do anything wrong, but the cat still grabbed her and carried her away. Momma, that cat needs to be killed."

Victoria was stunned by her son's simple and clear logic. But she wasn't ready to go that far yet.

"Remember Marc, `Vengeance is *mine*, sayeth the lord.'"

"Okay momma," he answered, although he was far from convinced.

Jack Morgan had enough of this cat. He called Sam and George together for a confab. Sam had two blue tick coonhounds and one old redbone. Jack figured that between his hounds and Blackie and Brownie, they could finish the cat. The hunt would begin the following morning.

## CHAPTER FIVE
## The Devil in His Eyes

The men gathered at Jack's house at four o'clock in the morning. They drank coffee and checked through the provisions. Sam's coonhounds were put in the fenced in yard with Blackie and Brownie. Initially, the two pit beagles itched to attack the intruders, but Jack and Sam's stern voices prevented any such skirmish. Once the introductions were made and ground rules made clear, a begrudging tolerance settled in.

The three coonhounds took half the fenced in yard and Blackie and Brownie took the other. Sam's old red bone hound was appropriately named Red and the two blue-ticks were Blue and Bluebell. They were formidable hunters and fighters in their own right. They were much bigger than Blackie and Brownie. They would win in fights against most any breed of dog except a pit-bull, and they would offer a stiff challenge even for them. They were bone lean and tough. They could hunt all night and they had a hound's relentless endurance. These were tough, experienced old coon dogs, but presented one serious drawback—they had never hunted a cat. They were great fighters and specialized in treeing prey and holding it at bay until the men and guns arrived. If the prey jumped out of the tree as the men approached they would by instinct all rush in and try to tear it apart. Thus the prey had three choices: it could try to kill all of the dogs, which in the case of coons was unlikely; it could try to run until the dogs wore it down again; or, it could go back up the tree until the men arrived.

In the old days these kinds of dogs were the choice of

cougar hunters. These dogs had never been in a cat hunt so had much to learn. Blackie and Brownie were to be set loose first to locate the cat; then the others would be released to join them. This hunt might well linger into the night and therefore the old method of using a pack mule to carry supplies was employed. Sam carried a cell-phone, a map of the land, and the names and phone numbers of those who owned each parcel, so that permission to hunt could be obtained and recorded with battery loaded recorder, before the party would cross onto a farmers land. The coon hounds were muzzled so that they wouldn't start to bay too early and scare the cat before the hunt had a chance to begin in earnest.

Jack was known to be an atrocious cook and, having no wife to assist in that area he often ate out. The men didn't like even his best dish, mulligan stew, so they had eaten at home and seen to their own provisions. The topic had given them all a good laugh with the coffee earlier.

By five thirty they were out the door. They had to be careful not to be discovered by those who wished to stop them from pursuing the great cat since hunting it was illegal. Coon season was in, however. That would provide them with the legal cover they needed to explain themselves if they were asked any questions by nosey personnel from the division of wildlife.

Prompted by the sheep killing, the hunt had been thrown together at the last minute; therefore the dogs hadn't been trained to work together as a pack and the men weren't as prepared as they might have been. The fact that it was not a legal, sanctioned, hunt, also put a bind on how far they could go and what they might be allowed to do. The odds, therefore, favored the cat.

Ol' George knew it and said as much before they started. He also knew that the men wouldn't be persuaded into waiting to work the other dogs into an efficient hunting pack. Because of his age, he'd brought a horse to ride and he tied the lead rope of the mule around his saddle horn. He would be the cook if the hunt went into the night. He worried about that, too. At night the cat all of the advantages. As a boy George had heard many stories about men that were attacked and killed trying to take a cat at night. He had a bad feeling about this hunt, but a thousand horses couldn't and wouldn't keep him away from being a part of it. It was, he figured, an old man's last great adventure. He didn't want to die in a rocking chair. If he had to die he wanted it to be on a great adventure with all of the marbles on the table and all of the money at stake. His life had been filled with adventure and he wanted to die in the manner that he had lived. That way he'd leave behind one final great hunting story that would be told and re-told through the ages.

A smile had crossed his weathered face. He had a wealth of cat knowledge that the 'young kids' who were with him lacked. They had the strength but he had the wisdom. He brought three masks along and made the others wear them. They would learn from this old man and he hoped that might save their lives. They might not believe it, but that *was* what was on the line here. Only he knew it for sure though Jack suspected as much.

Sam, who knew the ways of game, did not know the ways of the cat. He was the expert in the field and was smart enough to know what he didn't know. Sam was content, in this instance, to be the student. He was probably the best shot in the bunch, although nobody in this group was anybody's slouch in that area. He felt that he was where he should be. He was protecting the people from harm. It was a part of his job, even though he no longer held the job. He was still a game warden at heart.

No more than a mile into the trek, Brownie's keen nose picked up the scent of the cat. Within a second, Blackie confirmed it. Brownie started to bay and Blackie started to growl and snarl.

"It's the cat," Jack said.

The men moved to high alert. They were in the field where they had been when the cat killed the deer and where the fight occurred in which the dogs had drawn first blood. The cat, resting in a tree, saw them coming. He waited for them to follow the scent to him. His plan was in place. As they approached, the cat would spring from the tree and kill one of the two dogs as he met the ground. Then, he would deal with the other one.

Alone, either dog was no match for him. Only when they worked together, with one on each side of him, were they a real threat. The cat had previously learned that the hard way.

If only they would wander under his tree. He had been napping for quite some time, so he was fresh and breathing easy. Right now the odds were in his favor and he knew it. Then he heard the hounds. The odds had shifted. He yawned and showed teeth. He couldn't wait. He heard Blackie's growl. He had been discovered. How could that be? How could that dog have known? By instinct, Brownie began to bay with a different tenor in his voice; a tenor that proclaimed: "We have run him to ground and have him at bay."

The cat heard the hounds approaching. At that point he didn't like the odds at all. He sprang to the ground without a sound and charged Brownie. Blackie's teeth hit his tail. He spun around and swiped at the black dog with a powerful paw. Blackie ducked and Brownie hit the cat's tail with his teeth. It was a replay of the first fight. The cat leaped and in a second was well out in front of the dogs. He sped up. The dogs were following him. He liked the odds better as he separated the dogs from the group. This is what he had wanted in the first place. He hit forty-five miles an hour and left both dogs in the dust.

Blackie and Brownie continued in full pursuit as the three hounds entered the field behind them. When the cat was half a mile ahead of them he began to double back. Blackie and Brownie were way ahead of the pack when the dog whistle sounded. True to their training they turned and headed toward the sound of the whistle. The hounds, however, did not stop. They passed Blackie and Brownie and kept up a steady bay. Jack and Sam hit the field running. They soon saw Blackie and Brownie returning. Jack petted them and then shouted, "Go get 'em boys!" Blackie and Brownie took off at full speed; the baying grew frantic. Up ahead there was a yelp and then another. Blue and Bluebell had picked up the scent and were following it at full speed, with ol' Red trailing behind. The grizzled and old veteran of many a coon hunt was wisely content to let the younger dogs set the pace. He trailed behind by some twenty yards.

Suddenly, the cat came as if from nowhere. He snapped his jaws but took nothing but thin air. The cat was now on him. A huge paw jolted his head and broke his neck. Everything went black. The two blue tick hounds skidded to a stop and went for the cat. There was not an ounce of cowardice in them. They ran at the cat with Blue in the lead. The cat made a leap hitting Blue with a paw, raking him from shoulder to tail and knocking him down. Bluebell bore in and he sent her flying with another blow. Then Brownie’s teeth found the cat’s tail, as Blackie and Brownie joined the fight. The cat whirled to respond to Brownie's attack when Blackie's teeth hit his back leg. That bite was serious. It could not have come from an ordinary dog. Bluebell got up and re-joined the fray, although she was bleeding badly from the shoulder and side. The cat turned and hit Blackie. The blow, however, was a glancing one as Brownie's teeth hit him, where the tail joined his body. The cat leaped again, but this time he went over the dogs, and proceeded at a full run. Suddenly, he was just gone.

The ground shook, as George and his horse entered the clearing. Blackie, Brownie, and a badly limping Bluebell started baying on the trail. George blew the dog whistle and Blackie and Brownie turned on a dime and skidded to a halt. Bluebell took their lead and came back with them. George dismounted. They would wait for the others. In about a minute, George fired his gun into the air. He waited five minutes and fired again, so as the others could locate them. Soon Jack and Sam, running side by side, joined them. From seventy-five yards away, they heard the pack mule bray it's last. George rode towards it at a full gallop, cursing!

"That cat killed the mule," George bellowed.

"Damn!" Sam exclaimed. "I blew it by tying him off!"

George rode back into the clearing.

"This hunt is over for the time being," he said.

The men began to survey the damage.

"One dead dog, one dead mule, and three torn up dogs," George announced. "The cat wins this one."

Blackie trotted up to Jack and dropped a chunk of something in front of him.

"Well I'll be a son of a... Look at this George."

George stared in disbelief.

"It's a chunk of cat hide and meat. Well, I'll be a ..."

George looked at Blackie and patted him.

"It looks like you got the better of this exchange."

Brownie appeared jealous. He walked up nuzzling the others.

"And you are a good part of the reason," George said patting him as well.

Then he looked at Jack.

"We've got something real special here."

Unbeknownst to the men, the object of their discussion was no more than twenty yards away, watching them. Killing the dog and the mule wasn't enough for him. He wanted more.

Blackie and Brownie began growling. Bluebell joined the chorus.

"Where is he?" Jack asked the dogs.

Without hesitation the pack started for the cat. They moved into the brush. Jack blew the dog whistle and the three dogs returned. George understood what was going on.

"That cat wants some more but not on this day."

The men and the dogs started towards where the mule had been killed. Sam carried Blue in his arms. He was nearly dead.

Three and a half hours after the hunt had started, it was over. They loaded the supplies from the dead mule, onto the horse, and started back. Three hours later they were inside Jack's house. They rehashed the damage as they drank coffee. Red and the mule were dead. Blue had three broken ribs and a punctured lung. He had a fifty-fifty chance of living. Bluebell had two broken ribs but no evidence of a punctured lung. She would be fine in time. Blackie was bleeding along his shoulder but nothing was broken. He was fine. Brownie had escaped unscathed.

The cat had suffered two tail bites, which were painful. It had lost a good chunk from its right back leg, which was now bleeding badly. As the adrenalin wore off, the pain became intense. Sensing a safe field, the cat returned to the mule and began to devour it. It licked its tail and it's butt. The back leg was on fire. When it had jumped to run, Blackie still had a hold, and the chunk of cat meat just shredded and tore off the cat's back leg. It limped noticeably. The wound was a mere inch away from the hamstring. If Blackie had connected there, the big cat would have been disabled.

George brought the "cat meat" with him and he examined it.

"It probably didn't cripple the cat, but he came close," George announced.

They patched up Blackie and Bluebell. Sam left and took Blue to the vet. Only time would tell if he would live or die.

The cat was also ready to let the battle continue on another day. It had only once before felt a bite like that one. It licked its shoulder where Sammie had bitten him.

George set Bluebells ribs and Jack cleaned the gashes on both remaining dogs with peroxide. They put a plaster of Paris patch over Bluebell's ribs, and anchored it by continuing the patch over the backbone and down the other side. It resembled a saddle. George strung two straps, anchoring one end of each in the plaster. When it dried he attached a clasp on the end of one strap, ran the other strap through it, tightened it like a cinch, and pulled it snug.

"It will have to do. The ribs will heal. In about a month, we can take the cast off."

Sam returned from the vets. He was shaken about Red and worried about Blue.

"I simply didn't realize the power that animal has." He said, shaking his head. "He killed that mule in a second, and damn near got all three of my dogs. It's just hard to believe."

George remained quiet, eventually saying, "Something bothers me about that cat. Normally, a cougar will go to a tree or a high rock and stay at bay. This one is different. It has killed many dogs and seems to have figured out that by circling and doubling back it can kill them off and keep going. How he got dog smart, I don't understand, but he did. That's gonna make treeing him difficult; and we're gonna have to tree him, if we're gonna get him. He is not used to a bite like the one Blackie delivered and we know why. That bite just might allow us to tree him at our next encounter."

He grew quiet for a moment and then continued.

"It's moved to the night shift. It was in a tree when it saw the dogs commin'. It waited for them so at the exactly right moment it could ambush them. I saw the tracks where it landed and they were deep, which indicates that it jumped out of the tree to the ground. This cat is bigger than any cougar I've ever seen. Its paw size and the depth of the print establish that."

Sam confirmed George's suspicions.

"The expert who examined the feces and the paw print was amazed at the size. He estimated its weight at nearly two hundred and forty pounds."

George was stunned.

"They're not supposed to get that large. I believe two hundred and twenty seven pounds is the largest one ever recorded!"

He looked at Jack.

"Is there anything else unusual about this cat."

"Yes," Jack answered. "It is black."

George went to his books.

"It cannot be." He answered flatly. "While it is known that cougars do have the potential to produce a black phase cat, not one has ever been killed or captured in North America, and very few, in South America. Are you sure, Jack?"

"Not positively," Jack answered, "I saw it one time when I was in the woods. It was on a ridge in the afternoon, and it saw me walking. I didn't have a gun so I beat a path back to the house. I stared right at it and showed it no fear, but somehow, I felt that it knew I was unarmed. It looked right at me. I felt it's eyes and they were the Devil's own. Maybe it was just the angle I saw it from, but I could have sworn that it was Black—I'm not talking tawny brown. It's eyes appeared green, not yellow, and it was almost hypnotic looking at them."

George let out a soft, but long, "Geeeess," and then he said; "I thought they were exaggerating."

"Who?" Jack wondered aloud.

George's face paled.

"My great-grandparents," he answered. "They always talked about a huge panther that was black with green eyes. They said the same words you just said. That it had the devil's own green eyes. It, also, went to the night shift, almost exclusively, and slept by day. No one could tree it and it killed many settlers. They told me an old Indian story of another such cat. The Indian's called that one `the evil one's very own.' It supposedly killed hundreds of Indians. I thought the story was simply stretched. Now, I have to wonder."

"One thing we know for sure," Jack said, "it bleeds and it can be hurt. Blackie proved that."

"I wonder," George said in a near whisper.

"Wonder what?" Sam asked.

George shifted his gaze to him.

"Maybe this old man is going crazy, but if there were black ones in these parts in the past, then, maybe that is how they survived. The cougar was supposed to be extinct around here but maybe some of them went far away and came to hunt only by night. Breeding among themselves led to a strain different from the others in several ways, maybe a little bigger and maybe a little more isolated. Night brought them safety because of their black color. What if, because of color variation and night hunting, they adapted to surviving in proximity with man? My dad always said that they were not hunted out, but that most of them just left because the deer got scarce after the land got busted up for farming, and the trees were logged, and the mining for coal in these parts all worked to make it a bad haunt. The Florida Panther is dark but not black. I wonder."

George's brow cleared as he got an Idea. He called the Salem's. Victoria answered the phone.

"Ma'am, this is George Hogan. I have got a question, that I wanted to ask you."

"A Question? What is it?" Victoria asked, with clear curiosity in her voice.

"The panther that went after your sheep. What color was it?"

"It was black and it had pure evil in its eyes."

Her voice quivered just speaking about it.

"What color were its eyes?" George asked.

"I'm not sure, but I want to say they were green. It was all a blur, so I can't say green for sure, but I think they were. I'm not sure that it was jet black either, but that's the thing that comes to mind when I think back about it. Why?"

"I'm just trying to size up our opponent."

"You're not thinking about going after it? Are you?"

"No, of course not," George answered. "That would be illegal."

He didn't want to give the animal rights crowd any information that could be used against them during the upcoming court date. Although the Salem's had what might be described as an attitude adjustment where it came to the cat, it was still not complete. They were still vegetarians and did still believe in animal rights, although in a less active way than before.

"Thanks for the info." George said.

"I pray that it goes away," Victoria said closing the conversation.

Publicly, she and her husband waffled only slightly on their position about the cat, but secretly they wished someone would blow its brains out. She couldn't verbalize it with most folks but hoped that it would happen. Her tone was pleasant and George sensed a note of gratitude.

George looked across the table at the two men.

"She said it was black with green eyes; something less than 100% sure."

The answer lay right there before their eyes. George looked at the piece of hide and 'cat meat' that Blackie had torn from the animal. Clearly, the fur was almost black. He wondered how they could have missed it.

"Boys", George began. "We have got a lot of work to

do before we try to hunt this one again. We're gonna have to hunt the perfect hunt if we are to get it. The dogs must be meshed into a pack of hunters that work together and obey the dog whistle as a pack. We should all be on horseback and have one good mule along. There must always be one of us near the horses and mule with a rifle, and . . ." he paused for emphasis, "we have to develop an unbeatable night strategy."

"What do you mean a night strategy?" Jack asked.

"If I am right, and I think that I am, we are gonna have to be extra careful in our night camps or one or more of us won't make it home." He leaned forward and whispered; "It has the devil in its eyes." His voice trailed off. "The evil one's very own."

His delivery had been enough to send chills up the others' spines. They soon adjourned. There would be other days to plan for the next outing.

Jack began playing with fire in his mind.

"Me and these two dogs, all by ourselves, can get this cat. I just know we can."

He reached down and petted his dogs. In the near distance he heard the cat scream. He couldn't know, but as he sat there, the two green eyes from a very black and very angry cat were casing his house. The cat was perched on a large rock looking down from the hill at the back of the house. It hurt terribly. It wanted to kill the two dogs and the man—becoming the hunter and not the hunted. A chill shuddered its way down Jack's spine as he remembered the way the cat had visited his home during his last hunt with George.

He got his gun and laid it near his bedside so he could "reach out and touch it," at night, if such became necessary. The sun was setting and he was exhausted from the hunt.

"I think I'll go to bed early," he thought out loud.

He ate a sandwich and turned in. The two dogs were suspicious too. Instead of staying down the basement as he had ordered them to do, they snuck up the stairs and curled up, one on each side of the door opening into Jack's bedroom. Jack was immediately asleep. Had known what the dogs had done, he would have smiled and been thankful for their loyalty.

The cat sat on his rock and surveyed the house. Its gaze was that of a predatory animal looking at prey. Then on impulse, it got up, and went to finish eating the mule. It's back leg and tail were on fire. There would be another night. A night when the man was not expecting trouble and the dogs were locked outside. The cat gorged on the mule and then, for the first time in days, he slept at night.

In the morning, Sam got the report on ol' Blue. He was going to make it. He and Jack would soon be working all of the dogs together, just as George had suggested. The next hunt would not be a hastily concocted operation. Sam thought to himself, "I must be nuts. They have fired me for telling the truth about this cat. Nobody believes me. It is illegal to hunt it, so we are breaking the law. Why is it our job comes down to tying to save a bunch of people from their own stupidity?" He thought of April Gillespie. He wondered how she could have ever gotten that job. He shook his head in disgust.

For several weeks things remained calm. The catamount had finished off the mule and had become quiet. His back leg was slowly healing. He had taken some deer and a sheep from another part of his range. An eerie truce seemed to exist between the big cat and the men.

The townspeople had long forgotten the cougar story and had written it off in their minds. The children, who saw the cat kill the lamb had told their parents and they had reported the incident to the state Department of Wildlife. Predictably, they had gotten the brush off. The lamb people had told April Gillespie about the incident. She had persuaded Victoria and Edgar that the cat was only after livestock and that it should be spared. The Salem's went along with her, but Victoria, in particular, was having second thoughts. She couldn't get rid of the picture of that blur, coming from nowhere, to kill Katie and wreak such fright upon her and her family. They kept all of the information from little Teresa. She alone was now not only unafraid of the cat, but she wanted to see the "big kitty." She had been told that Katie had just wandered off. She worried about her lost and alone in the woods. Every now and then she would bring the subject up.

Victoria had convinced her that Katie was okay because, "God watches over little lambs." That thought brought her little girl's mind great peace. Soon she was looking forward to Easter Sunday.

The coming trial of the trespassing hippies who had been caught red-handed by the dogs and the sheriff's deputies, would take place in two weeks. The animal rights crowd was making a big deal out of it. If they won in court, then, no one who owned property would be safe from their interference. Jack didn't think that was likely. Everyone assumed that they would simply be sentenced to thirty to sixty days, or fined heavily and ordered by the court not to do it again or face real and dire consequences.

But if it came out in court that April Gillespie and therefore the State Department of Wildlife were involved, along with organized animal rights groups with money, and had in fact bankrolled and planned the operation, then all hell would break loose. Those who planned the operation would be in hotter water than the college kids who had been caught. That is what the prosecutor was hoping for. He was prepared to immunize any of the kids who were involved in exchange for their testimony. He wanted an end to this kind of activity in his county.

Rumors were rampant. The trial would be covered by local media, and national media had already picked up the story. Interviews with these 'children' were already being planned for national TV, by those who wanted to put their own spin on the issue. The battle lines were being drawn.

The lamb people were worried that their involvement might land them in trouble. Even worse, they were beginning to question their own involvement on a moral basis. The attack of the panther on their own sheep and the fear they experienced every time they heard it scream in the night was beginning to take its toll. They were close to breaking off their association with the group. They were, in the words of Victoria, "Having second thoughts." If they broke ranks and testified about the planning and the meetings then April Gillespie's job and reputation would be at risk. She kept the pressure on and the

Salem's were feeling it. They didn't know what to do.

On Easter Sunday the Salem's were up and about early. They dressed for church. Their church was having a service at ten o'clock and the family had a long drive ahead of them. Teresa was especially excited about it. Victoria had dressed her in a beautiful yellow and pink dress, with spiffed up paten leather shoes. Her blonde hair draped down to her shoulders and her blue eyes set it all off. She looked like a little princess and she loved it. She began to twirl in front of the mirror, causing her little dress to extend. For the first time in her life she felt beautiful. She was so excited!

After the services the family, some relatives, and some friends, went to their house for Easter dinner. Since all of the attendees were vegetarians, no one felt it odd that the meal had no meat in it. Victoria did suddenly felt strange. She looked at her beautiful little girl and remembered Easter's past. When she was growing up, lamb and beef were served. In spite of herself, her mouth was watering at the memory. She shrugged it off and served up the vegetables. As they ate they began to talk.

Teresa soon got bored with all of the old folks chatter. She wanted to go out and play. So did Marc. Victoria was firm.

"After we eat, we will all take a walk together. Maybe we will stop by Mr. Jack's so you can show him your pretty dress. We don't agree with his hunting, but he has been very nice to us. Would you like that, kids?"

"Yeah!" Teresa and Marc said as one. "Maybe he will even let us pet Blackie and Brownie!"

Victoria smiled across the table at Edgar and he smiled back. They were getting along better than they had in years. The children had sensed this the way children have the amazing gift to do. They were all smiles.

"This is going to be the best Easter ever!" Teresa said as she twirled across the living room, impatiently waiting for the adults to finish eating so they could begin the walk.

She looked into the mirror. Mamma had made up her face with eyeliner, face powder, and even a little lipstick. She felt wonderful! Edgar entered the room and looked at his little girl. He was so proud of her.

"Okay little princess, we are all ready for the walk."

She squealed with delight.

They moved out the door, across the freshly mowed field in back of the house, and up the hill to the road. On the road, they all stayed on the left side of the gravel lane so if a car were to come their way, everyone would be safe. The kids continued on ahead of the slower, less energetic adults. Teresa continued to twirl. She led the group by some forty yards—twenty yards ahead of Marc and his friend.

Mr. Jack's house was several hundred yards ahead. Teresa couldn't wait to show off her dress and her makeup and to get to pet Blackie and Brownie.

Suddenly she stopped twirling. She alone saw the cat laid out atop the bank directly in front of her. She pointed for the others to look. At first she was frightened, but her mother's words came to her. "It's just like a big kitty. It won't hurt you if you don't hurt it."

"Look at the big kitty!" She exclaimed. "Here kitty-kitty. Nice kitty. You're so pretty, kitty!"

Marc screamed out to his sister.

"You get away from there!"

He started to run towards her. It was too late. In a fraction of a second the cat leaped from the top of the bank above the road and onto the little girl. She started to scream.

"MAMAAA!"

The cat clutched the child in his jaws and scrambled up the bank. Teresa managed one final scream. Then all went quiet. The adults ran to the spot screaming. Edgar and the other men scrambled up the bank. Nothing was left to be seen. Marc ran up the road to get Mr. Jack. He pounded on the door.

Jack had slept in, as was his Sunday morning custom. He believed in God but he had not graced the church with his presence very often since Sue's death. It was hard going to church alone. He was in the bathroom shaving when he heard the pounding on his door. He wiped the shaving cream from his face and headed for the door. There he found Marc. The boy screamed.

"The panther got Teresa and carried her off into the woods. Please save her, Mr. Jack!"

"Okay Marc, come in here. I'm gonna need your help." Marc hurried into the house.

Jack grabbed a slip of paper and wrote George's number on it.

"You call George at this number and have him call Sam—got that? *Sam*. Tell him about what happened, while I go to the woods."

Jack opened up the back door. "Blackie! Brownie!" he hollered, "Come here."

The dogs scrambled into the house together. Jack threw on a shirt, grabbed his gun and whistle, and slung his ammunition belt over his shoulder. He looked at Marc.

"Where this happen?"

Just down the road there. My family's there now."

The moment they arrived, Blackie and Brownie had the scent. Up the bank they ran, baying and growling. Jack followed them up the bank, gun at the ready. He hollered at the others.

"Go to my house and wait."

Edgar convinced the others to do as Jack instructed. Then he ran after Jack.

"It's got my little girl! I'm coming too."

Jack looked over his shoulder and nodded his agreement. The dogs were on the Cat. Jack could tell. He ran forward. There, in the clearing ahead, the battle was on. Teresa was nowhere in sight. Blackie and Brownie were bloody. So was the cat. The cat saw Jack and leaped away from the dogs. Jack's rifle blasted. The cat fell to the ground. It struggled back to its feet and was gone. The dogs continued after him with Jack in hot pursuit. The cat was in full flight. Jack blew the whistle, and the dogs returned.

Jack backtracked to find Teresa. He came upon Edgar weeping, and holding what was left of his little girl. She had been viciously mauled and had not survived. Edgar wrapped his little girl in his sport coat and picked her up.

Jack put his hand on Edgar's shoulder. There were no words sufficient for that moment. They started back together.

"We'll put her on my bed at the house and we'll call the Sheriff."

Edgar looked at Jack.

"Thank you," he said. "She's gone. Isn't she?"

Jack nodded his head.

"Let me carry her so that you can comfort Victoria. The others don't need to see the body."

Edgar nodded through his tears and handed over the body of his precious child. Jack followed Edgar back to the road. The dogs were bloody and whining. Gingerly, they made their way down the bank. Victoria looked at Edgar. He shook his head.

"No."

He held her as she screamed and wept. Jack carried the little girl's body into the house and laid her on the bed. He covered her with a blanket and arranged a pillow under her head. Jack closed the bedroom door. He put the dogs in their place out back. He would tend to them later.

George pulled into the drive. He got out and entered the house, which was by then filled with people.

"Sam's on his way—He called me," he announced. He surveyed the faces of the people. "Are we too late?"

Jack looked at his old friend.

"The little girls body is on the bed. She is dead."

"Damn!" George whispered. Then he grew silent.

Sam arrived five minutes later. One look at the faces and he knew it was too late. He winced and hung his head.

Presently, the sheriff and the ambulance arrived. Hal Bonner got out of his cruiser. His face was set. He entered he house. Jack led him into the bedroom and showed him the body. He outlined what had happened. The two men exchanged sad glances.

"That is the worst thing these eyes have seen in a long, long, time. It's the part of this job I hate he most."

Jack nodded. They left the bedroom. Hal told the paramedics to load the body on the ambulance and see that the hospital issued a death certificate. The parents were to follow the ambulance.

Hal approached the parents and looked into their tortured faces.

"I am so sorry. I won't bother you further at this time. We'll speak later. I'll send a deputy along to fill out the report at the hospital. There is only one question. Are you absolutely sure it was a panther?"

"There is no doubt of that." Edgar said.

"Yes," Victoria added. "It was a cougar."

As the ambulance left, the media arrived. They were horrified by the story they heard. One cam truck headed for the hospital. One reporter cornered Sam.

"Then it *was* a mountain lion, after all."

Sam exploded.

"You knew that. You knew that as soon as you saw the report that I sent you. I proved beyond any doubt that the last incident here was the work of a cougar. You just let people go on believing it was a bobcat." He looked directly into the camera. "This young life was lost because you good people and the state Department of Wildlife chose to promote a fantasy rather than to tell the people the truth."

His voice trailed off. Then, with fire in his eyes, Sam uttered the words that would become the rallying cry for vengeance against the cat, and against those who sought to protect it by denying it's existence. "THIS LITTLE GIRL'S BLOOD IS ON YOUR HANDS!"

With that, he turned his back on the reporter and walked back into the house. Then, Sheriff Bonner approached the reporters and said:

"I agree with Sam Macafee. Now get out of here. You have got your bloody story. Now git!"

The reporters started to quibble about it. Jack pushed his way forward and announced: "As of this moment, you are trespassing on my private property. Get off of it."

Hal smiled and continued. "Do any of you wish to spend the night in jail?"

Without further ado, the reporters left.

On the evening news, a teary eyed reporter, who had earlier sarcastically trashed Sam Macafee, and cheered April Gillespie, told the true story of the killing of the little girl by the panther. She showed the footage of Sam's statement. The camera panned back to her face.

"You were right Sam. And this reporter accepts her responsibility. I believe we need a complete and thorough investigation of the state Department of Wildlife and a full explanation of the lies that were proliferated about the bob cat and the false insinuations that Sam Macafee created a hoax. This doesn't look like a hoax to this reporter. Sam, if you are listening, I promise you that this reporter will not rest until the truth comes out."

The camera panned to the paramedics carrying the blanket-covered body of Teresa into the emergency room. Then, a photograph of the smiling the little girl emerged from the tragic scene.

The Monday morning paper carried Teresa's picture, side by side with one of Sam Macafee in his game warden's uniform. The headline read: "Blood on our hands." The whole quote was explained. They also reprinted the independent laboratory's verdict on the cat evidence—the report that had been buried when it had first been received. The paper demanded a full investigation. April Gillespi refused to be interviewed.

In the capitol, the governor's phone rang off the hook. The state-wide press picked up the story. The governor's damage control team moved into high gear. Soon, they found their face-saving answer. They would clean out the entire state Department of Wildlife and prosecute those involved in the bobcat misadventure. Among a long list of charges would be evidence tampering.

"We have to put someone in charge who the people have absolute confidence in, or the press will start after you," the governor's chief strategist proclaimed.

"I know just the man, for the job." The governor stated. "By appointing this man; I become a hero."

"Who do you have in mind?"

The governor whispered the name in his ear and the advisor grinned from ear to ear.

"Yes!" He agreed. "That would do it."

When Sam got home from work the next day, he entered his house to a ringing phone. It was the governor's office.

"One moment please for the Governor," came a secretary's business-like voice.

Sam was stunned. From a long hard day at the factory to chatting with the governor all within a few minutes. His head whirled.

"Sam," the governor began.

"Yes Governor," Sam managed.

"I read the papers and saw the news. I am outraged! This mess must be cleaned up!"

Sam couldn't believe his ears so made no comment.

"I need a man of utmost integrity to run the department. Would you accept the job?"

Money and power were not things Sam had ever sought. He had never contemplated having the position. His answer, however, came easily.

"I would be honored, sir. But first I have one big piece of unfinished business I must take care of."

"What would that be?" The Governor asked, intrigued by the man's response. There was a note of concern in his voice.

"Sir," Sam began again, "I want to get the cat that killed the little girl. I would ask that I be deputized to go after that cat with free reign. That cat has now tasted human blood. It just has to be stopped. It will now prefer humans over anything else. It must be stopped immediately. I have a couple of men in mind to help me. They know the ways of the big cats. If we can have free reign to go after it, we may well save other children's lives."

The Governor was taken aback. It had been a long time since he had heard the sound of an absolutely honorable man who wasn't after money and power and prestige for himself. It was refreshing. It also fit well into his own, save-his-tail, plan.

Sam felt the Governor breathe an audible sigh of relief.

"Consider it done," the Governor pronounced. "I will appoint an acting department head who will serve until you get your cat. Can you be here in the capitol tomorrow?"

"Yes sir." Sam answered.

"Good. When you get here tell the receptionist at the Governors mansion who you are and she will see that you get where we need you to be. I will call a press conference for two in the afternoon to announce your appointment and acceptance. I will also commission you to get that cat with no interference, naming you as a special game marshal in charge of the project. You will have total power to hire who you need and to get whatever equipment you may require to get that cat."

"It is more than I had dared hope for, sir."

"We will see you in the capitol at 1:00."

"I will be there, sir."

"Good. We will see you then."

The Governor's aid had been on the extension. The two men felt they had engineered the coups of the century.

The aid chortled: "Governor Landsberry For President!"

The Governor smiled.

"It *does* have a certain ring to it, doesn't it? Remember, Macafee is to have cart blanche. Come now! We, have speeches to write!"

On Sam's end the atmosphere was quite different. Sam was in total shock. He responded to his wife's hug with a gently peck to her forehead. He looked her in he eyes.

"Do you realize that the nitwit you married just gave up a soft, high paying job, so that he could risk his life chasing a man-eater?"

Sally laid her head against his chest.

"Sam Macafee, you are my kind of nitwit!"

They clung to each other for some time. Then she said, "Don't you think you should get into your truck, and personally tell Jack and George that they have been deputized, with full pay, to help you get that cat."

"Yes ma'am!" Sam said, with a big smile. "I will get right on it!"

Sally grinned, "But first, you better give me another bear hug."

Sam rekindled his smile, picked her up, and twirled her around. Setting her down ever so gently he said, "What a woman I married! Do you want to come along for the celebration?"

"No. I have one of my own to plan for when you get home. So don't take too long."

They shared a laugh. In his excitement Sam had forgotten to call Jack and George, to forewarn him of his visit. Sally made the calls arranging for both of them to be at Jack's when Sam got there. She was thrilled. She also made one other call. It was to her employer. She thanked him for hiring her and told him the good news.

"I'll work two final weeks if you would like."

"No," he said. "We are thrilled for you and your husband. Somehow we will survive here without you. You are needed more where you are."

"Thanks for understanding," Sally said.

Sally felt lighter than air. She was grateful that they had hired her in a moment of trouble, but was she ever glad to come back home! She went to the cupboard, pulled out a cake box, and began to mix the contents. "Chocolate marble" she said out loud. "Sam's favorite—with chocolate ice cream, of course."

In twenty minutes, Sam pulled into Jack's drive way. Both George and Jack were there to greet him. They still had no idea what was up, but one look at Sam's face told them it had to be some kind of great news.

"Jack, how would you like a new job?"

"Hadn't thought much about it." Jack answered.

"George, how would you like to come out of retirement?"

George laughed.

"What? And *work* for a living, when I can sit home and collect for just sitting there? Coming from you it sounds interesting. What do you have in mind?"

"Well, we had better be sitting down when I tell you.

I'd hate to fall down, hit my head, and wake up from this wonderful dream! The Governor called me today—just a while ago."

"What!" the two men shouted, as one.

Sam related what had taken place and how his whole world had been set upside down since he and Jack had left work. The two men were stunned.

"The Governor told me that I could hire two special deputies at full pay to help me go after that cat. Will you help me?"

George got to his feet. His dream of one last great adventure had just come true. He realized that they were not in for a picnic.

"I'm in if you don't think this old man will slow you down too much."

Jack's response was short and to the point.

"I'm in if you will have me."

"Then it's settled!" Sam hooted, slapping his hat against his leg.

"I've got to get home," Sam said, "to a special lady who has put up with a lot lately. Would you tell the Salem's that we will get that cat.

"We'll go tell them, in person as soon as you leave."

"I've got to be in the capitol at one o'clock tomorrow afternoon. There will be a press conference at two."

"We'll be glued to the TV."

With that, Sam said his goodbyes, got into his truck, and drove for home. Jack called the Salem's and told them that he and George would like to drop by.

"Fine, and if you would, please bring some live ammunition for the gun."

"Yes ma'am." Jack answered.

The two men soon arrived at the Salem's. Their mood plummeted from joyous to somber as they crossed the porch. Edgar opened the door and invited them in. They sat down together. Jack handed Edgar the box of ammunition that had been requested. Victoria thanked him. Jack assured them that it was no big thing.

"Edward and Marc have a request," Victoria announced.

Edward began.

"You won't need to leave this with us long. In the morning Marc and I are going to a gun shop to pick up some good rifles and handguns for this family. The problem is that I don't know a good one from a bad one and I don't know how to shoot."

Marc looked at his father.

"Dad, do you really mean it?"

"You bet I do, son. If you and I are going to be the men in this family, then we had better learn to shoot so if that cat ever comes this way again it will be the last thing he ever does!"

Edward looked back at Jack.

"Would you help us in the selection?"

"Sure thing," Jack answered. "I will come by in the morning if you like."

"That would be great."

"Then it's set," Jack said.

Edward began again.

"Your kindness toward this family in our time of crisis will never be forgotten."

Jack smiled.

"You would have done the same for me."

"We have an additional request," Victoria added.

Jack turned toward her. "Whatever I can do."

"Would you teach them how to shoot?"

"Sure." Jack answered. "I'll be happy to. Now, I have some news for you. The Governor called Sam Macafee today, and put him in charge of the Sate Department of Wildlife. He accepted but told the Governor that he won't start the job until the cat is hunted down. The Governor has put him in charge of getting the hunt and he will deputize George and me to help. He just left my house and as his first unofficial-official act, he asked us to contact you and to let you know that none of us will rest until that cat is dead."

"Thank God!" Edgar said.

"It's not done yet. That is one vicious cat and it is now a man killer. We have our work cut out for us."

"Yes you do." Edgar agreed.

Marc looked up at Jack.

"Mr. Jack. You kill that cat good! Will you?"

"I'm gonna do my absolute best, Marc. Could you do me a favor?"

"What?" Marc asked, puzzled.

"Start calling me *Jack.* If we're gonna be friends, then lets get things on a first name basis."

"Okay. . . Jack," Marc said, tentatively. Smile met smile as the two sealed their new relationship.

They made small talk for a while. Soon it was time for Jack and George to go. They said a round of goodnights, and then George and Jack left for home. As they were exiting the truck at Jack's place they heard the cat scream. George raised his fist and hollered into the woods.

"Your days are numbered, cat, even if you are the devil's own. We are gonna be comin' for ya for killin' that little girl. Do you hear me cat?"

The old man shook his fist in the general direction from which the scream had come. He turned to Jack.

"He may have the devil in his eyes but before this is all over we're gonna send him to hell where he belongs."

Jack nodded.

"I'm sure glad you're gonna be in on this, 'old man'."

George smiled. "It ain't gonna be no picnic."

"I know it," Jack agreed.

Soon George was on his way. Jack went into his house and sat, exhausted, on the couch. He called the dogs in. They bounded in the back door, tails wagging and tongues out. Jack petted each of them.

"You are your mothers sons."

It seemed they understand. They had fought the cat to a standstill on several occasions, and both were ready for more. Jack went to bed. The dogs again slept by the doorway to the bedroom.

The cat, high atop a rock on the hill behind the house,

licked his chops. The taste of human blood had only inflamed his hatred for the man and his dogs. He lusted for more.

## CHAPTER SIX
## The Blood Lust

At two o'clock the next day the Governor held the promised press conference. He announced the complete revamping of the State Department of Wildlife. As he looked out at the assembled reporters he sensed their unasked questions. Why would his department appointees lie about the mountain lion? Why would they fire an honorable man like Sam Macafee? What went wrong? Governor Landsberry exuded confidence. He had the answers that they wanted to hear.

He began by announcing that a house cleaning had been ordered. He had fired the director. He had fired his assistant, although he had been a long-time friend and campaign aid who had been of considerable service to him. He had fired April Gillespie. He had declared that a full investigation would occur. He left the best for last. To insure that honor and integrity would be restored he had appointed Sam Macafee as the new director. Sam was standing by his side. A standing applause erupted at the Governor's announcement. The heat was now off. The Governor announced that Sam had a job to do before he began the job.

"Mr. Macafee told me that before he would assume the position he had a job he needed to complete. He said that he wanted to personally lead the hunt for the man-eater who recently killed a young girl. I promised him what I will now promise you: That he can name his own people, requisition his own supplies, work with the total cooperation of the Governors office and the State Department of Wildlife. I further told him that all of our prayers would go with him. Let me introduce to you, Sam Macafee."

Sam moved to the microphones. He felt out of place. Public speaking was not his thing. However, his sense of mission took over and all the right words made their way from his heart to his tongue.

"I am humbled. I have to tell you up front that this will not be an easy hunt. Those of you who think we will just go out there, get this cat, and go home, are wishful thinkers. The cat has tasted human blood. It now sees people as his first choice for food. We must take precautions. We must be ready. Children must not walk the country lanes alone. I will need your patience and your help."

He began by putting a thousand dollar bounty on the cat's head. He encouraged farmers to carry rifles with them when they went into the fields. He asked everyone living in remote areas to refrain from being on foot outside after dark. He announced that he was hiring two deputies to help him on the hunt: George Hogan and Jack Morgan. They would begin the hunt as soon as they were provisioned.

"With your help and God's, we *will* get this cat."

Thunderous applause greeted his words. He was surprised!

The Governor took to the microphone.

"You just heard from a man who put off a safe desk job so that he could hunt down a killer. He told me to ask you for your patience and your prayers. I assure you that he will have mine and I know he will have yours. I will sleep well tonight. I know that I have hired the best possible man for two very tough jobs." Then he added, "I want to assure Edward and Victoria Salem that we will get that cat. We as public servants often make mistakes, and your Governor has made his share. As Governor, however, I have always tried to admit when an error has been made, and do my best to make it right. We have children to protect. Neighbor will need the help of neighbor, and friend of friend. It has always been that way. It will always be that way. Teresa Salem reminded us all of that simple truth."

Applause interrupted the Governor and he waved to the

cheering crowd. The press conference was over. Sam Macafee waved at the crowd and departed for the airport and home.

When he got off the plane at the airport, a thousand people were there. They cheered him and he waved high and long. A sheriff's department cruiser was waiting for him with the lights flashing. Hal Bonner was driving. Sam climbed in. The sheriff was grinning.

"We got a reception waiting for you in town."

Sam was immediately embarrassed. The Sheriff re-assured him.

"The people in this town have a natural sense of justice. They have just seen justice done. Whether you like it, or not, or whether your ready for it or not, they want to celebrate the victory of the truth prevailing over the lie. It makes them feel good. It makes me feel good too, Sam."

Sam smiled.

"I feel like I woke up on a different planet. What am I supposed to do, or say?"

Hal looked him in the eye.

"You just continue to tell the truth—to stand for the truth. It has kept me in office for twenty years. The minute you or I change, the people will smell it."

"Thanks Hal," Sam said, "That's exactly what I needed to hear."

"One more thing," Hal added. "They have been waiting hours to see you ride into town. Tell them thanks."

Sam nodded. "I sure will."

Sam looked out the back window of the cruiser. He couldn't believe it! Dozens, perhaps hundreds of cars were following the cruiser in what looked like a giant funeral procession to Sam's way of thinking. He felt so out of place. He felt so unworthy. Then he realized what Hal had meant. It was the triumph of the truth prevailing over a lie that they were celebrating. Sam smiled. *That*, he thought, was worth it. He was just a symbol and he could happily live with that.

When they hit town the cruiser made a left and drove to the town square. It was packed with people such as Sam had never seen. They had red, white, and blue bunting everywhere.

A massive platform and podium had been erected, right in the middle of the main street.

The cars kept coming. Sam began to sweat. He didn't have a speech. What could he say? He'd just truthfully say what he felt. It was all that he could do.

The cruiser pulled directly up to the platform. Sam and Hal ascended the wooden staircase up to the platform. The mayor had been warming the crowd up. They broke into a sustained and thunderous applause as Sam and Hal came into view. The mayor, sensing that the time was right, hollered, into the microphone, "And now without further ado, I give you, our new chief game warden, in charge of bringing the man-eater to justice, Sam Macafee."

Sam stepped to the podium. He started by waving—both hands above his head. When the crowd quieted, he spoke.

"I hope all of you will forgive me. I am not a politician," he nodded to the mayor, "no offense intended sir." Raucous laughter broke out. "What I meant to say was that I am not used to giving speeches. The only thing I can do is to tell you straight from the gut how I feel."

The applause broke out again and again it was thunderous. Sam smiled and it died down. He began again.

"Put yourself in my shoes. I had been fired from my job for supposedly creating a hoax about this cat. I was working in a factory. The cat killed Teresa Salem. Jack Morgan and his dogs chased off the cat and recovered the little girls body. The press was there. I just got mad that nobody had listened and that a little girl had to die before people would realize the truth: the truth that there was a catamount in our midst. One that was killing dogs and sheep and cattle, and that soon it would attack people if we didn't go after it. I got mad and I said as much to the reporters. I had just gotten off of work at the factory and had gone home when the phone rang. It was the governor. Now suddenly, I have been given the responsibility of getting that cat. I went to the capitol and now I have come home. I want you to know that this old game warden never in his wildest dream, dreamed of ever seeing anything like this. Hal Bonner told me something, I will never forget. He said, `these people aren't celebrating you. You are just a symbol and a reminder that the truth has just triumphed over a lie. The lie gave life to a rabid bobcat that never was, and about hiding the fact that a genuine danger to public safety—a cougar—did exist and had to be dealt with. So, I am going to tell you the truth. We have a man-eater on our hands. He is dog smart, and trap wise. He looks upon people, as food. He has tasted human blood and he likes it better than anything he has ever had. He will eat children and adults alike. He will kill livestock. He is a threat that must be stopped. I don't want anybody here thinking that getting him is gonna be any kind of picnic. It may only take a day. More likely it will take months and it may take over a year. He typically hunts by night and sleeps by day. He is jet black in color. He is hard to see at night. I have, from the governor, a declaration of emergency for the affected area. In town you won't have to worry, but in the rural areas, a five hundred square mile area, the decree holds: So, First: Nobody in the affected area will walk alone at night. Second: no permit to carry a fire arm on your person, or in your car, will be needed until the emergency is over. I would advise you to have one handy at all times. Imagine if your car broke down on a country road and you were all alone knowing that cat out there somewhere. A flashlight and a gun might save your life. Third: a bounty of one thousand dollars is hereby placed on that cat. You shoot him and we will shake your hand and give you a thousand dollars. Believe me, if one of you gets lucky and kills that cat we will all be happy. I don't care who shoots him. I just want him dead so that no more little Teresa's get killed. I am just one man. I will do my best and spare no effort to get this cat, but I can not guarantee your safety. You, as citizens, must, in the final analysis, do that for your selves. You have now been warned. Take appropriate measures, to protect your selves, and your neighbors. Don't expect Sam Macafee to be superman. I am not him. I cannot be everywhere and I cannot do everything. I will need your help, your prayers, and your patience. This is a fight to the finish."

"The governor has allowed me to pick two deputies to help me get the cat. I have chosen George Hogan and Jack

Morgan. I ask them to join me here to be sworn in."

The men approached the podium. They wore suits, which were obviously both uncomfortable and unfamiliar to them. They exchanged smiles and hand shakes.

The swearing was not what could be called formal.

"George Hogan, I hereby deputize you as a deputy game warden, at full pay, with the special assignment of helping me get this cat. Do you accept? "

"I sure do." Sam took one of the two badges that had been placed on the podium and pinned it on George's suit coat.

He turned to Jack.

"Jack Morgan, do you accept as well?"

"I sure do."

"Good," Sam said and pinned a badge on Jack's suit.

Sam looked around.

"Does anyone here have a holy bible?"

The mayor walked to the podium with a big bible in hand. He handed it to Hal Bonner. George put his hand on the bible first. The mayor administered the official oath of office. George responded.

"I do, so help me God."

Then it was Jack's turn, and he answered, "I do, so help me God."

Then the mayor shook each of their hands and congratulated them. The applause was deafening. Sam began again.

"I want everybody here to know that no matter how old I get, or how long I live I will never forget this day and you folks who came out to share it with me. You have gladdened my heart. Because you demanded justice it has and will be done. I will do my dead level best to live up to the trust that you have placed in me. So help me God."

The applause resumed. The high school band struck up a chorus of *Hold that Tiger*. Sam looked out over the crowd. He saw many American flags. There were posters with Teresa's picture. Many of them read, "We will not forget." Others had Sam's picture on them, with the caption: "The right man, for the job." Still others had a simulated cougar's picture on them.

They had captions that read: "Wanted: Dead or Alive," and had "$1000 Reward" printed, in capitol letters.

The mayor stepped up to the podium.

"Ladies, and Gentlemen," He began, "We are all proud of Sam Macafee and his new deputies. I ask, that we give them and their efforts, our prayers. `Our Father who art in Heaven: Hallowed be thy name...'" The crowd joined in the recitation of the Lord's Prayer. Every one spoke with one voice. Sam was getting choked up. Everyone was getting choked up. "...But deliver us from evil. For thine is the kingdom and the power, and the glory, for ever, and ever. Amen." Then the band struck up, *The Battle Hymn of the Republic*. Every one sang along. The ceremony was over. It had been longer than necessary and more words had been uttered than had been necessary but it was what the people needed.

Sam, George, Jack, Hal Bonner, and the mayor, all waved back to the lingering, still cheering crowd. The P A announcer rendered the usual cautions about remaining orderly and having a safe drive home. Hal drove The Guest of Honor and his lovely wife to their home. Hal asked for a rain check on the offer of coffee and was told it was redeemable at his earliest convenience. Hal waved his goodbye and, at last, Sam and Sally were alone. It had been one grueling and wonderful day. Tomorrow, the work would begin.

That night, as the sun dropped below the horizon, the cat awoke and stretched. He was hungry. He wasn't hungry for just anything. He wanted another human. He began to prowl passing up a number of animals that would have one attracted his attention. He wandered along the bank above the road eventually descending to follow the creek bank. The creek meandered through many farms and emptied into a remote lake. He wandered throughout the night finding nothing to his liking. Near dawn he came upon a wide crevice in a rock bluff above the lake and denned up for sleep. Looking around one last time his eyes came upon a lone fisherman working his way along the bank of the lake—early spring bass on his mind. Sleep would wait. The cat began his stalk. He moved closer not making a sound. He remained concealed in thick brush where he waited patently.

The man was Roscoe Tanner. He was well known in the area as a dedicated bass fisherman. He was, by trade, an insurance salesman. He had his own agency now. He had done well and had others selling the insurance for him. He ran the office and had hired competent help. That gave him the time for what was really important to him: Catching the wily bass. Some of his trophies were mounted in his office but each time out he hoped for the biggest bass of them all—the monster of all monster bass.. It would take center stage in his trophy case.

It was early in the day. Maybe it was too early. He didn't care. There was a chill in the air but not enough to deter him from his quest. He had dressed for the occasion with thermals, a warm jacket, and a hat with ear flaps. He felt it in his bones; that this was going to be the day he'd catch the fish of all fish!

His wife had complained, as usual, at his getting up early. After all those years one would have thought she would be used to it. She managed a smile as he left. At least she knew where he was. He would rather fish, than do almost anything else so she felt certain that she didn't have to worry about another woman. Another woman didn't swim in water, and grab lures, and fight like a tiger, leaving the man with stories to tell that grew with each telling. Another woman would have no chance with Roscoe. Over the years she'd even grown to love the stretched stories her husband would tell. Truth be known, there was not much about the man she didn't love. Her early morning complaints were more part of their ritual than anything serious.

Roscoe cast and recast his lure into the water. The fact that he hadn't had so much as a nibble didn't disappoint him for he just knew that his luck was about to change. He worked his way towards a line of trees along the bank, as many of their roots under the water as remained in the ground. It provided the perfect habitat for trophy bass. He worked towards them, plugging the shoreline as he moved. The sun was just on the horizon. He reeled in his plug and moved ten feet closer to those trees. He made his way through the brush to the next open spot on the lake. He set his tackle box down and surveyed the beautiful new morning.

An uneasy feeling engulfed him. The hair prickled on the back of his neck. He shrugged it off.

"Must be getting old and feary." He said, to himself.

He had plugged this area for years and had never had a sensation like this. He sensed that he was being watched. He just felt a presence. His instincts made him look around. His eyes picked up nothing unusual. He shrugged and cast his plug out again beginning to work it as he reeled.

Something hit him from behind. He instinctively dropped his pole, threw an elbow into, whatever it was. As he started to turn, he fell. He saw a claw-extended paw on his shoulder. He screamed, then felt teeth invading the back of his neck. His body lost all feeling and control. His spinal cord had been severed. He couldn't breathe or move. His world went black.

The catamount pulled his kill into the brush and concealed it. He clawed away the clothing. He was soon pulling huge chunks of flesh off of the bone. The taste of human blood provided a rush like nothing else. He devastated the man's midsection. Adrenalin flowed as he lapped up the blood and other fluids. His eyes narrowed. He raised his head and launched a scream of triumph. He had just conquered the one creature that he had previously feared. A deer put up a much better fight – even a sheep. It had been easy! Catch the man off guard and strike from the rear. It was no contest. He would never look at a man in the same way now. Man could be eaten. HE was the king of the woods and the wilds. He gorged himself and then covered what was left with leaves and twigs. It was well concealed. Then the cat went back to the crevice in the rock where he would remain concealed throughout the day. He yawned and stretched in the manner of a housecat and went to sleep.

Later in the day Janie Tanner became worried. Four o'clock came and Roscoe wasn't home yet. He usually fished the morning and the early afternoon away, went to a restaurant for coffee, and then came home. That was especially true in the early spring. It was chilly out. She hadn't called the restaurant yet as she did not want Roscoe to feel that she was an old nag.

By nature, Roscoe was always considerate. If it was getting later than usual he would always call. If she wasn't there he'd leave a message on the answering machine so she wouldn't worry. This was just not like him. She called down to the restaurant. Nobody there had seen him all day. Something was wrong and she knew it. She called the Sheriff's department and a deputy had answered. He tried to re-assure her that Roscoe probably just lost track of time. She asked to personally talk to Sheriff Bonner. Hal picked up the phone. She told him of her husband's normal method of operating, and that this definitely did not fit his pattern.

Her thoughts ran wild. What if he had suffered a heart attack? What if some young punks on a joyride had attacked him? She was scared for him. She told the sheriff that nobody had seen or heard from him at Jim's restaurant, where he *always* went after fishing. Hal asked her if she knew where he would have fished that day. She told him he would always plug the shoreline of Spring Lake. That was all she knew. Hal told her that he would personally get on it and that she should stay by the phone for his call.

"This may take a few hours so don't worry if it's a while before I call you back. Do you know any of his fishing buddies who might know what part of the lake he usually fishes?"

Jane went to the Rolodex and gave the sheriff three names and numbers. Hal told her not to worry. He would find her husband.

Hal called Jim Sommers. Jim allowed that he and Hal fished the lake often so he knew exactly what part of the lake ol' Roscoe frequented. They agreed to meet at his restaurant in fifteen minutes.

Hal brought a deputy along. His name was Jeff Sanderson. Jeff brought Private Chopper, his canine friend. Chopper was a big German Shepherd who was trained to sniff drugs and contraband. He could also find a man by scent from a piece of clothing or such.

They stopped at Janie's house and explained to her that they would need an item of Roscoe's clothing to sniff to get him on the trail. Janie went to the laundry pile and got one of Roscoe's T-shirts. She handed it to Hal.

"Don't worry Jane," Hal said trying to reassure her. "We'll find your husband. I'll call you just as soon as we know anything."

Jane put on a brave smile but she was scared inside in a way she had never been before. She managed, a weak "Okay," but that was the best she could do. Something was terribly wrong and she just knew it. There was nothing to do but to wait. She was not good at waiting. Roscoe was like a time clock. She never had to wonder. She watched the sheriff's car pull out of her drive.

It was eight o'clock when Jim, Hal, Deputy Jeff, and Chopper met at Jim's Restaurant. Jim wasted no time. It was only a few hundred yards to the lake. Hal and Jeff brought their police radios, flashlights, and revolvers. When they reached the edge of the lake Hal handed Roscoe's shirt to Jim. Chopper sniffed it and, nose to the ground, started to bark indicating that he was indeed on the scent. Hal smiled. This shouldn't take long now. They kept Chopper on leash, so he wouldn't get too far ahead of them. It was just beginning to get dark. The flashlights were turned on, and Jim lit up his Coleman lantern. They followed the shoreline for most of a quarter mile. The age-old, well-worn, fishermen's path grew narrower. Soon, it was nothing but brush and took time and effort to negotiate. Jim soon saw the tree grove where half the roots were in the water. He told Hal that this had to be the spot. He was walking toward the trees when he stopped dead in his tracks. There, in the lantern's glow, was Roscoe's tackle box. Nearby was the man's fishing pole. Chopper began tugging at his leash. Hal told the deputy to release Chopper. Hal suddenly had a bad feeling. Up until then he had figured that ol' Roscoe had just over fished his clock. But it was dark and he knew him well enough to know that Roscoe wouldn't intentionally leave his equipment behind.

Chopper started to snarl. He barked and growled. He headed directly for the weeds ahead. Suddenly there was fighting. Hal pulled his revolver. Chopper continued the struggle. Then suddenly Chopper's barking stopped. They heard him whine and all went quiet. With some caution they moved their lights from spot to spot. Jim raised his lantern as they reached the brush where they had heard the commotion. There were two discoveries. Both were sad. Chopper was dead! It was as if the dog had been struck by lightning. One minute he was barking, growling, and fighting, then, with a final whimper, he was dead!

"Good Lord!" Hal swore. "What in the..."

His flashlight beam hit the remains of of Roscoe Tanner. The flesh was gone. There was some torn clothing, but no flesh at all. Of all of the strange things that Hal Bonner had ever seen, this was the strangest, and perhaps, most horrible! Hal and Jim shined their lights on the ground beside the body searching for any clue about what had happened.

Suddenly, Jeff Sanderson screamed from the shadows. He disappeared. He had been standing over his dog no more than twenty yards from the rest of them. Hal's flashlight beam caught a glimpse of something running in the weeds, lower and faster than any man. He fired at whatever it was. They moved to find Jeff. Deputy Sanderson's neck had been broken. His spinal chord was severed and only slash marks remained where his eyes had been. He was dead.

Something had jumped him from the tree above and killed him within a matter of seconds! Hal had a chilling realization. Two men and a German shepherd were dead. One of the man and the German shepherd had died within a matter of minutes. The other man had been pealed of his flesh. Whatever had done it was still out there!

Hal reached for Jeff's service revolver. It was still in his holster. Whatever had killed him had done so before he had been able to make a move for it.

Hal barked, "Retreat to the edge of the lake where we can cover our backs from whatever it is!"

Jim was not in a mood to argue. The two men backed up. Hal handed Jeff's revolver to Jim. The two men backed up to the lake. There was just enough moonlight to let them find the shore. They backed up to the water's edge. They stopped by a tree and searched its branches with lantern and flashlight to make sure that nothing was up there.

Hal pulled out his police radio. Normally, police etiquette required a sign on code and a lot of specialized lingo. Hal just yelled into it.

"Code blue! This is sheriff Bonner. We are at Spring Lake and something has killed Private Chopper and Deputy Sanderson. Whatever the hell it is, is still out here. Get me some backup with shotguns loaded with double ought buck shot out here NOW!! DO YOU COPY?"

The response was immediate.

"Roger Sheriff Bonner. Where exactly is your position?"

" Proceed due west from Jim's Restaurant to the lake and hang a right. Then follow the bank and you will find us. You are gonna need a couple of four wheelers and a couple of stretchers. Proceed with great care. There something deadly out there in the night."

"What is it we're up against?" The radio barked back.

"I have no damned idea; just get your red asses out here! DO YOU COPY?"

"ROGER. WE ARE ON THE WAY. OUT."

Deputy Anderson and his men were on the way.

Soon the car radio blared: "This is Grove City Police. We got your transmissions. Do you need assistance?"

"Roger, Grove City. We sure do."

"Swat team One is on the way. We will rendezvous at Jim's restaurant."

"Roger Grove City." And thanks."

The radio crackled again.

"This is State Highway Patrol. Can we join the party? "

"Roger State Highway Patrol. I think sheriff Bonner will appreciate the company."

Sheriff Bonner heard the transmissions. He cranked up

his radio. “This is sheriff Bonner. Do you copy?"

Deputy Anderson answered. “We copy, and we are on the way with a little help from our friends."

"Good," the sheriff answered. "Tell everybody to stay together with plenty of light. Whatever-it-is, that is out here is lethal and will not hesitate to kill a straggler. Do you copy?"

"Roger Sheriff Bonner. Will advise. OUT."

Jim and Sheriff Bonner were back to back with their guns at the ready. They thought that they heard motion. Jim shot in the direction of the sound.

"Hold your fire," sheriff Bonner barked. "We better save our ammo."

The radio cracked again. "Sheriff Bonner. This is Sam Macafee. Jack Morgan is with me. Describe the situation. We may be able to figure out what it is? "

"I just figured out what it is." Sheriff Bonner barked back. "The little Salem girl had the meat ripped away from her ribs on one side. You just jogged my memory. I think it’s that damn cat! It's either that or some kind of pre-historic monster. Do you copy?"

"Roger. We are on the way, with Jack's two dogs.”

"Sam. Do you read me?" Sheriff Bonner shouted.

"Roger. We copy."

"Whatever it is just killed a special k-9 unit without any trouble. Maybe you should leave the dogs behind. OVER."

"These dogs have fought that cat before. They are special trained. OVER"

"What the hell kind of dogs are they? OVER."

"They are pit-beagles. Do you copy?"

"You mean those little dogs of Jacks? OVER?"

"ROGER.”

"What the hell is a pit beagle? OVER."

"Hal, this is George Hogan. A pit beagle is half pit bull and half beagle. OVER"

"What the hell are they good for? This whatever it is just killed a hundred and twenty pound shepherd? OVER."

Hal could hear George chuckling over the radio.

"They'll hunt all day. Just don't try to take the rabbit

from `em. They have fought this cat to a stand-still before. They are low to the ground and hard for that cat to hit, and their jaws are the jaws of a pit bull. OVER."

Sam and George were trying to keep Sheriff Bonner's spirits up. It had to have been a long night for him.

"Well, then bring 'em on. OUT."

The sheriff felt some better. At least he thought he knew what he was up against now, and lots of help was on the way. The overpowering fear he had felt was under control. They had heard nothing move in a while. Jim was shaking. He still couldn't believe what had happened. He hoped that every one would arrive soon and join them. He'd had entirely enough of this situation.

"I hope ol' whatever it was is gone?" He offered.

Hal shook his head and lit up a cigarette.

"You and me both," he agreed.

Not twenty yards from them, a black form crouched. Its tail was twitching. The cat was waiting for one of them to move away from the other. His black coat made him all but invisible in the darkness.

"It has got to have left by now. The shots had to scare it off." Jim surmised.

"I'm not sure of any thing," Hal said. "All we have to do to stay alive for sure is to stay close together and keep our eyes peeled until help arrives."

At Jim's Restaurant, the reinforcements were arriving. There were two sheriffs cars and two vans. Three state highway patrol cars had arrived. They were starting to unload the four wheelers and the two stretcher trailers when the swat helicopter arrived. It shined a bright light on the assemblage below. Sam, George and Jack's trucks pulled in and the three men and the two dogs got out. Sam Macafee was laughing.

"What is so damn funny?" Deputy Anderson, demanded.

"This looks like Normandy beach!" Sam offered looking around. The leader of Swat Team One bounded out of the cargo hold and down to the ground.

Instantly, the battle plan was established. The men and

the two dogs were to proceed down the path. Jack had his faithful double-barreled twelve gauge. George carried a sawed of double barreled twelve gauge. Sam Macafee had a single barrel slug-loaded pump twelve gauge with six shots loaded. The sheriffs department had followed orders and six of them carried Mossberg 590 military 12 gauge pump shotguns, each with eight shot tubes, along with their side arms. The state police carried their Ruger Mini-14s, and their side arms. Grove City's number one swat team of five carried H&K MP5 submachine-guns, along with their standard issue side arms. The operation did look like Normandy beach!

It was immediately decided, to abandon the four wheelers and the trailers. The stretchers were loaded onto the helicopter. They would all proceed in columns of four, side by side, with ten yards between each group. The helicopter would light their way by flying above them as they worked their way towards the sheriff. When they located him, they would bring the chopper down at an open location, evacuate the sheriff and Jim, and would carry out the dead.

Just as they were leaving for the lake, two action cam vans from the television station pulled up. The circus had just come to town! The sheriffs deputies and the city police demanded that they leave. An argument ensued. Sam Macafee brokered an agreement that would allow one camera crew and one reporter to accompany the group.

The camera crew and the one reporter would follow the first group and stay six yards in back of them. Ten yards behind them would come a second group of state highway patrol officers; each spaced five yards apart. Sam, George, and Jack would take a point position ten yards ahead with the one dog on leash so that any cat in the immediate area could be detected. Brownie would accompany the back line, leashed so that if the cat somehow got behind them it would be detected. The reporters also had to agree not to run film live because the two families of the two dead men had not been notified. They would be allowed full coverage after the notification of the next of kin. The reporter would be allowed to view the dead but pictures of the bodies were not allowed, as they would be too graphic and too hard on the families involved.

The force, with the helicopter above it lighting the way, preceded forward. They followed the shoreline of the lake. After a half a mile the trail ended. The grove of trees was coming into view in the moonlight. As the light from the helicopter came closer, Sheriff Bonner saw movement in the brush. The cat had broken off the ambush as the commotion moved towards them. Hal was dumbstruck.

"Whatever it was, was right over there!" He pointed to the spot that it had vacated just a second before. "It's a good thing we didn't relax and start to move around thinking it was gone."

Jim started to shake. He had actually contemplated moving a few yards away to relieve himself, earlier. Sheriff Bonner had talked him out of it. It was a good thing, he thought to himself. Whatever it was might have killed him outright and then come back for Hal once he was alone.

"Sheeew," Jim uttered. "If we had moved apart, even just for a minute, it might have gotten us both."

"I think that is a safe bet from what I have seen here tonight." Hal allowed.

The men arrived and the chopper sat down. Hal relaxed for the first time since the cat killed Chopper. He led the swat team members to the bodies. The female reporter saw the skeletal remains of what had once been Roscoe Tanner. She started to weep. Jack escorted her away. Soon, the remains of Roscoe and Jeff were loaded on stretchers covered with blankets, and loaded onto the chopper. That is what the camera was allowed to record, for posterity.

As Chopper's remains were carried aboard, the reporter looked at that huge dead dog. She asked Hal how the dog had died. Hal gave her the entire story of the encounter from beginning to end. The reporter was aghast.

"What could have done this?" She asked.

At that point, after what her eyes had just witnessed, if Hal had told her that little green men had emerged from a spaceship with zap guns, she would have been hard pressed to disbelieve him. Instead, she got proof. George had found tracks where the big cat had been laying, a few yards, from where Hal and Jim had made their stand. Jack took a plaster cast of the imprint. When it set he showed the reporter. Then, showed her the other tracks. She was simply shocked beyond belief.

Soon, the chopper was loaded and airborne. The invasion force went back the same way it had come, with the chopper lighting their way back to Jim's restaurant. Jim was so glad to see his place of business, and safety, that he kissed the door before entering. Off in the distance they heard the big cat scream. It had an eerie, haunting, chilling effect on all who heard it.

Hal said his thanks to everyone and asked his chief deputy to drive him out to Janie Tanner's home. This was going to be the hardest day he had ever known. He knocked on her door. She could see the bad news in his eyes. She started to sob uncontrollably. Then, she stopped. Roscoe, she thought, would not want her to be that way. She thanked the Sheriff for all he had done and tried to do. She told him she would be okay. Sheriff Bonner had earlier called her sister, and she and her husband were on their way and would be there within minutes.

He had one more terrible stop to make.

"Let's go see Jeff's wife."

Deputy Anderson looked at Hal. "If you want to sit this one out, I can drop you home, and then go out there and tell Jeff's wife. You have had one hell of a night."

Hal smiled at him. "I want to thank you, for saving my butt tonight."

The deputy smiled. "It was just my turn, you saved mine last month."

Two strong men shared half a smile. Then Hal said, "If you had bought it; you would have wanted it to be me, that told your wife. I owe that to Jeff, and his wife."

Frank nodded his head. They went to the Sanderson's together. Thus far the news people had kept their word. The story had not aired yet.

The cruiser pulled into the Sanderson's drive. Annette

came to the door. She had thought that the cruiser was her husband and Chopper coming home after a long day. When Hal and Frank got out she knew the worst had happened. As she opened the door the tears were already flowing. She sniffed.

"When I married him, I knew that this day could come." Then she broke down. "But damn it, I prayed so hard that it never would."

Hal held her in his arms and she sobbed on his shoulder. She cried it out and then thanked both men for coming in person, instead of just giving her a phone call. Hal was overcome himself, and it showed. Annette could see it. She invited them in. The coffee had already been made.

Hal kept his word to the press and gave them the phone call he promised them he would, after the families had been notified. The television and radio programs were simultaneously interrupted by a special report. By that time the hospital had confirmed that the deaths were to be attributed to the cougar.

The entire area was now in shock, as Rebecca Monk, gave the report and the details. Her eyes looked hollow. She was shell shocked herself. The mayor and the county commissioners both proclaimed a day of mourning. The schools would be closed. The flags were to be flown at half-mast. Church services of every denomination would be held in memory of the dead. Jeff and Roscoe's pictures were splashed across the television screens that night and appeared in the papers the next morning. The man-eater had struck again.

Hal and Frank stayed at Annette's for a half an hour. They called Jeff's brother and parents. They were on their way. None of them wanted to be alone that night.

Frank dropped an exhausted Hal Bonner at his home. The two men shook hands. Then Frank headed for his place. It was a day that neither man would ever forget or ever want to repeat. Their families had prayers of thanksgiving in their hearts and deep sadness for the passing of two good men and a dog. Hal hugged his wife and went straight to bed. He was just flat-out spent.

Along the creek bed that led from the lake to the farmlands and eventually to Jack's property, the catamount stalked. He walked with an air of superiority. He had struck down two men and a dog. He had seen the helicopter again. At night, it had not pursued him. He would move north all night toward a part of his range that was quieter. The cat seemed to know that all hell was going to break loose in these parts. He would vacate this part of his range, for a while. Things would cool off later. His move was a tactical retreat. There would be less suspecting men women and children up north. They would be easier prey. The cat simply walked away, from this part of his range, and moved north. He denned in a cave, at night's end. There, he slept the day away, and continued north again by night. The dogs and the helicopters could look all they wanted. The cat had just vanished, into thin air.

## CHAPTER SEVEN
## The Trial

The next day came and the men and their dogs let no time waste as they deployed to get the killer. Sam sent Department of Wildlife helicopters flying over the hundreds of square miles that had been projected to encompass the cat's massive range. George and Jack began to break fourteen new coonhounds into the pack that would soon be unleashed against the cat. George had advised Sam to wait until the pack had been trained before chasing blindly off into the woods after the cat.

Sam agreed, in principle, but pointed out that, "We can't just be sitting here in the wake of two murders. The people will justly expect us to be about the business, of bringing the cat to justice, before it kills off more people, while we are `preparing to get ready.'" George acknowledged the problem. He understood that people wanted immediate action, yesterday; but, he told Sam, "If we go off half-cocked, then, all that is gonna happen is more dead dogs and hunters." He looked at Sam, right in the eye, and said, "the dogs and the men, must act as one, if we're gonna get this cat. And, we have to develop a strategy, to do just that."

The show was going to go on. Sam and Jack along with Blackie and Brownie hit the now, very cold, trail the cat had left by the lake. It was as if the cat had sprouted wings and just flown away. Sam carried a radio with him so he could call in the latest technology including helicopters should the trail become hot. He, Jack, and the two dogs, spent the entire day following a cold trail that eventually got lost altogether where the cat had crossed the creek and in so doing, diluted its smell in the water. It then crossed into a rocky area that was difficult for the scent to cling to. At the end of the first day, Sam and Jack loaded the bone-tired dogs onto the back of the pickup and headed for home in defeat.

The media had gotten their pictures of the men and the dogs and the helicopters hard at work trying to get the cat. The public was satisfied that they were getting their money's worth.

Meanwhile, George spent the entire day working the dogs and training them to the dog whistle, trying to get them to work together as a unit. He was a master at the art of dog training. All of his life, it was what he did best. He had been instrumental in showing Jack the ropes in the training of his two dogs, and that was a part of what had made them such a formidable team.

The rest was in their breeding. Their mother was woods smart and downright brainy as dogs go—and she had heart. Their father was a king dog: a fighter without parallel. Blackie was his fathers' son with all of his mothers' wood smarts and cunning. Brownie was his mother's son with much of his father's fight but more of his mother than his father. He had her nose and her loving nature. In a fight he was Blackies' backup—with the instinct to hit from behind, while the combatants were at it. Blackie, like his father, would want to charge in and get a hold of something vital and crush it in his jaws. Brownie liked to let the opponent know he was there with a powerful bite from behind. Brownie had the better nose and Blackie the better jaw. The cat developed a grudging respect for the two and an urgency to kill them. The cat wanted those two dogs and their master dead. It was as if all of them knew that it would eventually come to a final showdown. The cat, for his part, wanted the odds in its favor, and the man and his dogs wanted the opposite.

Unlike a lion or a tiger, this cat had to use stealth and odds in its fight against the men because it was smaller than a tiger. It relied upon craft and guile as much as outright brute force. This particular cat had an abundance of both for while it was smaller than a tiger, it was, pound for pound, stronger, and it was the master of the hunt and the kill. It was camouflaged to the maximum at night, and it had learned to sleep by day. Like a child's worst nightmare come true, it lurked in the dark places, in the hidden shadows, ready to appear out of nowhere. It was certain death to any unsuspecting person it might encounter. It had tasted human blood and it had a raging thirst for more. It had eaten of the apple and had acquired the forbidden knowledge contained, therein. No man, woman, or child, would be safe so long as it prowled. In the dark and eerie places of the woods and farms, at night, it could be anywhere at any time. A green-eyed monster roamed and prowled in silence: ready to pounce and tear flesh and bone with claws and fangs. It would then scream its victory into the darkness. It would echo through those dark places as a warning to all creatures within miles.

That day it heard the helicopters from deep within the darkness of its den. The helicopters had seen and heard nothing, and the men and their dogs were in the wrong part of its range. The cat was waiting for the darkness, in which he ruled supreme.

In town, the people mourned the deaths of two of their very best citizens. The church bells tolled and the flags were at half-staff. The families mourned and were consoled by their friends and neighbors, and even by strangers. The entire town was as one large family. The police and sheriffs departments held a joint funeral for the fallen officer and his dog. The Tanner insurance agency was closed, and cards and letters of consolation flooded in to Roscoe's wife. At the Sanderson home, a parade, of uniformed well-wishers continued into the evening.

As the hunt, and the funerals were going on, another drama was about to play out. The next day, the hippies who had trespassed on Earl, Jack, and George's land, were to go on trial. It would begin in the morning.

That evening, John Weston sat in his study going over his case. He had been the county prosecutor for twenty years. He'd seen the cases come and go—from murder to spitting on the side walk. He'd prosecuted the cases as the law required.

Somehow he saw this case as different. He had laughed for having taken himself so seriously.

"Since when is trespassing, more weighty than murder?" He'd mocked out loud.

He'd wondered why this case seemed so much more important to him than simple murder. In a murder case, one so-called human being took it upon himself to take away another human beings life. Often, the deceased had done something real or imagined to the perpetrator. Sometimes, the criminal was simply ornery and evil to the extreme. They had to be punished and put away, in any case, to insure the public safety. He was efficient at his job. His conviction rate was high. What he was more proud of though, was that in all of his twenty years he was convinced that he'd never sent an innocent person to jail. He would arrange plea bargains, where possible, and recommend leniency where he believed that was in the public's interest. He really believed himself to be one of the good guys, and, because it was important for him to see himself in that way, his conduct was in line with his self-perception. In short, he *was* a good guy.

Make no mistake about it, in the courtroom, he could strike an attorney, a witness, or a perpetrator, with an innocent sounding question, or statement, followed by a rhetorical death blow, as coldly, and efficiently, as any cobra ever brought down it's prey. He had a grasp for detail that was amazing, and he could, with almost breathtaking ease, glean what it was out of all of that detail, that was significant and important in the case at hand. Had he chosen, he could have gone to much higher places, but to him, what was important was his family, his county, and his home. In his spare time he was a fisherman and hunter who was out in his county, just living in it. He was a husband and father first, a neighbor and a friend second, and a prosecuting attorney third. Because of all of these things, his home county was well protected and well served. The county had been blessed and, in many ways, he was one of those blessings.

The answer to his question was soon before him. In a murder case, three things were important: Who had done it?

What, if any, extenuating circumstances were there? And, did the public safety and the public morality, require the death penalty in that case? As a prosecutor he had always structured his prosecution in such a way that these elements seemed to come out in the courtroom with the clarity of a well-written stage play. But never in a murder case had he seen a real attempt to say that murder was okay: That murder had been with us always and was a part of the human condition that was neither good, nor evil, but rather was simply to be adjusted to and be understood. This case was more important than a simple murder case, for precisely that reason.

In this case, there was a real and insidious attempt to claim that trespassing and taking away a citizen's right to liberty and the pursuit of happiness on his own land, was lawful and right. The high-priced socialist attorneys for the college kids involved were seriously asserting that trespass was not only not a big deal, but that the perpetrators were heroes because they were protecting the deer from being hunted. The deer, in other words, were given status of souled beings, not only on a par with mankind, but in many ways, they were asserting that they had rights beyond that of mankind and certainly above that of a man's property rights. It was as if he were prosecuting a murder case where the murder was being touted as an act of a heroic nature that was to be lauded and certainly not prosecuted. What was at stake, he realized, was property rights for the common man.

He knew that deer certainly wouldn't know, or care, about the out come of this case. Only the socialists had a stake in this one. For if the individual loses his property rights to the public interest, in this case, animal rights, then liberty would be lost for all citizens who own property. Instead, the 'Enlightened Ones', namely the socialists, would tyrannically force their statist ideology on everybody. Like thugs with a license, they could storm your property and mine, violate our rights, and lecture all of us on their politically correct views. Sooner or later the government would effectively own all of the property and the individual would become a serf instead of a liberty endowed citizen with 'unalienable rights'.

The national media was in town to cover the trial and they were essentially in league with the socialists. They were there to support animal rights, and animal rights activists, (hippies), and to make the hunters and the property owners appear like Simon Lagree: in this case, the oppressive hunter out to kill poor bambi and to despoil nature in an insidiously evil way. He knew that the national media, who's constitutional duty was to be a guardian of our freedoms and to alert the citizens to any danger to our liberties, were here instead to propagandize on behalf of the socialists and the poor oppressed college kids, who were just trying to protect bambi, from the terrible land owning oppressors who would shoot the beautiful animal out of `craven neanderthalism and machismo.' In short, the media was in town, to "Tell it like it wasn't."

He understood fully what was at stake in this case. It *was* more important than a murder case. That night he prayed for the wisdom and the words he would need to put an appropriate ending on a story that had the potential to be corrosive to our very freedoms. He was ready, almost eager, for the battle to begin.

Across town in a motel room, the defense team was hard at work. Sheila Longworth and Bradley Loftus, headed it. They worked for a national liberal liberties group that specialized in pushing the socialist agenda through the courts, where the people and their retrograde, voting habits could not come into play. Sheila had just finished a case, striking a Christian cross from a city seal that had been that city's seal for a hundred years. The courts had ruled that it violated the separation of Church and State provision of the U.S. Constitution, even though such appears nowhere, in that document. But, because, the Constitution says what the Supreme Court says it is, and because of two generations of liberal justices on the Supreme Court the cross had to go. She smiled as the citizens wept. She left that case triumphant and she was confident—almost overconfident—that she could prevail here.

"These hicks are going to get a taste of liberation and they are going to have to eat it and like it," she sneered.

"I'm not so sure," Brad answered.

He was just finished a case involving a group of parents who were fighting against a "pink triangle curriculum," that the National Teachers Union had introduced into a school system with the willing acquiescence of the school board. The parents had objected to their children being exposed to what they considered was homosexual lifestyle propaganda in the first, second, and third grades. They protested vigorously. A new conservative rights organization of attorneys had taken their case. There had been a lot of publicity, and, as the court case was working it's way through the courts, a funny thing had happened: there was a school board election and the new school board had more conservatives than liberals for the first time in a generation. The new school board had simply voted to drop the case and to change the curriculum to fit the parents desires, in the education of their *own* children. The National Teachers Union applied all of the pressure it could, but the local school board would not budge on the issue. Many of the teachers picketed the school board's offices, but to no avail. The end result was that the locals now knew which teachers wanted to "Teach that filth to the kids."

The presiding judge, while very liberal herself, had no choice but to dismiss the case because the School Board had dropped the issue. The National Teachers Union tried to object in court that it should continue, but the judge had to rule that curriculum was still the province of the school board. Brad was confident that he would have won the case in court, but the people had spoken in an election so the case he could have won was dropped. He had argued that the state had a compelling interest in the education of its children, and that bigotry against homosexuals, must be rooted out of the children through the schools, and the curriculum. The attorney for the parents had argued that the parents, and not the state, had the largest say in the education of their children. The election had been so spectacular in its results that the whole state was now talking about vouchers given to the parents by the state so that they, and not the state, could take the money and make the determination for their kids as to where they went to school, and what the curriculum would be. For now, however, the townsfolk in that state were foursquare behind the new school board and dead set against the National Teachers Union.

Brad looked at Sheila with concern.

"We have pretty well had it all our way for thirty years. It's going to get rough for us for a while."

Sheila sneered. "These hillbillies won't have a chance. Just wait and see them get dazzled and whipped!"

They were both concerned about one thing. The college kids had been caught red-handed by the sheriff's department. The county had picked up the prosecution of the issue. They had been charged with trespass and vandalism in the damaging of Jack's new fence when they'd breached it to enter the property. They all had been charged with incitement to riot because one of the students had crossed on to Earl's property, cursed him, and refused to leave the premises when ordered to by Earl. Because the kids operated as a group, state law made those charges applicable to the whole group. The arrests had been made by the sheriff's department who had witnessed the whole thing. The attorneys for the eight college kids rejected offers of immunity and reduced sentences in exchange for testimony relating to the *Friends of Animals* group for conspiring to deprive the civil rights of the property owners.

Sheila and Brad knew that Weston wanted to go fishing for possible illegal conspiracy charges against the animal rights group who had planned and bankrolled the entire operation. In particular he was fishing to catch April Gillespie and Robert Sanford, who were at the time employed in the state service for the Department of Wildlife. April was a charter member of the Friends of the Animals, whose generous donation to the Liberal Civil liberties group, had resulted in their being represented by them. Their plan was to feint for brutality in the arrests, get the charges dropped, and then to sue the county and the Sheriff department for conspiracy to violate the college kids civil rights for violating their free speech rights. They were going to play to the press, which would result in funds being sent to the group nationwide from animal rights supporters and other rich pro-liberation groups. Their goal was to get the charges against the kids reduced and then sue the pants off of everyone involved. Sheila could already smell the money and the publicity! She envisioned Hollywood stars protesting outside of the courtroom and the media throwing gala's for them after the victory was achieved.

To win, they had to plea bargain, seem amenable to settling the case as a child's prank, and then sue. So far the prosecutor wasn't buying any of it. He wanted to grant the kids immunity from prosecution only in exchange for information on the larger group of adults behind the effort.

The charges against the eight defendants added up to from six months to a year in jail for inciting to riot and refusing to leave along with the trespass, vandalism, and malicious mischief charges. All of the charges were misdemeanors, but they were high misdemeanors. These cases usually would be plead down and the offenders would get thirty days in jail if they pleaded, but the prosecutor was refusing all pleas, much to the consternation of the defense attorneys who needed those plea bargains and the resulting light sentences in order to claim, in a later civil suit, that the locals had overreacted and had, in their prejudice, violated their civil rights. Their goal was to trivialize trespass, vandalism and incitement to cause riot, as spitting on the side walk, type offenses, and to thereby describe, as trivial, the rights of the landowners and their property rights, while touting as important, their animal rights agenda, and it's socialistic goals. They wanted to martyr the students, display them as victims, and then go after 'the oppressors', in the civil case, and so penalize them and the county that stood behind them that others, who sought to protect property rights, would fear to champion that cause. They would plead for mercy for their 'innocent clients', and then show no mercy to those against whom they had trespassed.

So the strategy for the defense was set. In another part of town, Judge C. Townsley Smith was burning the midnight oil as well. He was looking at eight cases that were open and shut, or should have been. "Why?" He wondered to himself,

"Why would these kids not plea bargain down to a month, get a suspended sentence, and move on. What could John Weston be up to?" The judge knew him well. He was always reasonable and painfully fair. Why was he refusing to plea them down and be done with this case? All that he had offered them was immunity from prosecution or reduced sentences if they would testify as to the motives of others he was seeking to prosecute. The judge was mystified, but over the years, he had come to respect the prosecutor and his instincts. He knew of the reputations of the defense team that had just been employed, and he knew that they were going to try to make a circus out of his courtroom. "They had better all be prepared to wear balls and chains if they try that!" He thought to himself. Something fishy was afoot, and he smelled it.

At their initial appearance the students had demanded a jury trial on what seemed to him to be an open and shut case. Bail for all eight had been set and paid immediately. They had been told specifically the misdemeanors with which they were charged: disturbing the peace (which carried a fine, and a maximum of thirty days in the county jail), trespassing (which carried a sixty day maximum sentence and a fine), incitement to riot, for refusing to leave the land, as ordered to by the landowner, and for the incendiary comments that James Wilson had hurled at him in his refusal to leave (maximum of six months in jail), criminal mischief by reason of vandalism for the way they tore up Jack's fence when they crossed it in order to gain access to the land (which also carried a six month maximum). Finally, each had been pulled before the grand jury and told that they were under investigation on state charges of conspiracy to violate the civil rights of a category of citizens through a criminal conspiracy. No formal charges on that score had been filed but all of the defendants had been notified that they were under investigation by the grand jury, for that charge, which carried with it a five-to-ten year sentence and a huge fine.

It was that potential charge that had the defense team worried. Up to that point all of the students and all members of the *Friends of the Animals* group had marched in lock step and refused to testify in exchange for immunity. Weston was unmovable on plea-bargaining these cases and the judge suspected that the prosecutor had an ace or two up his sleeve. He had watched him operate for many years and knew that he had to be seeking the maximum on the misdemeanors in order to force them to seek immunity on the big charge and reduced sentences on the misdemeanors, in exchange for incriminating testimony against the *Friends of the Animals* group.

The judge was also well aware of the reputations of the defense team and believed they would try to make it appear that he, the judge, was partial to the prosecution, and that the whole proceedings was rigged and somehow unfair. They would try to make him into judge Roy Bean, and his courtroom, into a circus tent with animal acts. Clearly, they would be standing at the ready to play to the media, which was already invading the town in huge numbers along with busloads of demonstrators from the campus. The campus demonstrators would be trying to make enforcing the law appear to be an exercise in fascism. He also knew that he was not about to fall into that trap.

The cat also played a role. He had begun his killing spree just after the change of venue could have been requested (within seven days of the trial). The cat had struck five days before the trial. Sam Macafee, George Hogan, and Jack Morgan had been appointed to get the cat just four days ago. But the law was clear: A change of venue had to be requested at least seven days prior to the trial and no motion had been made. As a precaution, John Weston had dropped Sam Macafee as an initiator of the case, because of his new celebrity and because he was a witness and not a man who's land had been trespassed upon. He would, however, be called upon as a witness. The cat and his victims would cast a mighty shadow over this case and the Judge knew it. This town now saw where animal rights had led.

John Weston had a strategy all right. He was going to be so darned fair to the defense that he would give them all the rope they needed to hang themselves. He had a surprise for all of them. The Salem's had testified secretly before the grand jury regarding the activities of the *Friends of the Animals*. He had granted them immunity from prosecution even though they had not requested it. They, he reasoned, had already suffered enough. It was the loss of their daughter that had finally turned the tide for them. They *saw* where the Animal Rights movement led. They had buried their daughter as a result. Now, they wanted to make everything right.

The national media was in for a surprise as well. John Weston was going to educate them on the importance of property rights, as it related to the constitution, and to the framers view of their importance to all of our other liberties. They had downplayed the cat story nation wide. Now the killer cat was going to be front and center, before the cameras, and the victims families were going to get a starring role on court T.V. with his blessings. The judge would be stunned that Weston would not object to cameras in the courtroom. His trap was baited and ready for the slick city lawyers who were just going to self-righteously blunder right into it. He would just get out of their way and let them make colossal fools of themselves, ON NATIONAL TELEVISION!

Long before jury selection had even begun the hippies had gathered in great numbers outside the courtroom. They carried signs that declared: FREE THE GROVE CITY EIGHT!! Others read: ANIMALS LIVES, ARE MORE IMPORTANT THAN PROPERTY RIGHTS!!

Rock music was blasting from a number of their vans. The county had been expecting as much and had deployed both county sheriff's deputies and city police in a cordon around the courthouse. There were media vehicles and cameras there to record any misdeed of the police as those same cameras studiously avoided recording the provocations the hippies would be hurling at them. The sixty's were in bloom in the nineties. The smell of marijuana began to seep from the demonstrators. To add to the hippie carnival atmosphere, two students were dressed up in kangaroo costumes and were hopping about proclaiming that the KANGAROO COURT was coming into session. Others were dressed up as clowns and dancing bears. The heck of it was that the clowns didn't seem out of place. As a matter of fact, they seemed to fit right in.

The townspeople were quickly getting fed up with the antics of the hippies. Someone called the local chapter of the National Rifle Association. Another call went to the V.F.W. and to the American Legion. The president of the American Legion, no lover of hippies after his service in a place called Vietnam many years ago, got a brilliant idea. The town had a local group that did revolutionary war and civil war re-enactments. He called the chapter president with a grand scheme. He would need all of their people who wanted to participate in a counter-demonstration. The chapter president loved the idea. They all gathered at the V.F.W. and plotted out their strategy. Then, they gathered two hundred supporters and they got dressed up in revolutionary war, civil war, and then, modern military gear. The N.R.A. made up some pro-gun and pro-property rights signs. The American Legion made up some signs of their own, as did the V.F.W. It was agreed that an informal competition would be held among the groups for best signs and best costumes, and a panel composed of members of all of the participating groups would select the winners. These 'Minutemen', would cede to the hippies the first day of the festivities, but they would be gathering, drilling, and practicing for day two, of the town's, misdemeanor, 'Trial of the Century.' That afternoon and evening and all through the night, the women's auxiliaries of the four groups involved were whipping up costumes for four hundred counter-demonstrators. Old, "DON'T TREAD ON ME" flags, with the rattlesnake coiled and at the ready were made up as well. The townsfolk quickly got into the act. Telephones rang off the hooks. The locals were going to have their fifteen minutes of fame, tomorrow. It would completely overwhelm the hippies and their plan to ridicule the town and the trial.

The media, for its part, was having a field day making a federal case out of a series of common misdemeanors. Most of the journalists were middle-aged baby boomers, now re-living Woodstock and the Chicago Seven trial of their youth. National media Anchors on the big three television stations were casting this trial as determining the free speech rights of the college youth, pitted against the old-fashioned property rights of the landowners. They recounted the police action in the arrests. They were also lobbying the judge to allow them to have cameras inside the courtroom, and were amazed that the prosecutor also wanted the cameras in, once jury selection was complete.

Inside the courthouse, the judge was in chambers, preparing for his entrance into the courtroom. He was also wrestling with the camera issue. His instincts told him to reject the idea out of hand but both the prosecutor and the defense wanted them. The defense wanted them right away and the prosecutor wanted them only after jury selection so that no circus sideshow would go on in the jury selection process. The Judge asked John Weston why he wanted the cameras and John replied, "The other side is going to try to make this case into a contest between free speech rights and property rights, and the media would be in their support. The only way to counter them was to require that court T.V. carry the proceedings live, and thus both sides of the debate would have to be carried. We can win this debate with ease if the media and the defense aren't allowed to present only one side of the issue. By locking in complete coverage, our side gets heard and we not only win the case but we strike a blow for our property rights as well."

The judge was concerned, but he liked the prosecutor's logic. He was expecting the defense to try to demonize him as well. Maybe this was a way to counteract that strategy.

Soon it was time to begin. The prosecutor and his team were at his table, and the defense team was seated at theirs. Every seat in the courtroom was filled with spectators, both from the town and from the hippies. Soon the Bailiff called out, "All Rise," as the Judge made his entrance. "Court is now in session, with the Honorable C. Townsley Smith presiding." The Judge strode into the courtroom, took his place at the Judges' podium, motioned for everyone to take his seat, and sat down.

There was murmuring in the courtroom. The judge crisply banged his gavel and called for order. Then he spoke on some procedural issues. The first issue was in regard to the cameras in the courtroom. The judge looked at the requests. "Ms. Longworth, why does the defense request cameras in the courtroom for a simple misdemeanor trespass and vandalism case?"

"There is a larger issue here," Sheila said with almost sarcastic arrogance. "This is, we believe, also a free speech case, and a case which pits simple property rights against those who are acting at the calling of a higher law. It pits the lives of innocent animals, who were going to be mercilessly murdered, against the `sport' of slaughtering them without mercy. This is, we believe, the real issue of this case. This is why your town is full of idealistic youth demonstrating in your town square. This is why the media is here. This is the start of a national debate on this issue. Should those who have property be allowed to mercilessly slaughter `the peoples' wildlife, just because the poor creatures happened to wander onto their land? Should those who seek to protect them be mercilessly dragged off to jail, threatened with vicious dogs, and locked up for God knows how long, just because they believe that the killing must end? We believe that the American People have a vested stake in the outcome of this case. That is why the cameras are here. We ask that you include the American people in on this debate."

"I see," Judge Smith replied, looking at her over his spectacles. "So, you would challenge the property laws on the books rather than to contest the trespass?"

"We are conceding nothing and contesting everything!" Ms. Longworth shot back.

"We shall see, Ms. Longworth, we shall see. I will warn both the prosecution and the defense, right here and now, that any attempt to turn this courtroom into a circus will result in contempt citations."

His eyes met John Weston's.

"And what interest does the prosecution have in allowing cameras into my courtroom?"

Weston smiled. The defense had just betrayed their strategy. He would hold his fire for later. For the time being he would play the wide-eyed county prosecutor who was simply awed by the competition and the press.

"Your honor," he began, pausing, as if fumbling for words, "The prosecution sees this case as open and shut and if the American People want to see how justice works this prosecutor has no objection—that is, after the jury is selected. The people do not need to be bored to death with that process. I also do not want the names of the jury released, except by number, to the press, because their is no requirement that the jury be sequestered in a misdemeanor case. I do not want the jury tampered with by the media or by citizens on either side of the issues at stake in this case. I do not want their identities known or their phone numbers released. I request *that* as my condition for agreeing to media coverage in the courtroom. The jury's comings and goings NOT be photographed in any way. I further request that the jurors be given a police escort out of the courtroom and transported to a secret location by police van and that from that location they can drive their cars home."

Judge Smith nodded.

"Does the defense have any objection to that suggestion?"

"None your honor." Ms. Longworth announced.

She was simply flabbergasted at the prosecutor's agreement. She had figured that the press would be kept out side and have to do reports with drawings. Court T.V., wanted to do gavel-to-gavel coverage of the trail. This, she believed, was a dream come true for the defense.

The judge looked at both the prosecutor and the defense. "Before I rule on the motion involving the cameras I understand that both the prosecution and the defense have agreed that all eight defendants are to be tried as a group, simultaneously. Is that correct?"

"Yes, your honor." Each stated.

The judge smiled approvingly. He then began to issue his ruling on the cameras.

"So far," he smiled, "The civility of this court has been remarkable. It had better continue. I am inclined to give the cameras a chance in this courtroom. But," he warned, "If I get even the slightest hint that this courtroom decorum becomes, in any way affected by their presence, I WILL NOT HESITATE, TO HAVE THEM REMOVED FOR THE DURATION OF THIS TRIAL!! We will give this a try and it is for all parties involved to insure its continuance. Is that ABUNDANTLY CLEAR??"

Both the prosecution, and the defense nodded their heads, and said, "Yes, your honor."

The jury selection process went on for two days. Bradley Loftus took charge of that for the defense. He was an expert at selecting the kind of jury most likely to be sympathetic to the cause of liberation. He wanted one, preferably two blacks on the jury, so the analogies to Dr. Martin Luther King's campaign of civil disobedience in the south, during the civil rights movement could be used as a parallel to the animal rights activists' efforts. He wanted as many women as possible—especially those with an aversion to hunting. All he needed was one juror to vote against conviction and everyone walked. A hung jury was as good as an outright acquittal. He asked prospective jurors if they had anything against college students. He asked them if they believed in a higher law. His questions went on through a long list.

John Weston was very laid back in his approach. He asked each prospective juror one central question: "Do you believe in property rights as being one of the most basic foundations on which our very liberty rests." He quoted the federalist papers and asked the juror if he knew that in early drafts of our Declaration of Independence, that there was strong support, for "Life, Liberty, and Property," rather than, "The Pursuit of Happiness?" He looked each prospective juror in the eye and asked them if they believed that liberty was important and that property rights and ownership was one of the foundations of that very liberty. In short, he was less concerned with the array of sexual and racial makeup of the jury, than he was with whether or not they understood the importance of property rights.

At the end of day two, the jury was selected. Four men

and four women. One of the four women was black and one of the four men was black. A panel of eight jurors is the law in misdemeanor cases, with two alternates.

Outside the courthouse, the Street Theater was heating up. Day two saw the locals practicing in revolutionary war uniforms and the women dressed in colonial costumes. They had applied and been granted a parade permit. It had been done quietly so as not to attract the attention of the media who were busily photographing the hippies and their speeches about the corrupt society and the kangaroo court. The kangaroos were hopping about along with others, dressed in deer and rabbit costumes. The police had ordered all demonstrators to stay fifty yards away from the courthouse and the police had cordoned off the area, so that the noise of the demonstration would not interfere with the trial. Excessively loud music was shut off by order of the Judge so that court inside might proceed in an undisturbed fashion.

Suddenly, they heard the sound of marching and drums. The colonial fife and drum corps led the parade of the locals down both sets of sidewalks on either side of the main street which led to the courthouse. There were about two thousand of them. They came in columns down each sidewalk. Each column was led by a fife and drum corps in revolutionary war costumes, followed by revolutionary war soldiers in uniform and marching in columns. Their muskets may have been made of wood but the bayonets on the ends of them were very real. Following them were columns of union soldiers dressed in blue and the confederate soldiers dressed in gray. Soldiers of more recent vintage, in turn, followed them, from the World War Two and Vietnam era. The soldiers were marching to the fife and drum corps tune and the sergeant majors were calling out the orders of march. Ladies dressed in colonial costumes followed in horse drawn wagons. The hippies and the media representatives were completely nonplussed! The columns of soldiers proceeded down the sidewalks on both sides of the animal rights activists, who had gathered in the middle of the street. These soldiers carried American flags, and old, "Don't Tread On Me," rattle snake revolutionary war flags. They also carried signs, that read: THE RIGHT TO BEAR ARMS, WE HOLD THESE TRUTHS TO BE SELF EVIDENT, WE FOUGHT FOR YOUR LIBERTY; NOW WE DEFEND OUR OWN, and: THE RIGHT TO OWN PROPERTY SHALL NOT BE ABRIDGED. The pro-life groups carried signs that read: SHOOT THE DEER, AND SAVE THE BABIES. Others read: GOD, MOTHERHOOD, APPLE PIE, FREEDOM, AND PROPERTY RIGHTS.

Their parade permit meant that the main street would be closed to motor vehicles. Traffic into and out of the courtroom would come and go through the rear of the building and in the cordoned off area in front. The judge had made sure of that. Down the main street came the covered wagons filled with women dressed in revolutionary war era costumes—Ladies in pilgrim dress and men wearing white powdered wigs. Samuel Adams, Thomas Jefferson and other Founding Fathers got out and set up their speech making platforms. Local townspeople, who had been watching T.V., flocked to the area to join in the fun. The hippies were now completely surrounded. Their jaws dropped.

The local merchants seized upon the opportunity. Tables and chairs were set up outside of restaurants so food could be ordered, served, eaten (and paid for!). A local appliance store began to post big screen T.V.s, in strategic places along the sidewalk so the crowd could see and hear what was going on inside the courtroom as the Prosecutor, and the Defense, made their opening statements.

The media was also interviewing the Founding Fathers, the soldiers, and the townspeople, as well as the hippies. It was still early spring but it was unseasonably warm. As the courtroom broadcast was ready to commence, the gathering took on the tone of a football crowd, as each set of partisans prepared to root for their side.

One set of Pilgrims set up stocks. A local, dressed as a hippie, put his head and hands in it. A Pilgrim Lady, positioned her self behind him. She wielded a corn broom, and would swing it making contact with his rear end. "BUMMER!!" the Hippie would cry out as it made contact.

Laughter exploded from the locals. The Animal Rights Activists, looked at the spectacle in shocked disbelief,

Meanwhile, a stern looking 'Judge', in a white powdered wig, pounded his oversized gavel on his makeshift judges podium and screamed, "ORDER IN THIS COURT."

Surprisingly, everything did get quiet, as the television screens showed John Weston preparing for his opening remarks.

Inside the courtroom Judge C.Townsley Smith banged his gavel. He looked at John Weston. Is the prosecution prepared to deliver its opening remarks?

"We are, your honor." John Weston replied.

"Then proceed," the Judge ordered.

"Yes, your honor." Weston got to his feet and prepared to address the jury, the television cameras, (meaning the American People), and even the crowd outside the courtroom, (which the prosecutor had no idea had grown to contain so much support for his position). He looked at the jury and then he began:

"Your honor; the prosecution contends that on December the second, in this, the year of our Lord, the eight defendants, ignoring the posted no trespassing signs and beware of dog signs posted on Jack Morgan's land, did breach his fence, destroying a part of it in a malicious manner, did then proceed to the fence line and interfered with the hunting rights of the owner of the land, adjacent to that property, Earl Johnson; did willfully trespass, over his protests, did interfere with his hunting rights on his own land, and further, not only did not disburse upon his ordering them off of his land, but instead did taunt and use inflammatory language against him, thus inciting to riot, and did refuse to leave, until guard dogs chased James Wilson off of his land. Since the eight defendants were acting as a group and have a documented agenda of interfering with the lawful hunting activities of the owners of the two properties, the incitement to riot charges apply to all members of said group according to statute law. (He quoted the statue and the section of the law for the jury). In as much as this kind of activity had happened before, Earl

Johnson, Jack Morgan, and George Hogan, who own adjacent property, had installed fences and signs warning of the presence of dogs patrolling the grounds and did post the land with an abundance of no trespass signs, it could not have been an innocent act of a group of unknowing citizens making an innocent and honest mistake. Because this had happened before, the Sheriff's department had been called and deputies had been concealed upon the said property owners lands. These deputies did also witness the aforementioned crimes and did duly arrest the perpetrators on the spot. Citizen Sam Macafee did also witness the crimes, as did land owners Jack Morgan and George Hogan. The prosecution has an open and shut case. The witnesses mentioned will testify to the violations of the law, along with law enforcement officers present. The offenses consist of criminal vandalism of Jack Morgan's fence, two counts of trespass for violating the land of Jack Morgan and Earl Johnson, incitement to riot as outlined in the complaint, and refusing to leave said premises until the dogs and the law enforcement officers ended the crime spree. In addition, the prosecution will call two additional witnesses who will document the motives of the group known as `*The Friends of the Animals*,' in harassing these two particular landowners, and targeting these particular landowners for harassment. These two witnesses have submitted affidavits to the grand jury pertaining to this case and others. These witnesses will only be called in this case if the defense, as expected, challenges the trespassing law itself. If that becomes their defense—rather than the defendants did not commit the crime—the debate on higher law and requesting jury nullification of existing law then opens up, to the prosecution. It additionally allows the prosecution to pursue the real motives of the larger group involved. In addition, the prosecution is prepared, if and only if, the defense claims the higher law defense, to show that what they advocate is not only *not* higher law, but is in opposition to the higher law upon which our very constitution and our higher law is based. I am also prepared to call additional witnesses who will testify as to the tragic consequences that can and have resulted from a fools nonsense, masquerading as higher law, and how that misapplication of higher law, has resulted in the victimization of people right here in our county."

The prosecutor paused and looked at the defense table. Sheila Longworth looked apoplectic, and was furiously scribbling notes. Brad Loftus flushed red. The country bumpkin about whom they had laughed, had just become a cobra, and his strike was rapier quick and out of the blue. They were wondering who in the group could have broken silence. Now they were really worried. They had also been put on notice that he was ready and willing to wave the bloody rag, of calling the relatives of the dead, which the cat had left in its wake.

The prosecutor continued:

"When I got this case I was deeply troubled by it. I have tried murder cases that were a great deal less troubling. I have never had a murder case where the only defense was not whether the accused committed the crime, but that instead that murder has always been with us and was neither good nor evil, but rather, was a condition we must come to terms with and accept. This is what is being proposed here. It is going to be argued that trespassing is a minor violation that should be dealt with as a `boys will be boys' attitude. It will be asserted that these `kids' simply were doing what they believed in. That they were protecting the poor deer from slaughter. The problem with that is that this was not a `boys will be boys' type of crime. There is premeditated motive and malice here. There are, and were, other adults involved who used these young people to step on the rights of some small, `little guy,' landowners. The motive is clear: first you barge onto someone's land because he is engaging in a perfectly legal activity with which you disagree. The constitution gives you free speech. But speech is not *action* as the Federalist papers clearly point out. The constitution also supports this. When you become so self righteous that you believe that your point of view is higher law, and that somehow that gives you the right to step on someone else, then you have crossed the line from idealist to oppressor.

“These `kids' thought only of animals and gave them more rights than the constitution gives every citizen of the United States of America. If you step on a little guy’s right to life, liberty, property, and his pursuit of happiness as he sees them, and when he tries to fight back by building a fence, posting his land, and warning you that it is guarded by dogs, you take that as an open invitation to violate his rights again. Then when you get caught red-handed by the sheriff's department you expect boys will be boys treatment. If you get a slap on the wrist instead of real punishment then you call in a group of rich adults to sue the landowner whom you trespassed against, and try to sue him. Because he doesn't have the money to fight your rich friends in court, even though he would win if he could afford the fight, you have denied him his property rights that the constitution guarantees him. These are not innocent kids at work here, these people are conspiring to take away one of the most precious rights guaranteed a citizen by our constitution: the right to enjoy his pursuit of happiness, on his own property. This is no small violation. This is why the sheriffs' department sent the deputies and this is why this prosecutor picked up this case and refused to plea bargain a citizens rights away, thus leaving him at the mercy of those with deep pockets, who would use our court system to bankrupt a little guy out of his most basic constitutional rights.

“The kids here are not the injured party. The little land-owning guy is the injured party. Just look at the power of the oppressors: They have high powered, high paid, attorneys who will try to convince people that wrong is right. The only reason that the National Media is here is to fight on the side of the oppressors and step on the little property-owning guy, and to use their massive power to persuade the American People that property rights are insignificant and that animal rights are more important than the rights of man. Look at the powerful array of money, media, and political muscle they have put together against two little men and one little county. I, as the prosecutor, am the champion of these little guys. The kids were pawns in a much larger game played by big money and media players. I will not allow them to nullify the constitutional rights of the little guys, in my county. That is why I am here.

"In summery, the prosecution has an airtight case in the enforcement of the existing law. The defense will try to persuade you, the jury, that the law doesn't matter and that what is really important is their animal rights agenda. They will try to persuade you, the American people, that a mean county prosecutor is trying to railroad some innocent college kids, out of some kind of sinister prejudice against college kids."

He looked right into the camera as he spoke.

"This is not about animals at all. Do you really think that the deer will know about or care about this verdict? Of course not! They will be grazing for food as they always have, and always will, in increasing numbers, I might add, due to the good herd management paid for by, you guessed it, the hunting licenses. The only people who will profit are the socialists who want the state to control all property rights and all game animals, so that no individual has any rights over them.

"One final note; those who say, `All power to the people,' are really saying, `All power to the state.' As George Orwell pointed out, the individual will have no property rights if `The People' own it all. The *Animal Farm* is now upon us. This prosecutor is fighting for your right to own property and to be left alone to enjoy it, to pursue your happiness, without the socialist thugs storming your land to tell you what you may or may not, do on it." He looked at the jury. "Do you want to live like that? Ultimately, it is up to you, the jury, and you, the American people. This ends the prosecution's opening statement."

With that, John Weston walked back to the prosecution's table and sat down. On court T.V., the media was engaged in damage control and the commentator was trying to sell the idea that the prosecutor was merely trying to justify his actions by blaming the media. Outside in the square, even the animal rights crowd was sobered and thinking about what was said, while the locals were cheering. Inside the courtroom, the gallery was clapping and cheering. Judge Smith banged his gavel repeatedly and reminded the spectators that they must not outburst like that again. Order was quickly restored. In his heart, Judge Smith was cheering, too, but he was wearing his best judicial poker face. Then he looked at the defense.

"Is the defense prepared to give its opening statement?"

Sheila Longworth realized her case had just suffered a sizeable blow. The prosecution had anticipated her defense tactic of ignoring the violations of the law and instead attack the law, the prosecutor, and even the judge, if necessary, to the effect that either the jury would nullify the law out of sympathy to the "kids," or, failing that, to get the prosecutor to plea bargain down the sentences, so that they could later claim, in the civil suit before a federal (liberal) judge, that the arrests were brutal, and out of proportion to the crime committed. She would lay it on a bigoted little town that was oppressive to anything progressive and liberated.

Her case had just been made into a shambles on national TV by a prosecutor she had obviously underestimated. If she went with her, 'the law is oppressive approach,' then the conspiracy could be revealed and the big fish would be caught along with the little ones. If she had been aware of the TV coverage of the townspeople's counter-demonstration and the impact it had wrought upon even the supporters of her cause she would have been even more shaken.

She began by requesting a change of venue. The judge looked her right in the eye.

"What has this court done to give you the impression that you or your clients have been unfairly treated here?"

"Since there has been an animal who has killed here, the people of this town are therefore biased against our animal rights ideology that is the basis of our case."

"Why didn't you ask for a change of venue earlier, prior to the seven days before the trial as provided in the law?" The Judge asked.

"The cat didn't do its damage until after the deadline."

"That was an act of God, legally speaking, of course. By statute, this court has no choice but to reject your motion on the basis that it was filed after the legal deadline has expired."

He looked her right in the eyes. "But then, you knew that, didn't you, Ms. Longworth?"

Having failed miserably before the judge, and having been humiliated before national television, she began the original defense, which she had planned before the bottom had fallen out.

"Very well, your honor, here is the basis for the defense. First, none of the defendants has ever been in court before for any offense whatsoever. Their records are clean. Secondly they believed that what they were doing was the morally right thing to do. They wanted to stop the slaughter of innocent animals. They put their futures on the line, just as surely, as did the Reverend Dr. Martin Luther King when he was willing to face jail to end segregation in the south. I will call a university ethics expert who will testify to the effect that it is immoral to murder for sport. I will encourage this jury to exercise its right of jury nullification, which as the founding fathers stated is the jury's way of knocking down laws, which are oppressive, by refusing to convict people who violate these unjust laws. I believe that the prosecutor has a bias against liberal college youth. There is no conspiracy here just a group of well meaning kids trying to make the world into a better, more just, place. They and I believe that animals deserve to live unmolested by evil men who like to kill them for sport. I believe as they believe that we no longer need them for food and that by sparing them from man's base, killing, nature, that we can strike a blow for a more just world. At most, these kids deserve a slap on the wrist, but certainly not the nine months to a year that this vindictive prosecutor would make them spend in jail. This court needs to view these young people as the hope of the future instead of common criminals. They and I believe that theirs is the way to a better world. Thank you."

"Is that all?" the judge asked her.

"For now, your honor, yes."

At the prosecutor's table, Weston smiled to himself. The defense had just opened the door that he hoped they would. They were going to challenge the law and not the facts. He could call in the victims of the killer cat's families to point out that their Higher Law meant dead children and adults alike. He believed that they were not going to be able to wiggle off the hook he'd just set.

The judge looked at his watch and allowed that court would recess until the following morning at nine o'clock. At that time the prosecution could begin to call its witnesses. The court, stood adjourned.

When they got to their motel, and began working to resurrect their case, Sheila started to cry.

"That dirty bastard just kicked my ass on national television!!"

Brad looked at her.

"It's worse than that. We are now in a conflict of interest situation. We both know that Weston has got the goods on the *Friends of the Animals* group that hired us to represent them and the kids. We both know that it would be best if the kids plead and cooperated with the prosecutor in exchange for leniency on these charges and immunity from prosecution on the State `Rico', organized crime, statute that Weston will surely use against the *Friends of the Animals*. The way to do that is to cut our losses in this case and keep ourselves out of ethics trouble. I will represent the kids and negotiate the best deal I can for them. You represent the *Friends* and try to beat the `Rico' charge outright. What do you think?"

Sheila looked at Brad.

"I think that you are a very good attorney. And you are right. We shouldn't sacrifice the kids to protect the adults, so let's keep our butts out of legal trouble."

They called the parents of the youngsters involved. Even though many of them were members of the *Friends of the Animals*, they all agreed that it would be best for them to take their chances than to permanently damage the kids. It was the kind of honorable resolution with which both John Weston and the judge would agree.

They had their clients come to the motel room that evening. The young people agreed to tell what they knew, truthfully, and were obviously relieved that, in all probability, they were not going to have to do much, if any, jail time for their crimes. The information they would provide would mean big trouble for some adults and the group knew it. They would have to go to work on that case after this case was resolved.

After the others left, Sheila looked at Brad.

"Thanks," she said.

"Sure," he answered. "And, if it's any consolation, I wouldn't have fared any better in that courtroom today than you did. We cannot take anything for granted in the big one."

Sheila smiled for the first time since before court had opened that morning.

"And this time I won't underestimate that bastard!! This is the first case in five years that I've lost and I don't like the way losing feels. I don't intend to make a habit of it."

Although it was very late, they called John Weston and then the Judge. They asked for a conference in the judges chambers at the beginning of court in the morning. John Weston slept well that night. So did the defendants. The first, of the cases against, the *Friends of the Animals* was all but over.

## CHAPTER EIGHT
## Terror In The Dark

After court adjourned the crowd in the square began to disperse. The animal rights activists talked among themselves. Many began expressing second thoughts about their position. The prosecutor had, if nothing else, gained a mountain of respect among all but a hard core few of them. Even though there was a sense among most of them that they were not going to win, they seemed addicted to the trial itself and to the townspeople as well. Few would ever forget the majesty of the soldiers from the country's past. They seemed to leap out of the pages of history and confront the present.

Students gathered at restaurants to eat and talk. Bob Hendricks was one of them. He and his girlfriend, Jane, had come to take in the festivities. Both were sincere believers in animal rights. Thoughtfully, she looked across the table at her boyfriend.

"I felt like I was having a dream set in colonial Williamsburg. I felt as if the founding fathers would like to spank us and to tell us to wake up and fly right."

"Yeah," Bob agreed, sheepishly, then made a suggestion.

"I've got some weed and a tape player in the van. Why don't we take in some of the rural scenery?"

"Okay. Sounds great?"

They were soon driving through some of the most beautiful country they had ever seen. Before long they were high on marijuana and tripping on the scenery. They turned onto a narrow, one lane, road that climbed gently into the lush, forested, foothills and were soon lost. Bob turned the van around and searched for a way back to town. There were no houses in sight. The sun was starting to set. Fear creep into their hearts. Realizing they were hopelessly lost, they put away the marijuana. Bob found a small cleared spot beside the road and pulled in.

“This seems like a safe little clearing beside the road,” he said. "I think we better park it here for the night and then try to find our way back when it gets daylight."

"That's a good idea," Jane agreed. "We can make good use of the beer and weed and have lots of time for . . . snuggling. As the sun set the air became surprisingly cool so Bob left the van running and turned the heater on high. While Jane put some light rock on the tape player he locked the van’s doors. They proceeded into the back of the van, reclining on the mattress there. Jane was feeling frisky and without prompting slipped off her top. Just as fast, Bob was off with his shirt. He reached out to pull her close.

"Not yet, Snookems," Jane teased. "I want another beer, first."

Bob raised the lid of the cooler and fumbled to open a can. At that moment the engine of the van quit. He moved into the front seat to investigate. He had gas but the engine had overheated.

“I've got to go check it out,” he said, clearly upset with the sudden turn of events.

Bob was neither unintelligent nor unprepared. He went into the back of the van and got a gallon of anti-freeze that he kept for such emergencies. He popped the hood and moved through the pitch black toward the radiator. The nearly full moon was blocked by the tall trees so he had difficulty locating and opening the radiator cap. In the process of managing the cap he got burned—severely burned on his palm. He reacted by cursing and pounding his fist on the fender. He cursed again and shook his hand.

Something hit him from behind. It was as if the blackness of the night itself had attacked him. The invisible adversary was all over him and began tearing at his flesh. The pain was excruciating! A blow to the back of his neck caused him to lose control of his arms and his legs and all sensation. He tried to gasp for breath but it would not come. His breathing stopped. His senses faded—sight, sound, touch. Memories flashed but even they were muddled and meaningless. He could mount no warning for Jane. Within moments the young man was dead.

The driver's side door was still open. Jane felt the van shaking and heard something. She called out for Bob. There was no answer. She struggled back into her top and climbed forward into the front seat, pulling the door closed. She could make out nothing in the darkness. She turned on the headlights and met the horrendous scene with the scream of all screams. There on the ground, bathed in beams of light, lay Bob's bleeding and disfigured body. The huge black panther was pulling flesh from his mid section and took little note of the van or its lights. She screamed again as she tried to start the van. All the starter did was grind. She hit the horn hopping it would either attract help or scare off the big cat. It did neither. The cat now sensed her presence.

Methodically, it made its way for the van. It leaped for the windshield managing only a glancing blow since the hood was up. As it moved out of the light she lost sight of it. She froze in terror as the truth hit her—the cat was coming for her! She locked the front door. She figured she would be safe as long as she stayed in the van but just in case she scrambled into the back and located the tire iron. She climbed back into the front seat from she had the best view.

Suddenly, something hit the left front window. The shattering glass slashed her face and arms. Instinctively she scooted toward the right door. She swung the tire iron at the huge black paw of the cat as it reached through the window. She hit it with all the adrenalin driven force she could muster. The cat screamed and withdrew. Presently it returned standing on its hind legs and placing a paw on each side of the window. Its huge head was suddenly inside the van. Its gigantic open mouth revealed sharp, bloody, teeth. Again she swung the tire iron missing the cat and hitting the window frame. The cat was tiring of the game. He already had a kill. He was unwilling to exert the necessary effort to shatter the other window and extract a second victim. It returned to Bob's body and continued its carnage. Jane couldn't look and yet she had to. From time to time it stopped long enough to cast a lingering glance in her direction—taunting her. Its eyes glistened green in the light orchestrating the devil's own hypnotic spell.

Eventually, it grabbed Bob's body by an ankle and dragged it off into the night. It—they—were gone. She heard it scream from somewhere deep in the woods. Quiet returned to the 'safe little clearing' beside the road.

The headlights grew dim and became useless. She turned them off. Maybe the battery would recharge by morning. She kept her hand on the switch in case it was needed. Her right hand held the tire iron in a death grip. She sat there paralyzed with fear and terror the remainder of the night. She sobbed quietly.

In her desperation she turned to God. "Dear Lord," she whispered, "I know that I have been bad but please save me. I promise that I will never doubt you again. In Jesus' holy name, Amen."

The night had lasted an eternity. She had relived her life, moment by moment. Finally, the first light of day touched the clouds above, with faint, though dependably brightening, ever-changing, swirls of mauve and pink. It was the first cause for hope she had experienced. She wept aloud, uncontrollably.

As the full light of day began bathing the area, a sheriff's patrol car appeared and stopped. It was the first time she could remember appreciating the presence of police. She looked toward the sky and whispered: "Thank you Lord."

Frank Anderson had drawn first shift since he would have to be in court at eight thirty. His attention was immediately drawn to the van—its hood raised, window shattered, with a lone woman in the front seat. He pulled along side and rolled down his window. In kind, Jane rolled her window down. She was sobbing uncontrollably.

"Please help me!" she called.

As Frank started to get out of his cruiser she screamed, "Don't get out or the panther will get you!"

Frank reached for his shotgun, checked its load, and cautiously opened the door.

"Did you see a panther?"

She nodded. Her hollow eyes and sobbing told him all he needed to know.

He scouted the immediate area shotgun at the ready.

"It's gone now, Miss," he said hoping to reassure her.

She managed a moment of control.

"It killed Bob—my boyfriend—and then it broke the window and tried to get me. It ate him right in front of my eyes. I thought for sure I was gonna die that same, terrible, death. It had horrifying green eyes. They glowed. Can that be?"

Frank opened her door and helped her out. She clung to him and sobbed into his shoulder.

"It's okay ma'am. If I had been alone in a van at night by myself without a gun and saw what you saw I would have also been terrified. Let me take you to my house. My wife will attend to your cuts and fix you something to eat, okay?"

"Thank you."

She nodded still sobbing and reluctantly separated herself from his strong arms. Frank helped her into the front seat of his cruiser and drove for home.

"I found God last night," she said breaking a short lived smile.

Frank smiled back.

"Maybe... And Maybe He found you."

"Yeah," she whimpered, "Maybe He did."

Frank pulled into his driveway, shut off the cruiser, and escorted Jane to the front door. His wife, Sally, was still asleep. He called to her and she soon appeared in robe and slippers.

Frank quickly brought her up to speed. Sally looked at Jane and said, "First, you get a hot bath. I'll have P.J.'s and a robe waiting for you when you get out."

She escorted the girl to the bathroom.

Bath completed, she slipped into the clothes, feeling clean, somewhat renewed, and very much more alive. She was grateful for those things and for the kindness being shown her when she had needed it the most. She combed her hair and then emerged a very different looking young lady.

Frank left the women and made his report at the station.

Jane picked at the breakfast offered. She was exhausted, but feared she couldn't sleep. Sally provided a sleeping pill.

"When you're married to a cop," she said, "You worry continually. Every time that man walks out the door may be the last time that I get to see him alive," she said. "So, I often have trouble sleeping. I take one of these and in a half an hour, I'm asleep."

"That must be hard," Janie allowed. "Why does he do it?"

"Because he loves." Sally answered. "He loves his home, and this county. He loves protecting folks who are threatened. Every once in a while he knows he is able to make a difference."

"He sure made a difference for me," Jane said.

She started to cry.

"Poor Bob...He is really dead. That cat was the most frightening thing I've ever seen."

She shook uncontrollably as she thought back.

"Easy now child," Sally said, pulling her close as she sobbed. "Easy child. That cat is the devil's own, you know. It killed one of Frank's friends on the force and two other people. One was just a little girl. I don't envy Sam Macafee, Jack Morgan, and George Hogan—the men assigned to find and kill the animal. May God watch over those brave men."

The names rang a bell for Jane.

"Aren't they the landowners who had the college kids arrested and chased them with the dogs? Aren't they the ones?"

"Yes they are." Sally answered. "Those kids, as you call them, went on their land illegally and bothered them. So, they put up fences and posted signs and ran dogs to warn them away. Even with the men's efforts to warn and protect the young people, they still came back, refused to heed the warnings, and did it all again. In my mind, they got what they deserved. Frank was one of the arresting officers. Did you know that the cat had a role in all of this?"

"How?"

"Well, Jack Morgan lives just a mile down the road from two animal rights activists. They were mad at Jack for his hunting and because he told them they should get guns because the cat was around. They didn't believe him and within days the cat killed their little girl right in front of their eyes. That is why they testified before the grand jury. The Governor appointed Sam Macafee to get that cat. He hired George and Jack to help him. Those are very brave men. The dogs didn't hurt those college kids; they are to well trained for that sort of activity. The men just wanted to show the kids that what they were doing was a serious breach of constitutional rights."

Jane was stunned.

"Why hasn't any of this come out in the trial?"

"Because the defense lawyers claimed it would be prejudicial to their animal rights arguments, which were the foundation of the original case. Could you talk about the `rights of animals', after what you saw that cat do to your boyfriend? Human lives are more important than any animal's right to wander where it pleases."

"I've never thought about it in that way. Bob and I came down to protest the treatment of the kids who were arrested. They're from our school. We thought that everyone down here was a bunch of hillbilly's intent on killing for fun. We just wanted the deer to roam free. We don't like hunting."

"Do you think that cat should be hunted down and shot?"

Jane looked directly into Sally's face.

"I'd like to pull the trigger myself!"

"I'll bet you would. I'll bet you would. But I'll bet you wouldn't like to be the one chasing him off into the woods, where he's the king of the hunters."

"Are you kidding?!" Jane said in horror. "I may never go out at night again, even in the city."

"That is what Sam Macafee, George Hogan, and Jack Morgan volunteered for."

"Why would they do that and risk so much? It can't be making them rich?"

"Love, honey;" Sally whispered; "Love. They don't want

to see any more dead kids. That's love. They will take their chances to save others. That is love."

She got up from the table, got her bible, and returned.

"You said you found God last night. Is that right?"

"Yes, I did. Or, as your husband told me, `Maybe He found me'."

Sally smiled. "Here is what God said: `Greater love has no man than this: That one man lay down his life for his friend.' My husband loves like that. So does Sheriff Bonner, Sam Macafee, George Hogan, and Jack Morgan. They are all heroes to me: especially my husband. That's why I can finally go to sleep at night, even when I'm worried sick about him. If he has that much love in him, then I'm gonna help him stay strong, even when I'm scared. If he dies one day because he loved so much, then I'll see him in heaven. I love too. That is how I help. It is very basis of our life in these parts."

Jane was puzzled and clearly deeply troubled.

"How could I have been wrong about so many things?"

"In many ways you are still a child and, believe me, you will be 'til you hit forty."

Sally changed the subject. "I'm sure you don't know it but those men learned that love in Vietnam?"

"Vietnam? That immoral war?"

"We disagree there, Jane. I don't believe it was immoral. Our leaders were trying to free a people and protect our freedoms. It seems to me that those who said `make love not war,' were really saying `make sex not love.' Those men loved, too, and when they got home many of them got spit on for that love—spit on by people who knew nothing about what real love was."

Jane looked puzzled.

"What about racism, and sexism, and homophobia?"

Sally was ready with her answers.

"Those men would all line up to stop anyone from going after Frank. They would love and they would fight to stand for what they believed was right. Sexism is women trying to be men. God made us different and told man and woman how to act. Read and follow," she said, handing Jane the bible. Then she continued. "Homophobia means fear of homosexuals. We don't fear them but believe they are acting immorally. We are not going to call what we believe to be wrong, right, even if that's popular nowadays."

"Do you know that you have just turned my whole world up side down?" Jane asked.

"No," Sally answered, "that's what they did to you at college. I'm just trying to set it right side up for you again."

Jane could stand no more. She had to give her a hug. Then she started to cry.

"I could have been killed so easily by that cat. Poor Bobby; he never had a chance. I thank God for you and your husband."

Sally smiled and added, "God says, `you are welcome.' Remember, God is love. The devil thrives in arrogance, self centered ego, and contempt for love." She paused. "You just have to be wrung out. Take this sleeping pill and get some sleep."

"I can't sleep," Janie said. "I've got to go to court and tell my friends that they are wrong and that Bob was killed by one of their `beloved animals.' Could we wash my clothes and could you take me down there. They will listen to me. Bob was their friend too. Let me show my love as you have explained it to me. Okay?"

"If that's what you really want. We can be ready in an hour. Why don't you catch a nap until your things are ready?

"Okay, but be sure to get me up. I think that it is important for me to try to set the record straight."

"You are quite a young lady, Jane. "Quite a lady."

"How can I ever thank you and your husband?" Jane asked.

"It would be nice if you would drop us a line now and then, to tell us how you are doing. We have an investment in you now."

"You bet I will."

Jane gave Sally a lingering hug and was soon asleep.

In the courtroom, Judge Smith called the morning session to order. He looked first at the prosecution's table and then at the defense.

"Well, I hope a good night's sleep has done wonders for everyone's perspective."

The television cameras were rolling and the judge was looking forward to the announcement that he was going to be able to make. It would stifle any chance the media may have had to vilify him. He felt good—damned good!

"It has come to my attention that the parties involved want to negotiate a deal in chambers. Is that right, Mr. Weston."

John Weston stood up and agreed.

"That is my understanding your honor."

"And the defense?"

Brad Loftus stood.

"It is our intention to meet with the prosecutor and settle on his terms. Also, since we were retained by the *Friends of the Animals*, who may be facing charges later, we decided that I would represent these defendants in the plea bargain negotiations and Ms. Longworth will represent the Friends group. In that way the defense eliminates any possibility of conflict of interest, between these defendants and the *Friends of the Animals*. In short, Yes, your honor."

The judge was reverting to his normal, and more personally comfortable, folksy, manner, now that the heat was off, from the out of towners and the media.

"I guess with attorneys, that is about as `In short,' as it gets!"

Laughter erupted in the courtroom. The judge beamed and allowed it to run its course without interference.

"This court will be back in order. Now, if the defendants and the attorneys need to use my chambers, I suggest that you hop to it! Have the bailiff notify me when you have ironed out the details. The bailiff will escort all of you to my chambers."

He poised the gavel to end the session when Sam Macafee entered the courtroom. He was twenty minutes late. The courtroom burst into applause with his entrance. He was clearly embarrassed but waved tentatively to the gallery and took his seat.

"The court recognizes the 'late' Mr. Macafee. What happened Sam?"

"Your honor, the cat has resurfaced and we went looking for him last night. Unfortunately he got clean away. I'm sorry about being late."

"Not a problem Sam. As it turns out the defense wants to negotiate away the differences in this case. We may not even need your testimony today."

Sam nodded that he understood.

The representatives of the national media were scratching their heads.

"What cat?" they asked.

Frank Anderson stood up.

"Your honor."

"Before I recognize you, Frank, I must declare this court in recess for the next hour."

He banged the gavel.

"Now, deputy Anderson, what could possibly be so important as to take up this courts time?"

"Your honor," he began again. "If the witnesses are not going to be needed, and the court is out of session, then I must inform the court that the cat killed another man last night. His name was Bob Hendricks. He and his girlfriend, Jane Lefforts, were lost and pulled their van off the road near Brooks Point to await daylight. When the engine stopped from overheating he got out of the van to take a look under the hood. The cat was waiting and it killed him and dragged his body into the woods. Jane Lefforts survived after a very close call as the cat tried to get into the van. I found her on my rounds early this morning. She is safe, now, at my home. Since Sam is here, and since we are not going to be needed as witnesses, I would ask that you let Sam accompany me to the scene of the killing so he and the dogs can get on the trail before it gets cold."

The judge's face was clearly saddened as looked over his glasses. Gone was his courtroom demeanor.

"Is there any chance that the boy is still alive, and your leaving early could save him?"

"No your honor. The cat devoured him while the girl

watched. She went through a night of hell. I just wanted to get as quick a jump on things as possible. Since it's a killing, I would like to offer my services as a sheriff's deputy to Sam, George and Jack."

"If I could, I'd just turn you loose with my blessings and say `go get um,' but until the deal is struck your testimony may still be needed. I promise you, thought, that at the first instant the legal obligation is fulfilled, I will do just that. For now, we wait. I'm sorry."

Outside, the demonstrators were stunned at the news. The television monitors had just played the news of the killing. The national press began asking the locals about the cat and the killings as if it were new news. They got their answers. They were referred to their local affiliate stations. Soon the local station's film footage was being shown on court TV, with narration provided by Rebecca Monk, the reporter who had covered the story from the beginning. She quite ably recounted the whole story. She answered the Court TV anchor's questions about the local men involved and the various roles they played.

The animal rights activists, except for a fanatic few, were now on the same page as the locals. They, too, had lost a friend to the cat.

New signs appeared from within the crowd. They showed a picture of a black cougar with the caption, *"Wanted: dead or alive: $10,000 reward"*. The bounty had gone up because the various police groups took up collections and the Roscoe Tanner Insurance agency, in the person of his widow, added five thousand to the reward kitty. The signs were sought by the hippies, many of whom were rethinking their position.

Presently a car entered the square. Sally and Jane got out. The students who knew Jane rushed to her. She said that she had something to say. She was escorted to the founding fathers' makeshift speechmaking platform. They turned on the microphone. She told the story of the cat's killing of her boyfriend and of how it almost got her. Then she said. "Animals don't have rights above those of people. When they hurt and kill people they have got to go. I was wrong. We were wrong. The prosecutor was right. It took Bob's death to make me see it."

She started to sob. Many pressed close and hugged her. The demonstration was over. Cat posters were everywhere. She wanted to meet Sam Macafee, and to give him a hug, and a *'go git `em'*, as far as the cat was concerned.

In the courtroom, Judge Smith got the call from his chambers and sat with the prosecutor and the defense attorney. John Weston had gotten everything he sought. He had signed affidavits from all eight defendants attesting to the role that the *Friends of the Animals* had played, and he got much, much more. Even Brad Loftus was clearly amazed by many of the revelations. They were kept under seal and all parties were sworn to secrecy.

Later, Brad would privately approach both John and the Judge and let them know how he appreciated the way they had handled themselves and the proceedings. He had gained new respect for those hillbilly courts.

Soon the Prosecutor and the Defense were back at their respective tables. The bailiff called for all to rise. The judge brought the court to order. Then he looked at the defense table and ordered the defendants to stand.

"How does the defense plead on all charges?"

"We plead guilty, your honor."

Then he looked at the other table.

"Does the prosecution have anything to say?"

John Weston stood.

"The defendants were very helpful in providing information. Therefore, the prosecution grants them immunity from prosecution on the upcoming felony charges being brought against the *Friends of the Animals*, and further requests leniency on the charges before this court."

"Very well," the judge announced.

He looked at the jury.

"The jury is dismissed with our thanks."

A member of the jury stood.

The judge spoke. "Would you like to address the court at this time?"

"I would, your honor."

It was Dick Stratton, (formerly known as juror number one). The jury has requested that I ask for your permission for us to remain here to hear the sentence. We would like to stay until it is over. Would that be okay?"

"You all may stay and hear the sentencing, with my blessin's and my thanks."

He then turned his attention back to the eight defendants.

"Do you realize the seriousness of your acts?"

They all nodded and said, "Yes, your honor."

"I truly believe that you do. You realize that even with the prosecutor recommendation for leniency, three or four months in jail would fit that bill."

The defendants nodded, some wincing—other pulling at their collars.

"Before I pronounce sentence is their anything you have to say?"

"Yes your honor." It was James Wilson. "I was the worst offender. I went on a man's property without permission and refused to leave, spewing a long line of obscenities in his direction. I was terribly wrong. I realize the law says that everyone was as guilty as me, but I would ask mercy for them. I am the one who deserves a harsher sentence."

The judge studied the young man over his spectacles. "You have just done yourself credit, son. Tell me this, will I ever see you as a defendant in this courtroom again?"

"No, Sir, your honor. So help me God."

The judge smiled, compassion showing through his weathered face. He looked at the others:

"So say you all?"

"Yes, your honor."

"Very well, then, here is the judgment of this court. You will all serve two weeks in the county jail. That is a given. Beyond that, I have a choice for you. You can serve an additional three months in jail, or engage in an alternative activity. It appears to this court that your education is seriously lacking in terms of constitutional law. You don't seem to have an appropriate grasp of what our founding fathers meant by phrases such as, 'Life, Liberty, and Property,' and 'Life, Liberty, and the Pursuit of Happiness.' Therefore, in lieu of the three months in jail I sentence those of you who so choose, to take a constitution class from Mr. John Loudon at the public library. He holds regular, six month class rotations, on the constitution and the supporting writings of our founding fathers including the Federalist papers. I hope you will come to understand the underpinnings of all of our freedoms. You must pass the course to his satisfaction or serve the sentence in jail. He will, I trust, have your undivided attention for the duration of the class. In addition, during four summer weekends in July, after you have finished the course, you will work in supervised litter control along our county roads. You will wear your deer and rabbit costumes while you pick up that litter. So, now, how many of you will take me up on this alternative exercise?"

All eight hands went up.

"Very well. Will the officers escort the prisoners to the county jail?" (It was not, of course, a question.) They left.

"Before I adjourn this court, I want to thank the media for taking this case into millions of homes of American citizens through the good offices of court TV, and for their decorum during the process. I hope the American people learned something from these proceedings regarding the importance of property rights as an underpinning of our VERY LIBERTY that we all to often take for granted."

He turned to Sam Macafee, George Hogan, Jack Morgan, and deputy Anderson.

"You 'ol boys better git after that killer cat, now. And, may God be with you."

"Yes you honor!" they said as one.

They stood and headed for the exit. Outside, they were met by Sally and Jane. Jane hugged Frank and started to cry. Jane's parents had arrived. Her father made his way to Frank.

"Words cannot say what I feel. Thanks for saving my little girl."

He reached out for Frank's hand and the two men shook. Sally hugged her husband and said—for both men to hear—"She's gonna be a different girl now. She found God."

"Is that right honey?"

"Yes daddy. I did. But I think maybe He found me."

She winked at Frank and he smiled back.

The three men were then on their way to try once more to rid the area of a four legged killer.

Inside, John had collected his papers into his briefcase and was ready to leave when the unrobed Judge called to him from the door to his chambers.

"John. He hitched his head for the man to join him."

Court being adjourned, John responded with, "Sure", instead of your honor. The two old friends moved into the judges' chambers. The bailiff was there with a bottle of aged Kentucky bourbon and three glasses.

"John, that was one great prosecution."

"Thanks Clarence."

"Ah say, that's C. Townsley, to you ahll!" he came back with grin that mocked himself.

"When youah mama names ya *Clarence*, well, special remedies are necessarily employed."

They all laughed together. The judge passed out the cigars—expensive ones—and the three men lit up.

John chuckled, "Well, it seems we all got to keep our good names in spite of the national media, the animal rights socialists, and even the National Liberal Liberties Union."

"Sure did," Clarence agreed. "They all quite unexpectedly ran into a loaded gun."

The bailiff took his cue and raised his glass.

"To Smith and Weston: The loaded gun."

"And to divine providence," John added.

"HERE! HERE!" They said as one.

They sat there talking together for an hour, just three good men, enjoying their premium cigars and the best whiskey money could buy; well, at least, the best *their* money could buy.

Tom, the bailiff, said, "I pray that Sam, George, and Jack get that cat quickly and come back safely."

Clarence allowed that none came any better than those three.

He looked at John and said, "May God watch over all of us and this home county that we love."

"I second that motion," John agreed. Then he puffed on the big cigar and smiled.

"Clarence, you know we're not done with them yet."

Clarence was savoring his drink and cigar and lapsed into his folksy accent:

"Ah realizes that, Johnny. But let trouble come anothah daay."

"Yes," John agreed. "Anothah daay."

He took another puff on his cigar and raised his glass.

"To the end of idiocy."

"Naw," said Clarence, "If we got rid a idiocy, we would all be unemployed. Ah say let's jist vow to keep the idiocy well under control."

The three old friends laughed.

"Seems like we got a good start on that today," Tom observed.

"Ah'm here ta tell ya we did!" Clarence agreed.

"To liberty," John offered.

"To liberty. "Here! Here!"

## CHAPTER NINE
## The Crevasse

When the five of them—Frank, Sam, Sheriff Bonner, George, and Jack—left the courtroom, they drove for George's house to gather up ‘the pack’. George was far from satisfied with their progress. His suggestion was to take Blackie and Brownie and leave the coonhounds for his further training.

"The pack doesn't have a leader yet and until they recognize one, they will be as erratic as a runaway missile. Blackie will emerge as leader because of his natural fighting ability and his assertive nature. He was born to be a king dog, a natural leader, but they haven't even worked with him yet. They have tentatively selected a leader but he won't be able to hold them when they meet Blackie and Brownie. They will have to settle that when they meet the way dogs settle such things. We'll have to be close by or Blackie will kill him outright. In the meantime they will still be fighting amongst themselves until they settle things for good. Blackie, Brownie, Blue, and Bluebell have worked together before and they recognize Blackie as their leader and Brownie as second in command. Take those four dogs and leave the rest of `em to me."

Sam reminded George that Blue and Bluebell were still too torn up to work.

"It's gonna be a good two weeks before their casts come off from their first fight with that cat," he allowed.

Jack reminded the others that Blackie and Brownie had taken that cat on alone several times and fought it to a draw.

“They are all the dogs we're gonna need for now," he

said.

Sheriff Bonner was skeptical.

"Jack, I don't mean to sell your dogs short, but I saw that cat kill a huge German Shepherd like it was a wet behind the ears pup. How can those little dogs possibly handle him?"

George laughed.

"Hal," he began, "I'll give you that pit bulls are not big dogs and they don't fight all that often. They get their reputation because when they *do* fight they are always the last dogs standing. Those two dogs of Jack's, especially the black one, may be half beagle, but when it comes to jaw pressure and body style, they are pure pit. The beagle gives them their woods sense and their endurance on the trail and the nose to follow game, in this case, predators."

Then he told Hal one of his secrets that only those who train and love dogs know:

"When that cat hit blue, his paw landed on Blue's side, and broke his ribs and punctured his lungs. When he hit Bluebell, she was a little lower to the ground so his crosswise swipe hit the top rather than the middle of her ribcage, fracturing two ribs. When that cat hit Blackie, he was lower to the ground, on shorter, but stouter legs. The crosswise strike from the cats paw hit higher on his body and glanced off. Blackie didn't even lose his feet and he bit off a piece of one hind leg. Before the cat could strike again Brownie had hit him from behind with a bite the cat will not forget. Your shepherd is about the same height at the shoulder as these coon dogs and he was by himself. There was no companion dog to hit the cat from behind and draw off his attack. Either of these two dogs alone would stand no chance. But they work together as a team and that is what gives them an edge, an edge the cat has come to both fear and respect."

Sheriff Bonner remained skeptical but he deferred to George's experience in such matters. Frankly, the cat still left him in awe. He had come too close to being killed by it himself. He was no coward, but the cat presented a severe test to his confidence. He would fight him again, but he had a mountain of respect for this opponent.

George summed it up.

"We have a long way to go before we will be ready to deal a death blow to that cat. He is on a killing spree that will not stop until we get him, but we have dogs to train and if we get overcome by the immediacy of the menace, we will go off half cocked and get a lot of dogs and maybe even men killed because we are not ready. You go after him if you must, but you get out of the woods by night. We are not ready to confront him in the dark without a foolproof plan."

Hal nodded his agreement.

"I have seen what that cat can do at night, and George is right. There is no way that we are ready."

Sam's temper exploded.

"I am so damned sick and tired of putting people in graves and seeing people look to me for answers and that cat getting away with it Scott-free! I'm tired of waiting. I want to kill that son-of-a-bitch and I want to do it yesterday!"

Jack sympathized.

"Sam, that cat tore up my house and wants to have it out with me and my two dogs. Maybe that's our edge. Maybe I should go out and confront it—just me and the dogs and let the outcome be what it will. I believe me and my two dogs alone will have a chance because it will come to fight and not to run. Let me take `em and go."

Sam looked into Jack's eyes and determined that his words were no idle boast. He smiled.

"I believe that I picked the two best men I could find for this fight. As mad as I am, I will not let the cat pick us off one at a time. We will do as George said. We will take the two dogs that are trained and we will go together first thing in the morning, and we *will* be out of those woods by dark."

George looked at his two friends.

"I want to go so bad I can taste it. But I have got to get these dogs ready for what I believe will be the main event."

Hal nodded his agreement.

"Then me and deputy Anderson will return to our work and leave the cat to your care. Give us a holler by radio when we can help with cruisers, men, and helicopters. As of now, you are our priority number one."

At five o'clock the next morning, Sam and Jack took the two dogs to the site of the cat's last killing. The crime scene was still marked off, although the van had been moved in order that it be returned to Bob's parents. The scent was faint, but Brownie picked it up. They were now in a far northern part of the cat's range—one that Jack had never hunted. They followed the dogs and watched their compasses as they worked their way into the unfamiliar woods. Soon they found the trail leading to a great rocky slope rising higher and higher ahead of them. Jack concluded that the cat had a lair somewhere in that steep rocky terrain. It was a natural.

About a mile into the mission, Blackie and Brownie began to whine in a way Jack had heard from them only once before. Blackie had whined that way when he found his mother's bones.

"I think we have found our victim." Jack announced.

He was right. The two dogs came to a stop and Blackie went to Jack and looked up at him with a look of almost human compassion. Brownie joined him, whining and crying, with the gentle eyes of his mother—not the fierceness of his father. The beagle had come out in them and the sad eyes of the hound told Jack that he had indeed been right. There, concealed in brush and half-covered with twigs and leaves, was all that remained of what had once been a human being. Only his bones remained. Sam took pictures. They had brought along a body bag for such an eventuality and they carefully placed Bob's remains in it. For both Sam and Jack it brought back terrible memories of a war fought long ago and far away. Still, it was yesterday. It was Vietnam. The two men looked at each other with the grim look of hardened soldiers: hard on the outside and torn apart on the inside; hard enough so that the untrained eye could not see the inside. But you could not fool the trained eye. Jack could not fool Sam and Sam could not fool Jack. Jack finally put it into perspective.

"It never gets easier. Does it?"

"Hell no." Sam agreed.

They left the bag for pickup on the return trip. The cat

would not come back to this kill. It had been stripped of all but the bones.

Jack called out to his dogs. "Blackie, Brownie. Let's get that son-of-a-bitch!!"

The dogs seemed to understand and took off, their noses to the ground. They seemed as determined as the men to put this cat away for good. The men followed and were as alert and resolute as they were when they were in that faraway war, so long ago. They were back in it now. They moved with the same determination: another menace had to be stopped and this time the government was not in the way. This time, as far as it related to the cat, it was all out war!

Five miles up the trail the dogs picked up their cadence. The trail was not yet hot but seemed to be getting warmer.

From inside his lair, the cat heard the dogs. He recognized their bays and barks. These were not just ordinary dogs. These were the two he had marked as mortal enemies. They were out of place. He had never heard them in this part of his range. It was only early afternoon. It was not the cat's time. It was the time when the man and the dogs had the edge: at least *that* man and *those* dogs.

The cat figured he had a good deal of time before the dogs could climb up, around, and over all of the rocks and boulders that led to the entrances to his cave. He would move before they approached that close. He did not want those dogs to locate his lair because then he would have to abandon it. He stretched and then went out to see how he could best go about killing his enemies. They were on yesterdays' trail.

He proceeded down the rocky slope toward the more gently graded and greener hills below. He intercepted his old trail there and proceeded off to the right. He ran for a hundred yards. Then he waited at the top of a hill from where he could clandestinely see both the men and the dogs. The dogs came into view first. They were out ahead of the men: almost far enough ahead. Suddenly, the tenor of Brownie's bay and Blackie's growls changed.

Jack pulled the dog whistle out of his coat pocket and blew. Both dogs skidded to a stop and turned back toward the men. The cat understood what it meant. The men were not going to let the dogs separate too far ahead. If cats could curse, he would have. He opened his mouth, showed his teeth, and screamed!!

The men took off on the run towards the dogs. For Brownie, the cat's screaming was almost too much. He turned and stopped. He wanted to start the chase immediately! Blackie growled. *He* was tempted, as well. Both dogs glanced back and forth, first over their shoulders and then ahead toward the sound of the cat. Jack blew the whistle again. This time, the dogs returned on a dead run.

Soon the men and the dogs met. Jack wasted no time in giving the command: "Okay boys, GO GET UM!!"

The dogs left as if shot from a gun. There was no quandary now. They understood it was get the cat time! At full speed, they proceeded to where the scream and the scent told them that the cat would be. The cat accelerated, immediately hitting top speed, which put a good distance between it and the dogs. Then it began to double back. There was no pack to be concerned about, just the two dogs that the cat hated above all others. It might just be his time. But daylight gave the men an edge. It would all depend on how far behind the men got.

Blackie and Brownie raced on ahead with Jack and Sam doing their best to keep up. Feet became yards. Yards became a mile. The chase kept things in the cat's court. He took a position on a rock ledge above where his original trail led. He could hear the dogs coming. Then he heard the dog whistle and saw the dogs come to stop just feet from where they needed to be for his ambush to work.

The cat couldn't let it go. He let rage overpower wisdom. He sprang down in front of the dogs and went for Blackie. Brownie was on him before the big cat's claws and teeth could make contact with Blackie. The cat whirled and Blackie hit its hind leg with a deep, savage, bite that damaged the flesh and caused great pain. The cat whirled and struck at Blackie again. The big cat's paw raked his shoulder but did not knock him down. Brownie made him pay by hitting his other back leg. It tore away flesh and hide. The cat screamed as much in rage as pain. He'd never seen dogs stand up to his attacks before. He lashed out with a claws extended paw, and knocked Brownie off his feet. Blackie's next bite just missed the Cat's right rear hamstring. It was more than the cat could take and he leaped over the dogs and beat a retreat, bleeding and hurting, into the woods. He would not falter in wisdom again. He had learned his lesson. To kill even one of these two his ambush must be perfectly set.

The men came upon the scene just as the cat was disappearing among the trees. The dogs had begun their pursuit. The cat easily managed a hundred yard lead. He then scaled a rock ledge that led to a crevasse. The gap was twenty feet wide. The cat turned positioning himself for the attack and waited. He had one last trick in his repertoire. As the dogs came into view he charged them at full speed, jumping the crevasse with ease.

Between the two ledges was a hundred foot drop—straight down. At its base were sharp, jagged, rocks and a creek that would insure death to any who fell short of the jump. At the edge of the ledge the dogs pulled to a halt. Both dogs were eager to continue the pursuit and gave strong consideration to attempting the leap. The whistle sounded and they returned to the men. The cat made its way into deep cover and waited.

To say that the men were winded was fully insufficient. They bent over, hands on their knees, as they worked to catch their breath. Seeing the dogs were in good condition, Jack sent them off again. They made for the crevasse. The cat appeared on the other side and laid down, obviously taunting them to try the jump he knew they could not make. Brownie backed off and started to run for the crevasse. Blackie barked and growled as if to launch a warning. Brownie stopped. The two dogs barked and bayed and showed teeth, daring the cat to come over and to have it out with them. As Sam and Jack arrived they saw the cat. Each of them got a shot off. The cat jumped behind an array of boulders a mere second before the shots rang out. They hit the rock harmlessly.

Then, he was just gone.

"We might as well head for home. It would take us hours to get to where that cat got with one big jump," Sam allowed.

Jack just nodded, clearly disappointed.

So it was that the men and the dogs—bruised, chewed, clawed, and dead tired—turned and began the trek home.

Sam was depressed about the misadventure.

"How in the hell are we gonna get that son-of-a-bitch? It can hide anywhere. It can jump places we can't even imagine. He can see in the dark as if it was day, and he can kill us with one blow or well-placed bite. I really thought we could just go out and get him. In spite of what George told us, I did believe in my heart that we'd get him. Now, I wonder if we ever will."

Jack looked at his friend.

"He won today but the dogs got in their licks too. He felt this battle and one day we will get him. We just have to keep trying."

Sam flashed a grim smile.

"When `the pack' is ready."

Jack nodded.

"George is working his magic on those dogs even as we speak."

They men nodded in reluctant resolve.

Unbeknownst to them the battle of that day was not yet over. As the men and the dogs turned around and were safely out of sight, the cat jumped the chasm and was once again on their side of the gorge. The cat was hurt and bleeding, far worse than the men could have known. He was enraged. He became the hunter and they his potential prey. He circled ahead of them and lay in wait off to the side of the trail.

Brownie stopped and started to growl. Blackie then took up the chorus with snarls of his own.

"Drop it!" Jack ordered.

It was getting to be too late in the day for the dogs to go chasing off into the woods. Jack, for one, wanted to be sure everyone was out of the woods by dark. Things seemed to subside and the men and dogs proceeded down the trail on the way to the body bag. They knew the cat had come to fight and that vigilance was the order of the day. It could be anywhere out there, which made it the hunter. The sun was setting. Jack knew that they could not dally around. Rest, as much as it was needed, would not be in the cards.

They each grabbed an end of the body bag and proceeded to move for the clearing and their vehicle. The men each silently noted how light it was. The drooped heads of the dogs showed their disappointment. The cat, for its part, continued to shadow them from just beyond the underbrush.

It was waiting for any misstep, any sign of inattentiveness or carelessness on the part of dogs and men. When it felt the time was right it emerged from the brush, showing its teeth. They dropped the body bag and went for their guns. The cat disappeared behind brush before the men could fire. The dogs broke for the cat. Jack blasted the whistle and they returned. They wanted to continue the fight but Jack understood the cat's tactics—delay their return to the vehicle, until after the sun went down. They picked up the bag and carried it the final mile to the clearing. They remained on alert because they felt sure cat was nearby. The dogs' behavior verified the fact.

Fifteen feet off trail, the cat was poised, ready to strike from behind a brush-covered log. Brownie rushed towards it brushing Sam's legs and making him falter. Blackie converged to the same spot speeding past Jack. The men set down the body bag and went for their guns. The cat's ambush plans had again been foiled by the dogs and by the quick action of the men. The dogs would not be lured to follow it, which was a necessary part of the cat's strategy. Never had the cat confronted such a well trained group of men and dogs. He disappeared into a thicket. His hate for these men and dogs grew with each encounter.

The pack was nearing readiness. Each day brought closer the time when the odds would shift in favor of the men and dogs. For the time being, the men were just glad to get out of the woods before dark.

They soon emerged into the clearing where the hunt began. It was the place where the cat had killed Bob. Sam's Game warden van was now parked there. The men loaded the dogs and the body bag into the back of the vehicle and climbed into the front. Only after the motor was started and the doors were locked did they put away their guns and start for home. It hadn't been a game of horseshoes—close didn't count.

The sun set and twilight spread its broad beauty across the sky. The cat watched the van and emerged in plain sight. Sam swore an oath and Jack grabbed for his gun, knowing full well that it would be gone before he could ever open a door and get off a shot. He was right. They continued on their way. It was time to meet with George and to figure out what their next move should be.

The cat was in great pain. His legs had been severely injured and he was exhausted. The wounds burned. His rage grew. He was hungry. He walked back into the woods in search of a meal and place to rest. He would sleep and then he would move on to another part of his range. He knew where the man and the dogs lived. Their time would soon come.

The cat was roaming the northern part of his range. It was sixty miles over winding country roads back to where George lived. Sam called the sheriff on his cell-phone and told him that he had recovered what was left of Bob's body. The Sheriff had men at George's house waiting to take the body to the county morgue.

Jack filled in everyone about the recent events. George listened as he patched up the dogs. Blackie had been hit on the top part of his shoulder and was bleeding where the flesh had been torn. Brownie had been hit a little lower, and while he had no broken ribs, he had sustained shoulder muscle damage that would take a week or more to heal. George advised that it would be best to keep both dogs out of the cat's way for at least a week because they would be stiff and sore, which would cost them mobility that could cost them their lives.

Sam asked George about how long it would take before the pack was ready.

"One more week should do it," he announced proudly.

"They have come a long way." Then he looked at Jack. "Since Blackie and Brownie are out of commission for a while, we should take advantage of the situation by working them in with the rest of the dogs so they have a leader."

Jack nodded his agreement.

Sam was still upset and went on about it.

"I've never seen such a creature. How do you kill what you cannot see? It jumped a twenty foot wide crevasse and just left us standin' there like we were nothin'."

George urged patience.

"Killer cat's are the hardest creatures on the face of the earth to bring down. They are not like ordinary big cats. Once they have tasted human blood they become bolder. They've lost their fear of man but not their caution of man. Unlike most prey, man is both their adversary as well as their prey. But these cats know that under the right circumstances they can prevail over a man. It's a lesson well-learned by this cat, I'll tell you that for certain. Man is not invincible to him. Most big cats give man a wide berth. Like other wild creatures they fear man outright.

A cat with a fear of man and dogs will tree out of fear. A killer cat will first seek a way to kill the men and the dogs, rather than just to climb a tree hoping for safety. Killer cats do not happen every day but when they do they are truly a threat, for they represent the most vicious nature of the breed."

"What would cause such an anomaly?" Sam asked.

"My father and my grandfather believed that cats like this one are the evil one's very own. The Bible talks of demons being cast into or taking over animals. As far fetched as this may sound, those who have looked into his green eyes, swear that they contain hell's own fire and burn with the very essence of evil. I had heard their tales of such cats. I thought them to be exaggerated, rather like a fish story. Yet when I studied the habits of the big cats all over the world, from the Tigers of India and Asia to the Lions of Africa, the Leopards of both places and even the catamounts of this land, the stories are remarkably similar. Cats that kill in rampage and seek to taste the blood of men are few in number as compared to the others, but they are the evil ones. They are the devil's very own."

Frank looked at George.

"That is how Jane Lefforts described the animal she witnessed from the van. I thought she was exaggerating because of the terrible night she had. She said it was evil and that it had the devil in its eyes. As incredible as it sounds, you just may have it right."

Hal shook his head.

"None of what I say, now, may ever leave this room. When I encountered him at night, I knew inside what you say is true. I've been in combat. I've been shot at as a police officer. I have never in my life known fear as I did on that night by the lake. I sensed the presence of an evil the likes of which I have never known before or since. It thrives on terror. It is strengthened by it. Such things feed its spirit and that spirit is the essence of evil itself. I believe that *it is a demon*!"

"Oh that's just great!" Sam said throwing his arms in the air. "So what are we gonna do to kill it? Are we to perform an exorcism? Are we to pound a stake through its heart?"

"No," Jack answered quickly, "We, who are good, are going to overcome it."

"Well, we have major problem here," Sam pointed out. "The dogs and the rest of the pack are down for a week. I think I will gather some trappers and contact the armory for some military equipment to bring down this demon, as you call it, while you two get the pack ready to go."

"That's a very good idea," George allowed. "We will introduce all of the dogs to each other in the morning.

With that, the men adjourned and went their separate ways. Jack let the two dogs sleep in the house that night. Something told him that he should.

In the morning he and the dogs returned to George's, to meet the dogs George had been training and give them a chance to work out the leadership role. George had the coffee ready and the two men talked.

George offered an observation.

"Sam will recruit some scientific trappers of big cats and they will their use modern technology, but I tell you, it will not work."

"How are you so sure?" Jack asked.

"Because they will treat this animal as if he were typical of the breed. They will use a camouflaged net with rockets or charges to spring it into the air and over the cat. They will attempt to tranquilize and capture it. It will fail miserably."

"Why?" Jack asked again.

"For one thing, the cat will catch their scent and find where they are hiding. This is not a weak cat that is old and starving. It is in its prime, alert, cunning, and powerful. They will bait the trap with a sheep or a cow."

"Why wouldn't that work?"

"They are using the wrong bait." George answered. "This cat eats men. While they will be hiding in wait for it to take the livestock, the cat will only be interested in them. It will do its best to kill one of them. These people are used to catching and tagging big cats for research and fitting them with radio collars so they can track its movements. They have never dealt with a man-eater."

"Did you tell Sam that?"

"No. Sam is going to have to learn that for himself. He doubts my assessment and has cast his lot with the scientists. He will have to see it with his own eyes or he will never believe it. I did tell him to make sure they carry real guns loaded with real bullets and he agreed. That may save some lives. Also, the cat will not be out in the daylight, which is what they expect of this breed. He had learned the better ways of the night."

"Surely you warned Sam about that?"

It had been a question.

"Yes I did, and I told him to order them to wear the masks. You know they won't do it. They think they know all about the big cats, and they *do* know a lot. But they know nothing about a man-eater."

George changed the subject.

"Your dogs took a beating on that last hunt and I suspect that the cat was chewed up pretty good too. I doubt if we hear from him for about a week. He will move to a different part of his range. He will heal and stay out of the way for awhile."

"He was limping as he ran. I did notice that from the van." Jack answered.

Sam returned to the dogs.

"This pack is going to need two leaders. The cat had good success working the crevasse so he'll prefer that setting. He can leap back and forth. We will need a group of dogs for each side. The dogs on each side will need a leader. The cat's heart is small so it can only run fast for a while. It can't pump enough blood and oxygen to maintain that pace so its system must rest often. That is one reason so many of them just naturally go to tree. This one backtracks and kills a dog or two and then rests during the resulting confusion. We have got to wear him down."

"Let's send Brownie out to meet the dogs first," George said. Their temporary leader is a redbone hound named Ringo. He will challenge Brownie but even torn up Brownie is more than a match for him. Then, when you release Blackie, Brownie will submit to him, and the rest of the dogs will get the picture. If you'd send Blackie out first, they would both have to fight to establish two leaders, because Blackie will not give way to Brownie."

Blackie and Brownie were on the floor under the table as the two men had been talking. Brownie heard his name being bantered about. He sat up and looked at the men as if to ask, "What do you want of me?"

"C'mon boy," Jack said.

He led Brownie out the back door and let him into the back yard with the other dogs. Brownie walked down the stairs and out into the yard. The two men watched so that they could break up the contest before Ringo was too badly hurt.

Upon Brownie's entrance into the back yard, several of dogs came up to him to sniff noses and other parts of his anatomy. Then Brownie set his jaw and growled. He was much smaller than the other dogs and they were taken aback at his lack of fear. They backed off and began to growl. Then

Ringo emerged, approaching Brownie with his well-established authority.

Ringo was a large and powerful redbone coonhound and he towered over Brownie and began a low, steady, growl. Brownie met growl with growl and bared his teeth. Ringo was clearly puzzled. Most dogs Brownie's size would have shrunk from him, whining. The new comer would have then been relegated to establishing his place in the pecking order with the others dogs. It was becoming clear to Ringo that the pecking order was to be set from the top. He showed his teeth.

The two dogs began circling, keeping each other in full view. Brownie wanted the bigger dog to make the first move. He growled fiercely, signaling his complete lack of fear. The hair along his spine stood up.

Ringo had enough from this small upstart. He would make quick work of him. Ringo charged. Brownie stayed low so that shoulder never met shoulder. Ringo's neck was now directly above Brownie's jaw. Brownie lunged straight up and had Ringo by the throat. Shocked and surprised Ringo tried to shake him off. Brownie clamped down driving his teeth further into the flesh. He held on like a vise, chocking the dog. Ringo's shaking tactic was not working. Soon he lost his feet. Except for the men's intervention he would have been dead meat then and there.

In those five minutes the issue of dominance had been unquestionably established. Ringo limped off fighting for breath and for life. The other dogs followed. Brownie advanced toward the lot of them and dog sniffed dog. There was one final, fully important step to be taken. Brownie strode up to Ringo and growled. Ringo whined and submitted. The new leader had been crowned. Jack and George went back in and watched as Brownie whipped the dogs into shape. He had been accepted as leader.

George and Jack left him there alone, with the others for about an hour as they continued talking. Then they sent Blackie out. The other dogs sniffed and sniffed. Blackie growled with such ferocity that the others whined and turned away; even Ringo. Then Blackie and Brownie faced each other and started to lick each others faces. Then it was over. Blackie now led and Brownie was second in command. The pack had met and accepted their new leaders.

That afternoon the men worked the pack. When the dog whistle sounded Blackie and Brownie skidded to a stop and returned to the men. The other dogs followed their lead. By the end of the week of training, from coons to deer, George pronounced his verdict:

"They have learned as much as they can this way. Now they must learn to trail and fight big cat. Only the cat can teach them their final lessons."

The cat was out there somewhere waiting. Sam had dropped off Blue and Bluebell and they fit in immediately. They were glad to see Blackie and Brownie and seemed to remember how those two had bailed them out just when it had seemed that the cat would kill them. At the end of the week George called Sam and pronounced that the pack was ready.

## CHAPTER TEN
## The Trappers

When Sam arrived home after the hunt he was frustrated beyond measure and did not know what to do. He had bitten off one big chew in wanting to take on the cat, and he was realizing just how big it was. He wondered if he and his team were up to it. The big cat had made it look so easy.

He complained to his wife: "You sweat and you run and you carry your supplies until you are about ready to drop and what did all the blood, sweat, and tears get you, besides exhausted? And then, old George tries to tell you that you are fighting a demon and not a cat. That would be bad enough if you didn't half believe that he was right."

Sally tried to put things in perspective. "Do you know of anyone who is more qualified than the three of you to go after it?"

Sam thought for a long moment and then realized that his wife's words rang true. He smiled.

"I'm just upset because people keep getting murdered by the cat and we are not able to bring it down. Now the dogs are out of commission for at least a week and I just can't bear the thought of layin' around here that long. I'm afraid that the people who put their faith in me will be let down, and I'd rather die than to let them down."

"Put down your guilt load honey," Sally advised. "These things are in God's hands, and you are doing your best. That is all any town or county or woman can ever ask of a man."

Sam reached out for her and pulled her close. He

wanted to never let go. Sally melted into his embrace.

The next morning Sam called the armory. He had an idea or two he wanted to bounce off the military. He told them about the cat jumping the crevasse and he wanted to know if the military had any kind of pre-made bridges they could place there so that men and dogs could follow the cat across. He was informed that the military carried tank bridges on vehicles that could be used for such situations and that they could be lowered into place from a chopper. Sam explained that it would need to cover a twenty foot gap and be capable of holding men, dogs, and horses. He was told that the bridges were made of metal grating, braced in the middle, and had side rails about three and a half feet high. It was four feet wide and had a back bracing of three feet on each end. Each bridge weighed about nine hundred pounds. It could easily support the specified load. To cross it was simple and safe. Two such bridges could be assembled in a week and delivered with an installation team.

He also needed a barred structure capable of holding three men, three horses, and a mule and up to sixteen dogs. Simple enough, he was told. The structure would be seven feet high and thirty feet square. It would be made of metal bars, and would have no floor. It could be subdivided into three sections divided from the others by bars. One compartment would hold men and they could pitch tents inside it. A second compartment would hold the dogs, and the third would house the horses and the pack mule. It could be quickly dropped and picked up by helicopter with a phone call.

Sam now had a strategy for following the cat across the crevasse and could keep his party safe on site with the night shelter. The bars would keep the cat out so the men, horses, and dogs could rest unmolested at night and start fresh first thing each morning. At the end of each day the hunting party could locate a field, call the armory and a Chinook would deliver the sleeping cage to their coordinates. This would enable them to wear the cat down more easily and would allow the men and the dogs to keep the pressure on it with significantly less rest for the cat between encounters.

Sam thanked the commandant. The Governor *really*

had given him carte blanch! Sam was feeling better already. The commandant, General Thomas Weberly, also recommended some night vision equipment. Sam accepted the offer and thanked him. The general left him with only one admonition, "Just get that damned cat!"

"I'll save you a picture of the son-of-a-bitch when we do," Sam promised.

"I've got just the place to hang it," the General said.

Sam allowed that he would deliver that photo personally.

"You've got a deal", the general laughed, "and if nobody wants the carcass, we'll stuff it and mount it in the officers quarters."

"First we have to get the SOB; then we'll talk about where the carcass goes," Sam laughed. He thanked the general and hung up. He was feeling better about the down time already.

His next move was to call the university to find out if they had any research grants in the area of studying and capturing the big cats. There was such a team and it and had studied the Florida panther extensively. The team could be made available to aid in the capture of this cat. Sam could meet with the team's director in a matter of days. Again it had been good news.

A meeting was set for later in the week. Dr. John Haskins was the team leader. The two men were introduced and quickly got down to business. This team, Sam was told, had trapped and studied all manner of cats from all around the world, and had trapped both for research and to supply zoos.

At the outset, Sam had a question: "Have you ever dealt with a man-eater?"

Dr. Haskins, who looked more like an aged hippie than a scientific researcher, answered.

"No", but big cats are big cats."

Sam raised his eyebrows.

"This cat has killed four people already and his attacks are getting more frequent."

The doctor hesitated. His career had focused on

capturing *normal* big cats. They were dangerous enough, but a man-eater in his prime was another matter. It was the stuff of stories he had heard from natives in Africa and India. That it could be happening near by seemed surrealistic. It would be more of a challenge than he had anticipated. Yet, there might be a very positive side to it all. Maybe it could be captured and studied to see what traits if any could be identified as contributory factors. His mind was already working on a capture plan. He would need to know where it was last seen and the extent of its range if he were going to get started—and he couldn't wait to get started.

He was intrigued that it was a black phase cat and that it killed at night almost exclusively. He was further amazed by its reported size, but attested to the probable accuracy when shown the plaster impressions of the tracks. In fact there was not much about this cat that did not surprise him, starting with the fact that it was in an area that should not be home to any mountain lions.

He asked Sam what he thought had triggered the turn of events that made him a man-eater. Sam replied that it started with attacks on dogs, then livestock, and finally on man. That began with a child and progressed to adults. He related how it had invaded Jack's home. The doctor was amazed. He had heard stories about lions and tigers doings such brazen things, but he had never heard of a cougar doing such a thing. The Florida panthers he had been studying were shy and stayed far away from men.

Sam cautioned him to carry guns and live ammunition. At first the doctor protested but upon reflection he acquiesced. He did not want to get any of his party killed. Sam gave him George's address and phone number and arranged to meet him there in the morning.

When they arrived at George's the next day, the old man was full of questions and skepticism. Dr. Haskins continued to have confidence in his methods. George suggested that he use the masks, carry live ammunition, and be out of the woods by dark. Dr. Haskins listened respectfully, then promptly disregarded all of the advice. He believed that he was the expert and that the old man was simply exaggerating the dangers the cat posed. George had warned them. It would be their funeral if they chose not to listen.

Sam took Dr. Haskins to the cite of the last encounter and gave him a map of the cat's range—complete with markers to indicate where within that range the cat had killed and the dates of the attacks. Dr. Haskins sought to obtain the services of a local who knew the country and Sam introduced him to a local coon hunter of some renowned. His name was Pete Donnigan. The professor promptly hired him as a guide.

Three days later the professor and his team were provisioned and set out to find signs of the cat. It soon became apparent that the cat had moved to a different part of its range, some forty miles to the southwest.

Normally, Dr. Haskins team used vehicles as transportation, but the timbered terrain lent itself better to horses and mules, so the doctor and his team of three went into the woods in search of the cat on horseback. Donnigan led and the Doctor his assistant, Dawn Gerlach, and a graduate assistant, Walter Peterson, into the woods in search of fresh sign of the cat. To the south and east they found a creek that had cat tracks along the bank.

"This must be the part of his range the cat has selected," Donnigan announced.

They spent the day studying the game trails. They picked two trap spots and called in their helicopter to bring equipment and provisions.

Their plan was to build two traps. The first one was a pit, dug fifteen feet deep and ten feet square. It was deep enough that a cougar could not leap out and its width of only ten feet made it so there was not enough horizontal room for a running start. The walls were to be completely vertical. Students would be airlifted in to do the digging. The hole would take them a week. Then the hole would be covered with a grating of crossed wooden sticks, too weak to support the weight of a big cat. On top of the stick grating, leaves and grass would be used to completely camouflage the hole. A sheep would then be tethered on the side of the game trail away from the cougar's den so that as he came down the game trail toward the bleating sheep, he would have to cross the hole and fall into the pit. Dr. Haskins had caught lions, leopards, and even tigers in this manner. He was confident that the cougar could be caught in this way as well.

Once this first trap was built, he would place netting on the other side of the sheep, so that, should the cat circle, instead of coming down the trail as expected, charges would shoot the netting into the air, and over both the cat and the sheep. The one side of the netting was to be staked down so that the 'charged side' would shoot over the cat. The trappers would then secure the net and shoot the cat with a tranquilizer dart so he could be transferred to the waiting cage. The plan was that anyway the cat chose to get at the sheep he would be caught in one trap or the other. The sheep would bleat at the first scent of a predator, making it an even more obvious target.

On the very first night in the woods, Dr. Haskin's well-laid plan began coming unglued. Donnigan carried a rife with live ammunition. He would not agree to guide them without it. As a forced concession, Dr. Haskins agreed to carry a sidearm. Ms. Gerlach and Walter Peterson were adamant in their refusal to carry live ammunition and armed themselves with tranquilizer darts in their rifles. The provisions for the first night arrived by helicopter—a generator for lighting the camping area, tents, cold weather sleeping bags, and rope. The mule had carried the foodstuffs and other basic necessities. They pitched the tents and strung rope around the perimeter of the area so the horses and the mule could be tethered. Outside the rope line signal fires were built. The logic was that cats feared fire so would not venture into the camp. Lights were strung and the generator was ready to power them at the first sign of a disturbance. This method had worked well in Africa, India, and in the Florida Everglades when they had been working there in pursuit of the big cats. Dr. Haskins was confident that the tactic would work there as well.

He would be very wrong. As the sun went down on the first night, Dr. Haskin's smug complacency was the first casualty. The tents had been pitched and the signal fires built and the rope line strung. Darkness had crept in. As Dr. Haskins crawled into his sleeping bag he heard the catamount's call. Its scream seemed like a challenge. The horses and the mule went crazy and broke the rope line, running, panic stricken into the woods. He was overcome with panic like he had never known before. He hit the generator switch just as the mule brayed its last. The lights came up just in time to show a black form leaping into the brush behind the dead mule.

Donnigan and Haskins ran for the mule, guns at the ready. Its neck had been broken and the spinal chord had been severed. They heard the sounds of a terrified horse, and then its fall to the ground. They dared not go look for it. It was beyond the signal fires and the generator lights. Finally, they heard a second horse neigh, rear, and collapse. Two more of the horses wandered back into the camp. The fire had attracted them. They were spooked and capturing them was a challenge. Donnigan grabbed one rope halter and held him while Dr. Haskins and Peterson re-strung the rope line. Dawn grabbed for the rope halter of the second horse. It reared and knocked her down. Eventually, Dr. Haskins and Peterson were able to calm the animals and secure them to the line.

Donnigan decided to stand guard with his rifle the rest of the night. They had piled wood in huge piles to keep the fires burning. They built up those fires and then all but Donnigan tried to get some sleep. They decided to leave the floodlights on as a further precaution.

For several hours all was quiet. Donnigan refueled the campfires and then sat down propping his head up with a bedroll. He kept his rifle at his side.

A bit later, the horses again reared and frantically pulled at the ropes. Donnigan rushed to them and tried and failed to calm them down. They had been hobbled and tied quite securely this time. One of them fell and the other got tangled in rope. Dr. Haskins, and his assistants ran to assist, when all hell broke loose. They tried to untangle the horses and to calm them down.

Unbeknownst to them, while all the chaos was going on, the cat paced and watched just beyond the circle of light.

Concealed in the darkness he moved silently about the perimeter. He was looking for any opening. None of them had heeded George's warning to wear the masks on the back of their heads. They simply had given no credence to that idea, even though Dr. Haskins was familiar with the practice in India. It would prove to be a fatal oversight.

While the men wrestled with the horses, Dawn Gerlach busied herself with re-fueling the fires. She had always been the one woman in what had always been a man's world. A devout woman's libber, she had also always received preferential treatment for her gender, as was the fashion of the times. She compensated for her lack of physical strength with a vicious mouth. She was terrified inside but afraid to show any outward sign of her fear. She continued to work the fires.

It was then she made her first and last mistake. She turned her back to the fires, watching the men across the clearing as they continued to struggle with the horses. Something hit her from behind. She felt claws in her flesh. She felt a blow to the back of her neck. She screamed once, but her scream was drowned out by the ruckus with the horses. Then she could scream no more. Her spinal chord had been severed. Her limp body collapsed to the ground.

While the men were occupied with the horses the cat dragged her body off into the brush. Fifty yards away from the campsite, the cat began his feast, one eye on the others as he ate.

The horses seemed to sense that the immediate danger was over and settled down as the men re-tied them to the rope line. It was then that they noticed her absence. Dr. Haskins figured that she had gone into her tent. He called out to her. There was no answer. They hollered at the door of her tent. There was only silence. Donnigan swore an oath. He saw the cat tracks and the blood in the soil. He saw the sign of the body being dragged through the dirt and the grass. His every instinct made him want to make chase and find her. His woods smarts overruled his instincts.

He knew in his heart she was dead, and that chasing through the darkness would only insure that he would meet the same fate. The others crowded around him and he pointed out the signs.

Dr. Haskins started for the woods and Donnigan grabbed him.

"Doctor," he said," She is already gone. If you run out into those woods you will be too."

He nodded at Donnigan and took a seat on the ground near the center of the compound. The others joined him.

Donnigan sighed. "I've hunted these woods all my life without ever seeing a sign of a cougar until this last year. Occasionally I would see a track or a deer carcass. I figured, correctly at the time, that it would stay far away from the dogs even as I coon hunted at night. I will not hunt coon at night in these parts until the cat has met is maker. I've never seen anything like this in all my life. I sense evil in that cat the likes of which I've never sensed in man or beast before."

The doctor nodded his agreement.

"I have trapped big cats all over the world and never have I witnessed anything even remotely like this. The old man was right. This animal's behavior is not like any big cat I have ever witnessed. I have heard natives in India and Africa talk of such cats as being demons. Inside, I ridiculed their superstitious foolishness. It was, I believed, just the superstitions of uneducated tribesmen, who lived, in an unscientific world of the past. We were the future of mankind, I believed. They were remnants of our ancient past. They were like children, afraid of the dark. Now I am like them. Now I know that their stories—those I had written off as fanciful superstitions—may have been completely true. As strange as it sounds, I have no better explanation for what happened here tonight than they would have.

"They would say that an evil spirit had taken over that cat and that it had demonic powers. I can no longer say `Nonsense,' and assure them that it was just a flesh and blood animal whose behavior was predictable. The natives would always say, `With this cat perhaps, but a devil cat, you have never seen.' I couldn't believe that George Hogan, a westerner with some education and a lot of knowledge of the big cats would offer up the same type of mumbo-jumbo as they did. Now I know that he was right, and I, the educated one, was the fool muttering in ignorance. We are going to call for help and get the hell out of here before it gets us all!"

With that the professor got on his cell phone and called Sam for help. Sam, of course, was in bed asleep at the time and was understandably groggy. He woke up in a hurry once he heard what had happened. He told Dr. Haskins he would call for a helicopter and that help was on the way. Then he called Sheriff Bonner to make it happen.

By the time the copter arrived it was daylight. They evacuated the party and informed Sam that the extraction was complete. The horses were taken out over the trail by Donnigan. First, he had tracked the cat to the tree and found the half buried body of Dawn Gerlach. It was half-eaten and covered with twigs and leaves in the manner that a big cat leaves a kill that he may return to. He wrapped the remains in blankets and strapped it to the back of the injured horse. There was no other choice. The wounded horse initially protested the load but carried the weight without much trouble. They would make their report to Sam the next day.

While all of this was going on, Sam and the military had been busy. The bridges and the `cage' were ready three days ahead of schedule. Sam met them at the crevasse. Two black hawk helicopters hovered overhead. Each lowered a four-man installation team, two on each side of the Crevasse. The bridges were secured in place.

They were located about two hundred yards apart, so the cat could not lead the dogs in circles and then jump the crevasse. When the cat jumped the dogs could follow. The cage was ready to be dropped wherever it was needed, whenever it was needed.

The afternoon before the trappers bailed out of trouble, George had called to announce that the pack was ready. Sam was just beginning to feel optimistic when the call from Dr. Haskins brought him back down.

The principles involved agreed to meet at George's home that evening to plot a unified strategy. It would take all of them and all of their various skills working together if the cat was to be had. Sam was going to make sure that happened. They congregated around the big dining room table. Dr. Haskins spoke first.

"Let me begin by saying that I am very grateful to be here at all. Most of my training and experience with the big cats seems useless on this one. I have never in my life experienced anything like this. This cat defies all scientific explanation. It does not act like a normal big cat. From now on," he looked at George, "I am the student and you are the teacher. You called this one from the beginning."

George responded. "Until you have dealt with a man-eater, you could not know. You can use your knowledge to great benefit to us all. I will get to that later."

He turned to Sam. "I have something that I think you will like."

Sam smiled and asked, "What's that?"

George pulled out a roll of paper, got up from the table, and unrolled it so they could all see it. It was a topographic map of the complete area of the cat's range with red dots glued to all of the locations where the cat had killed. The outline of the cat's range was emerging.

"This", George began, "is my best estimate of its total range. I may be off in places, but I don't think by much. Beyond this line," he said, pointing, "there have been no reported cat sightings or man killings. Inside here is where all of the killings, sightings, and most of the livestock killings within the past year and a half have occurred. Somewhere within these boundaries we ill find cat. Here, is the Crevasse. Here is where he killed the Lefforts girl's boyfriend. Clear down here is where he killed Roscoe Tanner and over here is where he killed Sanderson and the dog. Here is where little Teresa Salem was killed. Here is Jack's house and here we are. This is where he just killed again."

He pointed to the spot where the cat had killed Dawn Gerlach. He looked at Dr. Haskins and Donnigan and sighed.

"We all grieve for her."

Dr. Haskins nodded.

"This is where he killed the sheep and the dog at the Phillips ranch. His range is huge. But I believe that if we start here," he pointed at the north end of the lake where Roscoe Tanner and Deputy Sanderson were killed, "and work our way north, we will drive him to the crevasse. We will split the dogs into two teams and cover both sides of the crevasse as we force him to climb into the high rocks here. This," he pointed, "is where we need to drive him so he cannot double back down."

He pointed to the trail that led from the spot where Bob had been killed to the crevasse.

"Dr. Haskins, if you and your team can, by day only, set your traps here, (he pointed to a spot on the trail that was about half way between where Bob had been killed and where the crevasse was located), we may very well be able to drive the cat into your net or your pit as he is running from the dogs."

Dr. Haskins was impressed. "I believe it is a brilliant plan. You can count on my team to do its part." George nodded his thanks. "It will have to be dug and ready in three days."

"I don't have enough manpower to do it that fast," Dr. Haskins said, sadly.

Sam smiled. "George and I called some mine operators and they have volunteered the services of fifty miners with picks and shovels. They offered to pay their wages but the men volunteered to do it for free. One phone call will have them on site within an hour and a half."

Dr. Haskins was overcome by the gesture. "God bless them!" He exclaimed—not the phrase one would expect from a life-long atheist.

Hal Bonner spoke next.

"We will have a police helicopter and a swat team at the ready." He looked first at Sam and then at Dr. Haskins. "One call to 911 will have us on the way within minutes. You all are priority number one.

There was the sound of a vehicle entering the driveway. Then a knock on the door. There, big as life, stood General Weberly and his chief aide. They removed their hats and entered. Room was made for them at the table. Sam and

George brought them up to speed. George had some further thoughts about the use of the cage.

"The horses and the mules will go stark ravin' crazy when they smell the cat. They won't understand that they are safe behind the bars. They will rear up and likely injure themselves. We cannot have horses with us after dark."

The general smiled a knowing smile. He knew that the old man was, as usual, dead right.

"Well then, we'll just have the Chinook take them out at dusk and return them at dawn."

"That would solve the problem," George said, then added, "I believe that with the Generals help we now have a night strategy that we can use that will be cat proof!"

He thanked the General and shook his hand. The general responded.

"My thanks will be that cat's stuffed body in the officers quarters. Just go out and get that son-of-a- bitch!"

"We are gonna do just that," Sam assured him.

With that, the plan had been set and the meeting adjourned. The hunt and the full implementation of that plan would begin at dawn the next morning, so a good nights sleep was in order. The odds had suddenly shifted in favor of the men.

George was now going to be able to participate in his final big adventure. He could hardly wait to get started. As he moved to the bedroom, pains spread through his chest. He cursed and fished around in his shirt pocket for his nitro pills.

"Damn this old ticker!"

He settled the pill in under his tongue waiting for it to dissolve. No one else knew that he had been living on borrowed time for the past six months. He knew that this would very likely be his last adventure. He knew that he might well not survive it. Even so, he believed, it beat the hell out of dying in his chair. Ten horses could not keep him from going.

## CHAPTER ELEVEN
## O'Malley's Luck

The next morning the trappers entered the north section of the cat's range. They passed where Bob had been killed and moved about half way up the trail to the crevasse. The volunteers from the mines followed them and were rarin' to get started. They began to dig the pit that they all hoped would put an end to the killer cat. The work went amazingly fast. At the end of the day the first pit was complete and covered. It was decided to dig three more in the area, aligned so the sheep used for bait would be in the center of them. They posted signs along the trail to warn people not to continue because of cougar traps. At the end of three days all of the pits were dug and the trap was baited. Dr. Haskins thanked the miners and shook each ones hand as they left. One miner summed it up for all of them.

"Get that cat. That's all the thanks we want."

Meanwhile, in the southern most part of the range the men and the dogs charged into action. This time George, Jack, and Sam were riding horses so the dogs could move faster. They also had a pack mule to carry the essential provisions. They began by crisscrossing the area. The dogs worked hard but it was apparent the cat had not been there in a long time. The trail was not only cold, it was nonexistent. Nonetheless, it was their job to make sure, so they continued north-by-north east. Sooner or later they would hit a hot spot and then the trailing could begin in earnest.

As dusk settled over the area Sam located a field that would be suitable for the night. Then he called for the cage to be dropped. The horses were picked up within a half hour. They built a campfire on the ground inside the cage that was to be their sleeping quarters and pitched the tents within its safe confines. Blackie and Brownie were allowed into the section where the men slept so they were close at hand if the cat did show up and also to demonstrate to the other dogs their special status as the leaders.

Meanwhile, miles away from the men and the dogs, the cat awoke to do its nocturnal hunting. He had vacated the part of his range where he had most recently killed. He had seen and heard the helicopters again so had moved on. Hunger stirred within him. It wanted another human so began to stalk the banks by the road. Cars passed and kept on going. He was waiting to see if one stopped and parked like the van.

He came upon a well-lit farmhouse. A dog started barking. In the barn two horses became restless in their stalls. The door to the farmhouse opened and a man with a double barrel shotgun emerged. The man called out to his dog and it came running. With his flashlight in his left hand, the man and the dog went into the barn to settle the horses. He shown the flashlight around the inside of the barn to make sure all was well. He saw nothing, although the dog began to growl deep within its throat. Something was around somewhere and the man knew it.

The cat had concealed itself in the hayloft directly above them. The horses would not settle down. The man made a mistake. He set his shotgun down as he tried to settle the horses. The dog smelled the cat and went up the stairs to the loft. The man heard fighting and then the dog's final whine. All was quiet again. The man picked up his gun. It was too late. Something hit him from behind with such force that the man fell face down. He tried to roll over and to shoot whatever was on top of him. The cat had bitten deep into the back of his neck. Within a minute he was gone.

The cat heard the door to the farmhouse open again and a lady with a gun made her way toward the barn. She had heard the dog barking and wanted to make sure her husband was all right. She carried a flashlight. When she entered the barn she saw her husband on the ground. She screamed and ran to him. In an instant she lay dead beside her husband.

The cat concealed himself and waited. There was no further sound from the house. Finally, the horses broke free and ran out of the barn. Seeing and hearing no further noise, the cat returned to the man's body and ate until he could eat no more. He grabbed the woman's ankle in his jaws and dragged her out of the barn and across the road. Finding suitable cover he stored her body in brush. Then he went to his den, yawned, stretched, and went to sleep.

Six hours later he awoke and went to find the woman's body. It was still dark but daylight was not far away. He started to claw away at the woman's clothes and proceeded to gorge again. Filled to capacity, he moved the body to an even more concealed place and re-covered it with leaves and twigs, before returning to his cave.

At about three o'clock in the afternoon, Charles 'Skinner' O'Malley teed off in the cow pasture. "Fore," he screamed at the top of his lungs. There was no one within miles of him to hear his call. He swung his club and sent the dimpled little white ball sailing high into the air. It landed about two hundred yards away. Skinner admired his accomplishment. Then he hopped on his four-wheeler and went in search of the ball. It was a very small ball laying somewhere in the midst of a very large pasture which could best be described as one massive "rough," in golf parlance. He downed a hefty portion of whiskey as he weaved through the field. In his mind, or what was left of it, he heard the oohs and aahs of the gallery admiring his massive T- shot.

He couldn't find the ball.

"Where's my damned golf ball", he bellowed out to no one. "It's gotta be here somewhere."

He staggered some as he turned in circles. Another slug from his bottle, and he was on his way to nowhere.

"Where's that damn ball?" He bellowed.

Miraculously, he saw it lying there as pretty as you please, within three inches of a massive cow pie.

Skinner smiled, doffed his cap, and waved at the

imaginary gallery, which, in reality, consisted of a chipmunk and a ground hog scurrying out of view.

In Skinners mind it was the P.G.A. It was the Masters, the British open, and every other money course on the tour. This was for all of the marbles, as they say, doubly important since Skinner had lost most of his over the years. He begged the galleries indulgence, and proceeded to drain what was left of his second bottle of the day.

"Have no fear," he announced. "Another is waiting." He cut a circuitous path to his four-wheeler, reached under a seat, and produced number three. "Irish mist", he proudly announced to the gallery. He popped the cork and, just for luck, guzzled down another slug.

He then sidled up to the ball. "So there you are," he sighed, as if he were chastising a child who had been hiding from its parents. He addressed the ball. The ball had to be struck in such a way that it would clear the cow pie lying directly behind it. Skinner swung, striking both ball and cow pie. The ball went about a hundred yards and dropped at the edge of the woods. There was something very unpleasant on his golf club, and remnants of that unpleasantness were every where. The man had finally answered the ancient Chinese question—originally posed by Wu Flung Dung. The answer was, Skinner O'Malley himself. He reached into his pocket for a handkerchief, realizing that he was in deep doo doo. He cursed his luck and threw the filthy handkerchief away. Then, he started his hunt for the ball all over again.

Asleep in his den, the cat had been awakened by the man's boisterous carrying on and came out to investigate. It crouched in the brush at the edge of the field. It was far from hungry and was more curious than any thing else. He watched as a strange acting man with a stick, swing and hit a foul smelling ball in his direction. It landed twenty feet from him at the edge of the woods. Presently, the strange acting man, in his strange looking vehicle, moved in the cat's direction. The animal crept toward the white ball to investigate. The man soon pulled to a stop nearby. The cat seemed bemused. O'Mally struggled out of his vehicle and took another belt from his bottle. As he slipped it back into his pocket, he spied the cat lying in the brush. In his confused state, he thought it was a dog. It was the biggest dog he had ever seen. The cat showed his teeth. To poor O'Mally, the white glint could only mean one thing—that big dogs had HIS golf ball in his mouth. This was not to be dealt with lightly during the final round of the greatest of all the great tournaments that there ever was. O'Mally cursed as he walked over to his golf cart and grabbed his nine-iron.

"Okay Rover," he commanded, "you've got me golf ball. Now give it up!"

With that, he unleashed a mighty swing that tore the brush. The cat eluded the club with ease, and was not sure whether the gleaming stick could shoot flame and death or not. He had looked O'Malley in the eyes and had seen no fear; only insane belligerence! The cat decided to get out of Dodge! He leapt out onto the field, sprinted across it, and disappeared into the brush at the far end.

O'Mally's toot was so complete, that any trace of his Irish accent disappeared. He was now spouting fluent West Virginian.

"Dammit Fido! Bring back my ball!"

He let out a string of curses, fired up his Golf cart, and set out in hot pursuit.

While all of that was going on, the farmer who owned the pasture where the greatest of all of the great tournaments was being played, returned home to O'Mally's unruly cursing and ranting. He called Sheriff Bonner. He described the scene.

"We'll be right out." Sheriff Bonner said. He turned to his deputy, Frank Anderson:

"Jack Dalton called and said theirs a man on his pasture cursing at nothing and acting totally insane. And guess what?"

"What?" Frank answered.

"He thinks he's playing golf."

"Not again!" Frank said shaking his head. "O'Mally?"

"Could be none other than Himself!" Sheriff Bonner answered.

The sheriff called out to one of his deputies.

"Bring the paddy wagon and follow us! And make the padded cell ready for a guest.

As he and Frank were moving with all deliberate speed towards the Dalton farm, Hal reflected on the situation.

"You know Frank, he came from a wealthy family. His mother keeps him solvent to this day: poor woman. They said that as a boy he had great promise as a golfer. He won all of the junior awards and then he went to college and was the best player on his college circuit. In his junior year he discovered that alcohol did something real special for him. Once he started drinking he just never stopped. He quickly went from being golf's brightest young up and coming star to being banned from every course he stepped on because he carried a flask. He'd get so nasty that he was eventually banned from playing. So, he took to playing on cow pastures and using that damned four wheeler as a golf-cart."

"He has to know that there isn't a cup out there to put his ball into, doesn't he?" Frank asked.

"I quit trying to figure that one out long ago, my friend. He does add some predictability to my life however. Once a week I can depend on his coming to visit the drunk tank. By morning he'll have no idea how he got there."

Frank shook his head, some in disgust and some at the sick humor of the situation.

"Well," Frank said, "every town seems to have its town drunk. Even Mayberry had Otis."

"Yeah," the sheriff chuckled. "And we've got Otis with an attitude! So lets go pick him up—again."

As they neared the Dalton place they heard the most god-awful crashing and crackling sound you could imagine. There in front of them, O'Mally and his four wheeler came crashing down the bank and out onto the road. He was oblivious to everything—even the police cruiser he'd narrowly avoided! He was weaving down the road with one hand on the wheel and the other waving his nine iron and cursing.

"Where's my G D golf ball!" He raged. Then, he whistled, as if he was calling a dog. "Dammit fido. Give me back my damn golf ball."

He weaved across into the oncoming lane of traffic, looking down the bank.

"I know you're out here somewhere, so give it up doggy!"

Hal turned on his lights and siren. That finally DID get O'Mallys attention. He skidded to a stop. Then he staggered toward the cruiser.

"Sheriff," he began, "I would like to report a theft!"

"This had better be good, O'Malley."

"Well," O'Mally began all quite seriously, "I was playin' the back nine, and hit a chip shot off by the trees. I know it was a chip shot because I got some on my golf club. So, I went off to the edge of the woods, and there he was!"

"He who?" The Sheriff asked, playing along.

"He who?" O'Mally answered. "Only the biggest blackest dog I ever saw in my life! But he wasn't gonna scare Skinner O'Mally with his growlin'. No siree! I got my nine iron and decided to show him who was boss! I gave it a mighty swing and he took off—with my golf ball in his mouth! He ran into the brush right over there!"

He pointed with his nine-iron. It was in the general direction from where he had just come crashing onto the road.

"And I've got to find him and get my ball back or it's gonna cost me a stroke! I can't afford a stroke in this tournament or 'cause I gotta win. And Skinner O'Mally ain't a gonna lose this one."

The Sheriff had heard all that he wanted to hear from O'Mally on that particular day.

"You are in big trouble this time Skinner."

"What for?" O'Mally asked, fully surprised.

"Drinking while driving," The Sheriff answered all quite matter of fact.

"Driving!" O"Mally shouted. "I was in the rough! And there ain't no law 'bout drinkin' in the rough!"

"You're not gonna pull a Clinton on me, Skinner O'Mally!" The sheriff said. "Better put this walkin' bottle in the cooler for a while."

Two deputies grabbed O'Mally's arms, recoiling at the

odor.

"You gonna come peaceful or are we gonna have to wrestle you into the wagon this time?"

"You and who else!" O'Mally said, sticking out his chest.

"Me and Frank, if necessary," The Sheriff answered.

"Well, seeing that there is . . . one. . . six . . . ten . . . of ya, I guess I'll go peaceable this time. But you're damn lucky that ya brought a army."

"We knew that we'd need it, Skinner."

"And *right* you were!"

With that, he walked a wavy line to the paddy wagon and climbed in. The deputies grinned at each other.

"Better get him a shower and then right into the padded cell before he starts singing again all night long," the Sheriff advised.

"Yes, Sir".

The deputies grinned again. Then took off for the county Jail and their special, padded, noise proof, cell. O'Mally was through for the night.

Sheriff Bonner smiled.

"Judge Smith ain't gonna be happy to see him again, and that is for sure."

Frank just rolled his eyes and nodded.

They were in the process of moving the four-wheeler off the road when Blackie and the other dogs broke through with their noses to the ground. Blackie recognized Sheriff Bonner and moved close to get petted. The Sheriff accommodated him. The dogs waited for their men.

A few minutes later the three men on horseback rode up and dismounted.

"We can't be more than ten minutes behind that cat," George announced.

"What?" Bonner exclaimed.

"He was in the brush over on the other side of the field up there. He crossed it and came right down right here.

"Well I'll be a son-of-a ..." Frank said. "That means that the huge black dog O'Mally was talkin' about was probably the cat?!"

"Sure must have been," the Sheriff answered.

Sam listened, wondering what they were talking about. The Sheriff brought them up to date on the latest escapade of one very intoxicated Skinner O'Mally and the story he'd told.

"I can't understand why it ran from him." George said, wondering aloud. "Unless it had just eaten."

Sheriff Bonner had the answer.

"Otto Von Bismarck of Germany once said, `God protects idiots, babies, drunkards, and the United States of America.' That's the best explanation I can come up with."

The sun was setting, so the men called the military and the helicopter with the cage was on the way. They would set it down in O'Malley's golf course and camp there that night. The dogs indicated that the cat was nearby but Jack called them off. It was getting to be too late in the day to safely pursue him.

The Sheriff and his Deputy headed back to the jail. Sam, Jack, and George rode into the field to await the helicopter. Brownie went to the edge of the trees where the cat had laid. Jack went over to him to investigate. There, right in front of him, was a badly soiled golf ball, and back amongst the trees in the soft soil, was one big cat track.

"It's unbelievable that it didn't go after him out here all alone like that." Jack announced.

George knew better.

"I believe we will find a body in the morning," he said grimly.

"I hope that you are wrong," Sam allowed.

"Me too," George said, but he knew that he wasn't. It was the only explanation.

Soon they heard the chopper, right on schedule. The cat watched. It hid in the brush as the cage was lowered and the horses taken aboard. That cat decided he needed to move on – too many dogs and one too many helicopters. The dogs were raising hell. George knew that the cat was nearby. It continued to watch them as they set up camp inside the bars.

From around the top of the cage, the generator lights came on and lit up the field. The cat was hungry. With the men and the dogs safely behind bars it was time to eat. He went to the body of the small woman and finished it. Then it walked boldly into the barn just two football fields away and finished the man. It then proceeded north by northwest to the rocky climbs where it would be hard for horses and dogs to follow. He was going to put as much distance as he could between himself and the man and their dogs.

The men built their campfires and set up their tents. Then they fed the dogs and let them bed down. George was busy cooking up something for the men—hamburger, beans, and corn bread. It was good, it was filling, and it was quick. George liked the night strategy they had developed but he couldn't miss the irony.

"We keep big cats behind bars, at the Zoo, when we're in control. This cat has got us behind bars. So far it and not we are in control. I'd like to change that real soon."

"Me too," each of the others agreed.

"I'm damned glad we don't have any horses or mules to spook in here," Sam allowed.

The men talked for a while and then turned in for the night. Soon the crickets and the tree frogs began their nightly chorus and everyone slept.

Throughout the night the cat moved steadily toward the high ground. He knew he was being hunted and had some tricks that the men and the dogs were unaware of.

George continued to have an uneasy feeling that the cat had killed again. The morning would prove him right. The attacks on men were becoming more frequent and the percentage of the cat's kills, which were men, was also going up fast. *Too* fast, George thought.

At first light the Chinook helicopter returned to take the cage and drop off the horses. The men waved their thanks as it took off again. They packed their provisions on the mule, saddled up their horses, and soon Jack was calling to the dogs.

"Okay Blackie and Brownie, go get `em."

The dogs rushed ahead, joyously. Almost as soon as they had started, Blackie and Brownie came to a dead stop. They began to whine.

"There is the kill," George announced.

The others nodded and prayed that it was a deer or some livestock. Instead, they found the body of Molly Madson. It was completely unidentifiable.

Sam called Hal Bonner. He told him the bad news.

"Sadly, George was right. The cat had just eaten."

Brownie had left the others following his nose down the bank, across the road, and into the barn. He returned and tugged gently at Jack's pant leg. He whined softly.

"What's the matter boy?" Jack asked backtracking the dogs trail with his eyes.

The dog indicated that he wanted him to follow. He mounted his horse and they moved out. When they came upon the barn Jack dismounted and followed Brownie inside only to discover the second body. It was John Madson, but he, too, was mangled beyond recognition. Then Brownie led him up the stairs to the hay loft where they found the uneaten body of the dog. Jack and Brownie made their way back to the others.

"Looks like he killed a man and his dog in his own barn", Jack announced.

George's face fell.

"He is getting even bolder. We better get him quick so we can keep this body count from rising any further."

Soon, Hal and Frank, and another squad car full of deputies pulled up, lights flashing. They took them to the first body and then the second. They body-bagged the remains of what had been John and Molly Madson. Hal had known them.

Sam was upset. He was taking it personally. He was feeling as if he were letting the people down. He didn't like that feeling. Now, he had official duties to perform that would buy the cat even more time. He would be needed to witness for the Sheriff's department on how the bodies had been found. It was all routine, but it also was time consuming. All the while the cat was getting further ahead. He hated that the worst. He asked George and Jack to go on ahead without him and he would meet them from the helicopter when it dropped the cage for the night. The two nodded and started off after the cat. It had already gained three more hours on them after daylight. It was time to cut into that lead as much as they could before dark. George was satisfied that the dogs had a warm trail to follow. The first three days had been spent walking in circles searching for a cat that hadn't been in that part of the range for weeks or months. Now the trail had moved up a notch to warm and the dogs could actually begin following the cat. That, at least, was an improvement.

In the northern most part of the cat's range the trappers were hard at work. It was amazing to Dr. Haskins just how many critters would like to eat a sheep. The first morning when they checked their traps all four of them had a capture. Some coyotes had ventured through and had fallen into the pits. The trappers tranquilized them and then released them into the woods. They decided to check the traps in the morning and at noon as well as late afternoon, because a sprung trap would catch no cat. On the second day a pack of wild dogs had taken the bait and had fallen in. They were destroyed because they were not of nature and would either kill stock or starve to death. On the third day they got closer to what they had been looking for. A bobcat had fallen in. It was tranquilized and released.

On one occasion they heard the unmistakable snarling and screaming that could be coming from only one animal. Cautiously they approached the edge of the pit and peered down into the hole. It was a cougar but was not black and weighed in at a mere hundred pounds. It was not their man-eater. They tranquilized it, lifted it into their cage, and transported it out of the woods.

Dr. Haskins, immediately noticed something very strange about the way this female acted.

"She is used to being caged," he announced. "This is very strange indeed."

They called Sam to report the capture and the observation that went with it. Haskins did not seem surprised and he *was* thrilled with the find. He was thrilled that the trap had yielded a cougar. Maybe they would get lucky and catch the man-eater. Maybe he could walk out of this situation with his head up. He was also grateful for the lessons he had learned but grieved for the loss of his assistant.

The dogs had trailed the cat all day and not a glimpse of it did they get. It had too big a lead. George was glad to note that it was heading north and east. It was just what he had prayed for. The cat couldn't know it now but the noose was tightening. They found a field, and called for the cage. Sam arrived with it. They pitched their tents and fixed their supper. They went to sleep. It would start again in the morning. Finally, the chase had turned in favor of the men. Sam talked with George and was assured that all was going according to plan. They slept well that night.

## CHAPTER TWELVE
## The Secret

The next morning the men and the dogs hit the cat's trail at the crack of dawn. George believed that they were making good time and were cutting into the big cat's lead. The men and the dogs worked hard but still didn't catch up with the cat.

Sam went to town for the funerals for Ms. Gerlach and for the Madson's. A memorial would also be held for Bob Hendricks who had been buried earlier in his hometown. His parents were grateful for the town's expression of love, and agreed to come. Jane Lefforts would be in town for the service as well. George and Jack wanted to pay their respects but considering the over all situation they let Sam speak for them.

At the end of the day the trail had become warmer and the dogs' excitement level reflected that. By the time the trail got hot it was dusk and time for the helicopter to deliver the cage. They found a field about ten miles from the crevasse.

George had a feeling that Sam was going to miss the kill but he didn't mention it. Sam had the same feeling. He really didn't care who actually killed the cat. He just wanted it dead. He also decided that the softer job in the capitol would not be such a bad thing after all. He was, he felt, getting too old for this stuff. He marveled at the old man still seemingly quite able to handle all of it. George was a marvel.

On he other hand, Jack *did* care who got the cat. It had become personal with him. In his dreams he saw the cat running right at him out of the darkness. He had the cat in his sights and was whispering a silent prayer that his aim would be true. In his dreams he had trouble getting a bead on the cat. The dream always ended just before he pulled the trigger. *He* wanted the chance to pull that trigger.

The cat was nearby when the Helicopter arrived with the cage. Sam and the horses left. The cat stayed, staring at the structure that protected the men at night. His instincts told him that he should leave and he did. He went down the trail by the edge of a country lane. A car was off to the side of the road. The cat poised himself behind brush at the top of the bank the led down to the road. He waited. Soon, the driver's side door opened and John Samuleson got out. He went to the trunk, opened it, and got out a spare tire and jack. He was not a happy camper. He' had a flat out in the middle of nowhere. He loosened the lug nuts on the left rear wheel and began to jack up the vehicle. He removed the lug nuts, pulled the old tire off, and set the new one in place. The car was between him and where the cat lay in wait. The cat crept down the bank until it was within one easy leap of the trunk. John soon had his spare on. He tightened his lug nuts and lowered the vehicle onto the spare. He picked up the flat and gave it a heave into the trunk. He was now ready to resume his trip. He closed the trunk.

As the trunk slammed shut, something slammed onto his shoulders pushing him over the trunk. The car was all that had kept him from falling to the pavement. He turned around into the eyes of the cat. He was filled with terror as he saw the devil himself in those green eyes. He ran for the car door and safety. He was three steps too slow. This time when the cat hit him he went down on his face in the road. He lost control of his arms and legs, and felt his own blood trickle from the back of his neck, down over the front of his neck and mouth. He couldn't breath. He couldn't fight. He couldn't even move. Blackness overtook him. He was no more.

The men and the dogs in the cage heard the cat's triumphant scream. Then all was quiet. The cat grabbed the dead man and dragged the body up the bank and back into the brush. Then he began to tear away the clothes at the midsection. He took an enormous bite of flesh and slurped at the blood. He approached his kill differently from most of the others. The cat licked away all of the fluids but ate no more flesh. It was as if he knew that he had to put as much distance between himself and the pack as he could. If he gorged himself, his body would demand rest and sleep at a time he couldn't afford either. He concealed the body in the brush. Then he left again north by northeast. He kept to a fast pace all night long. At daylight, he came upon a familiar cave. He entered, yawned, and went to sleep. It was as if he knew that he was going to need all of the rest and sleep he could get. He also seemed to know that when he killed dogs or men the search was delayed and he bought huge chunks of time for him to rest or to put more distance between him and his adversaries.

Around the campfire, inside the cage, George and Jack talked. Blackie and Brownie were enjoying their special status as guests in the men's quarters. They had all eaten their fill. The dogs seemed to be listening as the two men talked into the night.

"It looks like Sam won't miss the kill after all," Jack began.

"Maybe not," George answered. "But we are not going to get this cat tomorrow, either."

"What makes you say that?"

"That scream told me all I need to know", the old man answered. "It has killed again, just as sure, as you and me are sittin' here."

"I sure hope you're wrong".

"Me too. But I'm not. That scream was a scream of triumph and a challenge to us too. That demon is almost supernatural. I sensed his challenge.

George called Sam. Sam was at home with Sally for the first time in way too long. He seemed out of sorts when he answered. Hearing George's voice his tone changed.

"Oh no," Sally heard him say. "That son of a bitch. Thanks for calling George. I'll be there with Sheriff Bonner, and Deputy Anderson in the morning. Goodnight."

When Sam hung up Sally could tell that the amorous moments they had been sharing were to be put on hold. She made the best of what looked to be a bad situation.

"What's the matter honey?" she asked.

"That was George. He thinks...Hell he *knows* the cat has killed another person tonight. That old man is uncanny. I can't figure how the hell he can possibly know that from the sound of a cat's scream in the night? But he knows and I wouldn't bet a penny against him. I won't be hunting cat tomorrow. Me and Sheriff Bonner are gonna be filling out more of those damned police reports on another dead body. I will have to leave early and be out there so George and Jack can keep on pushing that cat. I wish it would die. I wish it would just die."

Sam was somewhere between rage and tears.

Sally looked into his eyes.

"You can get mad at that old cat in about four hours but until then, Mister, you are mine."

Sam raised his hands above his head and sat up in the bed.

"I surrender", he grinned. "I will come peaceable."

Sleep (eventually!) came easily, that night.

Too soon the alarm clock announced the morning. Sam felt half dead and the other half didn't feel like it was worth saving. As he shaved she made coffee.

Back in the cage, George and Jack had talked half the night away. They genuinely liked and respected each other as men and they talked on about what it was going to take to get that demon. Jack told the old man about the dream that kept repeating itself. The old man smiled.

"Sometimes dreams like that come true. If it does, I hope your aim is true and I hope I'm there to see it."

A few moment of silence passed. George turned serious made a strange request.

"When I die, I want the church to sing the song, `W*hen the roll is called up yonder*' at the funeral. If something bad should happen would you see to that?"

Jack looked at his old friend.

"I pray that nothing does, but if it should, I will personally lead the choir."

George looked into the night and changed the subject.

"How come you never re-married?"

"I haven't met the right one yet." Jack answered lamely.

"Don't wait too long," the old man said. "It's hell living alone when you get old."

"I will remember that, "Jack said. "I'm finding it's is hell living alone when you are middle aged, too."

The old man smiled and nodded.

The conversation went on for some time before the men decided they had better get some sleep.

At first light, the Chinook arrived. George and Jack helped lead the horses and the mule down the ramp. They left Sam's horse on the copter. George was that sure that he wouldn't need it for the day. He was right. Five minutes later the dogs located the body. George looked at it and cursed.

"That son-of-a-bitch didn't eat enough to even slow him down. The bastard ran all night!"

Twenty minutes later Sheriff Bonner and Sam were at the site with a body bag. Sam was taking it all very hard—too hard. George started to say something but Sam cut him off.

"Just kill that son-of-a-bitch! Will ya?"

Then he looked at his two friends and realized that they hadn't been off the trail in nearly ten days.

"I'm sorry," he said shaking his head. Jack looked at him.

"You and me and George are gonna get stinkin' drunk once that cat's dead."

Sam looked at him and nodded. George nodded and wiped his hand across his mouth as if he were already thirsty. Then he and Jack and the eighteen dogs were off again.

That time that cat had only gotten a very short respite, from the pressure of the hunt. The dogs seemed to sense that this was going to be the day. There was greater excitement in their bay and more pep in their step!

The cat had a surprise in store for them. At about four in the afternoon he heard the dogs coming. He'd been expecting it. The den was a cave, a tunnel, actually, that ran for about a hundred yards through a hill between the two exits. The cat didn't even take the far exit. He came out the same opening he entered and made a circle up the seep hill and then re-entered the cave. He then exited through the back door and began a parallel circle to his old trail of the previous day.

The grade was becoming steeper. It was too rocky and two steep for the horses. The men would have to come by foot. That would slow down the down, too, as they would be whistled back more often. One of the men would have to stay with the horses and the mule. If ever a cat smiled an evil smile this one was just that. Is first step was to start cutting down on the number of dogs that were after him.

The tail they were following had gone up another rocky cliff, which was hard for men and dogs to follow, and impossible for the horses. They were in the hills, now, and there wasn't a field for some miles. Either the men would have to give up early and go miles out of their way, or they were going to have to sleep out in the open. The grade was too steep for the helicopter to land and there was no level place for the cage.

At the base of the hill, Blackie, Brownie, and the rest of the pack began to ascend the slope. Higher and higher they climbed. The trail narrowed to a point where the dogs were forced to follow one another in single file. Behind a group of boulders, about thirty yards to the right side of the trail, the cat waited in deep cover. Blackie and Brownie, and many of the others, went right past him, their noses overwhelmed by the strong scent on the ground.

He waited for the last four dogs. He pounced killing one hound with a quick paw to the head. Then he struck the next, and the next. The last dog turned and ran back the way he had come. The dogs ahead of him had trouble getting turned around on the narrow ledge. The cat pursued the last dog and pounced on top of it. The coonhound never had a chance. The cat leaped onto a boulder above where the dogs could not follow. Blackie and Brownie turned around and returned to the scent that led back up the trail.

George and Jack rode up and sounded the dog whistle. George cursed.

"That son of a bitch will kill them one at a time, single

file that way. Even Blackie and Brownie are no match for him on a steep grade in these rocks. The cat could simply kill them all."

George grabbed his chest and fell off his horse. Jack dismounted. George waved him off. He fumbled around in his pocket for his nitro pills. He asked Jack for his canteen. In ten minutes he was back on his feet, seemingly, as good as new.

"I'm getting old", he said. "I am gonna need a day to rest. Then I'll be okay."

Jack was concerned. George looked him dead in the eye.

"Ticker is goin' bad," he said. "Could die today, or tomorrow, or anytime, whether I'm out here or settin' home at the table. I'll rest at home for a couple of days. Then I'll be okay."

He put his hand on Jack's shoulder.

"Please don't tell Sam. I want it this way."

Jack could see it would kill his spirit to have to die at the table. This hunt was the frosting on his life's cake. He couldn't take that away from the old man. He wouldn't.

"Old man, I didn't see anybody fall off any horse if that is the way you want it."

"Thanks. I mean it. If the worst happens to this old body, just know that this was the way he wanted it. You gave an old man his last wish."

Jack nodded somberly. He understood.

When Blackie and the pack returned to the men, George was ready to retreat for the rest of the day. Caution overruled the proximity of the cat. He got out his map and they laid out the route to a field where the chopper could land. It was a good five miles away.

Sam didn't miss the kill, after all. He came in with the chopper. George told them that the horses would all have to be mules in the morning. The army agreed to make the switch. The grade would simply be too much for horses to handle. They had also gone from eighteen to fourteen dogs and the four lost could not be replaced with untrained recruits. The cat was cutting down the odds. That day had been his.

George stayed with them in the cage that night to give them his last minute instructions. In the morning he would head home to take a couple of days off for some much needed rest. Sam told him to take them with his blessings and apologized for the fact that it had been so grueling.

That night it was Sam and Jack who did the cooking. The old man protested. Sam smiled.

"I had two nights with the prettiest woman I've ever known. Both of you deserve some time off, but I can only spare one man at a time. Jack if you want a couple of days off when George gets back..."

Jack interrupted him.

"It's personal between me and this cat. I will rest when he is dead. He has killed one of my dogs and torn up my house and killed a neighbor girl. It's personal."

Sam and George nodded their heads. Sam had long ago decided that if Jack had the shot it was Jack's to take no matter if he could get it off just as well. It was Jack's cat, if it was close.

After dinner Sam reached into his saddlebags and pulled out a bottle of Kentucky bourbon whiskey and some cigars.

"Judge Smith sent this along for us to enjoy. He said it was his way of saying, `Godspeed,' to us."

"Damned thoughtful of him," George allowed.

He was grateful for the change of subject, as well as for the aged whiskey and truly premium cigars. Soon all three of them were drinking and puffing. They needed that R and R. if only for a few hours.

The cat, for his part, had changed strategies. He liked the odds right where he was. He gorged on dogs that night. The men heard his screams of triumph. George felt sure knew what it meant and outlined a strategy for the following morning. He hated to have to leave. He prayed that he wouldn't go away in his sleep while he was home in bed. He prayed that he would be there for the finish of the last great hunt and adventure of his life.

George loved to tell a good story. Now, he had a

chance to live one. As the helicopter lifted off, he prayed a silent prayer.

"Dear Lord. I know that my time here is short. Please grant me the wish that I am able to take the time I have left, and to make it count. Amen."

He felt a warm tingling sensation all through his body. It told him that his prayer had been answered. He smiled all the way home.

When he got there, he found his driveway filled with cars. The press was there. He waved at the cameras and tried to walk past them into his house.

Rebecca Monk met him at the door.

"George, I have been on your side ever since Sam told us off. Will you talk to me?"

George looked at her, and sighed.

"Yes, you have been. But I would like to do it inside where I can sit down."

"There is a surprise in there for you. You better talk here briefly first."

George was trapped. He was going to have to tell a hunting story to the press. He had dreamed of this opportunity. Now that it was here, he didn't really want to do it. The first question came from the national press, and it was hostile.

"How come with so many men and dogs and helicopters and horses and trappers after just one animal, you haven't gotten it yet?"

George looked at the reporter and said:

"As we were chasing it up a rocky cliff yesterday, it killed four full grown and trained redbone and blue tick coonhounds in less than a minute. It leaped ten feet straight up in the air to an overhanging rock ledge, and was gone. I will tell you what, madam, if you think that you can do a better job, I can give you a gun and set you at the base of that hill. Would you like for me to arrange that?"

Laughter erupted from the assembled reporters and the snippy reporter moved back in humiliation.

Then, George said, "Nobody wants that cat dead more than the men who are trying to get it. Sam is so frustrated he is about to tear his hair out."

A second reporter asked him why he was here, instead of out there, trying to get it, if he truly wanted it so bad.

"I have been on horseback chasing that cat through brush and trees and up rocky cliffs for ten straight days. I've slept on the ground at night. I am seventy years old. Sam and Jack, told me to take a breather." He then added, with a grin, "An old fellah has to take care of his ticker and you wouldn't deprive me of a bath once every ten days, now, would you?"

Another asked, "Why are you doing this at seventy years old, instead of sitting back with a secure retirement and just relaxing and enjoying life?"

George smiled. "All of my life I have studied the ways of the big cats. My father got the last one in these parts over sixty years ago. They need me. I trained the dogs. I don't want to see any more dead people. Does that answer your question?"

Rebecca chimed in and changed the tone.

"I don't believe that this county has three better men than the three it has chasing the cat. I also believe that the whole country would have to look long and hard to find their equal."

She looked out over the other reporters with disdain.

"I had the chance to be along when the cat had killed two people and a dog down by Spring Lake early this spring. It was the most frightening thing these eyes ever beheld or my heart had ever felt. I want to personally thank you, Sam, and Jack for what you are doing and the risks you are taking."

She gave old George a long-held hug. The assembled reporters began to clap.

The door to George's house opened and Jeff Sanderson's widow, Roscoe Tanner's widow, and others who had lost loved ones to the cat emerged. They led the old man into his house.

"Surprise!!" They said as one.

George did not recognize his own home. The inside was completely repainted and re-carpeted. His perennial mess had been cleaned up. The dishes were done!! George had to steady himself!

At the dining room table, places were set and the guests were seated. George walked into his home. The others were all dressed up, and there he stood, smelling like sun-warmed, road kill. Janie pointed him toward the bathroom. There he found a complete set of clean clothes in a freshly painted and redone bathroom.

The ladies told him to take his time while they put the last touches on supper. The tub was full of sudsy, hot water. He laughed seeing a rubber ducky bobbing there—Marc Salem's addition.

Soon George emerged with, what was left of his hair, slicked back and with a big grin on his face. He just could not believe all of the trouble everyone had gone to. First, he had a score to settle. He pulled the rubber ducky, out of his pants pocket, and gave it a squeeze. It squeaked.

"And who", he asked, "is responsible for this?"

He looked directly at a red faced, grinning, Marc Salem.

"UH- HUH!"

The old man began to laugh. He reached out and patted Marc's shoulder. The table erupted. He looked around at the faces, many of which he didn't even know. Rebecca stayed after the rest of the press had left. Around the table were the relatives of all of the victims of the cat. They had formed an association and had decided that one way that they could deal with their loss was to do some thing nice for those who were risking their lives to get the killer. They explained to George why they were doing, what they were doing.

He responded: "I wish we had gotten him for you, but the hunt is closing in on him now."

He offered a prayer for Sam and Jack, as the hunt was coming to a critical point. Then he looked around the table, and said, "You didn't have to do all of this. I really don't feel that I deserve this."

Annette Sanderson spoke.

"My husband was like that. Every day he risked his life for others. He took that for granted and others took that for granted. Then one day he paid with his life. We don't want you to have to wait and miss hearing our appreciation. I want you to know how much peace it gives us to know that men like you and the others are out there risking your lives for the safety of others—so this group doesn't have to grow larger. You see, we could sit around and grieve, and we do some of that, but what helps most is to be able to let the hunters of that killer know that we love them."

George got teary. He wiped his eyes. Then he said. "To this old man, this is no small thing and, 'thank you' is one very inadequate phrase for me to say, to all of you."

They ate and they talked, and then it was time for the association to leave and for an old man to get some much needed rest. He shook every one's hand as they left and gave each woman a hug.

The old man crawled into his soft bed. It had clean sheets and blankets for the first time in months. He folded his hands in prayer.

"Thank you, Lord, for all that you have given me. Please help me to be able to help the others get that killer. Thy will be done. In Jesus name we pray. Amen."

He was immediately asleep. He would not wake up for twelve hours as his system worked to cleanse all that was exhausted from his mind and body. He woke up somewhat refreshed but as weak as a kitten and famished. He fixed eggs, bacon, and toast, and went right back to bed. He never had felt as old and as tired as he did right then. By the end of the second day, however, he was a' chompin' at the bit, to get back on the trail of the cat. He drove to the Sheriff's department, caught a police chopper to the armory, and rode out with the cage to meet the others. He was rarin' to go. As it turned out, the others would need him more than any could know at that moment.

## CHAPTER THIRTEEN
## The Cave

The plan George had outlined before he had left was a very straightforward method for running the cat to ground. The men and the mules were to split into two groups, one positioned on either side of the rocky gorge. The dogs would start up the rocky slopes on two sides. Blackie and Jack would take the west side. Sam, Brownie, and half of the hounds would take the other. They would work to the middle, climbing ever higher, until both teams were at the base of the highest and rockiest of the hills. George believed that the cat would quit running and try to pick off the dogs as they worked their way up the steep rocky faces of the gorge. On such a nearly vertical grade the cat had all of the advantages against dogs.

Somewhere up there was its lair. If it could be chased into its den, they could simply smoke it out of there. If it had left the immediate area it was George's guess that it was headed for the crevasse where it had previously left men and dogs behind by jumping to the other side. Now, through the help of the military, bridges had been installed so that men and dogs could follow immediately. Without them it would take nearly a day to traverse the crevasse from the floor below, while the cat bounced back at forth at its pleasure above.

The plan had several serious drawbacks. First, it meant that Blackie and Brownie were separated, each leading a pack of six other dogs. Consequently, their well-practiced tandem style of fighting the cat, was out of the question. The six other coon dogs, formidable as they were, were secondary in the cat's mind, because it had found that killing them was much easier. If it could kill either Blackie or Brownie, it would enhance its chances of survival against the men and the other dogs.

The second drawback was that the men were separated as well and would have the mules following them as they proceeded up the grade on foot. The cat's mere scent could spook the mules, so one man would have to try to hold the mule to tether. All things considered, the cat had a better shot at both the lead dogs and the men. It was a high stakes gamble, taken because of the terrain and the plan to drive the cat to high ground.

Sam and Jack had started the day with fourteen dogs and two mules. The pack mule and the horses had been eliminated because of the steepness of the terrain and because George was not there to tend them.

The cat had circled the area several times and day old cat scent seemed to be everywhere. It had slept in its cave for part of the night, awakened early, before the sun came up, and staked out an ambush location to await the men and dogs. It was a bushy area concealed behind some large boulders. The dogs would pass close chasing day old scent. The cat took to the high ground to wait and to watch.

When the sun came up he was ready. The fireworks would not be long in the making. The cat could afford to wait them out. He had gorged on coon dog the night before. He was rested and full. He had slacked his thirst at a nearby creek. He was, as the saying goes, good to go.

Sam circled the gorge and went to the west side of the area. The dogs began to work their way up the high rocky terrain. Jack and his dogs started at the east end. They would meet at the top of the highest hill at days end and, if all went well, they would have the cat cornered and finish him off.

It was as if the dogs were expecting the climax of the hunt that day. Sam and his group of dogs were on a very steep incline. He was leading his mule. The dogs were on a game trail that went up the sheer face of a rocky hill.

It was at that moment that all hell broke loose. Sam's mule reared. He pulled on the lead rope with all his might, battling the mule when the cat hit the dogs again. Going with what had worked so well before, he went after the last in the line, quickly killing two more dogs. He jumped to a ledge high above and with one more bound disappeared from view. Sam had no prayer of getting a shot off because of the mule's antics. He wanted to shoot the damn mule himself!

The six dogs Brownie had been leading were suddenly four. They headed back up the trail. A hundred yards ahead the grade became more gradual and Sam was able to ride. It allowed him to remain closer to the pack. The dogs were a hundred yards ahead when his mule went crazy again. Fighting the mule and trying to stay in the saddle, Sam somehow managed to blow the dog whistle. It probably saved his life. The mule fell over on its side. Sam's right leg was pinned under it. It had stepped into a hole while it was rearing and had broken its right back leg. It was braying and fighting to get up. Sam could not get out from underneath it. He grabbed for his rifle from the scabbard and put the wriggling mule out of its misery.

Using his rifle as a pry bar, he worked to get the heavy mule off of his leg. It was to no avail. The mule was too heavy. Then he looked behind him and swore! The cat, seeing the man down, emerged from the brush and the rocks. He walked toward Sam. Sam shot into the air as he was fighting to get himself turned around to get a well-aimed shot at the cat. The dead weight on his leg was unforgiving. He could not turn around. The cat closed on him. He saw its body above him and tried to shoot at it from on his back. It was all up side down. Sam would save his last shot for when the cat was almost upon him. It was his only chance. He looked right into its evil, green, eyes. Its tail twitched. The cat was going to come in one rush. Sam prayed that he could make his last shot count.

Just as things were looking their darkest, Brownie, with the other dogs at his heals, arrived as if out of nowhere. Without hesitation they headed straight for the cat. This time Brownie did as Blackie would have done. He charged in from the front, rather than circling behind for a bite. As the cat turned and prepared to deliver a fatal blow to the brown dog, the others charged in from behind. Brownie got in a powerful bite to the cat's front leg. Then Ringo and the others bit the cat from behind. The cat was overwhelmed and beat a forty-five mile an hour retreat back up the trail where the dogs had just come from. Brownie didn't try to follow. He sensed the man was in trouble. He licked Sam's face. Sam was never so glad to see a dog in his whole life!

Brownie barked once and the other dogs seemed to understand that he wanted them to stay with the man. Then, going the opposite way that the cat had taken, Brownie was off to find Jack and the other dogs. The cat crouched a mile up the trial waiting for dogs to follow. That was Brownie's good fortune. The other dogs sat on Sam's command and waited for Brownie to find Jack. Sam tried to call Jack, but his cell phone had been damaged by the fall.

Brownie seemed to know that he was vulnerable by himself, so he remained quiet and moved deliberately, staying within cover as he could. He made the half circle to the other side of the gorge. He sniffed to follow the scent of Blackie and the others. He started up the grade, as fast as his legs would carry him. After some five miles he spotted Jack just ahead on his mule. It was then he began to bark.

Jack turned around and saw a brown dot below him, moving up fast. He blew his dog whistle to call Blackie and the other dogs to return. He needn't have bothered. Blackie's keen ears picked up Brownies bay and he immediately turned the pack around and headed toward the sound. He got to Jack before Brownie and rushed past him towards his partner. The two dogs sniffed noses and licked each others faces before heading towards Jack. Brownie barked and started back in the direction from which he had come. Blackie and the other dogs followed. Jack brought up the rear on his mule.

When they arrived it was clear that Sam was hurt severely and that circulation had been cut off in his pinned leg. Jack dismounted, got his rope, tied one end to his saddle horn and the other around the mule. He called Blackie and put the lead rope of the mule in his mouth. Jack went around to Sam, who already had his rifle under the mule. Jack wedged his rifle on the other side of the pinned leg and called out to Blackie, who immediately tugged on the mules lead rope. But the stubborn creature would not cooperate. Brownie nipped at the mule's hind leg, dodged a flying foot, and growled. Eventually the mule got the message and moved forward. After a few struggling steps the carcass inched off the leg just enough to pull Sam free. As the blood rushed into it Sam screamed in agony.

Fifteen minutes later the pain began to subside and Sam could wiggle his toes. With Jack's help he hoisted himself up into a standing position. He gave Brownie a hug and Blackie a pat.

"They are such damn good dogs!" he said.

Jack nodded his agreement. Sam limped badly but he *was walking*. In his mind he was thanking God for that.

The cat screamed its challenge from above.

"What do you want to do Sam? Don't you think we better call this off for a day or so?"

"Let's get after the bastard. I'm not so crippled up that I can't ride a mule!"

"You're crazy. We can't split up again with only one mule, and we risk chasing him off this hill, which gives us our best shot at getting him."

Jack had a flash of inspiration.

"Here is what we might be able to do. What if you take Brownie and what is left of his pack and go to where I was on the east side of the gorge? Don't try to climb it. You and the mule and the dogs just find a spot where you can see if its working it's way down towards you. If you do; blast the SOB! Me and Blackie will wait twenty minutes for you to get into position. Then we'll go up the west slope, here, and drive until we meet you at the base of the other side."

"Sounds like a winner to me." Sam agreed. "That way I won't slow you down and I can still be useful."

With Jack's help, Sam mounted the remaining mule and called for Brownie and his pack. They proceeded around the base of the gorge to where Jack had begun the day. They would work their way up only so far as the grade was favorable. At the point where it began to get steep they would find a recon point and wait.

Jack gave them twenty minutes, then started Blackie and the larger pack up the slope. Jack was worried about Sam's leg and believed that he should get medical attention for it, but he also knew that Sam was too bull-headed to do it. He just shook his head. Soon Blackie was growling and snarling and the coon dogs were at full bay. The cat's challenge had just been answered.

The cat proceeded another three hundred yards up the grade to set up another ambush point. There was no mule this time, but there *was* a man, by himself, on foot, lagging well behind the dogs. If the man were to pass his ambush spot he would be easy prey from behind. The cat knew this man's scent and above all others he wanted him dead.

Blackie moved quickly up the grade when something odd hit his nose. He was on cat scent, all right, but the wind shifted for just a moment and it brought a fresher cat scent into his nostrils. He veered off the trail to the left and made his way along a ledge leading to a flat, rocky, area.

The cat was now faced with the prospect of fighting six coonhounds and the black dog on almost level terrain. He didn't like those odds at all. He moved on further up the rock face of the cliff where he knew no dog could follow. Blackie turned and led the pack back to the main game trail they had been following.

The cat was now two thirds of the way up the grade towards the cave. Everything was familiar to him up there. Nothing was familiar to the dogs. Not wanting that Black dog following his scent, he crossed the game trail some hundred yards ahead, and headed north towards the crevasse, ten miles northeast. He was just one, twenty-foot jump, away from losing the others.

When Blackie hit the hot trail, he again veered to the left along a level ledge. He and the others were getting too far ahead so Jack blew the whistle. They worked their way back to towards him and when they met he sent them off again.

Watching the movement of the dogs, he determined the spot where the cat made his left hand turn. He pulled out the topographic map of the area. He saw where the cat was headed: away from the capture point at the top of the highest hill and northeast towards the crevasse. He called the dogs off the trail, followed the game trail to the top of the highest hill, and led them down toward where Sam should be waiting. In less than an hour they located the others. They ended the day in the same field from which they had started—two dogs and one mule short.

Sam was badly banged up but he was too proud to admit it to Jack. So, when the helicopter dropped the cage and took on the one remaining mule he remained.

The cat worked his way back to the cave after he discovered he was not being followed. So far, he liked the way the battle was shaping up right there. There were more mules, dogs, and men to be killed. He certainly hoped they tried to follow him again the next day. After darkness set in, he returned to the mule and gorged. He had eaten well—even if it wasn't his *favorite food.*

The cat screamed in triumph, just to let the men know he was still in the area. Sam and Jack looked at each other not knowing whether to curse or cry. In two days of gut busting effort they had lost six dogs, one mule, and had a badly injured man. They needed a better battle plan.

"I wish George was here," Sam said.

Jack nodded, but was privately glad he wasn't. He didn't want the old man to die from lack of rest and a bad ticker. He wanted to tell Sam about George but he had given the old man his word, so he wouldn't. In the morning they would just have to try it all over again. Jack had begun to feel the effects of eleven straight days on the trail. He wasn't going to take any time off just yet, but he felt the toll, none the less.

The next morning Sam could barely stand. His leg had swollen badly during the night—to nearly twice its normal size. Jack tried to persuade him to go in and get some medical attention for it but Sam was adamant.

Jack reminisced. "I had a guy in my unit like you. He

stepped on a sharpened bamboo stick the enemy had left for us. He was so gung-ho that he wouldn't go back and get it treated until our mission was completed. Then the monsoon came and no helicopter could get through. The leg got gangrene."

He looked Sam in the face. "We were out of morphine and our medic bought it. As the first lieutenant it was my job to get him drunk with what whiskey we had left. While the others held him down, I had to cut his leg off with a knife. I still dream of his screams. You may be in charge of most things here, but not on this matter. I made a vow to God to never again let a brain dead moron lose a leg out of stupidity. Sam, either you take the chopper into town tomorrow or I'm done with this hunt altogether!"

Jack pulled out his bowie knife.

"Let me see that leg."

Sam was whipped and he knew it.

"I can't roll up the pant leg. It is swollen too bad."

"I figured." Jack said.

He reached for the leg and began cutting away the pant leg. Sam offered no further resistance. The leg did hurt and he wanted the pant leg off it. Jack's Bowie cut through the denim like butter. Then Sam and Jack saw what both men feared. The leg had a huge black clot and red streaks running down the leg under the skin.

"You are outa here as soon as the chopper arrives. Me and the dogs are just gonna have to do our best tomorrow by ourselves."

Sam looked at him nodded, then added his simple, "Thanks."

Jack returned the nod and said, "I will try not to let you down while your healing."

Sam sighed. "If we never get that cat, I want you to know that neither you or George ever let me down. I haven't let the people down either. That is just one hellatious animal out there. I'm off my guilt trip now. We are just three men trying our best. It will just have to be good enough, or not, as far as anyone else is concerned."

Jack smiled. "Besides, it's got personal with me any

way."

"Personal?" Sam repeated. He grinned for the first time in days. He patted Jack on the shoulder. "Personal!"

They made breakfast and ate together.

When the chopper arrived, Jack took on one mule to ride. He traveled light with just enough in the way of provisions to get him through the day. It was he and twelve of the original eighteen dogs.

"The dirty dozen," he laughed to himself, and from the odor that filled the air, it seemed he was right.

Sam boarded the chopper. Jack waved to them as they left with the cage. He turned back to the task of the day. In his mind, he heard ol' George talking.

"Why did that cat follow the ledge as I left the top of the hill?" The answer was immediately obvious: "Because he didn't want the dogs to discover his lair."

Jack pondered his possibilities. 'Let's just go up and see what's there.'

With that he started up the east side of the gorge. If the cat ran west, the traps were set and waiting. If the cat took the ledge northeast, the crevasse was ahead and he didn't have the manpower today to split up the dogs.

'I'll just drive him west.'

He liked the idea that Blackie and Brownie were working together. That way the cat could not try to kill one, without the other being there guarding it's back. The other hounds were to tip the edge from a stalemate to victory. Blackie and Brownie would be the keys to this operation. Why drive the cat to a place where they have to be split up?

That triggered another idea—a question, really. 'Why have Blackie and Brownie at the front of the pack so the cat can kill the dogs that lag behind? Why should the man and the mule be left without dog protection, so that when the mule rears out of fear, the man is in jeopardy?'

He was on his own and decided to try a whole different approach that today.

He called out: "Blackie and Brownie, drop it. Ringo go get um."

Ringo and the hounds were off, leaving Blackie and Brownie confused and whining. They were puzzled about the apparent demoted. Jack patted each one. Then he started off on the mule. Whenever either dog started to get ahead he called them back to heel.

He talked to them and they soon accepted their lot.

About a third of the way up the rocky slope, the cat lay in ambush. The dog whistle blew just in time. The dogs rushed back to Jack and the mule. Once regrouped, he sent them back at it, still holding Blackie and Brownie in reserve.

Once the first eight dogs passed him, the cat attacked the last two. At the commotion Jack called out: "Blackie and Brownie, go get um."

The two dogs understood and lit out at full speed. The cat had killed the next to last dog. The trailer turned back toward the man but the cat was too soon on top of him. It was at that moment that Blackie and Brownie joined the fray. It threw the cat off balance. He hesitated and paid with a bite to the shoulder from Blackie. It tore tendons and flesh. Before he could strike the black dog, the brown one hit a back leg coming close to crippling him. The whole pack converged and he took nearly a dozen bites within a few seconds. He screamed in pain and ran in the opposite direction—toward the cave. He was immediately inside. He had never known such pain.

The dogs were soon at the entrance and bayed the victorious bays of dogs that have brought a quarry to corner or to tree. Soon Jack joined them. He moved the dogs back and shined a light into the cave, his rifle cocked and ready. It was not a shallow cave but one that snaked back for what seemed forever. He ordered the pack to stay put. Then he called to Blackie and Bownie and urged his mule forward into the tunnel. As he emerged from the other side he saw a black form slinking along the ledge towards the crevasse. He pulled his rifle and aimed. Fire and smoke belched from his rifle. The cat turned a corner and the bullet sent rock splinters in all directions.

“Damn it! Damn it! Damn it!”

Instead of trying to follow along the narrow ledge to the

crevasse, he turned his mule around and called Blackie and Brownie to heel. He wasn't about to let that cat catch him from behind. He cut a branch of a tree, wrapped cloth sacks around it—ones from his saddlebags used to tote plaster casts and such— and soaked them with kerosene from his emergency fuel supply. It became his makeshift torch. He tied off the mule and ordered Blackie and Brownie to stay there with it and guard the cave entrance. He let the cloth and set off to see what was inside this cave.

What he found made him sick to his stomach. Bones; Human bones; The bones of a child.

Further in there was more trouble. The cave came to a room like opening. Branching off it were four tunnels of varying diameters. It caused the hair to stand up on the back of Jack's neck. The scream of a cougar echoed through the cave. His torch flickered and died. He backed out of the room and made his way toward the light marking the spot where he had come in. The cat was in one of those tunnels—it or possibly another one. Earlier, the trappers had caught a young female cougar. He didn't know for sure what was going on, but he did know enough to move immediately to the safety of the outside! He backed out to the dogs and the mule. Blackie was growling and snarling and Brownie was baying and snarling.

This hunt was over for the day. He rode the mule and led the two dogs back to where the pack was waiting. This cave was going to require more manpower and more equipment than he had at his disposal. Blackie and Brownie led the dogs down the hill behind Jack and the mule. They returned to the middle of the field—the one that was beginning to seem too much like home—to await the delivery.

Jack was more than just tired. He was full out spent. He secured the mule by a neck rope and removed the bit from its mouth so it could graze. He built a campfire and warmed up a can of chili from his pack. The dogs went to the little creek and romped playfully drinking their fill. Rest was in order for the balance of the day. Jack bet that George would arrive that evening with the supplies and the cage. He could have waited to re-join them in the morning, of course, but Jack knew that old man; he would be in that chopper that night.

He was right.

## CHAPTER FOURTEEN
## The End of the Trail

When Sam arrived at the armory he was immediately air-evacuated to the hospital. Advanced blood poisoning and the precursors of gangrene were apparent. He also had a cracked femur and a broken ankle. The issue of his keeping his leg was very much up in the air. The helicopter landed on the helipad on top of the hospital and they carried Sam inside. He thanked God that Jack had stood up to him and sent him home. The media was there but hospital security kept them from seeing or talking to Sam. The surgeons went to work. His wife was waited for word.

On the local television station, a teary Rebecca Monk reported that Sam had been severely injured in pursuit of the cat and that he was in surgery. The town began to respond immediately. Cards and flowers poured into the hospital. The media was covering the vigil as if it were the President of the United States, whose life was in peril.

The wives of the victims of the cat were allowed in to be with Sally while she waited, hoped, and prayed.

The surgeons asked her permission to take her husbands leg if need be. The last thing he had said to her before being moved into OR was: "No matter what happens, don't let them take my leg. I do not want to live as a cripple."

Sally kept her promise. The surgeons were then confronted with the task of saving all of him or none of him. She prayed that she had done the right thing. She and her friends prayed and waited together.

Ten hours after the surgery had begun, an exhausted Dr.

Edwin Martin entered the lobby and asked for Sarah Macafee. She looked into the drained eyes of the surgeon and, for a split second, feared that she had lost her husband.

The surgeon's smile brought immediate relief.

"He is one tough somebody. He is going to live with all of his parts intact!"

Her friends moved to give her a hug. Sarah was not going to go home. They set her up with a bed next to Sam's in his hospital room. For some time she just stood looking at him, holding his hand. Eventually she gave him a long, tearful, hug, lay down on her bed, and fell into a fitful sleep.

When Sam awoke in the morning he found tubes everywhere. He was in a cast from his hip to his toes. It had been uncomfortably elevated but he was sure it meant the leg was all in one piece. He looked around. The room was wall-to-wall flowers. Best of all, his wife was there with him, still asleep.

When she woke up she saw Sam smiling at her. She moved to his side and they embraced—as much as the tubing would allow. She sat on his bed and started opening and reading the mountain of cards that had arrived at the room. Sam was overwhelmed.

They had not gotten the cat, but the people still loved those who continued to try. It made Sam realize that the only one who had felt that he had let them down, was he, himself. He tried to call Jack and George. There were no answers. He figured they must be up to their necks in trouble. He would try back later.

When the cage and provisions arrived by helicopter that evening, George hopped out of the cargo-bay with a smile on his face and a sparkle in his eye. Jack was glad to see him, even as concerned as he was about his health. That aside, the fact was that he desperately needed him. The helicopter took on the lone mule. George told Jack that Sam was in the hospital in very serious condition. He had not received word on the outcome. Jack called the hospital and was informed that Sam had come through the surgery okay, but that he was sleeping. That put his mind at rest.

He told George of his grim discovery— that there were bones of a child found inside the cave, and that it had many entrances. He didn't have the slightest idea of even how to go about exploring the cave, let alone getting the cat trapped inside it. George had several ideas.

The military had agreed to bring a body bag when it dropped off the mules and picked up the cage in the morning. They dropped off the clean set of clothes Jack had requested. George looked at his friend and thanked him for keeping his secret. Jack smiled. Jack walked to the creek and took a bath.

"I'll probably freeze my ass off, but at least I'll freeze to death clean."

"Good idea," George joked, "because we can't have the cat smellin' *us* coming."

They laughed and talked well into the night. George, for his part, was ever so grateful to be back in action.

George called the Sheriff's department and set up a rendezvous. He requested that they come in by horseback because they were going to need their help in the cave. The military had also agreed to provide some long burning torches for their cave exploration.

The helicopter arrived at dawn. The men unloaded four mules. Sheriff Bonner and Deputy Anderson jumped to the ground.

"Why should we ride horses all the way up here, when we could fly in?" The sheriff explained.

"No reason at all," George laughed.

They ate the breakfast George had prepared. That over, 'sweet smellin' Jack,' and the others mounted their mules and headed up the west end of the gorge towards the cave. Sheriff Bonner and George, along with Brownie and his smaller pack, went part way up the eastern slope and settled into a good ambush spot should Blackie and his bunch chase the cat down their way.

While all of that was going on, the cat had left for another den by way of the crevasse. The night before he had not killed or eaten. They had no way of knowing any of that. Also, they could not have known that Sam's off-balance shot had hit the cat on top of his right shoulder. He did not need a fight on that day. He needed to rest and to heal. He had more than a dozen severe bites and he was in far worse shape than the men could know. The cat was running for his life.

The men had solved many of the riddles of that gorge. The pack was now down to ten dogs, but ten dogs represented lots of power—especially with two of them being a healthy Blackie and Brownie.

Jack and Bonner started up the west end of the gorge. Again, Jack called out to Ringo. "Go get `em", and Ringo and the hounds took off up the trail. Blackie was again held in reserve. That time he seemed to understand that the change in tactics was not a demotion. Besides, he liked the special attention and being able to stay close to Jack.

From the dogs' reactions—or lack, thereof—it was soon apparent to Jack that the cat had not been in those parts the night before. By the time they got to the ledge, which led to the crevasse ten miles to the northeast, the trail seemed to begin getting warmer. That told Jack all he needed to know.

He called George.

"Better meet us at the cave because the cat left for the crevasse last night."

"We're on our way," George answered.

Within forty-five minutes, both sets of dogs and hunters congregated at the east entrance of the cave. Blackie and Brownie met and licked each others faces. The men dismounted and began discussing strategy.

"While we are here we might as well see what is in this cave," George said. "That way, if we ever run him in here again, at least we will know the layout of his lair."

Frank and Jack rode around to the other entrance. It lay near the trail that led to the crevasse. George and Hal started to explore the near one. The mules were tied and the dogs were told to stay. Brownie kept his pack close to one entrance and Blackie kept his close to the other.

Jack lit two torches. He and Frank entered the cave. About fifty yards inside, Jack showed Frank where the bones were. The two men set about the grim business of putting the remains of what had once been a child into a body bag. Frank sighed, "Somebody's baby died here."

"Yup", Jack agreed.

There were no words that could express the combination of sadness anger, rage, and total helplessness they felt. They could do nothing but put the bones in the bag. Life was hard. The death of a child seemed so unfair. They would both have gladly changed places with those bones, so that someone's mamma and daddy would still have their baby. It gave them renewed determination to get the killer so it could never kill again; so that no more parents, or wives, or girlfriends, or husbands, would have to keep burying loved ones, while the killer remained free, to kill again. The men had a common cause and a common enemy. They were both on the side of good against a common evil.

The men began to move foreword down the tunnel with their torches lighting the way. Two hundred yards ahead they came to the room—the hub— where the various tunnels met. George and Hal were already there. It resembled a medieval chamber of horrors.

George looked at the others and announced: "The cat has been hurt bad. We found dried blood where it slept. We could follow these tunnels forever, and never explore all of them. He left because he doesn't want us to discover his secrets in here. For now, the cat leads and we must follow if we are going to have a ghost of a chance of getting him. Let's leave the body bag by the far entrance and take the trail to the crevasse. We can pick it up on our way back to the field. We are just gonna have to follow and see where it all leads."

The men nodded in agreement. Outside, George and Hal mounted their mules and Brownie and the dogs followed them as they rode around the gorge to once again meet up with Jack and Frank and the other dogs. Soon, four men, four mules, and ten dogs made their way down the trial that led to the crevasse and, hopefully, the cat. Once again, the hunt was on.

The detour had cost them a good chunk of the day. The cat was sleeping the day away in another den, waiting for the first sound or smell of the men and the dogs. The den was near the highest point on a hill near the crevasse. He would wait until they got close. Then, he would simply jump the crevasse and leave them to wonder as he simply walked away. It was going to be easy. His new, bold, scent would keep the dogs from ever discovering his second den. The cat felt certain he could guard that secret. He would be very wrong.

He did not yet know of the bridges that the men had placed across the crevasse. The impenetrable had indeed been penetrated.

Soon the dogs were in full cry. The cat awakened. He climbed down the rock strewn grade to the trail ahead of the dogs, and had waited until they were close. Then he walked to the edge of the crevasse. The sight puzzled him. He saw the bridge and realized his strategy would have to change. The cat ambled across the bridge, walked down the ledge to the other bridge, crossed it, and then made a loop up a hill, crossing the first bridge again. His plan was to get the dogs running in circles. He would kill again and then move to his private escape route where no man or dog could follow. He knew of places—miner's tunnels and a labyrinth of unmapped caves within the hills. He could hide there.

The cat now re-entered its den and descended hundreds of feet into the guts of the hill. He emerged at the very base of the crevasse. It was in the bank of the creek, below the men and the bridges they had erected.

As the men and dogs hurried across their bridges above, the cat watched as it lapped water from the creek below. It dined on an unsuspecting, nearby, doe.

The dogs were on scent but moved in circles crossing the bridges twice. George figured out what the cat had done. He split the pack into two groups, one scouting each side of the crevasse. Eventually, Brownie got the scent of where that cat had doubled back by jumping the crevasse.

One dog thought he could make the jump and in spite of Brownie's warning, fell to his death. The cat had marked the spot in his mind for something to eat that night.

Meanwhile, up above, the men and Blackie led the

combined pack, and proceeded to trail the cat to its den. The tenor of their bays soon announced to the men that the cat had been driven to ground. Jack and Frank joined Hal and George at the cave entrance. George took some kerosene soaked rags and put some black powder on it and secured it at the entrance. He then trailed black powder out to where he could light it. The black powder trail led to the kerosene rags, called a *spitting devil*, which should create enough smoke to drive the cat out and, with any luck, reveal other close cave entrances. Black smoke poured from the other entrance. Two men and six dogs went immediately to that spot. Since no scent was found to indicate the cat's escape, the men figured that the cat was trapped inside and soon would be driven out by the smoke. The men and the guns were at the ready.

Ten minutes passed, and no cat had emerged. George smelled a rat. When the smoke cleared, he lit a torch and crawled through the low, narrow, entrance.

Within minutes everyone heard him curse.

"That damned cat has done it again!"

He backed out of the cave and stood up.

"There is a vent to an ancient coal mine smack dab in the middle of this cave. Where it leads to, only God and that cat know! It will be like trying to find a needle in a haystack."

He threw his Stetson on the ground and stomped on it in total frustration.

To the others it looked humorous. Jack began to laugh. Then Frank and Hal joined in. The old man then realized how comical he must have appeared. Humor overcame rage. Days of frustration, anger, and fatigue poured out in uncontrolled laughter.

They went back to the field that evening, in defeat. The trail had simply ended. They were going to have to develop a whole new strategy. It was agreed that the men would take a few days off, try to get hold of the maps of those old coal mines, and study them. Jack was especially in need of rest. The pack needed nine replacement dogs.

George would make phone calls to the mine companies, the library, and the historical society to figure out how to get his hands on some maps. That night the helicopter loaded the men, the mules, and the dogs all on board, leaving the cage behind. It would be there when the men were ready to re-occupy it in a few days.

When Jack got home he had a surprise waiting for him. There were cars in his driveway.

"What in the...?" he muttered, as he pulled to a stop.

Unbeknownst to him, the group of people that had lost loved ones to the cat had been tipped off by George that Jack was coming in for a breather and they had fixed up Jack's house as well. Exhausted from nearly two weeks on the cat's trail, all Jack had wanted to find was a bed. Instead the house had been completely cleaned. Guests filled the place and good smells drifted from the kitchen.

Jack was overwhelmed. He thanked everyone but he was at a loss for words. What was he supposed to say or do? Victoria Salem broke the ice.

"We just wanted to say thank you for what you are doing."

Young Marc was next to chime in. "Did you see it up close, Mr. Jack?"

His eyes told of his excitement.

"Yes, we saw it. We did everything but kill it. It seems to have a sixth sense about it. For thirteen straight days, it's been killing our dogs, horses, and mules, and almost killed Sam. We drove it into its den and thought we surely had it but it just disappeared! It apparently escaped through an old mine shaft. That cat is hurt bad right now. Blackie and Brownie and the other dogs made it pay real good, but we didn't get it. It is out there somewhere recovering from its wounds while I sit here, like a bump on a log, dead tired, and hardly able to continue. . . . I want all of you to know that I am very grateful for what you did here, today. I just wish that I felt like I had earned it."

Marc took his hand and said, "Oh you have earned it all right Mr. Jack. We are all real proud and grateful that you are after it. Just that makes us feel safer." Then with wisdom beyond his years he added, "Every night when I go to bed, I think about Teresa. And then, in my mind, I can just see you, and George, and Sam riding your horses after it with your dogs on its trail. Every night I think about how scared I would be if it was me out there; and every night I pray that you will be okay."

Jack looked down into the little boy's eyes. "Thank you Marc. Maybe it was your prayers that saved Sam."

There was scratching at the back door.

"I wonder who that might be?" Jack chuckled out loud.

Marc looked up at him and smiled.

"I bet that it's Blackie and Brownie!"

"I'll bet it is, too."

Annette Sanderson had been quiet but was moved to speak. "We love you for all that you're doing."

Jack looked back at her—longer than may have been necessary. Then he addressed everyone gathered there in the room.

"I don't know what to say, except that as long as I live, I will never forget this night, and your kindness. Thank you all very much."

Marc announced that a tub had been run, and that clean clothes were laid out in the bathroom. Even though Jack had bathed the day before, and he had been royally teased about bein' 'sweet smellin' Jack', he had not had a hot bath in some weeks. He was not about to turn down the opportunity.

Twenty minutes later he emerged feeling clean and refreshed. Janie Tanner opened a box of cigars that the judge had sent along, and Annette Sanderson brought out some aged Kentucky bourbon to go with them.

"Can I pet your dogs?" Marc asked, being unable to contain himself any longer.

"Sure," Jack answered.

He got up and opened the door so Marc could pet them outside.

Annette said, "Ladies would you mind if we let them in?"

Jack had a word of warning: "They've been on the trail for two weeks without a bath and they smell it. Better let the boy pet them outside until I can get them cleaned up."

"I don't care," Annette announced, "I love those dogs."

The other women agreed, much to Jack's amazement, and so he called them in.

"Drop it," he ordered when they got inside. Blackie and Brownie hit the floor side by side while Marc took a spot beside them and administered the most complete petting any dogs had ever received.

Then Blackie cocked his head and looked up at Jack as if to ask, "May I meet the others?"

"Okay Blackie, but you be on your best behavior, you hear? We have ladies present."

Blackie didn't know what all the words meant, but he understood that it was okay for him to meet the others. He made the tour, got a pat from everyone around the table, and then returned to Marc. Brownie then made his tour.

Soon it was time for everyone to go. Jack thanked then again as they left. Janie Tanner was not going straight home. She was going to visit ol' George. There was something about him that she liked. Annette lingered behind. As she looked Jack in the eye, he thought he saw "that look" again.

"You are quite a woman," he said.

"I like strong men."

Her next comment hit him right between the eyes.

"And I would like to stay here with you."

Jack suddenly understood that hadn't imagined that look.

"Sure. As long as you like," he managed.

"I think I will, then."

She poured two glasses of whiskey and they sat down together on the couch.

"Let the dogs back in, okay?"

"Okay."

Blackie and Brownie went down the stairs to the basement according to their standing orders when company was present.

"They are real good dogs, Jack. They would die to protect."

"Yes, they are. And they would," Jack answered.

"Our dog was like that. It gave me peace to have him around. But I haven't been able to get myself to get another one to take his place."

"I know the feeling." Jack answered. "I was the same way about dogs, until their mother came scratching at my door, hungry, as a pup. Then she gave me these two. Now, I don't know what I would do without them."

"Mister," she said, "I lost a good man and a good dog. Now I am a' scratchin' at your door. What do you say to that?"

Jack looked at her and swallowed, hard.

"I'm half again your age. You could do better than me."

Annette smiled. The good men are always more concerned about those they take care of, than they are about themselves. She had, she believed, found a *very* good one.

"My husband and I were almost the same age. He died. Tomorrow you or I could die. All we have is today and tonight. He always said that the only way he kept going through, what he had to go through, was because he had a good and willing woman a' waitin' on him at the end of the day. I need a man. I want a good man. I want you."

For the first time since he had lost Sue, Jack was overwhelmed by a woman.

"Well then, I guess you've got me," he answered. "I can't believe that one man could be this lucky for a second time in his life."

"Or one woman." She answered slipping closer.

They sipped at their drinks. They held hands. It seemed natural. It seemed wonderful. It seemed right.

She took the glasses and put them on the end table. She snuggled close and looked up into Jack's face.

"Well then," she said, running her fingers through his hair, "I suppose we'd better get started on the rest of our life."

She was about to say more but Jack's lips got in the way. They kissed. They held each other close. Later, they went to the bedroom. Two of the best had found each other. There would be no more lonely nights for either of them. (Well, not once the cat was taken care of!)

## CHAPTER FIFTEEN
## Where Evil Lurks

While the men were figuring out what to do next, the cat was resting and healing. For four days it seldom moved from its lair at the base of the crevasse. He had been severely injured and knew that sooner or later the men and the dogs would be back for it. He knew it was going to be harder and harder for it to keep going. The men figured that sooner or later they would force it to ground or to tree if the cat were to remain out in the open for them to chase.

The cat had figured out that the dogs could only help the men on level ground. It could climb and jump to places the dogs could not follow. The ability of the men to climb was pitiful by comparison. The dogs and the mules could not follow at all. The cat had long been familiar with the cave and the mineshafts, and the entrances. The men, on he other hand, were lost as lambs inside those catacombs. The cat was not about to get caught out in the open again by daylight. At night he was the king. By day, the odds favored the men, unless he could lure them into his place where darkness ruled. There, without dogs, mules, and light, the cat would be the supreme ruler twenty-four hours a day.

His strength gradually returned. The men didn't realize how seriously he was hurt.

The next phase of the hunt would depend on how quickly the men were able to solve the riddles of the caves and the mines. Left alone, he could still kill an animal, drag it to the cave, and wait the healing to be complete. If they came back sooner, he would be in trouble. The cat needed time.

It was the men's plan to find out the secrets of the caves

and mines and get back on the trail as fast as was possible. They needed rest and left the area by helicopter for several days. For the time being, the cat would be safe. Nothing in the wilds was its equal, even in its injured state.

As each day passed the cat grew stronger. Its confidence was slowly returned. The men were resting and healing. Sam was pretty much out of the chase for the next six months. George was iffy. Jack was ready to go as were Blackie and Brownie. The remaining seven experienced pack dogs were footsore but could be pressed into service.

Jack and Annette went to see Sam in the hospital. He was still strung up like a trussed turkey with one drumstick secured with enough altitude so that lifting his head and shoulders off of the pillows required Herculean effort. He was still in great pain so was content just to lay there and heal. He was grateful just to be alive and in one piece. There was a constant parade of town folks in and out of his room. He was grateful for the outpouring of support, but he was tired all of the time. The morphine impaired his concentration

When Jack and Annette entered his room, his spirits lifted. He wanted to know everything that had happened on the hunt. Jack told him the whole story. Sam just shook his head. Hunting the cat inside such a cave would be extremely dangerous.

He managed a smile when told it had been hurt. It was reassuring to know that it *could* be hurt**.** Therefore, he figured, it *could* be *killed.* The two men talked. Sam acknowledged that the hunt was pretty much over for him but reasserted his confidence in the others ability to complete the mission.

Jack announced that he and Annette were going to get married. Sam was pleased beyond measure. "You two didn't waste any time deciding that one, did you?"

“When it’s right, it’s right,” Jack said pulling her close.

They left. Jack needed to get over to George's house and find out what the old mastermind of the hunt had come up with. It was the weekend so Annette didn't have to go to work or go back home. In truth, she didn't want to go back to that house and its memories. If she was going to get a new start on a new life, then it was time to get rid of the hurtful relics of the old one. She had loved her husband with all of her being, as Jack had loved his wife. They were both gone now. There was no changing that. What was wonderful was that they had found each other, and that they could truly love each other. She wanted to get started on her new life. It held much promise. They went to George's together to spring their surprise announcement.

*They* were in for a surprise, as well. When they knocked on the door, the old man answered. Janie Tanner was sitting at the table. Annette and Janie looked at each other and started to laugh. George had confided to Janie about his heart condition. Her husband had been in insurance for thirty years and had contact with all kinds of medical experts. She had made up her mind to contact some of them to see if any procedure existed that could fix this old man's ailing heart. She hadn't said a word to him about it. She had just told him that whatever time that they would have together would all be a plus. She liked the old guy and he felt the same way about her.

Annette announced their upcoming wedding plans. Hugs and handshakes were given all around. The men celebrated by smoking the judges' premium cigars and all four toasted with a shot of whiskey. Then the two women went into the kitchen and got busy fixing something to eat.

George got on the phone to find some maps. The mining companies knew who had owned the parcel of land and the old mines. It belonged to the Empire Coal Company. They discovered that the old tunnel maps they were seeking were probably been still in the hands of the former owners, the Kingsford Coal company. The search was on, directed by the President, himself.

An hour later George got the call. The documents had been located and were on their way by courier. They would be there within the hour.

"Just kill that damned cat", the President said when George thanked him for his help. "That is all the reward I need."

"We will get right on it." George promised.

As promised the courier arrived with the maps. Also, as promised, food arrived from the kitchen.

George set the package aside.

"All work and no play," George began, "makes Jack a dull boy."

"And we simply cannot have that," Annette piped in.

The table rocked with laughter.

Across town, John Weston was tying up the details of the recent, marginally legal, activities of the *Friends of Animals*. He was shocked by what he had discovered. A lot of people, including some prominent ones, would be going to jail. Among his findings was evidence that would send April Gillespie and Robert Sanford to jail for a long time. There was plenty to go around for other members, as well.

The tame female cougar the trappers had caught was just a part of the damning evidence. The group had an associate with an exotic pet license, and had used that license to purchase, and then release, several dozen cougars into the nearby wilds. The rational provided was to re-establish them in their ancestral habitat. Such a release was illegal as it violated public safety considerations. The state government would never have sanctioned such a program.

The Racketeering or R.I.C.O. statute, held the group liable for any and all damages created by those cats, and held it liable for punitive damages that could be sought by the injured parties. The evidence provided by he state prosecutor regarding the doctoring of evidence and the release of knowingly false statements to the press as well as the firing of Sam Macafee, were prosecutable in their own right. Malfeasance, dereliction of duty, the misuse of public funds, and many other provisions of statute law had been broken.

Ms. Longworth was going for her second dose of humility in as many encounters with "Smith and Weston." The trial of the animal rights group was to begin in two weeks.

When the full extent of the illegal subterfuge became exposed, the people would react with shock and with outrage. The question on the citizen's minds would be: "How could they have gotten away with it for so long?"

The prosecutor would prove an answer they probably wouldn't like to hear. "The people lose their freedoms only when they are not diligent in monitoring their own government."

He believed that was, more than anything else, where the real evil lurked. Like the cat, in its underground lair, hid and plotted his evil, so the secret groups with covert governmental connections and the cozy ties to the press had plotted theirs. The evil had been sprung on the people while the press played ostrich—even when confronted with the truth. It had buried the findings from the private lab in a small article on the back page, rather than demanding to know the whole truth on the front page. And so, the people slept in ignorance.

The people could have risen up against a press that deliberately parceled out to the people only that truth they felt the people needed to know, rather than providing the whole truth. Only after the people were led to the truth was justice served. For one thing, Sam was appointed. He had told them the truth about the cat from the start, and how hard it would be to get. Because of that, no one expected miracles.

So, while on one side of town, George and Jack mapped a strategy for catching and killing a cat, on the other side of town, a wily prosecutor was mapping his strategy for exposing and jailing the guilty human doers of evil. George and Jack were dealing with a physical killer, while John Weston was dealing with the behind the scenes facilitators of that killer. All evil has a common source. So has the good. There has always been a battle between the two. No victory is guaranteed until the end of all things temporal. But there is glory in the fight, and battles can be won as well as lost. For good to triumph it must discover where the evil lurks, pierce its safe-havens, and drive it into full public view.

George knew cats that hid in the caves and catacombs of mines; Weston knew lawbreakers and scoundrels, masquerading as public servants and interest groups, who hid within the labyrinths of the bureaucracies. The two quarries had one other thing in common. Neither could survive long in the light of day and both thrived in their dark and secret places, where they could lay hidden, strike at the human soul, and then hide in isolation.

Later, the core group gathered at George's house for a strategy session. Originally, just George and Jack were going to plot it out and then move from there, but Sam was itching to get out of the hospital and to be in on the planning. They had removed the tubes and had prescribed strong pain medication to keep him going. Sally wheeled him into George's house in his wheelchair. With one leg extended straight out, Sam looked like a refugee from WWI movie. None the less, he was present and accounted for, and feeling damn good about it. If he couldn't go on the hunt himself, he could certainly be in on the planning of it.

"Well I'll be damned," George said, chuckling, "I've heard of the wheelchair Olympics, but never expected it to take place in my living room!" Everyone laughed. Some clapped.

The women served up supper. George and Jack felt they were getting spoiled fast. The women were, too. It was nice to have someone to care about, especially when it was mutual.

After everyone had eaten, George brought out two easels, and put up the maps of the caves and the mines. With his pointer he began to explain his strategy. He started with the two caves at the very top of the maps.

"Here is the first cave. There is no known connections from here to the mines, but if the four tunnels go to, say, here, then it connects to all of this. If that's true, then both caves are connected to the mines. This is probably why the cat left the cave to go to the crevasse. I believe that they *are* connected and the cat did not want to give away the secret. He thought he could jump the crevasse and it would be goodbye men and dogs.

"My guess is that he was watching us from below as we were closing in on the den. It has miles and miles of crisscrossing tunnels to hide in. It would be virtually impossible for two or three of us to drive him out of those dark tunnels in order to resume the chase out in the open. It looks like checkmate. How in the hell are we going to drive him out of this maize of tunnels?

"We can't even use the dogs down in there. There's too much climbing where the dogs can't follow. It is as dark as a dungeon and the cat can see us as if it were daylight. We would be blind fools chasing a shadow in a black hole.

"Down here," he pointed at the stream at the base of the crevasse, "are no fewer than fifteen exits or entrances into the mines and nobody knows how many more cavern entrances there might be that lead into them somewhere off of this map. The timbers have to be rotten as hell, and we don't have any idea how many have collapsed or are about to collapse. Any sound could trigger a cave-in. What are the methane levels in these tunnels? The cat knows them all, you can bet on that!"

George was frustrated beyond belief and showed it.

Jack had a proposal.

"What if we set smoke bombs down below—here?"

He pointed to the entrances down by the river, at the base of the crevasse.

"What if we kept them going for however long it took to drive him out up here?"

He pointed at the seven known entrances from the first cave to the crevasse den.

"We keep the packs up here and here."

He pointed towards the two cave locations.

"We make no aggressive move till the cat is away from the exits. Then both packs begin to drive him downhill towards the traps—the pits—to the west."

"It's a long shot." George answered. "There are literally miles of caverns and tunnels where it can hide and where it can avoid the smoke. At least with smoke covering the exits it couldn't leave."

Then it came to him.

"We can simply set charges at all of the mine entrances and collapse them. Then the escape routes for the cat are few. We won't get them all but we will get a lot of them. As you suggested, we can have men and dogs waiting above. We will either trap him in there or drive him out when he gets hungry.

We might even get lucky and have a mineshaft or a tunnel collapse on him."

Sam was skeptical.

"There are too many exits for us to cover. What if we took, say, five hundred miners armed with rifles and went in there and just drove him up and out?"

"The rifles are a problem," George began. "One shot and the tunnels may start to cave in, trapping God knows how many men. But the dynamite might just get him, and if not, we might just drive him out.

"We can have the military make barred iron doors to fit the remaining exits that we discover, and then, one by one, we either bar him in or out. Sooner or later we will get them all. It's messy and a crapshoot but it's the best that I can come up with. Our only real alternative is just to wait for him to move to a different part of his range and try to drive him to ground there. That probably won't work because he is free to go wherever he wishes at night."

It was decided to adjourn and sleep on the information and new ideas now at their disposal. George was going to make three phone calls. One would be to General Weberly. He would also ask the president of the mine company to come or to send an engineer who could work out the technical details regarding the use of explosives, smoke, or whatever they decided to do. The trappers would be invited also, both as a courtesy, and to see if he had any trapping ideas that might be simpler. George was going to let his fertile brain go to work on it over night. Jack and Sam would focus on simplifying things as well. There *had* to be a simpler way.

In the morning, the newspaper carried the headlines that April Gillespie, Robert Sanford, and ten others had been indicted by the grand jury, and that arrest warrants had been issued. The charges were many and varied, and carried years of jail time upon conviction. Ms. Gillespie and Robert Sanford posted $100,000 bail. Many others in the group couldn't come up with the bond and would be living at taxpayers' expense until their trails. The most damning part of the article was contained in the charge that twenty or more cougars had been released into the three county area. That had people *linchin' mad.* The trials would begin in two weeks.

The paper's front page also carried another article. It told of bones of a child that had been found in the catamount's lair. They had been identified as a child named Cynthia Wells, age eight, who had been missing for almost a month. She had wandered off into the woods and had never been seen again. Her parents were frantic. Now, their worst fears had been confirmed. They told her story and the town prepared for another funeral.

Jack read the paper.

"Nine dead souls," he whispered to himself.

George had told him of cats that had killed up to four hundred people before being finished off. He just shook his head. This cat had already killed nine. That of course, didn't count the dogs, the horses, the mules, and the livestock kills. Still, he believed that the pressure they had kept on it, had saved numerous lives. What if it were free to roam, without having to constantly look over it's shoulder? It could spend all of its time stalking and killing people. He came to understand for the first time that if no other good had yet come out of all the efforts to bring it down, perhaps a lot of bad had been prevented. He took solace in that.

Then he read about the people who had released twenty to thirty cats into their midst. He reminded himself that most of them would stay away from people and would stick with deer and, occasionally, livestock. Another man-eater was unlikely. Those who had released them were ignorant idiots. Just because they used to be here, before men wisely drove them out to protect their families and their livestock, was no reason to bring them back.

"Does madness know no end?"

As he thought, it came to him. Softness and safety had bred a generation of naive folks who knew no fear. The old stories of cats killing people were ancient history to them. Some literalists really thought that the lion would lay down with the lamb in this world. They believed they could reason with the likes of Ho Chi Minh and Chairman Mao to resolve world problems. They believed that utopia was doable. When times get too good and life too easy, people go crazy. They create misery and hardship and oppression, because they could not take a life without challenge. They bring on tyranny just so that suffering would be revisited on them.

Thomas Jefferson said that every generation must renew and revitalize liberty or it would be lost. The present generation is in real trouble. He thought of his father laughing at his favorite *POGO* cartoon. Its caption read: "We have found the enemy, and he is we." He now understood where it was that evil lurks. It lurks in the hearts of the spoiled. It lurks amongst the utopians. The road to hell *was* paved with good intentions. Then, he mused about his grandmother's favorite saying, that, "Idle time is the devil's playground." He never understood what she had been getting at. How could anyone be against a little free time? "Have an apple Eve?" the snake had said when life became too easy in the garden. Now, he was beginning to understand what the old saying meant. Evil lurked in the heart of that man-eater, too. It came from a common source. He shook himself away from his musings. He was doing all that he reasonably could.

In the evening, the strategy session at George's home resumed, but this time, the heavy guns were called in. In addition to George and Jane, Jack and Annette, Hal and Frank, and Sam and Sally, were John Wainwright, the president of Empire Coal, and his chief engineer, Pete Fitzgerald, and General Weberly.

George smiled as if he might have something up his sleeve. He pulled the easels into the room. They still contained the topographic map of the area and the detail map of the mines tunnels and vents. Initially, everyone was taken aback by the enormity and complexity of the labyrinths that crisscrossed below the hills. A virtual underground city was displayed. Vacated for fifty years, no one could even guess what the conditions were inside. What had caved in, and what remained intact, was all speculation. It could well be a deathtrap of monstrous proportions.

The General began the discussion.

"Judas Priest! No wonder that son-of-a-bitch has been so damned hard to kill!!"

Pete Fitzgerald then joined George by the easels and outlined where the explosives might be placed to accomplish the most massive tunnel collapses. It was decided that some seventy different charges would need to be set. George marked each charge placement with a red circle.

The general would supply night vision equipment. The governor had authorized the use of helicopters and sharpshooters. If necessary, the military would construct barred steel covers for all remaining entrances. There were two options: seal the cat in, or seal the cat out. Either worked fine.

The scope of the project was huge! The National Guard would defray much of the cost. The miners had volunteered their time and the coal company had donated the use of their experts to assist.

George, Brownie, and half of the newly reconstructed pack of eighteen, would take position at the base of the crevasse and begin to track the area immediately after the explosion. Jack would take Blackie and the other half of the pack and comb the upper hills area by the crevasse and the ten or so miles to the most recently discovered cave. The helicopters would be on cat surveillance from above."

Jack expressed some reservations about so much firepower in the area, and hoped aloud that everyone toting a gun would exercise greatest caution.

The mine company would donate the explosives. The volunteer miners and the National Guard would begin training in the morning. It would involve two days of working together under the instruction of the military and the mine engineer. They would learn about the use of the explosives, the night vision equipment, and the silencer-equipped pistols. The General dubbed the mission, "Operation Lion." It would be carried out with military precision. The plans had been laid. The personnel had been trained and the equipment had been requisitioned. The operation was set to begin early morning three days hence.

Sam wheeled his way to the Easels and spoke:

"Now that the battle plan has been set, it is time for us to unveil the surprise."

He grinned. Jack and Annette saw that everyone else was grinning, too. A van pulled into the driveway. Caterers emerged with the biggest cake Jack had ever seen. Other cars pulled in and the group that called themselves, "the loved ones of the victims of the cat," arrived. Rebecca was there with a camera crew. Sam announced it was a surprise party to celebrate the engagement of Jack Morgan and Annette Sanderson. Jack knew he had been had. Annette was delighted and couldn't contain her grin. Film was taken and the newspaper prepared a human-interest story. Rebecca would announce it on the nightly news.

Of the hunters, Jack had been the quiet one who had, thus far, slipped under the radar screen of the press. Everyone knew about Sam and George but Jack was the silent type. He had managed to remain anonymous—until then. He was stunned! Embarrassed, he just thanked everyone from the bottom of his heart. Annette playfully seconded the motion.

On their way home, Jack asked, "I wonder why they did all of that?" He was genuinely puzzled.

Annette answered, "You were the iron man of the hunt. You were the one who never left his post, so that others could. This was their thank you."

Jack was still bewildered. "I really don't understand but it was nice of them, I guess. I get embarrassed easy. I don't like the limelight."

Annette hugged him. "I always did like the strong, silent type."

He hugged her back. "Why don't we end all of this folderol and just find a preacher tonight and be done with it?"

Annette gave him a look.

"You would deny the bride her big day?"

"Never!" Jack said. "It was just a thought."

They held hands as they walked to the house together. It was good not to be alone, Jack thought to himself. It was going to be a far different life than he had known in years.

The evening of the fourth day after the hunt had been

temporarily suspended, found the cat still feeling weak, though restless. He was uneasy staying there where the men knew he was. He set an easy pace southwest by night covering a paltry thirty miles dusk to dawn. He found a yearling buck for breakfast. The kill had been made within easy dragging distance from the den he had selected for the day. The cat ate and rested. With darkness, it moved another thirty miles south and west. He dined on groundhog.

He was headed to the southwest portion of its range and planned to stay away from men and controversy for quite a while. Only when it was completely healed would it take on another man. No one would hear or see it for an entire month.

Just as the men finally figured it was dead, would they start to die again. Inside its den, the cat yawned, stretched, and lay down to sleep. He was healing fast and growing stronger as he hid in the dark places by day and prowled for lesser prey by night.

It had been a tactical retreat, not surrender.

## CHAPTER SIXTEEN
## The Incursion

Back at the labyrinth, Man was about to invade and retake the underground city he had created so many years before. The seventy some charges would be placed where the engineers estimated the greatest tunnel collapsing would be effected. The atmosphere was like a preparation for a full fledged invasion of enemy territory. The sanctuary for the cat would be as close to closed as the men could manage.

George and Jack were once again back at work, readying the 'green' dogs to fit into the pack. All was going smoothly, as dog taught dog, faster than man ever could have. The day before the incursion was to take place they took the pack into the area and searched for the cat's scent. They discovered the cat's lair at the base of the crevasse.

There was cause for worry because there was clearly no fresh scent. The dogs wandered aimlessly.

George was particularly worried.

"I think that the son-of-a-bitch has moved southwest."

He openly wondered if it wouldn't be smart to run the cat to the north east and then blow up the mines. That didn't seem possible since this operation was on a military time schedule tied with the maneuvers of the National Guard. It was no longer a matter of the hunters convenience. The incursion would come in its own time and way. They just hoped that enough of the tunnels could be collapsed, and enough entrances sealed, so that the sanctuary would effectively be closed to the cat when it returned.

George figured it was always possible that the cat was

staying inside the tunnels and not venturing outside. Both men suspected that the cat was moving to a quieter area of its range in order to heal and to be relieved of the pressure of the hunt. If that were the case it was going to be very hard to find.

The pack spent the day combing and re-combing the rocky area from the first cave to the crevasse and down to the base of the crevasse. The dogs looked down right despondent as they went through the motions of tracking a cat that simply wasn't there.

As the sun began to set, the two men turned their mules down the trail toward the field where the cage was still sitting from the week before. That night the helicopter came to pick up the mules and to supply the men with provisions for the evening. Oddly, perhaps, it felt good to be on the trail of the cat again, even though the trail was cold. There would be no urgency for an early start in the morning. They were to hold their positions until the miners and the soldiers had set all their charges and the detonations had begun. The hills would be shaken to their core. They had been instructed to set up about a mile from the blast area and to just watch the fireworks. Once it ceased they were to re-scout the blast area for any sign of the cat. It was for sure any scent would be fresh. They were to be in place at high noon. Somehow that seemed most appropriate.

At 0600 hours the normally peaceful hills were treated to the sound of a full fledged invasion by helicopters of every size shape and description. Demolition teams were dropped at twenty-five locations at the base of the crevasse, the top of the hill, and at several points in between. Miners and their military escorts began to enter the mine at thirty designated locations. They were to proceed to the demolition points outlined on their mission maps, and to call in if there were tunnel collapses that prevented them from reaching their x-points.

The operation ran like clockwork. The general was personally conducting the operation, viewing it from his command chopper. Slowly, but efficiently, the various demolition teams moved inside the hill. The cat copters, with their sharp shooters, surveyed the area from above. A sighting would trigger a mass retaliation.

As the teams of miners and soldiers began to work their ways through the old tunnels, quiet, became the order of the day. One misstep could bring the tunnel tumbling down on them. They inched their way into the dank, forbidding, darkness. Some walked. Some crawled. Some moved on their bellies. George and Jack were in place early—at daylight—just to watch the massive operation. It truly was something to behold. They said a silent prayer for those inside the mine. As well planned as it was, anything could go wrong at any time.

Inside the mine, Jacob Reynolds and private first class Wallace Franz crawled along side by side. One carried plastic explosives and the other a pistol, silencer in place. They wore hard hats with lights and had night vision gear. They searched the shadows for any movement. They had three designated points at which they were to place explosives and detonators, which could be activated from outside after they were safely back outside. They had trained together and they were confident in each other's abilities.

One was there to set the charges and the other was there as an extra set of hands and as a personal bodyguard. They directed their lights along the time-weakened timbers above them. At one point their methane detectors went off. They broke out and donned gas masks.

The two moved on and found their first X- point. It was designated for plastic explosive to be placed at a point where two massive timbers met. Well practiced hands teased the putty-like plastic into place. The detonators were inserted and connected to the electronic receivers. That finished, they crawled on.

A timber gave way overhead and what had been tunnel became their grave. The earth shuddered, the ageing timber groaned and creaked, and the earth above met the earth below. The brave men were gone.

Dust and gas belched out of a hole in the rocks, and filled the air. The plume of thick, swirling, dust was the only visible sign to the outside world that two good men, had died, below.

There was nothing that could be done. Later, the roll

would be taken and the missing would be identified.

While the cat had directly killed nine, two more were as surely dead because of him as if he had done it himself. Operation Lion would not be casualty free.

By twelve noon, all of the others were out safely at their designated re-assembly points. The roll call was taken. Two identifications were made. They asked for volunteers for a rescue operation. Everyone volunteered. Only seven would be sent. They snaked along the aging caverns and tunnels, where Private Franz and miner Reynolds had crawled and walked before them. It took them an hour to get to the spot. They saw Private Franz's boots and they saw the magnitude of the collapse. They tried to dig the private out of the debris, when more started to fall. He was dead, no doubt about that, and so was his companion.

They radioed the news to the others. Their assessment was that any attempt to extract the bodies would result in more deaths. Reluctantly, the rescue team backed out of the mine as ordered. It was not easy to leave two of their own in the mine, but there was no real choice.

When the team emerged from the tunnel they were ordered to vacate the immediate area. The demolition commenced close to schedule. The ground shook. Rocks tumbled from the cliffs. Smoke and gas belched out of the top of the hill. Flames followed. A pall of black smoke and dust covered the area for miles. Fire and smoke belched out of dozens of cave entrances.

The blast marked the end of Phase One of the operation. It was time for man and dog to search the area to see if the cat had been driven out. Neither George nor Jack really believed the cat was still there. Still, they would comb the area thoroughly.

They split into two groups as they began to move towards the blast sight. George worked his way down to the base of the crevasse, while Jack began at the first cave and worked towards the top of the hill. Overhead, the helicopters and their sharpshooters patrolled the skies searching for a black form running the trails or creeping through the underbrush.

The men and dogs combed the area. In the end, there was not a trace of the big cat.

When George and Jack found out about the deaths of two good men, they were distressed beyond belief. The media was again saddened to have to report more cat related deaths. Again, the town made ready for more funerals.

It was soon dark. It was agreed that at the end of the day the helicopter would pick up the cage, the mules, the dogs, and the men, because either the cat was dead, trapped in the mines, or had earlier moved on..

Below ground, much of the mine remained as it had been, still providing many hiding places for a cat who knew the tunnels. In time, he would discover other entrances and tunnels. He would be inconvenienced for a while, but he would find his way. Many would think him dead while he recovered his strength.

Most of them wanted to believe that the threat was now over. They would soon grow careless again. Two men knew better. For now, both sides were resting from yesterday's battles, while both prepared for its renewal.

One week after the incursion, the men returned for another brief time, sealing up the obvious entrances that remained. When they left, peace returned to the wilderness. They erected a monument to the two men left behind, lest men forget.

One week later a much stronger cat returned to his old haunts and began to explore the area both above and below ground. He marked new den sites and discovered where he could and could not go. He then moved southwest again and was soon back to full strength. He felt the growing need to kill and to eat men.

At the funerals the dead men were lionized as the town paid tribute to its fallen defenders. The wives, sisters, and daughters wept, while the brothers and sons tried to maintain an outward show strength. The dead were still dead, and the living knew that one day, for all their human arrogance, they would join them in whatever place the dead go. For now, they had a harder task: to live as they should, and not just as they would.

It had come down to only Jack, George, and eighteen dogs patrolling the area looking for sign of the cat. They found none. Soon they would start where they had started begun the first hunt. They would start at the southwest most part of the big cat's range. They would comb the area, working ever north and east until dog smelled cat. The men and the dogs would try to close the distance and to bring it to tree or at bay, on top of a high hill, or in a cave. They rested while they could. Once they began again, there would be little rest until the cat was dead.

In the town and at the military base, the mood was up beat. They believed the threat had been ended. Only the General worried. He talked to the men who knew the most about this particular cat. They believed that it had moved out of the area of the operation. The General would provide the cage and the logistical support for one more combing of the area from southwest to northwest. Then, if sign was absent, all would proclaim victory.

On his couch, Sam and his cast struggled to accommodate each other as he watched the evening news, witnessing the blast second hand, on the small screen. It was only then that he learned the details surrounding the loss of the men. His wife held his hand as they watched and said nothing. He thought back about how long and how hard the battle against the cat had been, and, that in all likelihood it was not over, even yet. He hated the fact that he had been side lined, even as he was grateful just to be alive. His gut became a caldron of mixed emotions, as he watched the real life television drama unfold. In his heart he felt certain that the cat lived. He knew that this was just a lull in the battle that had claimed and had injured so many men and animals. All Sam could do for the time being was to sit on his couch and be a spectator. That galled him to his core.

His phone rang. It was John Weston. He wanted to see him in the morning to get a deposition from him regarding his knowledge about events that had transpired when the college kids had 'invaded' his property. Weston wanted to make sure that April Gillespie paid the price for betraying a public trust with deceit, malice, and corruption. The example needed to be made, so that others who would entertain such evil motives, might be dissuaded. He would meet with Weston at his office the next morning.

When he hung up the phone, he felt some better. While he was physically out of commission, he had been the catalyst that had brought all of this together. He had assembled the team and now, like a coach on the sidelines, all he could do was watch, and hope that his game plan was up to the competition.

George labored over another battle plan for the hunt he knew would eventually be necessary. He studied the maps of the cat's massive range. Janie wanted him to take a break. She had also set up an appointment for him at a well-respected cardiac clinic in the city to the north. They told her that surgery would most likely be necessary. George had gotten the exam, but ruled out the surgery until the hunt was concluded. He knew that Jack was going to need him.

Jack was enjoying the company of the woman who would become his wife. The hunt, if and when it came, was not immediate. In the meantime, love was conquering all.

Fifty yards from Jack's home the catamount stalked. A month had passed. The injuries were healed. He was on the prowl again. He climbed to the top of a forested, rocky, knoll across the gravel road from Jack's house. He leered down upon the spot where lived the man and dogs he both hated and feared most. The man soon called the dogs in for the night. The cat made his way back into the woods. One night, he thought, the man would leave the dogs outside. That would leave Jack and his woman alone inside. That night, when it came, the cat would break through a window and have his revenge.

## CHAPTER SEVENTEEN
## The Elopement

Jack and Annette's relationship was moving fast. She put her house up for sale and moved in with him. They wanted to move up the wedding so people would quit talking. The sharp-tongued gossip was that her husband's body wasn't even cold before she was involved again. That incensed her. She had been as loyal a wife as ever had been. She could do nothing to bring him back. She wanted to live again, to be happy again, and most of all to love and to be loved again. Jack suggested that instead of a big wedding and a lot of folderol that a quiet ceremony with just a few friends and relatives was all they needed.

"We are not eighteen year old kids just starting out. We know the ropes. If you want a big wedding it is okay with me, but for myself, a small quiet one where we give our vows to each other and to God is quite sufficient. It will shut up the biddies too."

Annette didn't need persuasion. She would have thought less of him if he were the type to leave his post in the middle of trouble. So she went him one better. Instead of a small wedding, she suggested that they just go down to the Baptist church and get the knot tied. She didn't need all the attention, and especially not all of the gossip that seemed to go with her newfound celebrity.

"Let's just get it done."

So, to the surprise of nearly everyone, they called George, Sam, Sheriff Bonner, and Deputy Anderson and asked them to come to the church on Friday night. Jack also called

Earl Johnson. Earl made a suggestion. He felt that since John Weston had picked up the charges on the trespass case, and, had been such a stalwart in protecting their rights that he should be invited as well.

Hal also had a suggestion.

"Invite Judge Smith and his bailiff. They ought to have a role in making all of this legal as well as moral. They would feel very left out."

Annette wanted to invite her parents and her brother and his wife. Before they knew it, a simple elopement had turned into a wedding anyway. Jack held his hands up in mock defeat.

"Okay then, let's do it right. I will have Sam and George as co-best men so that neither one of them will feel second best." He looked at Annette, "That's legal. Isn't it?"

"Perfectly," she grinned.

Earl Johnson would also be a best man.

"So that makes three. Now, who do you want as the maid of honor and the bridesmaids. Annette had no hesitation.

"I want Janie Tanner, Sally Anderson, and Shirley Bonner."

Jack smiled. "I can't fault you on any of those choices."

Then she asked, "Would you mind if I had my brothers little girl, Helen, as the flower girl?"

"Of course not," Jack grinned.

It was finally sinking in. He *was* getting married again.

"I don't know a young boy who would make a good ring-bearer," she said her brow furrowed.

The name, Marc Salem, popped out of Jack's mouth.

"Great choice!" Annette agreed, as she thought about the boy who'd lost his little sister, and to whom Jack had become a larger than life hero. It was the perfect choice.

Jack scratched his head. This was starting to get complicated.

"Why don't you leave the arrangements to me?" Annette suggested. "I have been a bride and I have been through it before. I promise that I won't break us financially."

She could almost hear the sigh of relief going through

her husband-to-be's mind.

"I would consider that a great kindness," he said.

Jack made the calls to George, Sam and Earl, and Annette called Sally, Janie, and Shirley. They agreed immediately.

That taken care of, they took a walk down the country lane that ran in front of Jack's house. The mission was to see a young man about carrying a ring. As had become his habit, Jack carried his forty-five in a holster.

Jack knocked. Victoria opened the door and welcomed them. Edgar was at work and Marc was upstairs doing his homework. Jack told her of their plans and asked permission to talk with Marc about being the ring-bearer. Victoria was moved and thrilled by the gesture. She called to her son and he came bounding down the stairs.

"Hi Mr. Jack," the boy exclaimed, clearly excited to see him.

"How you doin' Mark?" Jack said.

He shook the little boy's hand. Victoria motioned them to the dining room table. She put on a pot of coffee and then rejoined the others.

Marc," Jack began. "I am in trouble and I need your help."

Marc became serious.

"Sure. What can I do?" the little boy answered in puzzlement.

"Well, Annette and I want to get married but we have a problem."

"What is it?"

Jack kept a perfectly straight face.

"I need a good man I can trust to guard a very precious ring while everyone is gathered for the wedding—to make sure it doesn't get lost or stolen, you see. Then, he'll need to have it ready to hand over when the preacher tells me to put it on Annette's finger."

Annette continued.

"And I need someone to hold onto the ring that Jack will wear."

"We need someone we can trust and count on to keep them safe." Jack said," And I got to thinking that my friend, Marc, would be just the man for the job. Would you be willing to do that?"

"WOULD I!" Marc shouted with glee. He then became all quite serious.

"And I promise you that no bad guy will get his hands on those rings. I'll make sure of that!"

The boy meant every word.

"I knew that I could count on you Marc," Jack said seriously. "Thank you very much."

Marc was clearly on cloud nine.

Before the talking was finished, Jack had agreed to have Marc and his father over in the morning for some shooting practice. Then he said that he and his wife-to-be had to go so they could get started on the arrangements and asked everyone to please keep the secret of the wedding, as they still had hopes of pulling it off quickly and quietly.

They had planned for a quiet little wedding but the fates and their friends would move things in another direction. George called Sam, Hal, Earl, and Frank and asked them to sneak over to his place—*pronto*. He had an idea and he needed their help and advice.

Soon, the five old friends gathered around George's table to plot a different sort of battle plan than they had been used to recently. Janie served up the drinks as the conspirators began to conspire.

"We got a problem here," the old man began. "Jack is a shy one."

"Shy?"

Sam begged to differ.

"I've seen that man look that killer cat right in the eye and not even blink!"

"I don't mean shy in that way."

George began again.

"I mean shy as in shooting the cat and not being there when the pictures were being taken. He would just leave the area as if he had nothing to do with it. He never takes credit for himself. He would rather leave that for others and just go home."

"You are right about that," Earl piped in.

The others nodded their heads. George went on.

"The press converged on Sam and me, but they didn't notice Jack. It was not an accident. Jack sits in the background, does most of the hard work, takes more risks than any of us, and cuts out before it's time to take his bow."

Frank agreed.

"Yup, he is the strong, silent type. I hadn't really thought about that, but you're right. He doesn't like the spotlight. But now he is getting married he will try to deprive the citizenry of this county of ours the chance to properly celebrate the occasion."

"And, we simply cannot allow that." Sam piped in. "He was the first man to go after the cat while I took the bows and got appointed to run the hunt."

George nodded.

"And the press plays me up for being in my seventies, and still going after that while ignoring him. He thinks that he can just smile to himself away from the press, Scott free! Now, when he is marrying one of the prettiest and finest women in the county, do you think we're gonna let him just slip away, unnoticed, again?"

"Nope. Not in this life!" Hal piped in.

"Annette is just as bad in that way as he is." Earl reminded the others.

"Jack's been that way ever since he was a boy. When he lost Sue he never said a word about how bad he felt. It took a long time for him to find her equal and now he has. Do you think his friends should let him simply ride off into the sunset without taking a bow? No Siree!"

"I'm glad you all see it my way," the old man grinned. "So far he has invited all of us and the wives of those of us who have wives"—he winked at Janie. He has invited the Salem boy to be the ring-bearer. So his wedding party is set. But their guest list is woefully inadequate!"

"Who have they invited?" Frank asked.

Janie chuckled. "Annette is handling that and only I am privy to that list. I offered to help her with the invitations."

She produced a piece of paper and read off all the names. George grinned and clicked his tongue.

"You mean to tell me they haven't invited all the people who have lost loved ones to the cat?" He clicked his tongue again. "Or the trappers, or the General, who would feel terribly slighted, or the mayor..."

Hal chimed in, "Or all of the members of the force who were at her husbands funeral..."

"These are terrible oversights that simply *must* be corrected!"

"And what are friends for?" Frank chimed in, grinning an impish grin.

Then Hal spoke. "He has a limited budget. He could never afford a hall that could accommodate so many guests." Then he grinned. "But what if he didn't have to pay for a hall at all? What if the town simply roped off the square and vendors set up tables like they did when Sam was appointed? And, what if just for one night, the city council allowed alcohol to be consumed in that area, and a public dance was proclaimed."

"What if it rains?" George said, bringing the gathering back to the practical side of things.

"God simply would not allow such a thing!" Sam announced.

"But if the devil were so bold as to try to dampen the party, then wires could be strung and tarps laid across them, building to building. The rolls of plastic would not be that difficult to obtain for such a good cause.

The more the conspirators talked, the wilder and more bizarre, their ideas became. Soon the list included the miners and military personal that had helped at the mine.

It was June, and a wedding to celebrate their local heroes was just what the whole town needed. It would perk up the place where sadness had dwelled for so long! The icing on the cake involved Rebecca Monk, who promised her silence until the "reception" began, at which time "The Press" would be well represented, to chronicle "The event of the spring."

If Jack and Annette had been aware of what the town had in store for them, they would have run for cover more quickly than that cat ever had.

By Friday the whole town was buzzing and it seemed like everyone in the county had chipped in a buck or two to cover the expenses. Many had chipped in more than that. How it was that Jack and Annette were kept in the dark about it all, was one of the more major miracles. Even Blackie and Brownie were the souls of discretion.

Sam was not about to go to a wedding and reception with a cast all the way up to his hip. His doctor agreed. They cut off the huge cast and fit him up with a mid-thigh, walking cast. He still could not bend his badly injured knee, but he could get around far more easily. His morale soared.

Soon, Friday was upon them. The cat had not been seen or heard from in a month. The men and the dogs had not picked up its scent anywhere. Even George was beginning to wonder if the blast might not have gotten him. The atmosphere was light and festive. It was time for a good party.

Janie had persuaded Annette that the wedding should come early in the day rather than late, so that she and her new husband would be able to have a quiet afternoon and evening together. How she ever sold that bill of goods with a straight face, was more than remarkable.

So, early Friday morning the bride and the groom got ready for their intimate little wedding. It would amount to a quick trip to the church and out. The small group of close friends and relatives gathered at the church. Jack took note of the over-sized grins but wrote it off the as their just being happy for them. He thought no more of it.

The organist began to play and the ceremony was under way. The groomsmen stood and the bridesmaids, all on cue, came down the aisle. *Here Comes the Bride*, boomed from the organ. Jack watched Annette as she was escorted toward him by her father. She was a sight to behold. In his minds eye, he saw Sue's face. She was smiling and nodding, "Yes." Her blessing gave him great peace.

Soon the bride and groom were standing side by side,

as the Minister began to say the words. A very serious Marc Salem made sure that the rings were handed to the best man and the maid of honor so Mr. Jack and Annette would get them, safe and sound, just as promised. He had done his job and sighed a sigh of both relief and pride. It was an honor he would never forget.

The minister asked Jack and Annette if they would take each other to have and to hold, from this day forward, and to the surprise of no one, both said "I will" and "I do." In the end, the minister told Jack that he could kiss his bride, and he did, with a song in his heart.

Up to that point everything was going according to the bride and groom's script. All of that was about to go out the window, as the bride and the groom moved quickly down the aisle toward the door, dodging rice, and waving to well-wishers.

When Jack threw open the door, they came to an immediate stop. Standing there was a double line of soldiers in full dress uniforms. In back of them were two lines of uniformed policemen, with six cruisers, strategically placed, lights flashing. Behind them came the judge and the prosecutor.

Sheriff Bonner walked up to the couple with his Ticket book.

"You two are hereby cited *for failure to invite!*

"Whaat?" Jack managed, his face adrift in puzzlement.

"That's right," the sheriff repeated. "Failure to *invite*!!"

"Did you think that you would be allowed to get married without inviting all of the men who helped you in your fight to get that cat?!"

It had been the General whose face was set in a practiced military scowl.

"Ugh, well," Jack managed still stunned.

Before he could trip over another word the Sheriff continued.

"And without inviting all of the police forces that helped you?"

The union boss called out from the parking lot.

"And all of the miners!"

Then Dr. Haskins shouted out, "And the trappers."

"And the mine operators!" mine president, John Wainwright, added.

The Sheriff and the General called for the judge! The prosecutor recounted all of the charges and Jane Lefforts, who the Anderson's had invited down for the occasion, proclaimed that the "Kangaroo Court was now in session!"

Judge C. Townsley Smith, promptly pronounced the sentence: "Ahh say; you two ahh to proceed downtown foah immediate incarceration for all of the rest of youah days. You two ahh hereby; ah say, hereby, sentenced to life—together!! Ah, General, will you and the Sheriff escort the prisonahs downtown."

"With pleasure!"

The General barked out a command and the lines of soldiers and the policemen parted, revealing a shiny black limousine complete with military driver. A uniformed highway patrolman opened the back door of the limo and ordered the prisoners to get in.

Only then did Jack and Annette begin to understand what was going on. As directed, they entered the beautiful vehicle. Neither of them was the limousine type but once in a lifetime wouldn't be all that bad.

The throng escorted them to the square, waving and shouting the whole way.

Jack gave Annette an accusing look, but from the shock he saw on her face he knew immediately that she was not the perpetrator. He began putting things together and knew that the old man and his friends had to be behind this.

George *was* one the culprits all right, as were Sam and the others, but what the couple would witness that afternoon and evening, no one man could have orchestrated. This was a town, a county, and a whole lot of just plain people pouring out their love. They were celebrating a wedding, their friends, and themselves. The good poured out of everyone and no one who was present would ever forget. Such an event could not have been planned in the true sense of the word. The idea just kind of caught fire. It was as close to spontaneous combustion of the best kind that ever could occur.

As the limousine arrived at the town square, a huge banner was unfurled. It read: CONGRATULATIONS JACK AND ANNETTE. The two of them looked into each others eyes in wonder. Jack fought back a tear. Annette cried openly with joy. The "prisoners" emerged from the limo into a town square that was decked out in the fashion of a great banquet hall. They were escorted to a table.

Then the mayor and the council took to the podium. They mayor read his proclamation which stated that the town wished to congratulate the wedding of two of its most honored citizens, and that further, since the Fourth of July was only five days away, the city was going to celebrate early.

The military band struck up *Stars and Stripes Forever*, and everyone enjoyed the food and drink. After the eating, dancing began. Dozens danced with the bride and a roaring good time was had by all.

In the end, they asked Jack and Annette to say a few words.

"Well," Jack began, "You all got me good."

Light laughter rippled throughout the crowd.

"Annette and I will always be in your debt. May God bless you all—thank you."

The streets erupted in cheers and then the crowd demanded that the bride say something. Annette took the microphone.

"What can I say? It is you who pulled all of this off. We love you all..."

She broke into tears of joy and managed a final... "Thank you all."

During the rest of the evening the town treated itself to the best in food, drink, and dancing music. The fireworks exploded into its early July beauty and the town celebrated itself, its freedom, and those who were assigned to protect its citizens.

When it was time to go, the limousine took the couple home. They waved and said their goodbyes. The well wishers gave them their privacy. Jack understood that he and Annette were just the excuse needed by the town to celebrate the good in itself. This town had an awful lot of good and that was well worth celebrating, whatever the excuse.

That night, two good people thanked God for their many blessings and their town for its big, wonderful, heart.

## CHAPTER EIGHTEEN
## The Convictions

The catamount moved to the northeastern part of its massive range. It discovered that its caves and dens had been grated over with metal bars. The men had had done their best to destroy the cat's sanctuary. The cat searched for alternative entrances to the mines and the caves. At the top of the rocks on the hill on the other side of the crevasse was a cave that had gone undetected. It had three entrances, and inside, it led down to where the men had dug.

The men had done great damage to the mines on the first side of the crevasse. Two thirds of the mineshafts had been destroyed, but fully one third of the tunnels were as they had been before.

The cat spent days exploring what was left of his sanctuary. The barring of entrances was as much a mixed blessing for the cat as it was for the men. Although it would keep the cat in, it would also keep the men and their dogs out. Once inside, the cat had found another way to the bottom of the crevasse so it could still escape. The cat discovered a second old mine, which was completely unharmed by the man's onslaught. It was on the other side of t he crevasse. The men and the dogs would not be able to trap him there. The cat had found a secure hideout. His strength had returned. The swagger had returned to his gait. He had stayed on the far side of the crevasse for three weeks. It had been over a month and a half since he had heard the dogs and the helicopters, or seen the men and the mules.

The men half-believed that he was dead. The last effort

to locate him in the southern part of his range had left dogs and horses sore of foot and without any trace of his scent. Even George wondered if he might be dead. In their hearts, both Jack and George felt that he was out there somewhere, waiting to pick the time and the place to kill again.

As the cat prowled, he moved back south. He was hungry but not for just any prey. He lusted for the taste of the forbidden. He lusted for victory over his enemies. He worked his way forty miles southwest of the crevasse. He climbed to the top of the familiar rocky ledge that overlooked the county lane, and gazed through green eyes at the den of his most hated enemy. The dogs were inside, as was the man and his new woman. The cat stared at the house. His time would attack, and soon. He worked his way down the bank and crossed over the lane into the woods behind the house.

Soon he arrived at the creek that led to Spring Lake. He denned by the lake, overlooking the place where he had killed Roscoe Tanner, Deputy Sanderson, and Chopper.

The sun was not up yet, but the grey of dawn was gradually replacing the black of night. He heard talking. The cat watched the shoreline from his cave. Two boys were walking side by side. One wore cut-offs, the other jeans rolled up to his knees. Both were barefoot and carried cane poles. The taller boy began casting on one side of the trees and the other moved some thirty yards down the bank. The brush was thick. They could hear but not see each other. The cat crawled down the bank in deep cover towards the farthest boy. Soon he was behind him—just fifteen feet away. With one leap he was on him. The boy was completely helpless. He managed one scream. The other boy heard the commotion and went to investigate. What he saw filled him with terror. The panther was tearing flesh away from his friend's midsection. In terror, he screamed and began to run. He was not fast enough. Twenty-five yards later he felt something huge hit him from behind. He couldn't breathe and his arms and legs wouldn't respond. He was screaming inside but no noise was coming out. Then all went black.

The cat dragged the dead boy's body to the cave entrance

and then returned to the first. He gorged on young human flesh. Then he dragged what was left of it to his den. All day long he alternately ate and slept. That night he ate again. He remained there for two days evading the parents and neighbors who combed the area for the missing boys.

That same evening, John Weston was hard at work. The grand jury had returned all of the indictments he had sought. The trial of the *Friends of the Animals* would begin in the morning. He was confident, but never cocky. He reviewed the evidence and all of the testimony that he had. It was voluminous. He looked for any flaw he might have overlooked—any loophole that Ms. Longworth might be able to exploit. Then he smiled a thoughtful smile. To the best that he could reckon, his case was airtight. He turned off the light in his study and went to bed feeling confident about the days to come.

Across town, Ms. Longworth was far less confident. She knew that she was overmatched by the evidence, and what was worse, she knew that her opponent was going to be sure to get the maximum mileage from it. Her task in this case was much different than in the trial of the college students. Here, felonies had been committed. So, rather than to try to sell the jury that the felonies were not serious, she was on the hunt for any legal technicality she could use to get the case thrown out. She would protest the use of the R.I.C.O. statute by claiming it had been passed in order to stop organized crime bosses and therefore had no application in that case.

Weston would claim that since the statute had been used by her and others to punish, fine, and jail, pro-life advocates, for damages done to abortion facilities, that it certainly applied here because hunting is a legal activity, regardless of how immoral, the *Friends of the Animals* perceived it to be. The charges were, therefore, just as viable in that case.

There were other criminal charges. It had come out that April Gillespie was a party to the group's activities, even while she maintained her position with the state Department Of Wildlife. Furthermore, she had been instrumental in acquiring the services of the radical environmentalist with the exotic pet license. It had been he who had arranged to set several dozen cougars free in the area. Not all of the *Friends of the Animals* members had been privy to this. A radical sub-group had undertaken that without the knowledge of the others. The Salem's had not known about it.

April Gillespie and Robert Sanford were up on other charges as well. They had been charged with impeding a law enforcement officer (Sam Macafee), from executing his duty to enforce the game laws, and by falsifying material evidence that could have been used to warn the people of a clear and present danger to themselves, their children, and their livestock. They were also charged with the unlawful firing of an officer of the law. There was also misuse of state funds and corruption in office charges.

Sam, if he had wished, could have sued them for damages done, but he would not pursue that since his honor had been restored and he didn't want money gained in that way. He was content to let the criminal charges against his antagonists suffice.

There were also charges of endangering the public safety stemming from the release of the cougars into an area populated by people. The catamount's killings had provided ample evidence. One key piece of evidence was missing though. Ray Stokes Ellis, the man who the group had hired to obtain and to release the cats into the wilds, turned state's evidence in order to get a lighter sentence, (he would get five to ten years rather than twenty to life, by the plea bargain), testified that while he *had* released at least twenty five cats into the wild, he *had not released* a huge black phase mountain lion. He produced documentation about the cats he had obtained and released. He pointed out that black mountain lions were rare and had never been captured in North America. He swore that if he *had* obtained one of those its worth would have brought huge sums of money from zoos and collectors. On this point, he was right, and therefore the damages and the deaths attributed to that one cat were not of his, or the group's doing.

However, Weston pointed out that Gillespie, as a member

of the *Friends of the Animals*, had persuaded the Salem's not to go public with the fact that the mountain lion had killed their sheep. That enabled the "bob cat" lie to go unchallenged, and as Victoria tearfully testified on the stand, allowed the cat to roam without pursuit, "until one day it killed our little girl, Teresa." Victoria also testified as to how she and the others had set the college kids onto the lands of Jack Morgan and Earl Johnson where they had subsequently been arrested. They had promised the kids that their legal fees would be paid and had persuaded them that they would be changing the country for the better. Judge Smith had allowed that she and her family had suffered enough for their mistakes. Weston nodded his agreement. He granted them immunity from prosecution without their agreement to testify. That was the curveball that hit Ms. Longworth right between the eyes. She had been prepared to accuse the prosecutor with using the grief of the Salem's to get them to testify.

The obstruction of justice cases against April Gillespie and Robert Sanford were so airtight that a plea bargain had been obtained –a guilty plea and five years in prison.

The national media, so evident in the first trial, was conspicuous by its absence. They knew the position they were defending was in for a big loss, and they didn't want to advertise that fact to the American people.

If the national press was largely absent, the local paper and television station, led by Rebecca Monk, were everywhere. They had learned their lesson. From now on the local policy would be, "The truth, the whole truth, and nothing but the truth, given to a people with an absolute right to know." That phrase was printed on page one of every paper from that day forward. The television station also adopted a slogan: "We are pleased to tell the whole truth, regardless of who it pleases, or displeases." The state media picked up the story as well, as did talk radio. One commentator gleefully trumpeted the convictions as a sign of a nation rousing from its long national sleep.

April Gillespie and Robert Sanford would be convicted on all charges. In addition, evidence tampering charges also resulted in convictions of several of their associates. Dr. Haskins' testimony on the tame nature of the female cougar that had fallen into his trap was corroborated by the zoo keeping professionals who had taken charge of the cat. It was that testimony that resulted in Ray Stokes Ellis taking a plea bargain and fingering those who had paid him. In the end, the *Friends of the Animals* had twenty of its members convicted under the state R.I.C.O. charge.

All that remained unanswered was where the killer cat came from. They asked George to testify. John Weston had been of the belief that it must have been transplanted with the others, which would open the group up for lawsuits from all of the relatives who had lost loved ones to the cat. Sheila Longworth got some help there from a most unexpected source. George was given wide range to express his knowledge of the big cats and he related the stories that came from his grandparents about a black phase cat with green eyes that the locals referred to as "The Devil's Own," and of a cat the ancient American Indians from the area had, centuries earlier, referred to as "The Evil One's Very Own." He surmised that as deer multiplied and the land went back to the wild from the coal mining and logging days, the natural predators had worked their way back into their old ranges.

"It was inevitable," he surmised. "The animal rights activists, or the environmentalists, or the hippies, or whatever you might choose to call them."

The court room burst out in laughter. The judge, although chuckling himself, gaveled the court to – "Be in order."

George began again: "They claim to be on the side of nature and of its animals, but they don't trust nature to restore itself. They think that man and government must do for nature and for animals what they cannot do for themselves. If they could, they would put wild creatures on the welfare rolls and people would complain that for being so poor, they enjoyed the most expensive of coats."

The courtroom, including the judge, roared in laughter. The judge allowed nature to take its course. Soon the court was back in order and George continued.

"People don't have the power over nature and it's animals that they think they have. That power is reserved for their Creator. Man is merely charged as a steward."

Ms. Longworth couldn't resist trashing George's, "God and the devil," view of the cats. She called Dr. Haskins to the stand. She began by asking for a "more scientific view of how it was that the cat got here," and asked him to refute the God and The Devil view of the cat's that turn man eater. Her point was that surely science, and not (God forbid) religion could explain the phenomena. Her motive was to paint the locals as naïve, religious, fanatics, even if she lost her cases.

Dr. Haskins began by saying that he had trapped big cats from around the world, and that he had always believed science had the answer— that the tribesmen who talked of a `devil cat' were spouting superstitious gibberish. "But then I set traps for this cat, as I had the others, and it didn't work. Somehow it just knew. It attacked the horses and the mules. Then it killed and ate my associate. It screamed its triumph into the night, and science could not predict its next move. Only one thing could have motivated such a beast!!"

"What could that be?" Ms. Longworth asked.

"The essence of the devil himself—evil incarnate!"

A hush fell over the courtroom. Ms. Longworth queried him again.

"You cannot, with all of your scientific training, really believe that can you?"

"Ms. Longworth, *you* have not gazed into its green and evil eyes. *You* have not seen it tear flesh from human bones or sensed its evil purpose. For the record I will state here and now that science has no answer for this evil one and that religion has. It scared the devil out of me. I am no longer an atheist for I have seen the devil himself at work. If the devil exists, Ms. Longworth, then so does God. I now believe fervently in him and pray that it is not too late for all of us."

He looked right into her eyes, and said, "Ms. Longworth, Tonight I am going to pray—for you!"

That evening the judge, the prosecutor, and the bailiff

enjoyed more select Kentucky Bourbon Whiskey and premium cigars. Their county was safer, more secure, and freer from tyranny, than it had been in a long time.

The nightly news on the local and statewide stations carried the stories of the convictions and the sentences that were likely to be issued the next week. Ms. Longworth had vowed to appeal. The good had triumphed and the bad were on their way to jail.

The next weekend saw the convicted animal rights activists picking up trash in their deer and rabbit costumes. The locals would drive by and razz them. After the first day of trash pick up, the youngsters had an idea. They decided, of their own volition, to wear signs around their necks that read, "We are sorry," and others that read, "We were wrong." Dr. Louden's constitution classes and the courtroom experiences had persuaded them to look at what they had done and to understand their own errors.

The next day, the locals saw the signs, and their whole attitude changed. Rather than honking, and shouting obscenities, they slowed down, smiled, and waved. The "animals" waved back. The judge heard the news and suspended their sentences.

In the morning, Jack's phone rang. Annette answered. It was Victoria Salem. She wanted to know if she and Jack wanted to come over that evening for supper. Annette wanted to be polite, but, fried vegetables weren't exactly at the top of her dream menu. Victoria hastened to add, "We're doing ribs, on our new barbecue grill." Annette accepted immediately. That evening the neighbors ate barbecued ribs and laughed and talked as neighbors will do. Marc was the honorary chef and he performed magnificently.

They were having a wonderful July evening together when the phone rang and Jack got the news about the two boys at Spring Lake. He said some quick goodbyes and headed for the truck. Jack and George were on the way to Sheriff Bonner's office. They called Sam and gave him the bad news. George and the newly reconstituted pack would be ready in the morning. The general had been notified and the cage would be ready for the hunters when and where needed.

When Jack got to the sheriff's office Hal gave him the official word. “We found the boys this morning. Our K-9 unit located what was left of the bodies. They died where Roscoe, Jeff Sandeson and Chopper died. We found the bones in the cave. Two more kids are dead. According to our dogs the cat has left the area."

Jack scuffed at the ground.

"We will start in the morning: Me, George, and the dogs. Sam is still two torn up. We really could use a third man so George, can stay with the pack mule."

"Did you say that you could use a third man?" Pete Donnigan asked.

"Sure could!" Jack answered.

"Sam asked if I would stand in for him, but only if you and George, agree."

"We agree all right."

Jack smiled and shook Pete's hand. We will meet at George's house at the crack of dawn.

"Could you use a fourth?" a voice asked out of nowhere. It was Dr. Haskins.

"The more the merrier." Jack answered. "Glad to have you aboard."

"I have a good graduate assistant to check the traps. I’ve never been on this kind of a hunt before but I want to help bring that cat down."

Hal and Frank looked at them and spoke as one, "If you need anything, you just call."

"We won't be a bit bashful." Jack smiled.

## CHAPER NINETEEN
## A Strike at the Heart

The men assembled at George's house at five o'clock in the morning. George had loaded the pack into a horse trailer hooked on the back of his pickup. The men ate a hearty breakfast that Janie had fixed. Sam came with the others to wish them Godspeed. Dr. Haskins arrived ready to go. The old man smiled. He had, in George's estimation, come a long, long way back. Pete Donnigan looked grim. He was a woodsman so he had an idea of what to expect—a long and a hard ordeal. George himself fought the excitement he felt inside. He also harbored some concern that he might not survive the experience. The others had learned a great deal but they all still needed his knowledge and wisdom.

Soon they were on their way. Once the hunt began, it was trail by day and cage by night until the cat was dead or the men could follow it no longer.

They were soon at Jim's restaurant and they began to unload the animals from the horse trailers. A military helicopter dropped off the mule and the horses. The men again thanked them for their tremendous support. Jim came out to meet them. He had been with sheriff Bonner, Jeff Sanderson, and Chopper, on the fateful night when they were looking for Roscoe Tanner.

They rode to the trees where the trail ended and the tree roots went into the water. The dogs were on the bay. They went directly to the lair and started to whine. They had smelled the scent of death.

"It's moving north and east again, just like last time,"

George allowed. "But this time the dogs got onto the scent earlier. That is our edge this time."

The end of the first day found them only five miles from where they had started. The cage was lowered by helicopter and the horses and mule were taken aboard. George began to cook and the men began to talk.

Two miles to the northeast, two green eyes stared at Jack's home. The catamount was on the rock across the county lane. The dogs and the man were gone. But there was light shining through the window. The woman was inside, alone. The cat descended from its high perch, moving without sound and easily jumping the back fence. He moved cautiously to the back door. With one mighty leap, he broke through the window glass and he was inside.

Annette had just lain down to sleep when she heard the sound of breaking glass. She grabbed her thirty-eight that Jack had insisted that she keep near at all times when he was gone. She had complied, although she thought it was an over reaction on his part. Now, she was glad he'd been so insistent. She flicked on a light. There, out of the darkness of the doorway, were the green eyes of the devil himself. The cat was huge. She squeezed off a shot it its general direction, ran to the bathroom and slammed and locked the door. She propped her foot against the base of the door should the cat try to break it in. She listened but heard nothing. Not one sound. Had she killed it? Not likely. What should she do? She was shaking with fright. What *could* she do? The phone! There was an extension there beside her. She called her husband's cell phone.

Jack was sound asleep when his cell phone rang.

"Hel-lo."

Someone was whispering and he couldn't make it out.

"Speak up. I can't hear you.

Then, he recognized the whisper.

"Annette! What's wrong?"

"The cat is in the house," she whispered. "I'm locked in the bathroom."

He felt the terror in her voice.

"I'm on the way. Stay right where you are till I get there. Okay?"

"Okay," she whispered, "But *please* hurry."

He handed the phone to George, grabbed some night vision goggles, and called to Blackie and Brownie. Donnigan was at his side. They set a full-out run through the treacherous darkness. Branches slapped them and underbrush cut at their flesh.

Dr. Haskins called Sam and then Sheriff Bonner. He filled them in, while George gave instructions to Annette. He tried to keep her calm, and above all, to keep her from panicking and opening the bathroom door.

Jack kept the dogs close as they all ran side by side. Jack knew where the cat was and he knew where Annette was. The moon was bright and that was a blessing for Pete who did not have night goggles. The men's legs tired but on they ran.

They arrived at the grove of trees behind the house. The men and dogs vaulted the fence like hurdlers tight to the finish. Jack opened the back door, turned on the lights, and saw the black form on the floor just outside the bathroom door. He couldn't shoot at it for fear of hitting Annette behind the door. He thanked God that the door was still shut. He called out.

"Annette. It's me! Get low in the bathtub, 'cause their is gonna be some shooting. Okay?"

"OKAY. I'm there."

Before he could get off a shot, Blackie and Brownie were on the cat. The house was still mostly unlit. Black forms were fighting in the hallway and out into the living room. Jack hit a light switch and lit up the room. The cat was in the air flying towards the window in the front room. Jack snapped off two shots. He believed that he had hit the cat at least once. Outside, the low, black, figure melted into the darkness. The dogs jumped out after it. Jack heard cars slam on their brakes. There was more firing.

Sam pulled in first and then Hal. Both men had climbed out as the cat was airborne out of the window, as two shots went off from inside the house. Sam and Hal also both got shots off but in the dark they were shooting at a blur. Jack blew the dog whistle and the dogs returned. They would be no match for the cat in the dark.

Jack knocked on the bathroom door. Annette opened it and fell weeping into his arms. She sobbed uncontrollably. They held each other close. He let her cry it out. He thanked God for her survival. It had been too damned close!

Jack asked Sam to go to the refrigerator and to pull out the last of Judge Smith's whiskey. If nobody else needed anything, he at least, needed a good stiff drink. The dogs, scratched but not badly hurt, lay by the kitchen door. The men sat down at the table and wound down. Jack called George to let him know that all was okay and to thank him for his help. They would meet up again in the morning.

Across the lane, high on his rock atop the rocky knoll, the cat watched. Although three slugs had entered his body and he was bleeding, nothing vital had been hit. He was limping. As he prepared to move deep within the woods, he let out a scream. It was a warning that someday soon he would be back to finish what he had started. Then he vanished into the shadows.

The men boarded up the windows. Pete was offered accommodations at Sam's home until the morning.

At last Jack and Annette were alone. The dogs had been sent to the basement at night. They complied until they heard the bedroom door close. The dogs had been allowed into the basement for the night. As things quieted up above, they snuck up the stairs, much like mischievous children. They curled up, one on each side of the bedroom door, lest the cat return. They were good dogs.

In the morning, the men returned with the dogs, horses and the mule. It was decided that for the time being, it would be best if Janie and Annette stayed at George's house with his two pit bulls. It had become personal between the cat and Jack. Annette had protested about not running away from her own home but Jack persuaded her that it would give him great peace of mind to know that she was in a safe place until the hunt was over and they got the killer. Lovingly, she agreed.

While the wounds were not life threatening, they slowed the cat down to a limping walk. Until it's wounds healed, craft and guile—rather than confrontation—were to be the order of the day.

After a late start, the men and the dogs followed warm though not hot cat scent for the duration of the day. They found a field and called for the chopper. The cage arrived and they proceeded with preparations for the night.

Once the dogs were fed and bedded down, Jack called Annette to re-assure himself that she was okay. Both George and Jack now had women that were precious in their lives.

Sam, for his part, was limping around wishing that he could will his leg to heal faster. He was grateful that two such good men were on the trail of the cat. He also had great respect for Pete Donnigan. Doctor Haskins would lend great expertise to the group as would become apparent as the hunt progressed.

They didn't hear the cat scream that night. It had somehow managed to lengthen its lead.

That night as George cooked up the men's vittals, they talked. George wanted the others to know what Jack already knew about his heart condition.

"It is only fair to tell you that I may die at any time during this hunt. You are not to blame if it happens. It will have been what this old man wanted. I believe this hunt fulfills a great part of my purpose for being here in the first place. You might say that this is my calling. If I survive this hunt, then, I will go into the hospital and they will cut me up like strudel, in the hopes of being able to fix this old heart. If I go there, it is for Janie's sake, so that she feels she has done all that she can for me, who for some unknown reason, she has come to love. I don't hold out much hope for a cure, but I do know that I am supposed to be here, now. If I should go down, I want to go back to town over the back of a horse, not by chopper. I do not expect you young fellahs to understand that, but it is an old man's wish – please honor it. The men nodded.

"What is your wish if you don't make it back, Jack?"

"That someone comfort a woman who has already lost

one good man and might not be able to handle losing two."

Donnigan and Haskins nodded again.

"What about you Pete?" Jack asked.

"Me. I had not even thought about it? But, if it happens, I want my wife and my boys to know that their dad died loving and protecting them."

Everyone nodded.

"And you, Doctor Haskins?"

"Please," he began, "Call me Haskins, or call me John, but drop the doctor. I thought I was superior, a teacher of men, a philosopher. Here, I am the student of a wise old man and his woods smart friends. I want to live to tell this story to many students. If I die, then at least, I found the truth before I did. I lived a lie that I thought was the truth for many years. Now, I am free of the lie. I have found and made peace with my God. I fear no evil. I would like to share the truth I have found with the members of a lost generation, and to, in some small way, help to bring them home."

In the flickering firelight, somewhere in a field near the woods, in the middle of nowhere, four men made their peace with themselves and their God, as they closed in on a killer. Now, all that was left for them to do for the night was to join, the other day creatures of the world, in peaceful sleep amid the music of the tree frogs and the crickets.

While the men and the dogs were taking their rest, the cat was out to do what it did best. It walked the bank above a small country road. Then it saw a car pull off the road. There were four occupants. Everyone was ninety-proofed. They passed the bottle until they had all but passed out. One of them had to go. He staggered out of the vehicle and struggled with his zipper. At that moment the cat hit him from behind, forcing him down on his face.

The cat dined on him as his friends slept in their drunken stupor. They would find his body in the morning, along side the tracks of a cat. They would call the most unlikely of people for a bunch of rowdy drunks: the police. Hal and Sam would have another corpse to catalogue; three confirmed drunks swore off the bottle forever.

Day three of the hunt brought confusion. They followed old scent though it seemed to get some fresher as the day went on. Late in the afternoon the dogs hit fresh cat scent and they went crazy—except for Blackie and Brownie. George and Dr. Haskins—John, as he now preferred to be called—arrived at the same conclusion.

"We have two different cats. The dogs smell generalized cat. Blackie and Brownie, however, are scented in on one specific cat."

"Is that possible?" Jack asked.

The old man nodded. "It's rare, but it can happen. I believe it to be true in this case."

"Then what would you suggest that we do?" Jack asked.

"We have to cover all bases," George said. "Let John and Donnigan go after the fresh scent. If it is not the killer, use a tranquilizer gun and darts. You can tree him, tranquilize him, wrap him up in a net, and call the university to bring a cage. If it is the killer, use your rifles to send him to the next world.

Take Ringo and six regular dogs and run it to ground."

"It's a good plan. You keep your lead dogs, who specialize in fighting the great cat, and go on your way with out being slowed down," John suggested.

It was agreed. The party split up into two groups in pursuit of two cats.

George and Jack called out to Blackie and Brownie who readily took to the older, colder, cat scent, and with some bullying, persuaded the ten followers to do just that, even as the noses of the pack told them that cat was closer in another direction. Donnigan and Haskins set out toward the fresher scent. They would contact each other in a few hours by phone and set co-ordinates for a rendezvous before the sun set.

Two hours later, Blackie and Brownie led their pack out of the woods to a place on the road where cars were gathered and red lights were flashing. George and Jack knew all too well what it meant. They dismounted and went to see if they could be of any assistance. They couldn't be, but they were glad to see Hal and Sam. Sam told them that the killing happened the evening before. George filled him in about the second cat.

Sam looked up at his friends and said, "I wish I could sit on a horse and go with you."

"We know that," George with a nod. The Sheriff went back to the paperwork as the men and their dogs tried to cut into the lead that the cat had built.

The trail of the other cat remained hot. Ringo and the small pack went crazy. Twice Donnigan had to whistle them back. Four hours later Ringo and the pack announced that the cat was at bay. Soon the men came into view. The cat was up a tree. It was a big male. But this was not the killer. It was tawny brown, not black. John Haskins slid his tranquilizer gun from its scabbard, and promptly shot the cat right in the rump. Within seconds the cat fell out of the tree. The men wrapped it up in the net and called in a cage for the cat. It would be taken to a zoo nearby. It arrived within the hour.

Donnigan called George and relayed the message. Haskins and Donnigan would be there to meet them in the evening. Jack and George smiled at each other. Their 'help' had already more than proven themselves worthy.

They trailed the big cat until the trail started to get warm. The sun was low in the sky. It was time to call for the cage. George studied his map, located a field, and called the military. The cage was dropped and the men and the dogs were soon reunited. The fresh scent meant they were gaining on the cat. Perhaps it was severely hurt. Perhaps it had more man-blood on it's mind.

John cooked up the vittals that evening. George was given a rest from the cooking. He listened while Haskins told everyone about the adventure of getting a cat to tree and then to cage.

Donnigan summed it up: "He was child's play, compared to the killer."

Haskins nodded.

Donnigan allowed that it weighed in at one hundred and eighty pounds and was nearly eight feet in length. The killer by its track size will go over a record nine feet long and will weigh fully two hundred and forty pounds—also a record. A one hundred and eighty pound cat is a big one. But the killer makes it look small by comparison.

George brought the sad news.

"The devil killed again—last night. He killed a drunk who was taking a leak while his buddies were asleep in the car. They never heard or saw a thing until the morning. The town is preparing for three more funerals in the coming week."

Jack looked at the others and said, "Thank God it is not four." Then he called Annette. They talked for a while and then George took the phone and talked with Janie. He clicked it off, with a big smile on his face. The others wanted to ask him what had been said but thought better of it. Pete called his wife and talked to her and his son.

George started to laugh out loud.

"What is so damned funny?" the others asked.

"If I told my father that we were hunting a catamount, sleeping in a cage dropped by a helicopter, and talking to our loved ones by phone from the middle of nowhere, he would ask me what planet I was on."

The others also seemed to wonder at the marvelous technology and the resources that were available to be thrown at this cat. Then George said,

"But for all of this fancy technology and the hard efforts of many, I believe that this cat, too, would kill four hundred or more before we got lucky. As it is, we may keep him under twenty victims. He is at twelve now, plus the two who died in the mines—fourteen souls in their graves because of this terrible beast. I know that all of you think we will get him right away, but this old man tells you that if we keep his victims under twenty we have really done something special. This, I believe, is the finest pack of dogs and group of cat hunting men ever assembled. I am proud to be playing a role in it, Poopsie Wopsie."

Soon he was chuckling again.

"All right old man. What is so damned funny," the others asked as one.

"Do you promise not to laugh?," George asked.

"Yeah, we promise." The others grumpily agreed to anything so as to get some sleep.

"She called me Poopsie. Can you imagine that?"

Laughter erupted as the men howled louder than dogs ever did.

"Aw, c'mon. You promised," George admonished.

That brought an even louder uproar as men and dogs both howled and rolled on the ground.

It was late and the men were tired. The laughter took on a life of its own. It was out of proportion to the actual humor, which was in itself funny enough – especially the look on the old man's face.

Finally it died down. The men were about to fall asleep. Suddenly Donnigan couldn't resist the urge.

"Goodnight, Poopsie Woopsie," he called out in a high. Falsetto, voice. The cage shook from laughter s fatigue took over.

George had had enough.

"What did your wife call you?" He asked.

"I'll never tell?" Donnigan deadpanned.

Soon exhaustion overcame the laughter. The men and dogs surrendered to Morphius. George slept with a smile on his face.

With that, the old man rolled over and was soon asleep. Jack thought to himself about how close he'd come to losing Annette. He prayed that the old man would survive the hunt and have some good years with Janie. They both so richly deserved it.

At five thirty in the morning the chopper came to take the cage and to bring the mules. Men and dogs were still tired, but the mules were fresh. The men waved their thanks to the chopper as they mounted the mules. The dogs began to walk toward the area of last scent and picked it up almost immediately. Their bays reflected their fatigue. But coon dogs are coon dogs, and soon their pace picked up again, as they followed the scent of the cat. Day four of the latest chase was under way. George's face was pale. Jack suggested that he go home for a couple of days. "That way you will get back when we hit the high country, where we will really need your scheming brain."

The old man balked at first and then realized that Jack's words were true. He didn't have to kill himself, intentionally. To nearly everyone's surprise, the old man agreed.

That night the cat killed again. That time, it was at twilight. A couple was out for a romantic summer walk. They were no more than a hundred yards from her house. It might as well have been a thousand miles. The cat jumped them hitting the man in the back, pitching him forward onto the ground. His teeth found the man's spinal chord at the neck. The girl screamed and kicked at the cat. The man was as good as dead and the cat took after the fleeing woman. She got twenty yards before the cat brought her down and ended her life by smashing and breaking her neck with one blow of his massive paw. She was dead before she hit the ground.

Her father heard the commotion and came running out of the house with his shotgun in hand and his dog at his side. The cat heard the commotion and with one bound was back up the bank and into the trees. The man and the dog ran down the lane with a flashlight searching along their way. The dog ran into the woods after the cat in spite of the man's attempt to call it off. The man heard barking and fighting and then the final whine of a good dog. He picked up his daughter in his arms. Refusing to believe she was dead, he carried her to the house and called 911 for an ambulance and the sheriff. He felt guilty about not going back for the man, but he was sure that he was already dead.

In twenty minutes the sheriff's car arrived and Frank Anderson got out. The man's body was gone. The woman was dead, and the deputy was not about to chase a corpse into the woods at night.

Joe Hill was beside himself. His daughter Karyn was dead. Her husband to be, Rick Mason was missing and presumed dead. It was almost more than a man could take – the man put his head in his hands and wept.

In the morning the sheriff's department's K9 unit found the half eaten remains of the man, and later, the dead dog further into the woods. The sheriff and Sam were there doing their grim work.

The end of day five there was still no cat. The men went to the field and George took the chopper to the armory. Janie and Annette were there to pick him up.

The nightly news headlined two stories: the latest killings by the cat, and the sentencing of the *Friends of the Animals*. April Gillespie and Robert Sanford were taken to jail. They each got fifteen years. Twenty others also received sentences. They interviewed John Weston, and he proclaimed that justice had been done, and now that the example was set, he prayed that public servants, particularly, in what, is euphemistically called, civil service, would serve rather than trying to rule the people by means of lies and deceit. They interviewed Sam Macafee and asked him if he felt vindicated.

"Only when that cat is at long last dead will I feel any good at all."

With that, they all retired for the evening. The plan was that at the end of the second day the women would drive George to the Armory and the chopper would return him to the hunt.

It wasn't going to work out that way.

The cat had changed directions and George got the call for help from the others. He and Sam got together to study the maps. The cat had gone northwest instead of northeast. It meant trouble. Then they got the news that the cat had killed three teenaged girls. George wouldn't wait to go in with the cage that evening. The routine part of the hunt was over. It was time for the mastermind of the hunt to return and solve the cat's riddle before it escaped to kill another day. George wanted the cat dead at the end. His time was short and he knew it. The others were going to need his help or the cat was going to get away and they would all have to start from scratch.

George believed that he had finally figured out how to get this cat. It was a risky plan, but it just *might* work. George and Sam took a chopper to where the cat had just struck again. The mastermind of the hunt, now had a master plan.

## CHAPTER TWENTY
## A Shot in the Dark

When George left for his rest, the men and the dogs wasted no time getting after the cat. As before, it headed north by north east. It was headed for its sanctuary. Jack knew that, but as of that moment there was nothing to do but follow where the cat led. The cat's scent was heating up fast, as men and dogs were finally cutting into its lead. It had not doubled back to initiate contact. It was not time for that yet. That would come when the grade got steeper and the odds were more to the cat's liking. In the meantime it was content to kill, eat, and keep moving. Depending upon which route the cat would select they were still two to three days from the caves.

In truth, the cat had gotten injured early in this hunt because of its attempt on Annette. It had been almost five days and its wounds were still painful. The healing process drained the cat's normal energy level. It was also leery of circling and killing the trailing members of the pack, because of what had happened when Jack had held Blackie and Brownie in reserve.

The cat was built for speed and fight, but only for the short haul. Its heart was small for its size and when it tired or was worn down it would have to go to tree or escape into a cave or tunnel. Its heart would need time to re-oxidize the blood. It was by breeding, a sprinter, and not a marathoner. That was why the lean, bone tough, and relentless hounds were the perfect chase weapons for bringing cats to bay. This cat was dog smart and had learned to circle and to kill dogs and men in order to buy the time it needed. The cat would, from then on, look to see that the pack and men had passed before attacking the trailing dogs again. The cage had eliminated the cat's nighttime threat to the men and animals.

He wanted to lose the men and the dogs at the mines and then strike another day when the odds favored him rather than the men. His tactic of killing men to buy time was not working either. On the evening of day six he had heard the dogs just before darkness forced them into the cage for the night. They were closing the gap.

Day six of the hunt was now over. The men and the dogs went into the cage. The cat was out roaming as the men were bedding down. For the men to meet and fight cat, they would have to be close to him well before the sunset.

That night Sam called Jack to ask him how it was going and to tell him that the *Friends of the Animals* had been convicted and were on their way to jail.

Jack told him that they had not closed in on the cat until just before dark, but that late in the hunt the next day the first daylight contact should be made. Sam allowed that no killings had occurred that day and that he was grateful, but that he was not holding his breath, because, like as not, the cat would kill that night.

Sadly, he was right. The cat had waited six weeks before killing a human again. Now, he was making up for lost time. The two men knew that it would run into what was left of the mines again, and that it had probably found tunnels enough to hide in until it decided to go on another killing spree. How could they stop it? At night, it could simply do as it pleased.

That night the cat made a detour to the west. It knew of a place that would be hard for men and dogs to follow. They were closing the gap uncomfortably fast. At the present rate they would be on him before he arrived at the caves. The cat needed to put more distance between itself and its pursuers. Instead of going north by east as it had on the first hunt, this time it went due west to some high ground where men and dogs and mules would have to crawl along, while the cat could move at almost full speed. The cat needed rest and it was hungry. It had spent the night moving and had not stopped to kill. Even so, by the end of the next day he heard the dogs. They were closer than he had anticipated they would be.

He had a remedy. His range was rich with terrain that was favorable to cat and not to men. The grade was becoming steeper. It was to the cat's liking. As it approached four in the morning, he came to a country lane. He crossed it and walked through a field. There was no activity. He heard the rush of water. A stream was nearby.

He leaped across it at a narrow spot. It was still pitch black out. He turned northwest, moving without pause. There were hills ahead and a crevasse, which, while smaller than the big one to the north and east, would still force men and dogs to split up and would require them to waste precious time. A few hours seemed like an eternity to the cat. It meant the difference between fighting dogs on an uphill climb where the odds favored the cat, and fighting it out on level ground where the dogs would have the advantage. Time meant life or death for the cat. The cat ran all night at a measured, slow, pace. As dawn hit, he proceeded up the hill he had been seeking. He came upon a cave about two miles from the crevasse.

At his point of safety he stopped running, exhausted and hungry. He found a trickle of water where a seasonal crick still flowed. He drank his fill. He became curious about the circle of canvas tents ahead. He sniffed the air and it told him the tents were occupied. Dinner would be easy that night.

As it turned out it was Girl Scouts on a campout. Two hundred yards to the west was a Boy Scout camp. All were asleep in their tents. The sun would be coming up in less than an hour. The grey streaks of dawn were beginning to pierce the black of night.

In the midst of the pitched tents, death walked on silent feet. Dottie and Samantha were asleep in their sleeping bags. Samantha was sleeping on her side. She felt hot breath on the back of her neck. She figured Dottie was playing a trick on her. She rolled over. All she saw was a black form above her and two green eyes. She let out a scream of horror. Then she screamed no more.

Hearing the scream, her tent-mate woke up in a start. She felt, more than saw, the commotion. She screamed and tried to work her way out of the sleeping bag, and out of the tent. She died without knowing what had killed her.

Tents were emptied. Flashlights were lit. Girls ran in all directions. Rachel Simmons ran too close to the wrong tent. A huge black form hit her from behind. She screamed as she fell. Two teeth sink into the back of her neck. Then she could scream no more.

The cat dragged her body through the weeds and up to the den. Soon it was tearing away at her mid-section, eating the succulent flesh and organs and lapping up the fluids. Then it screamed its victory. It dragged the remains into its lair. It had been so easy. It spent the day undisturbed as it alternately ate and slept, with its ears alert for the sound of the men and the dogs. It would be ready.

The boys from their campsite arrived. They saw the collapsed pup tent. What they found brought horror of a kind they had seen only in dreams. This was far worse. This was real. There was blood everywhere. The wounds were worse than unimaginable.

The scoutmaster sent a den mother to drive for help. They took roll. Dottie Jamison and Samantha Wilson were dead. Rachel Simmons was missing. They all gathered together, as sheep do when they are frightened. A killer was out there somewhere. They had heard its scream. They did not know what it was. They had no idea of what to do except to arm themselves with sharpened sticks. They were terrified beyond measure. Some of the boys wanted to go into the brush and hunt whatever it was. Their scoutmaster told everyone to gather together and stay close until the den mother came back with the police.

The afternoon of day seven of the hunt brought the men and the dogs due west and then north by west. Dr. Haskins and Jack stopped to consult their maps. They knew where the cat was heading. There was some high terrain in that sector. They called George to get his opinion. Sam was at the house. The two men laid out their map of the area and George swore.

There were ravines, hills, and places the cat could cover in minutes that might take the men days to traverse. He told them to follow where the cat led and that he would have a plan of attack when he met them at the cage that evening. The preliminary part of the hunt was over. The mastermind was on his way back to his troops with a plan and a prayer.

They arrived at the scout camp at two in the afternoon. The cat heard the dogs. He moved from his lair and proceeded to jump the crevasse. Then he walked slowly to another den site, laid down, and went back to sleep. The men would not get there until it was nearly dark. Then they would have to leave and to find a field. The cat had asserted a tactical advantage, even as it seemed the men and dogs were closing in.

The men saw more red lights ahead and that meant more death. Sam had gotten the call. George wanted to go with him, so they went in by chopper, taking along a mule for George to ride. George did not want to wait for the chopper that night. He wanted to stop the hunt in its tracks, right there, and save some time.

Blackie and Brownie led the hunters into the camp. Jack saw the chopper and stopped to see what had happened. There were two police cruisers there also. Hal Bonner and Deputy Anderson were taking the details. The ambulances were being loaded. One girl was still missing. The dogs followed the trail of the cat.

George mounted his mule. His face was as grim.

“Up that hill is a small crevasse. You will find the body that way and cat scent so warm that the dogs will go crazy. Don't be fooled. The cat has probably already jumped the crevasse and is sleeping in a den somewhere on the other side. We are going to arrange a nasty surprise for him as he sleeps. It’s a shot in the dark but we might just kill a killer today."

A big army helicopter landed.

"Now," George began again, "Donnigan and Haskins can take Ringo and half of the dogs and follow the cat. They will find he remains of Rachel Simmons along the way. She was killed early this morning before the sun came up. Jack and

I will let the chopper drop us on the other hill that leads to the other side of the crevasse. We will take the fighting dogs with us because the cat will be on our side of the crevasse. If we are lucky, the cat will not realize that we are there until we are at the door of its den. Let Ringo and his pack make all of the noise they want. That will be music to the cat's ears. He will think that he is safe, and that he bought an abundance of time with these killing. Let him think that and he may remain in his den until we get there."

Two Chinooks took off from the armory that day. One dropped the cage into a field that George and Sam had pre-selected. The other came to act as an airborne ferryboat for George, Jack, and nine of the eighteen dogs, including Blackie and Brownie. The chopper took off away from the crevasse and made a detour around the area in order to drop its cargo on the other side of the cat's hill. It was about two in the afternoon. If all went according to plan they would be at the cat's door within the hour.

With that, the men and the dogs split up and went in two different directions. Sheriff Bonner and Deputy Anderson went with Haskins and Donnigan because they knew the body would be found somewhere on that hill. They were right. Barely seventy yards from where they started, Ringo began to howl and whine. The men went to where the dogs had stopped. It was a small cave. The half-eaten body was inside. Hal got on the radio. The others came to the spot with the body bag. Donnigan and Haskins left them with their somber duty and proceeded up the trail to the top of the hill. The dogs were in full bay. Ringo was leading the pack.

The cat heard the dogs but remained unruffled. He heard their bays of triumph change to confusion and frustration as they came to the edge of the crevasse. Only eighteen feet separated them from where the hot scent continued. One of the greener coonhounds couldn't resist the temptation to try to jump the distance. He plunged to his death, serving notice to the others what would happen if they were to try.

The cat stretched and yawned in its den. The men and the dogs might as well be dozens of miles away. He was going to rest well there—or so it seemed.

Meanwhile, the chopper carried George and Jack to the base of the hill on the far side of the crevasse. They muzzled the dogs until they got close to where they believed the cat was denned up. Then, they came upon the crevasse. George called Donnigan on the cell phone and asked him to see if he could set Ringo and the dogs to bay real loud. George believed that they were closing in. They unmuzzled the dogs and rode along the other side of the crevasse. Blackie and Brownie began to bay and growl. They had the scent. The cat woke up at full alert. He heard their voices and recognized them.

He quickly emerged from his den. The dogs and the men were within a hundred yards of him. George saw a black flash loping ahead along the crevasse. Donnigan was much closer. He got a bead on him and squeezed the trigger. The cat had been so intent on putting as much distance between himself and the dogs on his side of the crevasse that he seemed to forget those on the other side. The bullet hit its mark temporarily knocking the cat off its feet.

"I got him!" Donnigan shouted. Then, he cursed, as the cat struggled to its feet and disappeared behind a boulder.

The cat was badly hurt in the shoulder. It ran on for about a mile and jumped back across the crevasse. He made a trail and doubled back waiting for the dogs to run past. He was not out to kill dogs, this time. He wanted to kill one specific man.

Soon the coon dogs ran past the well-hidden cat. He attacked the last three, killing them in seconds. Then the others turned around and the cat was up a grade where the dogs could not follow. Haskins and Donnigan arrived. They notified the others that the cat was now on their side of the crevasse and had killed three dogs. The fighting dogs were now on the wrong side of the chasm.

George had been gambling that they would be able to get close enough to the cat's den to get it. He had gambled and lost. He cursed! The cat was now going to kill a lot of dogs, and maybe, two men. He told Haskins and Donnigan to keep the dogs close and to move slowly.

"It may be behind you already. It lays scent for the dogs and then doubles back on it's own trail to ambush the attackers," George warns Donnigan.

Donnigan observes that the cat was winged pretty bad.

"All the more reason to watch your back," George stated flatly.

Donnigan's mule started to go crazy—bucking and braying—until Donnigan was right at the edge of the crevasse. He jumped off just in time as the mule went over the edge and fell a hundred feet to its death. Donnigan's rifle was lost as well. Haskins got off of his braying mule and grabbed his rifles. He threw Donnigan the one loaded with the tranquilizer dart. It was better than nothing and Haskins had the legitimate ammunition that went with it. Donnigan ejected the dart, and loaded up with the real thing. He didn't want to tranquilize the killer. He wanted to kill the son of a bitch! Although Donnigan and Haskins didn't know it, the cat was behind and above them on a rock ledge. Haskins was still fighting his mule. Donnigan had his back to the cat. The light of day and Haskins had saved his butt so far, but this was not over.

Blackie and Brownie led the dogs and the men along the other side of the crevasse. Jack saw the cat above Donnigan and got a bead on him. Fire and smoke belched out of his rifle. Jack's mule bucked as he fired and that saved the cat. As it was, the bullet hit the cat in the shoulder and almost knocked him off the rock ledge. The cat limped behind a boulder and proceeded straight up the side of the rock and boulder strewn hill, making sure it kept something solid between it and the men with the guns.

George looked at the sky. The sun was beginning to set. The dogs were called off and the men, on both sides of the crevasse, went to the east side of the hills. They took the grade down to the field where the cage had been dropped. The chopper was waiting to pick up the mules. It would be one light on the trip home. They heard the cat's scream in the night. He wanted the fight to continue.

The cat was badly hurt. It limped into a cave at the top of the rocky hill and collapsed. It lay there for a full hour before it regained enough strength to put some more distance between itself and the others. The cat was getting desperate. It limped up another hill to the summit and started down the other side. Then it came to the county lane it had crossed further south on the way to the crevasse and, with what strength it had left, picked up it's pace towards the north east. The cave and the mines there represented his only chance for survival. It limped in pain to a den about fifteen miles from the cave—a place where the men couldn't follow. It collapsed at daylight inside a small cave that had only one entrance.

When the chopper left with the mules, the men gathered in the cage, pitched their tents, and George started to cook up the vitals. Donnigan silently thanked God, Haskins, and Jack for just being alive. It had been a close one. George had called the armory. They were going to need two choppers in the morning. They were going to place one group at the cave to lay in wait for the cat and hopefully to prevent it from going to ground in one of the entrances the men had not discovered. Once inside, George believed the cat would be into the mines and it would start all over again, later. This cat was responsible for nineteen deaths. George believed that they had to get between the cat and his safe haven or all would be lost again.

He also had a bad feeling about his heart. He had taken several nitro pills while the others weren't looking. He would take it as easy as he could without slowing the others down. The pack was down to fourteen dogs, but the cat was hurt too. It could not run as far, or as fast, as it once could. If men and dogs could stay between it and the cave, then that next day might be it's last.

Day eight of the hunt began as a scramble. Donnigan and Haskins were to follow the scent of the cat and try to keep the pressure on it. Jack and George were to be at the hill of the cave and would be located on the trail that led to the big crevasse. The cat could not run there or to the cave, without confronting men and dogs that stood between it and where it wanted to go. The chopper was to drop them and seven of the remaining fourteen dogs. They would stay hidden until dog got wind of cat. Then they would try to run it to tree, or drive it to the crest of a hill and have it at bay. Blackie and Brownie were to lead the charge ahead of Haskins and Donnigan's dogs, so the cat would not be tempted to try to have it out with the dogs, but would instead run until it could run no more.

Blackie and Brownie whined as George, Jack, and seven dogs entered the chopper. Haskins gave them a pat. Donnigan did as well. The men understood a dog's desire to be with its master.

Once they hit cat scent, they were all business as they led their pack after the badly wounded cat. The men followed behind the dogs on their mules and the chase was underway.

Twenty-five miles ahead, George, Jack, Ringo, and the dogs took their positions in the rocks along the trail that led to the crevasse. Their day would be spent in waiting and George, for one, was glad for the rest his ailing ticker so badly needed. He had a bad feeling about this day but he kept it to himself.

Four hours after they began, the cat scent got hot. The dogs and the men sensed they were closing in. Twenty minutes later the cat would hear their bays and Blackie's unmistakable growl.

The cat knew that the two dogs it hated and feared the most were closing in. He ran as fast as he could, considering its extensive injuries. He lengthened his distance between them to about a mile when it came upon a creek. He stopped and drank. He didn't linger long. There was no doubling back on the men and the dogs on that day. The cat was on his way to the cave and the crevasse and the mines that were his familiar sanctuary—the sanctuary that had served him well in the past.

He stopped in a safe haven and rested for several hours. It was time to test his body. He would run until he dropped before he would go to tree. At top speed he was fifteen minutes away. The problem was that he could not run at top speed—or even half or quarter speed. So, he ran until he could run no more and then walked until able to pick up the pace once more. The dogs had been running the whole time and while he could lose them in short bursts of speed, they could and would wear him down at some point so that sudden burst would not be there. The crucial question was, could he make it to the cave before that happened. It would be close.

The cat got to within five miles of the cave when he ran out of gas. The dogs were closing in fast and the cat was fully exhausted. He found a lair that had two entrances. He moved through one and out the other and then made a circle back to the first entrance. He made many circles and then jumped twenty feet and moved up the hill. He was slinking now. He was walking slowly—every yard a struggle. The cat was panting heavily when Blackie and Brownie came upon the entrance to the cave. Blackie stayed at the first entrance while Brownie ran to the second. They stood guard a full ten minutes before the men arrived.

Haskins called George and told him the situation. George told him how to make and light a spitting devil. If the cat didn't come out, then wait until the smoke cleared and see if there were other tunnels that led to other entrances. If not, then turn the dogs loose. As Haskins followed George's instructions, and Blackie and Brownie continued to smell for cat scent, the cat moved further up the hill. Ten minutes passed. They waited for the smoke to clear. Then they checked the cave. It was empty.

Donnigan barked out: "Go get um," and the dogs turned and started up the hill. They immediately picked up hot cat scent again and they were off. The hill gave the cat an edge. It was steep and the dogs were single file. The cat didn't want the fight there. The next hill was even steeper and it held a familiar cave and an abundance of mineshafts. If he could then get to the other side of the crevasse the men would have no chance!

The cat looked at the sky. It was only early afternoon and the sun was bright. Night would not save him. He was at the crest of the hill. He could make his final stand there. He considered his options. He was in pitiful shape, bleeding and limping badly on one front leg. He needed to rest if he were to kill the dogs and men; the odds looked bad. He made his way down the other side of the hill. He was now one hill closer to the cave. At the base of the hill was forest and brush. He ran until he could run no more. His limp became worse. He heard the dogs. They were again closing in. Ahead was *his* hill. Ahead was *his* cave. He began to wind his way up the hill. It was steep and presented more than the usual challenge for him. The dogs would labor for every inch. With the entrance in sight he believed he was home free.

He looked up the grade. Men had emerged above him. Jack and George had not yet seen him, but the cat had seen them. The way to the crevasse was blocked. The worked his way a third of the way up the hill, then stopped. He could run no more. He circled back down and waited for the dogs to run past him. He would be behind the men and the mules. He would be in position to kill the men. He lay behind a boulder in a brush-covered area where he could not be seen from above or below. Blackie and Brownie ran past. Then the rest of the dogs passed him.

He was behind the two men. Their mules became skittish. The two men fought to stay in the saddle. The cat jumped on top of Donnigan's mule and then onto Donnigan. Cat and man fell to the ground. The mule ran for its life. Haskins managed to pull out his rifle but he could not get a bead on the cat because of his mule and because he was afraid of hitting the other man. He fired over the cat's head and it ran for cover. Haskins jumped off of his mule and blew the dog whistle. He was going to need help. Donnigan was laying on the ground unable to move. During the fall he had landed on his head and shoulder and had been knocked out. Haskins believed him to be dead.

The 'cavalry' arrived on cue. Around a boulder came Blackie and Brownie with the other dogs close behind. Haskins moved directly to Donnigan. The big Irishman was alive but was badly shaken. The blow from the cat's paw had dislodged an arm from his shoulder socket. The bucking of the mule had saved him.

Haskins notified the others of the situation and then returned his attention to Donnigan. A practiced veterinarian, Haskins slopped the bone back into its socket and wrapped the arm, placing it in a sling. He wanted to call the chopper and have it air-evacuate him to the hospital. The big Irishman refused.

"These are not fatal injuries and my shooting hand is still good. If need be, I can leave with the chopper tonight. Let's get these dogs on the trail and let's kill us a big kitty!"

Reluctantly, Haskins agreed. He had developed a mountain of respect for the man.

On top of the hill, George and Jack were still waiting for the cat to make its move to the cave. Haskins and Donnigan re-mounted their mules—which the dogs had rounded up—called out for Blackie and Brownie to "Go get em," and the chase was on. Donnigan had to ride a more gingerly pace than the others. He told Haskins to keep up with the dogs and that he would catch up later.

The catamount moved around the base of the hill while the men at his back were getting re-organized. His attack on the man had bought him a precious half-hour of time. The cat gazed at the sky. A few more hours and the men would have to leave for the cage and he would be safe once more. He had worked behind the other side of the hill. The men were blocking his route to the crevasse but not to the one entrance to the cave that connected him with the shaft of the mine below. He crept up the east side of the hill, crouching low. It was steep and rough terrain, much to his liking.

The pain grew worse. To survive he would need everything to break his way. He would need time to recover. In his condition he could not fight the two dogs and win. The blood loss continued, leaving him ever weaker.

Then he heard a sound that told him all could still be lost. *Those* two dogs had picked up his scent and were after him again. He somehow managed to climb the steep slope. If he were lucky he would make it to his cave entrance. He moved as fast as he was able. He stopped in his tracks.

Jack, his mule, and three coon dogs were moving toward him. While they did not know precisely where the den opening was, they had done as the old master of the hunt had told them to do. They moved to a point where the dog's bays from below directed them toward the cat. George and the remaining four dogs guarded the open trail to the crevasse. The cat saw Jack, but Jack did not see the cat.

The cat got behind him and moved towards the man and dogs that barred his way to the crevasse. The cat was down wind of them so the dogs didn't catch his scent. The cat continued to circle. Soon Jack and his dogs were out of sight, and he moved further up the grade.

Climbing the hill, Blackie and Brownie were on the cat's scent. Their progress was slower than the cat's had been. They saw Jack and their bays and barks became almost joyous. Jack and his dogs fell in behind them as they trailed the cat. Haskins came in behind the last of the dogs and said Donnigan and Bluebell were about half a mile behind them. Blackie and the pack arrived. Jack and Haskins followed them on their mules.

The big cat moved further up the grade. Now he was on top of the hill. Below him, he saw George and four coon dogs. He worked his way down the hill and behind them. The wind kept his presence a secret. Suddenly, it shifted and George's mule reared with fear. The dogs smelled it too and started up after the cat. Blackie and Brownie headed down the slope from up above.

Below, the mule had thrown George to the ground and he was unarmed. The cat leaped to the trail and towards the old man. He did not move. The cat sniffed the old man wanting to make sure he was dead. Then there was movement. George's eyes opened. Above him were two green and evil eyes. The old man wanted to die fighting the cat if it was his time to die. The cat opened its huge jaws to strike. Blackie and Brownie were upon it. The cat leaped over the old man's body and climbed straight up the side of the hill. George struggled to stand but couldn't.

"Go get um," he shouted after the dogs.

The dogs did not obey. Brownie brought the mule by its lead rope. George popped a nitro pill and grabbed his rifle. He leaned back against a boulder, the gun across his lap. The pack arrived and stayed as per Brownie's instructions. George was moving in and out of consciousness.

Soon Jack and Haskins arrived. George rallied.

"Go get the son-of-a-bitch before he gets away!" he bellowed.

Haskins told him that Donnigan was about ten minutes behind. Jack looked into the old man's eyes and knew that something was wrong. George was adamant in his demand that they press the cat right away. He whispered something to Haskins. Haskins nodded. Then Jack, Haskins, and the pack were on their way. Ringo was ordered to stay with the old man. He whined and the old man gave him a pat.

The cat limped to the top of the hill. He was unstable on his legs—perhaps close to death. He heard the dogs again. He entered the cave and lay down behind a boulder. He panted rapidly but shallow. His body simply quit on him. He could run no more.

Soon the dogs were at his den's door. Jack and Haskins arrived. Jack spoke.

"Me and the two dogs are gonna go in there and try to get him. We aren't gonna let him live to kill another day."

Haskins smiled.

"The old man told me you might try something foolish like that. He told me to go to the entrance of the den by the crevasse and cover up the mineshaft there with my net."

Haskins called the armory. He had one more big job for them. Jack smiled. The old man had one last trick in his arsenal.

Jack took two flashlights, a Coleman lantern, and Blackie and Brownie; they entered the cave. He did not have the night vision goggles he wished he had. His plan, such as it was, was for him and the two dogs to follow the cat wherever it went. The old man had suspected that a tunnel connected the two dens, and that the cat would be heading for the vent in the second den from which he had escaped the first time.

Jack and the dogs moved on after the cat while Haskins waited for the chopper that would take him to the den and the vent to the coalmine, provided the explosion had not closed it.

The team of military specialists arrived at the entrance to the first den and quickly installed a barred and hinged grate, padlocking it. They slid a key under the grate, should Jack work his way back to the spot and need a way out. Then they loaded the dogs and two mules on board and proceeded with Haskins to the den by the crevasse. Once there, they cut the grate with a welding torch and went inside. They shined a flashlight down the shaft and could not see bottom. Ten feet down, they did see where a cave tunnel joined it. The cat could have used it to get away. Two military experts repelled down to that spot and installed a portable hinged grate over the opening. They padlocked it and, again, slid a key under the grate. They took care of other exits in similar fashion. They left a lantern for Jack in case he got that far. Haskins was given a master key: just in case. I was all accomplished with military precision in less than thirty minutes.

Haskins then called Jack to let him know what had been done. There was no answer. There was too much rock between the two men for the signal to penetrate. Jack figured that the other end of that cave would be blocked in some way—he counted on it! Pete and George waited by the trail that led to the crevasse.

The helicopter couldn't land there, so it unloaded Haskins, the dogs, and the mules, by the entrance to the first cave. From there Haskins tied the mules together and followed the trail that led to the crevasse. The dogs ran on ahead of him and the mules trailed behind. When he got to Pete and George the news was not good. George was fading fast and he had refused to be air evacuated out.

"If I am to die;" he repeated, "It will be out here and not in some hospital."

The sun was setting. The moon was rising. It would have been beautiful were it not that it meant the onset of the time of the cat. But that night the dark held no fear for the men. It would make no difference inside the cave tunnels where day was as night, anyway. Jack was now on his own with only the help of his tools, his dogs, and his God.

Donnigan and Haskins fixed supper. They kept the talk light so as not to worry the old man who was fighting for his life.

Inside the cave, Jack and the dogs slowly followed the cat. Jack knew that he didn't have to go faster than it was safe for him to go. If the old man was right, and this did lead to the tunnel that Haskins, and the military would grate up, then he could let the cat get out ahead--and run into a dead end. What he was more concerned about, was the cat somehow working it's way behind him and the dogs, where it could jump on him, from out of nowhere. He saw the huge pool of blood the cat had left behind, and saw more blood spots where it had walked. Maybe it was mortally wounded and he would just find it's body. He knew in his heart, that would not be the case. Jack could not know, that in truth, all he would have had to do was to exit the cave at the entrance he had entered from. The cat was closed in from all sides and if left in there, would have starved to death.

Ahead, the catamount was moving with as much speed as it had left. It now had the battle with the one man and the two dogs it hated and feared the most, and that battle was on it's terms--in the dark; but so critical was it's condition, that it did not want the fight. The two dogs and the men could wait for another time. Now, all the cat was concerned with, was in pushing it's injured body along the tunnel, where he knew that it would lead: to the mineshaft, where the men and the dogs could not follow. If it got there, it would live to fight, another day. If it had to fight the man and the dogs, the outcome would be questionable, at best.

At a crawl, the man, the dogs, and the cat that was ahead of them, moved through the cave tunnel that led wherever it led. The pace was very much to the cat, and Jack's liking. Blackie and Brownie wanted to step it up, but were called back, whenever they got too far ahead. Ahead, for what seemed like endless hours, the man and the dogs moved forward. Jack was shining his light on every overhang and crevice in the rock strewn tunnel, looking to be sure that the cat had not doubled back, behind him. The hair was standing up on the back of his neck. The dogs were not baying and growling now. An eerie quiet descended on everyone. It was as though all of the combatants were too tired for sound.

Finally the cat sensed that the air shaft that led to the mines was near. For the first time since it entered the cave and heard the man and the dogs coming, it sprinted. Ahead would be the air shaft that led to the mines. That would be where the chase ended. The cat was smelling victory. It bounded ahead--and skidded to a stop. The way was barred. The cat sniffed and batted at the bars with a powerful blow from it's paw. There was no give. The cat was trapped!

Now he would have to fight the man and the dogs. It ran from where it had just come from, at full speed. Then, it jumped to a ledge above the ground floor of the tunnel. It slowly worked its way back towards the man and the dogs. The dogs began to bay and bark at the spot, where the cat had speeded up. Jack kept having to call them back. Behind some rocks, the now concealed cat waited. He saw the dogs go past. The man would be coming--and soon. Then he saw the man. He passed under him, and called the dogs back. Soon, they were off again and the man, shining his lantern and flashlight, was looking at the area above him. The cat waited until he passed, and then crawled to the cave tunnel's floor. Then he bounded ahead.

The man was twenty yards ahead of him, feeling his way, in the dark. The cat could see, as in daylight. It got to within ten yards of the man, and then broke for the kill. He jumped on the man's back. The lantern flew out of one hand and the flash light out of the other. The lantern shattered on impact and the fluid spilled out on the cave floor--and ignited, lighting the cavern up like it was daylight. The dogs had been returning when the cat had leaped on Jack's back, forcing him forward on his face--and what should have meant, certain death. But the dogs were at just the right place, at the right time, and they jumped the cat, at just the right moment, before it's teeth and claws could seal the man's fate. Jack had hit his head on the cave floor and was momentarily out cold.

When he came out of it and shook his head, he heard the sounds of battle. The Coleman fluid was still burning, and lit up the cave, but it was dying down fast, and it was getting darker. Jack blew on his dog whistle, and the dogs returned from around a bend in the tunnel, where he had heard the fighting. Behind them came the cat. With a leap, it was past them, and headed for the man. It was getting dark. Then Jack realized that this was how his dream had gone. The cat was in his sights, but it was too dark to get a bead on him. It was coming straight for him he was ready to pull the trigger. This time, instead of waking up, he pulled the trigger. The rifle went off with a roar, that shook the cave and caused rocks to fall. Then all went black. For what seemed like eternity their was dead silence.

Jack braced himself for the impact of the cat slamming into him. Instead he heard a scream that sounded like Satan himself. It was half human in it's tone, and it too, reverberated throughout the cave. It was so eerie, and so mournful, that it momentarily, made the man sad. It was the death cry of the cougar.

Jack turned on his other flashlight, which he had strapped, to his belt in its holder. The beam came on, and he shown it ahead. It landed in the middle of two green eyes. Then, he saw the green light go out of those eyes, and what looked like a green mist, rising from the cat, as the life left it. Then it lay dead. The dogs were standing over it. Then they howled, the mournful howl of the wolf that was still somewhere in their blood, and moved for their master. They were themselves again, and sniffed at Jack who was sitting on the seat of his pants, with the gun lying next to him and the flashlight shining from his hand. Their tongues were out and they wanted a good petting. That, Jack delivered--in spades!

Then Jack fished around in his pack for his cell phone, and thankfully, it was undamaged. He called George's cell phone number. There was no answer. He would have to get to a place where the signal could get out of the cave, before he could make contact. He half walked and half dragged himself to the end of the tunnel where the military had grated up the vent. There, the lantern lit up the exits that were also barred. Maybe the cell phone would be able to reach the others from here. He dialed George's number. This time it beeped.

The old man answered it, in a voice that sounded like death warmed over. "George, this is Jack. The cat is dead. I'm where they grated me in, at the end of the tunnel. I am going to need help to get the dogs, and the body of the cat, out. Can you help me?" He felt the old man smile. "We will be there, as fast as mules can get us there." "Thanks George. It went, just like my dream, only this time, I pulled the trigger." George smiled, "I had a feeling about that dream," He said. "We will see you, when we get there."

The old man looked at Pete and at John.

"I was right," he began. "This is the finest team of cat hunters that was ever assembled. Jack has killed that demon and is waiting for us at the end of the tunnel."

Life seemed to rush back into the old man.

"Well I'll be a son of a...." Donnigan whispered.

Haskins just smiled. He looked at the old man.

"He would never have gotten him without your help."

"And yours," the old man smiled. Then he turned to Donnigan, "And yours, too, my friend."

Donnigan broke into a smile. If I were up to it I'd dance you one hell of an Irish jig.

"You have lost too much blood for all of that," the good doctor proclaimed.

The men shared a strained chuckle. George looked like he'd just caught the biggest bass in the lake.

"Well, are we just gonna stand around or are we gonna go get Jack?" George shouted.

"I think you two are gonna wait right here," Dr. Haskins said. "I'll take two mules and go myself. *Then*, we are all going to take a nice ride in the chopper—*to the hospital*!"

The two men looked at each other, knowing George was no up to such a trek.

George stood up and managed a few unsteady steps toward his mule. In mid-stride he came to a dead stop, clutching his chest. He fell to the ground and reached for his pills. The doctor assisted him.

"Give me ten minutes," he said weakly. The others sat by him and waited.

Ten minutes and the old man knew.

"I am not going to be able to get up. When the nitro works, I'm good as new. It is not working."

His eyes held no fear, but they were tinged with regret.

"Tell Janie that I love her. Will you?"

The two men nodded. George managed a weak smile and coughed. He struggled to keep his eyes open.

"It looks like this is it. Please, sing me into the next world?"

The others understood that this was, indeed, the end of the trail for the old man. Fighting back tears, Donnigan and Haskins began to sing:

"When the roll is called up yonder.
When the roll is called up yonder,
When the roll is called up yonder,
I'll be there."

At the beginning of the second chorus the old man joined in, mouthing the words. His eyes closed. By the third verse he was gone. Haskins searched for a pulse. There was none. His inclination was to resuscitate but George had departed this world.

Donnigan put a hand on Haskin's shoulder and told him what he already knew.

"They have taken roll and he is there."

Haskins nodded through his tears.

"Damn right he is!"

"Then let's do what the old man told us to do." Donnigan fairly shouted.

Haskins looked puzzled but only for a moment. Then he knew.

"Right," he said.

The two men picked up ol' George and gently laid him over the back of the mule. They secured him in place and covered him with a blanket. George looked dignified in death.

They made their way through the night to Jack and the dogs.

"Anybody home," Donnigan called as Haskins swung open the gate, which stood ajar.

A figure got to his feet in the shadows.

"Damn right I am!" Jack answered with a grin in his voice.

The lantern still lit the area. The men and animals rejoined each other. With ropes and mule power the cat was soon extricated from the cave.

Jack asked the question that both men were dreading.

"Where's George?"

He found his answer written on both of their faces. A sad look came over his own.

"At least he knew that we killed the cat. He died knowing, right?"

The others nodded.

"Then we don't ride home on a chopper. Do we?"

"Not on your life!" The others agreed.

Donnigan and Haskins tied the cat to the back of a mule. With that, the men mounted up and headed for the field where fresh horses would be waiting.

Jack was ready to return to his life of anonymity and spend time building his new life with Annette. However, there was a conspiracy underfoot that might delay all of that.

## CHAPTER TWENTY ONE
## **No Greater Love**

When the men got to the field, the chopper was waiting. The horses were too. The men, the mules, and the dogs rode to the chopper. Their horses were ready and saddled. The men dismounted. The chopper crew saluted them. They returned the salutes. Jack said, "Please tell the General that none of this would have been possible without his, and the military's, help. He will get the body of this catamount with our blessings, once the people of the town have a look at it." The officer smiled, and said that the General "sends his compliments on a job well done."

Dr. Haskins and Jack, were then assisted in the job, of taking George's body off of the mule. A white blanket was laying on the ground. With loving care, they wrapped the body of their friend in the blanket and then secured it, with ropes, so that it would not slide off. They hoisted George over the black saddle of the white horse that the military had provided for his last ride, and secured it, with rope so the old man, would ride, secure. The men, both civilian and military, saluted the old man. Then the men brought the body of the cat, down off of the mule, and secured it, over the saddle of another horse. Finally, Jack, Pete Donnigan, and the good doctor, mounted the horses, saluted the military men, said their thanks, and began their long ride back to the town.

Jack called to Blackie and Brownie and shouted, "Drop it!" Two of the best dogs that ever were, formed, one on each of Jack's heels, and the dogs followed in two lines, one on either side of the riders. Then they started for home. Jack led; then came Donnigan. The horse carrying George's body was secured to Donnigan's saddle. Dr. Haskins followed next, with the lead rope of the horse, carrying the body of the cat, secured to his saddle. As they rode into the trees, they saw the chopper take off, on it's way back, to its base.

Ahead lay six hours of riding, as the men followed the game trails through the woods. After three hours, Jack, who had not slept since the night before last, was so exhausted, that he made camp, for something to eat, and to feed the dogs, and the horses for the last leg of the trip. Jack built a campfire, rolled up a blanket under his head, and the three men ate. He slept, for about an hour. They could not afford more time than that, because they didn't want the body of their friend, to stink, on his last ride. They also had to make time, because of their condition. Jack was light headed because of his concussion and from fatigue, and Pete's arm and shoulder were badly swollen, and he was in great pain. He wouldn't show it to the others, though, such was his pride.

Soon they remounted, and started, on the final leg of their journey home. Dr. Haskins, used his trailing position, to best advantage, and got on the cell phone to Sam Macafee, and related their position to him. Donnigan looked over his shoulder at him and grinned and winked. Two friends were sharing a secret from Jack, who honestly did not have a clue, as to what would be coming.

Jack was slipping into half-consciousness. He was awake enough to find his way home, but he was nodding off, as he rode. He was hearing the old man laughing and talking, just like always, as he rode. Then, he heard the old man say, "If I have to die, I want it to be on a great hunt, who's story will be told and re-told, throughout the ages, with everything on the line, all of the chips on the table, and all of the marbles at stake. I don't want to die at my table, sitting in a chair alone. This is the way this old man wants to die. Do not feel bad if I go that way. You gave this old man his last wish." In his half-conscious state, a tear was working it's way down his face, and he was chuckling at the same time. It was a strange kind of mixed emotions. The fatigue and the headache he was feeling, put every thing into slow motion. He managed to look over his shoulder at the others. Donnigan was chewing tobacco, and his face was a mask of pain. Jack **had** to stay focused, regardless of pain and fatigue. He **had** to get his old friend, and his new friends home. He could not allow himself to quit. His body wanted to do just that. Only his spirit kept him going.

After what seemed like an eternity, the riders came to the county lane, that would lead to a wider road, that, in turn would eventually lead to the town and the hospital. They would stop by the courthouse, and turn the body of the cat over to Sam Macafee, who, in turn, would give it to the General. Then Jack would go to the hospital, along with Pete, who Jack noticed, was swaying in his saddle too. There would be some well-wishers, for the old man, before he was taken to the hospital for the proclamation of death to be made, tardy as it would be. When he got out of the hospital, Jack would go to a certain church and lead it's congregation in a certain song for a special old man. He looked over his shoulder at the wrapped body of his friend. He just couldn't quit now.

Suddenly, Jack stopped his horse dead in its tracks. There on the county lane were two police cruisers. His cell phone rang and, when he pulled it out of his saddlebags to answer it, Frank Anderson's voice rang out. "Me and the Sheriff are here to escort you into town." Jack smiled. "You wouldn't just let me sneak in and sneak back out. Eh?" Sheriff Bonner's voice rang out next: "Hell no! Besides, we brought a friend of yours along, and loaned him a cruiser." The two doors of one cruiser, and one of the second, opened up, and Hal Bonner, Deputy Anderson, and Sam Macafee, got out and walked up the bank, to the riders, who promptly dismounted.

Jack looked into the eyes of his old friend, who had hired him for this job, and for whom he'd used his contacts, at his old factory job, to give him employment, when he had been fired. "George is gone," he said sadly, "but we didn't let you down. We got the cat." Sam looked into the tortured eyes of his friend. "Let me down, hell! You saved my bacon, after I was too banged up to do it myself. I do have one beef, though." Jack smiled. He knew what was coming. "You got him before my leg healed, so I missed out on the kill," Sam continued. "Well, it got personal, especially, after he almost killed Annette." Jack allowed. "Personal. Remind me never to get on your bad side," Sam said, laughing. The two men shook hands. Their eyes spoke volumes of their appreciation for each other, as men.

Then Sam said, "Me, Hal, and Frank wanted to get a look at the big kitty, before the line forms, in town." Jack started to walk, with the others, back to the horse that the cat was tied to. As the men walked past George's body, they stopped, stood, and paid their respects. Jack said, "Without him, the cat would still be out their killing folks." The men nodded, and then Donnigan put his hand on the old man's body and patted it. "God watches over him now." The men nodded in silence. Then, they walked over to the body of the cat. "My God; what a monster it was!" Sam whispered.

Then the two dogs that played such a role in the killing of the cat walked up to get their pats. Haskins rubbed them up real good, as did all of the others. "Pit beagles," Sheriff Bonner whispered. "Who would have ever guessed?" Jack patted his dogs. "Only their mother knew. George and I laughed at them when they were born. Their mother knew."

Donnigan was in obvious pain. He tried to hide it and he could not. Hal and Sam offered him a ride in the air conditioned cruiser, but Donnigan would have no part of that. "I am going to personally help this old man get his last wish." He looked at the old man's body. Then he looked at the others, "And we must all play our parts, so the story is told and re-told, just as the old man wanted." Jack and Haskins nodded their agreement.

So, now it was time to mount up, and get to town, to let the people say goodbye, to an old friend, and to celebrate the demise of a killer. Jack needed help to get back on his horse, and Sam obliged. Jack thanked him and said, "but for the dogs, I would be as dead as George." Sam nodded. It was in his mind that the same was true for him. The dogs had saved him as well. Then the caravan proceeded down the county lane, until they got to the wider asphalt road that led into town. There, two more cruisers joined the procession. They had closed the main road to traffic, and now two cruisers led, with their lights flashing, and two followed the men on the horses who rode, single file with the lines of dogs formed at Jack's heels, walking along both sides of the horses, in lock step.

Then they heard a helicopter overhead. Jack looked up, and it was waving by juking back and fourth. In it were General Weberly and the pilot who had so often delivered the cage and the supplies. The men on the horses waved and then saluted it. The General had a smile that would not quit! Jack's cell phone rang again and the General fairly shouted, "You got the son-of-a bitch--Great job!" Jack smiled and hollered back, "Yeah, I got him, with the help of the military, two great dogs, some miners, and some others, and especially one old man who planned the whole damned thing. General, **WE** got him." The General laughed. **"WE sure did!"**

With that, the caravan paraded into town with Blackie and Brownie fairly strutting along side with big doggie smiles as the hounds joined in the spirit of the thing. The came around the last bend in the road, and the town square was in front of them.

What Jack and the others saw then nearly knocked them off of their horses. The whole town square was filled to capacity. Smack dab in the middle of the square, a bandstand had been erected. The military band and chorus was on the stage. When the cruisers and the riders came into view, Rebecca Monk was on the stage with a film crew. The microphone blared. "Here they are folks, Jack Morgan, Pete Donnigan, Dr. John Haskins, and the body of George Hogan; who's last wish was a chance to say good bye to the town that he loved. `For greater love has no man than this: that one man lay down his life for his friend.' So says the bible. Good bye George, and Godspeed."

With that, the drums began to roll, the military band began to play, and the chorus began to sing: WHEN THE ROLL IS CALLED UP YONDER, WHEN THE ROLL, WHEN THE ROLL, IS CALLED UP YONDER, WHEN THE ROLL, WHEN THE ROLL, IS CALLED UP YONDER, WHEN THE ROLL IS CALLED UP YONDER, I'LL BE THERE!

The crowd and the entire town square joined in. Jack, Pete, and the good doctor broke into song. A tear was working its way down many faces. Jack's eyes searched the crowd.

There were the miners, standing side by side, they waved and he waved back. The whole square was shaking with the sounds of the drums and the singing, as stanza after stanza was jubilantly sung and played.

Jack saw Mark Salem standing with his folks. He motioned to him, and the little boy ran to him. "You got `im Mr. Jack! You got him!" Jack reached down an arm and helped the little boy climb on the horse behind him. "This is for your sister." He said. "And all of the others," The little boy said. "And for all of the others." Jack agreed. "Now hold on tight." Mark did. As George's song was played and replayed, Marc and Jack sang along.

Jack's eyes searched the crowd. There was Judge Smith, John Weston, Thomas Swiggert, and their families, standing side by side singing their hearts out. Then he saw Sally Macafee, Sally Anderson and Jane Lefforts and her family, standing side by side. He waved, and the ladies blew kisses.

His eyes looked further down, and he saw a special lady dressed in black. It was Janie Tanner, and next to her was Annette. She looked so beautiful! Jack shouted to Mark, and they dismounted together, bringing the procession to a temporary halt. Then, Mark did, as he was asked and led the white horse, Jack was riding, towards the bandstand. Jack walked uncertainly towards Annette and Janie. He was almost out on his feet. They ran to him and he put an arm around each of them. The three of them walked to the horse that held George's body. Janie was sobbing, as she and the others, joined the whole town, in singing George's farewell song. That was the last thing Jack remembered. He was out on his feet, but Janie and Annette somehow kept him up.

Donnigan and Haskins dismounted, tied the horses together, and all of them walked together, along side the white horse, that bore the body of their friend and the master of the hunt. Donnigan's wife and son's ran out to be with their dad, and he put his one good arm around his wife, as they all walked together and sang the final stanza of the tribute to their friend: WHEN THE ROLL IS CALLED UP YONDER, WHEN THE

ROLL, WHEN THE ROLL, IS CALLED UP YONDER, WHEN THE ROLL, WHEN THE ROLL, IS CALLED UP YONDER, WHEN THE ROLL IS CALLED UP YONDER, HE'LL BE THERE!

And so it was, that a town and a county celebrated it's heroes, and the end of a killer. Somewhere up above, an old man smiled down on them. That feeling was shared by all. The good had triumphed, and the bad had been vanquished. That is always worth celebrating.

The next thing Jack remembered was waking up in his hospital bed with bandages around his head. His wife was sleeping next to him on a hospital bed that had been provided for her. He looked again, and Blackie and Brownie were sleeping by the door. They say, that the hospital made an exception, to it's "No animals in the rooms rule," for two exceptional dogs. He gingerly climbed out of his bed and Annette heard him. She got up, and gave him a monster hug. He had been out for ten hours and she had been very concerned. Now everything was going to be all right.

She helped him down the hall, and over to Donnigan's room. When they got there, he also was in the bosom of his family, with his arm in a cast, and a new sling, around his neck. Apparently the hospital had made some more exceptions to the rules. He had a glass of whiskey in his good hand, and a premium cigar in his mouth – and he was loving it! Apparently, the judge had paid him a visit. He had paid Jack one as well. Annette had control of the contraband, and it would be a few days, before Jack could indulge. He and Donnigan shook hands.

Then he got the news that he could go home. He and Annette walked out together, escorted by two of the best dogs that ever wagged a tail. They simply got in their car, and drove home.

The next day, a young man was knocking on their door. His name was Jeff Hogan, and he was the youngest of George's grand children. He and his wife, had taken over the old man's place. He had just graduated from college, with a degree in forestry. Jack told him he not only was welcome, as a neighbor, but that if he needed a job, that it could probably be arranged. You see, as the new special game warden, in the area, he could hire a couple of men to specialize in cat control, since cats were now into the area, either because of the bad work of the "Friends," group, or the fact that the cougars had migrated back to their old hunting ranges, because the deer had multiplied, and the habitat had improved, depending on which ever interpretation, you accepted. Besides he had a friend that was the head of the State Department of Wildlife. Donnigan would also be hired, and Dr. Haskins would serve as a consultant from time to time.

The Governor was running for re-election already, although the election was not until November. He had a new campaign issue. It seems, that he had noticed that the crime rate had dropped even lower than it usually was, since the people of the three county area, had been allowed to carry guns, because of the cat. There was great public support, for that policy to be carried out, statewide. The Governor had read the polls; and then decided that it was a **wonderful** idea. Jack was laughing hard, about that one. He escorted young Hogan out, as he was getting ready, to return to his home, for supper.

Suddenly Blackie and Brownie were barking like crazy. Jack walked out to where they were carrying on. There, in his garden, were four sets of cougar tracks. A female and three cubs. "Blackie and Brownie," he called out, "We'll worry about that on another day." He reached down and petted his dogs.

A half a mile away, into the woods, a female cougar and three cubs were out for a walk. She had one spotted female kitten, a larger brown and spotted male kitten, and a third kitten that looked more like a half-grown cat. He was fully a third larger than the brown male kitten. He was also black, and had green eyes--and, he **was,** his father's son.

For so it always is and will be, that just when the good has triumphed over evil, and celebrates that victory, that evil re-appears, on the horizon. Sometimes, if the good are vigilant, they triumph again. But should they ever be tempted to just rest on their laurels, a price will be paid, that is far from pleasant. So it is, in the quest to retain anything good. For as surely as there is no rest, for the wicked, the good cannot rest for too long, on their laurels, either.

The story of the hunt however, may be told, and re-told throughout the ages, for selflessness begets triumph, and the lessons are more valuable than the events, themselves.

The end is not in sight.

Printed in the United States
137366LV00003B/3/P